THE DAMNED AND THE DESTROYED

RICOCHET TITLES

The Crime on Cote des Neiges by David Montrose

Murder Over Dorval by David Montrose

The Body on Mount Royal by David Montrose

Sugar-Puss on Dorchester Street by Al Palmer

The Long November by James Benson Nablo

Waste No Tears by Hugh Garner

The Mayor of Côte St. Paul by Ronald J. Cooke

Hot Freeze by Douglas Sanderson

Blondes are My Trouble by Douglas Sanderson

Gambling with Fire by David Montrose

The Keys of My Prison by Frances Shelley Wees

The Pyx by John Buell

Four Days by John Buell

THE DAMNED AND
THE DESTROYED

Kenneth Orvis

A
Ricochet
Book

Véhicule Press

Published with the generous assistance of the Canada Council for the Arts, the Canada Book Fund of the Department of Canadian Heritage, and the Société de développement des entreprises culturelles du Québec (SODEC).

 Canada Council   Conseil des arts
for the Arts   du Canada

Canada   SODEC   Québec

Series editor: Brian Busby
Adaptation of original cover: J.W. Stewart
Special assistance: Michelle Hahn-Baker and Eliza Prestley
Typeset in Minion and Palatino Linotype
by Simon Garamond
Printed by Marquis Printing Inc.

Originally published in 1962.
Copyright © Véhicule Press 2019
The publisher is pleased to respect any
unacknowledged property rights

LIBRARY AND ARCHIVES CANADA CATALOGUING IN PUBLICATION

Title: The damned and the destroyed / Kenneth Orvis.

Names: Orvis, Kenneth, author.

Description: Series statement: Ricochet books | Reprint. Originally
published: 1962.

Identifiers: Canadiana (print) 20189067594 | Canadiana (ebook)
20189067608 | ISBN 9781550655230   (softcover) |
ISBN 9781550655292 EPUB)

Classification: LCC PS8529.R95 D36 2019 | DDC C813/.54—dc23

Published by Véhicule Press, Montréal, Québec, Canada
www.vehiculepress.com

Distribution in Canada by LitDistCo
www.litdistco.ca

Distributed in the U.S. by Independent Publishers Group
www.ipgbook.com

Printed in Canada

ACKNOWLEDGEMENT

To the addicts, the pushers, and the connections whose counsels have, during the five-year period of research devoted to this work, aided me in representing, as faithfully as my ability permits, the story of drug addiction and trafficking in Canada, and the endless, terrifying consequences of same, my sincere appreciation.

For his kindness in affording me access to his precious case-histories of Canadian addicts, and for sharing with me his experience of many years as a student of addiction, its causes and effects, and my deep gratitude to:

The late Gordon W. Phillips S. Th., Consultant at the Allan Division, Royal Victoria Hospital, and Chaplain Montreal prisons.

For her interest in and dedication to the purpose of this work, my heartfelt thanks to:

Miss Sharon C., Narcotics Anonymous, New York, N. Y. And to:

The late Miss Billie Holiday, singer; Barney Ross, boxer; and Francisca de Ramirez, guitarist, my most affectionate gratitude.

To
Florence E. Van der Voort Le Mieux, my wife,
who took me into her heart and showed me
many wonderful things.

INTRODUCTION

On the Trail of Kenneth Orvis

Brian Busby

I first came across Kenneth Orvis's name five years ago in an old ad that ran from late September through early October, 1983 in the *Globe & Mail*:

An internationally published author with eight works to his name? A writer of such stature that he could hold a workshop at the pricey Four Seasons Toronto. Why had I never heard of Kenneth Orvis?

My initial thought was that the bibliography was inflated, and that Orvis himself was something of a charlatan who had seen eager, aspiring novelists as easy targets.

All these years later, I'm not sure I was entirely wrong.

As it turned out, Orvis *had* been published internationally. Hardcover editions from large- and medium-sized houses on both sides of the Atlantic, followed by cheap paperbacks from Pan, Digit, and Belmont. Publishers come and go in Orvis's bibliography, but eccentric Englishman Dennis Dobson stands out as by far the most committed, publishing four Orvis novels. I expect Dobson might have kept going, had he not died of a brain haemorrhage on a train back to London from the Frankfurt Book Fair. The author's next publisher was Robert Hale Ltd, a British house that had come to specialize in genre fiction. In 1974, it published two Orvis thrillers, *The Disinherited* and *The Doomsday List*, after which the author fell silent.

By 1983, when Orvis was selling lectures on "plotting, characterization, revision, manuscript preparation and dealing with agents and publishers," his novels were all long out of print. Orvis would publish just one more book, the 1985 memoir *Over the Table and Under: The Anatomy of an Alcoholic*. A product of Montreal's now defunct Optimum Publishing, its opening pages present a variation of a familiar story: young Kenneth grows up in a comfortable Montreal home with a distant father and a fragile mother. He's a bookish child, but not a great student. At some point, Kenneth discovers Hemingway, Faulkner, and Wolfe (Thomas, one assumes, Orvis only uses surnames), which leads to dreams of becoming a novelist. Teenage Kenneth leaves the family home to take a job with a Toronto trade paper, convinced that the experience will give him the material and skills required to make it big. Several other publications and many, many bars follow. In middle age, Kenneth achieves his dream by publishing his first novel, but is saddled with alcoholism.

Kenneth Orvis's debut, *Hickory House* (1956), is all about one man's struggle to reinvent himself. The protagonist, a crook named Alfredo Rossi, has made good money running numbers, but is tired of moving from town to town ahead of the law. And so, he uses his ill-gotten gains to become respectable Al Ross, proprietor of a swanky nightclub somewhere on the shores of Lake Michigan.

However, Rossi dooms his own efforts by resorting to theft and blackmail in order to establish himself. Early in the novel, he looks to use the services of Lou Kovaks, a crackerjack safecracker who happens to be serving the final days of a stint at the prison in Dannemora, New York. Rossi—hell, he'd prefer we call him Ross—checks into a nearby motel the evening before Kovaks' release:

> For a while he listened idly to the rain drumming relentless fingers against the windows. Then he began thinking about the man lying behind Dannemora's high stone hedge, sweating out the last hours of his sentence, waiting impatiently for a reluctant dawn. The gambler wondered briefly what a man would think about at such a time.

What makes this rather bland passage noteworthy is that Orvis knew precisely what a man would think about at such a time; *Hickory House* was written when the author was in prison for passing false cheques. In actuality, Kenneth Orvis was a man named Kenneth LeMieux (aka Kenneth Lemieux), who was known amongst police as a 'Saturday noon operator,' appearing just as banks were closing for the week. According to the May 8, 1947 edition of the Montreal *Gazette*, LeMieux—hell, he'd want us

11

to call him Orvis—was 'a personable, well-educated man who seldom aroused suspicion.' I don't doubt it. A Montrealer, Orvis was raised in privilege as the son of businessman Malcolm LeMieux, general manager of the Studebaker Corporation of Canada and founder and president of the Canada Marble and Lime Company.

Orvis never reveals his true surname in *Over the Table and Under*, and claims that his debut, *Hickory House*, was written over the course of seven sober months in a small furnished apartment not far from Montreal's Berkley Hotel. When that first novel was published, Orvis writes, he was undergoing treatment for his alcoholism at the 'Crescent Street Hospital,' an institution that never existed. 'My novel had opened many new doors,' the author boasts. 'After several radio and TV interviews and short pieces in local newspapers, more copywriting accounts than there was time for were easily available.'

What Orvis fails to mention is that the publisher of *Hickory House* was Harlequin Books. A cheaply produced mass-market paperback, it was sold during the month of August, 1956 at Canadian newsstands. The next month, it was gone. There were no foreign editions, nor was there a second printing. I have my doubts about those radio and TV interviews, just as I have a hard time believing that *Hickory House* brought a slew of writing gigs.

I can't give a description of Orvis's second novel, *Walk Alone*, because I've never seen a copy. Has anyone? The title isn't recognized on WorldCat, and it doesn't appear to have been reviewed or even advertised. In my years on the trail of Kenneth Orvis, not one copy has appeared for sale online. And yet, beginning with *The Damned and the Destroyed*, *Walk Alone* is a constant in the bibliographies published in Orvis's books. The sole reference to the novel in *Over the Table and Under* is fleeting: '*Walk Alone* didn't shatter any sales records, but it did better than average and, as well, its spin-off

367 Gamblers and Politicians
had a high stake in . . .
35¢

HICKORY HOUSE

AN ORIGINAL NOVEL · NOT A REPRINT

A HARLEQUIN BOOK

benefits like copywriting contracts were lucrative.' As far as I know, the only other mention—*anywhere*—comes courtesy of a 1965 Montreal *Gazette* interview, in which the novel is referred to as *I Walk Alone*, the basis of the Hollywood film.

I Walk Alone was released in 1948, eight years before *Hickory House* was published. The first of seven movies to star Burt Lancaster and Michael Douglas, it was adapted from a 1945 Broadway play *Beggars Are Coming to Town* by Theodore Reeves.

Oh, why bother? Why bother with Kenneth Orvis?

I suppose much of my interest has to do with my work on that self-described "accomplished liar" and "great practitioner of deceit" John Glassco. I spent many years on a biography of the man, pursuing what Michael Gnarowski—Glassco's friend and mine—refers to as "the knowable truth."

I wanted a new case.

Orvis was never nearly so accomplished a liar, but then, he wasn't nearly so good a writer. Frankly, I'm not sure his heart was in it. He seems a man who was not so much attracted to writing as he was to being published; it was often more about being recognized as a novelist than actually writing novels.

This is not to say that that Orvis produced nothing of note. *The Damned and the Destroyed*, his very best book, is essential reading for anyone at all interested in the decades Montreal reigned as Canada's sin city. Its opening scene takes place on October 25, 1954, the very day champion of morality Jean Drapeau won his first election to the mayoralty.

The second scene, which sees private detective Maxwell Dent responding to the summons of a prospective Westmount client, echoes the beginnings of the city's earlier Montreal noir novels like David Montrose's *The*

Crime on Cote des Neiges (1951) and Douglas Sanderson's *Hot Freeze* (1954). In this case, the private detective is tasked to break up a dope ring.

In 1954, Montreal was the drug capital of Canada, had the most brothels, and housed the most gambling dens. It's no wonder that Orvis chose to set *The Damned and the Destroyed*, his best novel then, rather than 1962, the year it saw publication.

Kenneth Orvis put more into *The Damned and the Destroyed* than any other novel. In the acknowledgements, he describes five years of research. Amongst others, he thanks the late Rev. Gordon W. Gordon, Chaplain of Montreal Prisons, who just happens to have been a close friend of my parents. His wife, Bluebell, was the first writer I ever met. Coincidentally—or perhaps not—her first book, a memoir titled *Adopted Derelicts* (1957), was also published by Harlequin. In it we find "Our Beloved Alcoholic", a chapter devoted to a man whom she and her husband had worked hard to save from the ravages of drink.

I can't say that Orvis was that sorry alcoholic, but I aim to find out.

What I can say is that Kenneth Orvis's second-best novel is *Cry Hallelujah!* (1970), about a young woman preacher who strives to make a better world for the fallen and a just world for the persecuted. It stands alone in Orvis's bibliography as the only novel that doesn't deal with crime or espionage. And yet, at its centre is a mystery: seven missing years in the preacher's life, a time very nearly equal to that Orvis spent in prison.

'There are always parts of everyone's life they try to hide,' says one character. 'Skeletons hidden in their closets.'

After five years on Kenneth Orvis's trail, I'm still finding closet doors.

Brian Busby is the author of ten books, including *The Dusty Bookcase: A Journey Through Canada's Forgotten, Neglected, and Suppressed Writing* and *A Gentleman of Pleasure: One Life of John Glassco, Poet, Memoirist, Translator, and Pornographer*. He is the editor of *The Heart Accepts It All*, a selection of John Glassco's letters published by Véhicule Press, and is the series editor for Richochet Books. Portions of this essay were first published in *Canadian Notes & Queries*.

Sad silent sages of the night
. . . on windy corners dwell
Their eyes on bleak tableau of fright
. . . horizons touched on Hell
From 'Streetcorner Vespers'
by Kenneth Orvis

1 Some days go to rest in one's memory as having been entirely spectacular.

On such a day, in winy October, the most electrifying upset in Montreal's violent political history took place—and the tragic Ashton drug case exploded into my unprepared lap.

A hurrying passer-by splashed a puddle of water over the shoes of the man standing beside e in the doorway of the city's main post-office. . . . 'Voila!' said the wetted one with an amiable grin that was a crooked arrangement of teeth, chin, and lip. 'A fitting tribute to a day that has already convinced me there *is* a fate worse than death.'

The man brought his thin hand up from his side and pointed it not too accurately towards the City Hall. 'Drama there!' he said succinctly. 'Like in the movies, eh? Consider it, my friend. For better than twenty years we live in a city running wide open under a wise old political-fox of a mayor—then, pouf! Suddenly before today's election we find we have in our midst an angry Civic Action League. That League is sponsoring a Johnny-come-lately, a crusader full of reform zeal and fire. The fat begins to sizzle. What happens next, eh?'

I laughed. I was enjoying this man with the wet feet. His opinion would be the first post-election one I would hear. The polls were still open, it was true; but in this city so long constitutionally opposed to do-gooders and vice-probers, the fledgling reform party had already scored a spectacular *fait accompli*.

'Well—what happens, eh?' the man repeated insistently.

19

'The mayor-incumbent bows out of the election race at the final moment. . . .'

'. . . Ha! But only after a roughhouse blasting from the simon-pures of the Civic Action League.'

'. . . So, free of all real opposition, the noble Johnny-come-lately reformist triumphs,' I smiled.

'Exactly—and phew!' my companion retorted, ad no longer sounding amused he added, 'So the new mayor's sidekick—a man who takes big pleasure in being called *crime-buster*—promises without delay to put vice on ice in Montreal. Ha!'

'And he just might succeed in doing it!' I retorted.

A deep sigh, then—'Ah, Montreal!' said the man with the wet feet. 'Montreal, the second Paris. To be frivolous and gay, perhaps even a little bit bad, it is in our veins, our blood, no?'

'No, not really,' I countered. 'Frivolity is only our habit.'

'*Eh bien!*' he retorted. 'We shall see how this new purity works out. Perhaps our reformist is not the type that wears well. And causes, you know—causes seldom survive their champions.'

'*Sometimes* they do,' I said with a smile—and left him with a friendly nod.

'But you are not interested!' he shouted after me. 'The lights are already going out in our city, and you are not interested. You are not interested!

It sounded like an accusation.

Actually, it wasn't at all that I was not interested. But the bright part of my day had been spent completing a lengthy security-case report and getting it into the mail. Moreover, my vote wouldn't' have been for reform. When all the fuss started—the Civic Action League's screams of police corruption and their outraged exposés of vice pay-offs made by the boys with the pro-tection edge, the Petrula-Greco hoodlum clique—I'd decided to take the reformists' bright promises with a stiff dose of scepticism. Experience had forced upon me the strong, prodding conviction that reform government had no grey-haired future in this second-largest French-speaking city in the world.

So the spectacular election day began to draw in its shadows. Pushing through gossips standing on the bottom steps of the post office, I walked along towards Place d'Armes. The square was as busy as a Brueghel painting. The sun was almost gone and immaculate office windows threw off sparks of refracted light so that the air seemed to be alive with a golden glitter. Subconsciously, I listened to voices falling from small, gathered knots of loudly malcontent voters.

One group was grumbling irrationally about the mayor-elect's vice-probing sidekick. I passed a second group where, with a half-dozen men in semicircle before him, a sceptic with a dark, betrayed face leaned forward grotesquely. He was shouting furiously: 'Don't give me that bushwah! It's not a question of vice. I tell you, get wise to yourselves. Nothing will be closed up. Not a single night-club. Not one single gambling house. Nothing. This won't last. It's all typical election footzy!'

'There's always been ruddy police protection and tolerance in this city. Always!' shouted out another. 'This reform stuff is for the birds!' he shouted directly at me. 'Damned right it won't last.'

His listeners were standing stoically, except for an old one, who smiled with contempt and shouted something about the last days of Babylon. I walked on past them, along to my office. My mind began churning over my own problems. My telephone had not rung since I'd finished my security case two days ago. My one-man, independent agency was getting a very unusual cold shoulder from the big city.

I think I finally stared my unco-operative telephone into action. Anyway, it rang.

21

No psychic sense stirred when I answered the telephone to warn me of impeding violence and horror. When I picked up the receiver and said 'Hello' I was aware only of a tense, agitated voice inquiring urgently: 'Am I speaking to Maxwell Dent?'

I said, 'Yes, Dent here.'

I heard a dry, nervous cough—then again the tight voice: 'This is Huntley G. Ashton, Dent. I must talk with you. Tonight. No later than eight o'clock. It's imperative—urgent. Come to my home at that time, please.'

I tried to hurry Huntley G. Ashton to a point. 'Why, Mr. Ashton?'

Again, the embarrassed cough. Then the voice—growing a shade edgier as Ashton said, 'Can't we discuss that at eight o'clock, Dent?' There was a long, pregnant pause while the wire crackled as though in a storm, then . . . 'Do come. Come, please, Dent. Believe me it is more urgent than I can say.'

The tightening feeling of having to start everything all over again that comes with each new case washed over me. The psychic sense stirred then—shot warnings at me, warnings that this assignment might well be a crucial one. My hand reached out for the city directory. I checked Ashton's address.

Huntley Ashton lived on one of the secluded terraces encircling the mountain that towers picture-postcard fashion over Montreal. I made careful note of the street and number. It seemed odd to me, even at this early point, that a man of Ashton's obvious standing would send out such a frantic call. Nevertheless, I decided not to form hasty opinions. Frantic calls aren't new to me. I started my agency after a tour of ops and some off-beat duty in Korea, and in the following years have experienced much of the unexpected and unusual. I closed the directory with a slap, shrugging off a foreboding sense of uneasiness.

I decided to fill in time until my eight o'clock appointment across the street at Louis's—my favourite café in this city of cathedrals and cafés.

Louis's was jammed—Montreal lower-town style. Reform talk filled the room. Newspaper reporters, elbows leaning hard on Louis's bar, their limp shirts open at the collar, their ties, knots loosened, hanging twisted about their necks, talked in excited bursts and drank. Street girls, violently roughed and unsteady on spike heels, kidded in shrill voices with equally shrill headquarters detectives. Uniformed cops from the next-door Criminal Courts Building argued in staccato French with worried political hangers-on drifting in from the emergency-lighted City Hall, visible from Louis's slamming front door. A pair of white-collars from a near-by St. James Street brokerage office pounded the bar for fresh drinks without interrupting their excited comments.

One was saying: 'Did you get a good look at the bulletins, Harry? They say the new clique will shut up the city tight as a Baie Ste Anne clam.'

His companion snorted. 'Bosh! The people will never go for that gruff. Anyway, it's only a phase. This new la-de-dah City Hall doesn't even have a snowball's chance.'

Voices rose and fell like a rolling of drums. I pressed closer to the bar. Louis pushed his tub-shaped body my way, grinned brightly at me. He handed me a bottle and my special glass, his sharp, Gallic eyes alive with business. I drank. Beside me, a tall, over-dressed, pencil-thin Frenchman stroked a black line of moustache. He bent to the platinum-haired girl complaining at his shoulder, spoke in smooth and silky tones: 'Time for you to go, little one. Tonight you will solicit in the uptown bars. But with care, *n'est-ce pas?* Tomorrow I find out if the fix for bar girls is still good.'

The girl tossed her head contemptuously. Her laugh was loud and high-pitched and jangling, as though she were having her feet tickled. The sound was off-key and chalk-on-blackboard shrill. 'No more feex!' she screamed, stamping her foot. 'Thees new wan in the City Hall is craze. His head it is in the clouds. No more feex. The business is feenish for sure!'

I dawdled over a whisky until a few minutes before eight, then pushed my way through ever-thickening bar groups to the door. My car waited across the street in the City Hall parking lot. I paused there for a moment, with my car keys in my hand.

The night curled coolly around me like giant leaves of silk. Instinctively, my eyes lifted to a sight that to me will never cease to be a thrill.

From where I stood in the darkening lower-town financial district, the dirty, harbour-bordered hem of Montreal, the city swept upward in a series of abrupt but graceful inclines that reached to the peak of the mountain forming its centrepiece. Beyond the mid-town shopping area, belted neon-scarlet now about the mountain's fat waist, broad light-splashed residential ledges followed closely one upon another to create the almost eerie illusion of vast golden steps. Higher again, and towards the north, stood a gigantic Cross—an incredible, blazing symbol of faith that watched silently over the sprawling city.

I drove uptown. The city lay soft neon-scarlet, filled with evening hush. Few cars were on the streets. Most moving vehicles were taxis carrying the first theatre crowds. I continued quickly north up the steep hills to Westmount Boulevard, and pushed up over the last light-sparkling ledge to the tapering roof of the mountain.

A cement drive curved like a finger-nail paring in front of a huge stone house. The house was traditional in its suggestion of wealth without ostentation. Manorial stone steps led to a wide, flagged terrace. Several windows on the lower floor were golden with light. The house did not look at all like a place where destiny, set in motion by a fearful horror, would place violent hands on my life.

I found a vine-obscured bell button, pressed, and waited.

A trim French maid, provocative in black crêpe and a spot of lacy white apron, opened the door. She made a cute, saucy sort of half-curtsy, and said, 'Monsieur Maxwell Dent?' I nodded. The maid stepped back. 'Thees way, please,' she smiled. 'Monsieur Ashton waits for you in his study.'

I followed buttocks that shook like small black rubber loaves to the end of a long hall that had a groomed, cared-for, and graceful look. The maid stopped before a panelled door. 'Go in, please. Monsieur Ashton, 'e is inside.'

I stepped forward into a large sunken living-room, and down a shallow fall of steps. The dark blue draperies at the windows were drawn. Wall lights drew gleams from fine pieces of furniture rubbed to a mirror-like smoothness, shone tranquilly on high bookcases, quietly coloured satin chairs, and a half-dozen fine paintings punctuating the ivory walls. Sofas flanked the white fireplace mantle under which a cannel coal fire waited unlit.

Ashton stepped forward to greet me. He stood tall and thin, with a noticeable slight stoop, his greying hair brushed smoothly back from the high forehead of his handsome aquiline face. There was courtesy but no pleasure in his greeting. It was obvious at once that Huntley Ashton did not expect to enjoy this interview. Suggesting that I join him in an after-dinner pony of brandy, he turned off to a small table at my nod, and I studied him closely. His skin was a bad colour, and he was obviously extremely ill at ease. Still, it wasn't only that. There was a queer fixity to Ashton, as though within his body his spirit had crumpled and was dead, or dying.

I sat back in a comfortable chair. For the first time, reaching for my brandy, I looked directly into Huntley Ashton's eyes; they were tragic eyes, tired and crowded with restless, writhing ghosts. Something had recently given this man's life a new meaning; in fact, a new dimension. Whatever that something was, it was mean, twisted—not anything nice to be near. It had the pallor of death.

And the man seemed incapable of making a conversational start. He fiddled with a sheet of typed foolscap, peered at it, flipped it over, and sat down. His fingers, as tell-tale as his ashen face, fluttered over a gold humidor as he chose a cigar and carefully lit it. Grimly, he stared at the cigar's thickening grey cap of ash, then at last back to me.

He found words with a wrenching voice he seemed to be bringing from far, far away. 'An extremely serious matter has made it necessary for me to summon you here, Dent,' he said. 'It is . . . it's a thing—a horrible thing—that has happened, is still happening. A family matter. A matter concerning my . . . my, ah, younger daughter."

I waited. Ashton shook his head with an odd, embarrassed savagery. I looked sharply into his face, then got up and crossed the room and turned off the bright wall lights. I pondered, and I waited. My tightening nerves jumped uncomfortably.

My silence had a curious effect on Ashton. He began speaking through it, but as though entirely against his will, with an air of pulling his words one by one from a sack, as though fearful of what he would draw next. 'My daughter desperately needs help,' he ground out. 'Help and protection.' He drew a deep breath, and charged bull-like through his fear and horror to get the fact out—'God help us, Dent—the thing is, my daughter has become a dope fiend. That's it; that's the hideous fact. My young daughter is a helpless *dope fiend!*'

Slowly, my fingers tightened over my glass. I attempted a calm reply. A cold, clammy feeling was creeping up to my lips. I've had active experience with people caught by the drug habit. People who sew themselves up in a tight mental sack. Lost ones full of worry and pain and afraid to let life get close enough to touch them. I knew now why Huntley Ashton looked out upon the world past ghosts that lurked in his eyes.

In his queer, far-away voice, he repeated: 'Yes, my daughter . . . a dope fiend. Heroin, I suppose. Or morphine. I don't really know what narcotic addicts use. All this is nightmarish and unreal to me. It's . . . aah, God! it's unbelievable. But the point is, my daughter is now so utterly helpless that immediate action must be taken. Very discreet action. But this hellish thing *must* be stopped.' Ashton pressed his finger-tips to his forehead. He seemed confused and drunk with the hurting emotions inside him; not entirely rational as he concluded, his eyes nailing mine: 'All right, Dent. I've told you. Now you know. You know about my daughter—*and you know why I summoned you here.*'

2 I sat up so suddenly the back of my chair moved in to slap at me. Obviously, Ashton had already made plans. He was preparing to ask questions, make a proposition. And I knew Huntley Ashton would be the type to settle only for the answer he wanted. I said, 'I know only that you have a serious problem. How could I know exactly why you called me?'

Ashton leaned closer. For the moment, he looked the way he was intended to look. Like a top executive being sauve about proposing a vital idea. 'Who else *but* you?' he challenged. He picked up the typed sheet of foolscap, smoothed it out with very great care. 'I've had you checked, Dent. Screened thoroughly. I respect what I found. You are the only non-policeman in this country who completely understands drug ring operations. In fact, you are probably one of the few people *anywhere* who does.' He tapped his typed sheet significantly. 'I've your

27

entire record here,' he said in a strengthening voice. 'All of it—going back to your school days.' He began to read from the sheet: 'You were educated in Montreal public schools. You studied Law at McGill until the outbreak of war in Korea. You left university then to enlist in the R.C.A.F., obtained a commission in '50. Later, you were transferred to Intelligence M-5. While on that duty you played a major part in smashing an enemy ring supplying narcotics to U.N. forces for the purpose of troop demoralization.' Ashton cleared his throat, concluded briskly: 'Following your discharge from the services, you opened your present independent agency.'

Somewhere in the house, a clock ticked. The sound grew until it was around me, inside me, like an amplified heartbeat.

The war. Korea. A full realization of what was churning in Ashton's desperate mind was now getting through to me. I said, hurriedly, 'See here, Mr. Ashton; during that Korean affair I was under oath to the Crown— U.N. Intelligence, to be precise. I had their facilities, their protection. Emergency powers were used to the full. That's a considerable factor in an involved investigation. Now I have nothing—not even official authority.'

Ashton nodded impatiently. His inner tautness thrust aside, he spoke now with the clipped curtness of a man long conditioned to having his orders carried out to the letter: 'Good!' he said. 'In fact, excellent. Official authority is precisely what I must avoid. I don't need men who can ask questions, I need a man who knows the answers. This filthy Montreal drug syndicate must be exposed and smashed. Smashed completely. I know that is a big order. A huge undertaking. Nevertheless, I want the people that are selling black-market drugs to my daughter run out of business and jailed. I want to see them punished to the full. I want it done without my daughter being involved or implicated in any way.

You see now,' he said with careful, deliberate emphasis, 'why I need a particular type of man. A man capable of carrying through an extremely dangerous investigation with utter discretion. A highly trained man. A specialist. You, Dent.'

I sat for a moment, thinking, before I finally said, 'I must ask you to bear well in mind that in Canada offences against the Narcotic Act fall under the jurisdiction of the R.C.M.P. The R.C.M.P. wouldn't like your present attitude. Another thing—it would be extremely difficult to expose, try, and convict your daughter's suppliers—the drug ring, and those operating it—without the full fact of her addiction and guilt becoming known to the police.' I drew an uncomfortable breath. 'After all,' I reminded Ashton reasonably, 'you must remember that each time your daughter buys drugs from a local pusher—which, of course, she is doing daily—she is guilty of a serious breach of the Act. She is laying herself wide open for arrest and conviction.'

Ashton drew hard on his cigar. 'I am familiar with the Narcotics Act,' he said, a little peevishly. 'I realize, too, the extent of my daughter's guilt.' He thought for a moment, his eyes becoming almost sly, then asked cautiously: 'Suppose information leading to the arrest of the drug traffickers were turned over to the Mounted Police—conclusive evidence—would they insist on prosecuting a comparative innocent like my daughter?'

I let the question wait. One of a set of thick, floor-length drapes forming a side door had moved. The soft stirring could have been caused by a random draught. Or it could have been started by someone who had become careless listening behind the drapes. I waited. Silence usually forces a listener to fidget. Not this time. Whether the restless fluttering had been caused by a draught or by an uneasy body, it held its breath. The drapes hung straight, flat and utterly motionless.

'No,' I said in considered reply to Ashton's question, 'I don't believe the Mounties would prosecute your daughter if events were arranged so they are handed a wholesale drug ring grab. Not unless she is actually caught in possession of narcotics, that is. Mind you, I'm not suggesting the Mounties would make a deal. The R.C.M.P. don't do that. But I don't think they'd try to build a conspiracy or guilt by proximity case against your daughter simply because she's an addict. But there's another angle. Sometimes the City acts in drug cases. Independent of the Mounties. If somewhere along the way they got on to your daughter, their attitude could be pretty nasty. Definitely so, if some conviction-happy Crow Prosecutor thinks she might break down and be a useful witness in an illegal-sale case.'

Ashton said with assurance, 'Forget the City, Dent. Put that worry out of your mind. You know the City can always be handled.'

Scepticism must have been naked in my eyes. When I didn't speak, Ashton said with tight-lipped disdain, 'Reforms don't necessarily succeed at altering policemen's personalities. I can handle the City.' He leaned forward. 'Accept this case, Dent,' he urged. 'Forget about police action. Consider the case a personal challenge. Find these criminals, then leave the rest to me.'

Ashton stared at me; let me get uncomfortable looking into his eyes, which were again desperate. 'You must know what this frightful habit is making of her, Dent. She's going to pieces inch by inch, and she doesn't even care. She's either stumbling about in a weird sort of trance, or acting like a hunted animal. You must help me,' he insisted harshly. 'You must. Because I know that very soon even *your* help will be too late.'

I felt trapped. I thought fleetingly of Korea; of that nightmare of drugs, the fantastic and highly complex crosscurrents of intrigue and counter-intrigue, the personal vendettas between rival black-marketeers and the hate and destruction and vengeance. And I knew that such evil exists anywhere there is trafficking in drugs. Ashton's demand for a quick exposure of the drug ring was worse than comical.

I could only say—'I don't know.'

Ashton persisted. 'If you do refuse me,' he said unfairly, 'you are permitting my daughter to die.'

'But you're asking me to climb a glass mountain,' I retorted, exasperated. 'To free your daughter from her habit, you expect me to work my way inside a vicious drug syndicate and smash it—a terrorist group that no doubt has been operating successfully here in Montreal for years. A protected, established group!'

Cords tightened in my neck. 'Don't you realize that drug traffickers are the tigers of the underworld?' I demanded, completely aroused now. 'Can't you at least try to *imagine* the fantastic precautions traffickers take? How close to impossible it is to trap them with the single shred of evidence needed for conviction? Aren't you even aware that right here in Montreal—with every police trick being used against them—addicts, pushers, and traffickers are running the authorities ragged?'

Ashton's mouth dropped open, hung foolishly. 'Are you telling me, do you mean to say, that addiction and trafficking is a major police problem in this city?'

I snapped out at him: 'Here! yes. So much so that in Montreal as well as in most other cities across the country illicit drug operators are keeping the R.C.M.P. sleepless. Narcotic squads are held on the *qui vive* night and day. Those squads make arrests, yes. But they keep arresting the same small-fry addicts and pushers. They pick them up and jail them time after time, until everybody gets dizzy. But that is as close as police ever get to smashing the trafficking ring—and it's not worth a ruddy damn. Because while those small-fry arrests are being made, Mr. Big sits protected and smug well back in the underworld shadows.'

31

Ashton simply stared. I began experiencing a sense of oppression in breathing. It grew difficult to keep emotion from showing on my face.

I continued bitterly: 'You've tried everything with your daughter, haven't you? Before you called me, you exhausted every hope. You tried committing her to hospitals. Forced her to take cold-shock and reduction treatments. You tried pleading with her. Perhaps you even threatened her. You tried to squeeze out the unnamed thing that haunts her and drives her screaming to the release of drugs. You tried to dig down and find the weakness, the horror or fear somewhere in her life her mind can't anesthetize without a shot of heroin. But it didn't work. It never does. She wouldn't even listen. Of course she wouldn't. Because, once people are addicted to drugs, they're far beyond threats or reason.

'So now you've another idea, Mr. Ashton. You've come up with a plan for straightening out your daughter without her being harmed more than she already is. You want her supply of heroin cut off directly at its source; but to accomplish that I'll have to come very close to performing a miracle.'

Ashton continued to stare at me. His mouth was clamped tight, and his eyes were narrowed and intent and smouldering-bright and seemed to be looking at me, but not quite seeing me. He was so frantically unhappy, tortured, and in such a dangerous state of worry that the feeling of him sitting there, stiff and straight, was all through me, like a sadness.

I came to the edge of my chair. 'If you knew a few facts about drug traffickers, you'd understand me better,' I said defensively. 'At least, you'd have a glimmer of what trying to reach them involves. To begin with, as I've already told you, they're the top money-makers of all criminals—their black market profits are unbelievable. And every dollar of that profit is fungus ridden with their victim's blood and sweat. Another thing. Like all underworld boss-men, traffickers always reduce their personal risk component to near zero. They take no unnecessary personal chances. None of them, not any, ever sell heroin directly to a user. They use agents for that.' I stared pointedly. 'Will it give you an idea of how utterly ruthless traffickers are,' I asked, 'if I tell you they even succeed in victimizing their own agents—the pushers?

'Most pushers are addicted before they are hired,' I explained in a voice I was trying to control. 'If they *weren't* addicted, the traffickers wouldn't trust them not to weaken under police pressure and turn stool pigeon. Because they are addicted, pushers willingly accept the biggest part of their pay in capsuled heroin. So most of their earnings go right back into the ring. Like all addicts, the drug comes first with them. Nothing else has any real meaning. They're like zombies. They live in a tight, silent circle. Trying to break into their circle to build evidence against a trafficker is an almost mad undertaking.'

Ashton looked stunned.

'The top men in drug rings are constantly protected from every side,' I went on relentlessly. 'The addicts and pushers and district connections all protect them. They do so because they're terrorized into caution and frightened stiff of their own supply of drug being cut off. Not only that—the traffickers themselves are supernaturally suspicious of everyone, including each other. Being able to victimize everyone one touches, to deal in death in capsuled form, requires a peculiar, mad sort of talent. Traffickers have that talent. That's why when anyone gets nabbed actually handling the drug, be sure it's someone small-fry—a pusher or a district distributor.'

Ashton fluttered the foolscap on which my record was typed. 'Traffickers can be caught,' he argued. 'The fact still exists that you've once accomplished just such a thing. You have the right training. You know your way about Montreal. You are respected and welcome just about anywhere you choose to go. For instance, I'm told you are very well received in Chinatown in this city. That's unusual, and, I think, perhaps might be quite useful now. Chinese and drugs . . . ah, those two are synonymous, I believe.'

I smiled at that. Ashton was completely wrong. Chinese and drugs are no longer synonymous; not here in Montreal, not anywhere on this continent. As well, Ashton's investigators had drawn bitter tea on the reason for my being *persona grata* in Chinatown. Chinese, regardless of where they live, are independent, isolationist people. They prefer to settle their problems without involving official authority. So, when a clique of thugs began waylaying Chinese café owners and robbing them about a year ago, I was called in by a tong leader named Ling Tan. Later, I became friendly with Ling's family. There was a daughter studying physics at McGill. Her Chinese name was Pansiao. Pansiao looked exotically beautiful in Chinese gowns, quaint and lovely in Western dress. I liked Pan, and we were sometimes seen together. But after a while I suggested to Pan that we break off our relationship. I realized it would be better that way. It's clever in my business to stay welcome in places like Chinatown. Not to offend. However, I let Ashton stay lost in his illusion.

He was bursting again to ask his big question. I saved him the embarrassment. In spite of all I'd said, I knew I had already let myself get too emotionally involved to refuse this incredible case. 'Let's set one thing straight,' I suggested. 'So far, you're judging my ability on my treatment of a few unusual local security cases and on the methods I've used to dispose unofficially of a group of minor hoodlums. As well, you are laying a mountain of importance on the special duty work I did in the armed forces.'

'Why not?' Ashton interrupted. 'You showed remarkable dedication to purpose while on your Intelligence M-5 duty.'

'But I am trying to make you understand that my service record doesn't have any real bearing now. Nor do the local things I've accomplished. There's a whale of a difference, remember, between loosely-knit minor hoodlums' activities and the set-up you want smashed. If it weren't for your daughter's critical position, you realize, of course, what my advice would be: call in the R.C.M.P. *fast*. Very well, you daren't. But you must understand this: should I get close, even within hailing distance, of whomever the local drug king turns out to be, I'm going to holler for R.C.M.P. backing in one devil of a hurry. And that, regardless of what objections you may offer at the time.'

To Ashton, that jelled it. It meant just what he wanted to hear. That Maxwell Dent would take this unbelievable case. His hand slid into his desk. He took out a sealed envelope. 'Fine, Dent!' he said, much as if he were rubbing together his patrician hands. 'In this envelope, you'll find a check for what I'm told is your usual *per diem* and expense advance. Another check, suitably larger, will be mailed to you the day you succeed at smashing the drug ring.'

He sat back, added, 'In this envelope, you will also find a letter. The letter will tell you a little about my addicted daughter. Helen is her name. Of course, at any time you choose, you may try to see Helen. But I'm afraid you'll find her damned difficult. Now, one last word. According to my investigators, you are considered something of an authority on music. Sometime ago, Helen showed a great deal of interest in music. Not for long, but for longer than she has recently shown an interest in anything. Something for you to think about? Perhaps. It might have some meaning.'

I smiled, slipped the envelope into my breast pocket. Ashton stood up. 'By the way, Dent,' he said, again with his baffled air. 'I must admit I'm curious. You spoke about vast profits being made by drug traffickers. In fact, you mentioned that several times. I must confess I don't understand those vast profits at all. Would you be kind enough to explain? . . .'

No easier way existed for me to convince Ashton of what we were really up against than by doing just that.

I answered the question with fresh grimness. 'Trafficking in drugs makes mining diamonds look like a poor-house operation,' I said. 'The trafficker's profit is endless—it doubles, triples, and quadruples itself at every turn.' I drew a sharp breath and detailed it quickly. 'One ounce of pure heroin retails legally for about nine dollars. The drug-ring trafficker pays about four hundred for it on the first black-market. Then he cuts it four to one by mixing it with powdered sugar milk and turns the cut portions over to his district connections, or distributors. The connections are the ring sales-managers. They put the cut mixture into capsules over to the district pushers.

'In this city, the pushers sell the caps in various rendezvous-points for five dollars each—earning a small commission, usually a dollar a cap, for themselves. And remember! the addicts are always hanging on the door-knob. The demand for illegal drugs always by far exceeds the black-market supply. So there you are,' I concluded simply. 'Considering the 480 grains to the ounce, simple multiplication will show you that by the time the pure drug is cut, capsuled, and offered to addicts the same ounce of heroin that originally cost nine dollars has pyramided in black-market value until it's worth a fortune. That's free enterprise—jungle style!'

I sat back uncomfortably.

Ashton simply stared.

'Jungle style!' he repeated, at last. 'Good God! that's incredible. At five dollars for an eighth of a gram, it must cost a staggering sum to maintain a drug habit.'

'Yes, it does. If your daughter is in the condition you say she is, if her habit has progressed to the point where she's injecting directly into her veins—as I imagine it must have—she's spending tremendous amounts on drugs. And like every addict, she must be in terrible fear of not being able to get enough heroin to keep her from going mad.'

Ashton nodded bleakly, gazed numbly into the unlighted fireplace. The man had had enough. I stood up.

I made only one provision. As I prepared to leave, I said, 'Mr. Ashton, you know your daughter is addicted to heroin. I think you also know that somewhere along the way before this case is finished, I am going to find out why. When I do, I believe it will turn up something damned hard for you to face. You'll need advice then. I'm going to insist that you take mine. As well, if I think special action is necessary, and you don't agree to it, I warn you I'll go ahead, anyway, without your consent.'

Ashton pointedly neglected to reply as he saw me to the door. He said good-bye without looking at me. I felt a returning prickling annoyance, knowing, as I had from the very beginning of this interview, that important, extremely usable facts were being deliberately held from me. Then the door clicked softly behind me, and I was alone.

I paused on the dark front terrace of the house for a moment. I watched the city lights flashing like huge firefly swarms below me. And there, during that moment, I had a sudden wrenching presentiment of what was to come. I resented bitterly the way this man had worked on my hatred of drug traffickers to force me into a vicious, dangerous, almost ridiculously impossible case.

A quick, unreasonable rise of anger pinched at me. I stalked up and down the terrace for a full minute. Then anger and bitterness washed away and, in spite of myself, I felt a tremendous surge of excitement.

I realized that—come what may, whatever hardship or horror, or whatever Hell—there was no denying that bright adventure, too, lay ahead.

That thought in mind, and with Ashton's fine brandy still burning comfortably within me like an inner charcoal brazier, I got into my car. If I was alert to anything external, it was the soft whispering sounds my tyres made as I coasted my car down the curving cement drive.

Suddenly, my eyes were caught by a face reflected palely in my rear-view mirror.

On reflex, my foot floored the brake pedal. All four wheels jammed. The car slewed forward two inches to the ultimate of the slack in its springs—then to a dead, sickening stop.

A half-erect body catapulted helplessly forward across the back of my seat. I reached out, and my fist closed over something soft and rounded.

Whatever else I had expected to hear, it wasn't the startled gasp of a female. I relaxed my fingers.

I jabbed desperately at the overhead light switch.

3 She sat back under the winking domelight. She looked steadily at me from bottomless blue eyes.

I stared unabashed at her face—a very rare thing, fine bones and full, arched cheeks and clear, clear damask skin. Perfect white teeth. Her hair, coal black, worn in tight coils, fitted her head closely, with a look of spirit and bravery like a Grecian youth. From a purely physical standpoint, she was breathtaking. A man, I realized, could easily be blinded by this perfection. But there was a great deal more. An undertone of intelligence and understanding and sensitivity, even a bright spark of fun that showed now to give her completion.

While I stared, she murmured in a calmed, almost amused voice, 'I know that hiding in a man's car is not the approved way of arranging a meeting. Sorry, I can't help it. I can only tell you that I am Thorn Ashton. Helen's older sister. And that I think you should know Daddy held out some facts on you. Some tragic but important facts it seems I'm left to tell.'

The voice fitted her perfectly—it was warm and friendly, and more than a trifle exciting. But, right now, my mind wasn't sympathetic to exciting voices. I opened the rear door of the car, then the one opposite where I sat. 'Change seats,' I instructed. Thorn Ashton changed seats agreeably.

I waited for her to speak. Looking up with a sudden anxiety on her face, her astonishingly blue eyes followed my hands closely as I took a cigarette from my package. She said, 'Can't we go now, please, so that we can talk privately?' She glanced towards the brightly lighted house. 'I think we'd better go downtown,' she suggested uneasily. 'Somewhere we can be quiet. I—well, there's rather a lot I need to tell you.'

'For God's sake!' I said, still recovering.

'Well,' Thorn retorted. 'I had to do it this way. You *do* want the whole story, don't you?'

I released the brake and coasted the car the rest of the way down the drive. We'd go to Louis's, I decided. The little lower-town bar would be deserted by now.

I turned south down the hills. It was on the tip of my tongue to ask Thorn if it were she who had been listening behind the suspiciously stirring drapes. Somehow, I didn't. Intuition warned me Thorn Ashton had a difficult story to tell. Her story would come easier if she told it without prompting . . . her own way.

I parked outside Louis's. We walked across the cracked sidewalk, now almost obscured under wraith-like harbour mists. A wind sent scraps of paper kiting along the gutter. A street light and Louis's angled neon sign splashed lonesomely into the gloom.

The opening of the door brought Louis bolt upright.

39

He turned in his comfortable bar chair, startled from the bold-faced headlines of his *La Presse*. Instinctively, he rose and reached for a bar cloth and began swabbing. Then he recognized me and he laughed, and the laugh was pleasant and contagious. 'But I do not expect you back this night,' he cried. 'No. Then you arrive, and weeth a lovely lady. Ah—mon, Max, these is veree nice!'

I led Thorn quickly to an end booth.

She sat opposite me and smiled across the narrow table. Her eyes met mine and told me things. Nice things. That she liked people and wanted them to like her; that she trusted people and wanted them to return her trust. I looked up from the deep blue of her eyes to be startled by Louis who was at the end of the table, bent extravagantly in a cavalier's bow. He served the drinks—and with a great air of being diplomatic, walked almost on tip-toe back to his bar chair.

Silence rooted in the little booth, and grew. Thorn dabbed at a corner of her lips with a bit of lace. I lit a cigarette for Thorn, one for myself. Louis walked heavily around the bar to the silent juke-box.

The long, low room filled with music. My kind of music—in fact, my record, one I'd given Louis, Haydn's London Symphony, his last. I knew If Thorn and I waited long enough before speaking we'd hear the best part— the part at the beginning of the last movement where the oboe joins the strings. Everything here was stage-set to be perfect. I was listening to wonderful music with a beautiful and exciting woman. Yet, nothing was really good. Nothing could be. Because lights had just gone out in my beautiful woman's eyes. And intuition told me she was thinking that, somewhere in this dark brooding city, her sister was alone and desperate, and perhaps at this moment waiting for some sleazy weasel of a heroin pusher to sell her relief.

It was not a time to attempt being diplomatic about disaster. I leaned across the table into a faint tease of perfume. 'Louis put on that music so we can talk without being overheard,' I said. 'Louis is a very understanding man. Gallant, too. But we're wasting it. So far, you haven't said one word.'

'I can't think where to start,' Thorn replied unhappily. 'You see, while you were talking with Dad, I listened from behind the living-room drapes. Until you noticed them moving. Then your eyes warned me you might rush across the room to drag me out.'

I waited.

Thorn hesitated, frown fixed. 'I knew you'd be at the house tonight,' she went on. 'Yesterday, Dad borrowed my portable to type the data he has on you. That foolscap sheet was on his study desk this morning. When I went to get my machine to make out some charity lists I noticed it, and I read it. Then, early tonight, I overheard Dad telephoning you. It wasn't hard to put two and two together.' Thorn paused to stare at me, her eyes terribly dark. 'You see,' she said, 'I know Helen's a drug addict. I've known it for some time. Long before my father learned about it. But I've been too horrified and bewildered to do anything constructive about it.'

I said, 'Well, at least *we two* know where we stand. Helen's an addict. We both know it. We both want to help her. She needs help. Not pity. But you'd better tell me everything you know. Beginning with the things that are too grim for your father to mention.'

For a moment, Thorn just sat. Our booth filled with thickening tenseness. The Haydn selection reached the oboe part—melody segued and started to build.

'Some things,' Thorn said, 'Dad was ashamed to talk about. He couldn't tell you that lately articles have been missing from the house. He can't quite face the fact of a daughter of his stooping to steal. Helen's stealing has been going on for a long time. Ever since she decided to move downtown. To take an apartment of her own.' Thorn sighed, stared off at nothing in particular. 'At first we all overlooked the stealing,' she said. 'We pretended not to notice things were missing. Missing after each time Helen came home for a visit. But the stealing grew steadily worse. A few weeks ago, Dad missed something really valuable. A ring. Part of a ring, tiara, necklace set that belonged to my mother. After mother died, Dad put the set away in his wall safe. Well—now the ring is gone.'

'I see. Have you an idea what the ring is worth?'

Thorn shook her head. 'A great deal. I should say, about ten thousand. Each piece of the set is individually insured, and that's the amount payable on the ring. I know because I saw the policy lying on Dad's study desk. He'd been checking it. He won't make a claim, of course. Because of Helen.'

I rubbed my cigarette out in one of Louis's little blue porcelain ashtrays. I was thinking that Huntley Ashton had better go on quietly paying premiums on that ring. Insurance companies don't much care *why* valuables are stolen; their interest lies only in protecting their risks, which they do, regardless of who gets hurt. I said, 'When did you first find out about Helen? About her using narcotics?'

'Well, I first became *suspicious* a few months ago. I noticed her acting rather queerly then.'

'Queerly? Will you detail that a little, please?'

'I'll try. She . . . well, she became terribly nervous. Jumpy, sort of. And she began having a funny look. As though someone were chasing her through her dreams. And I heard her being sick—frightfully, violently sick— the minute she got out of bed each morning. Then it got worse. She began to lose weight rapidly. And her eyes always looked weird. Bright and hard, with the pupils tremendously dilated. Then, one day, I went into her room while she was dressing. I noticed the veins on her left arm were discoloured, ugly and bruised-looking. I don't know what causes that, but it looked ghastly. Then I found streaks of blood on one of her towels. And I became really frantic.'

There was only one sensible way to explain things: bluntly. I said, and I hated each word as I said it: 'Bruised veins are the confirmed addict's trade mark. Repeated punctures with a hypo cause the bruises. You found blood streaks on Helen's towel because that morning she was impatient for a shot. She tore a vein using the needle. Addicts often tear veins. They're so shaky and sick and frantic for heroin relief they can't wait to inject properly.'

A shudder rippled Thorn's lovely shoulders. 'I still wasn't sure,' she went on determinedly. 'Not until one morning when I found a hypodermic needle and some capsules on Helen's dresser. Apparently, she had fallen into a drugged stupor and left them there. I've heard of drug addicts, of course—I suppose everyone has. But I couldn't believe it of my own sister; I couldn't. So I took one of the capsules. I brought it to a friend of mine interning at the General. He had it analysed. It contained an eighth grain of diacetyl morphine-hydrochloride.'

I nodded grimly. 'Heroin. Did you tell Helen you'd taken the cap?'

'Helen accused me of taking it. She was furious. She cursed me. Called me a dozen filthy names. She told me that what she chooses to do with her life is her own business. The next day she made another terrible scene and moved out of the house. She has her own money— Dad would have told you that if he hadn't been so upset. Grandfather left her a life income.'

I said, 'Well, it's not big enough—her income. It can't pay for a drug habit that grows a little more outsize every day. That's why Helen steals. It's why—if stealing failed—she'd eventually become desperate enough to try anything. Even the ultimate female resort.'

Something retreated in Thorn's eyes. It was like watching fires washing out. Her voice grew thin, bewildered. 'It's all so futile . . . degrading,' she said. 'I know Helen's . . .

wild. Bored with life. But a lot of people our age are. I—I suppose psychologists would call it a basic insecurity. But Helen is just not the type to do insane things like using drugs and stealing. It—it's horrible.' Thorn's fists clenched. 'I can't understand it. I just can't.' Her lips trembled. 'We're counting so much on you, you know, Dad and I. Perhaps because you understand Helen can't do anything to help herself.'

'Helping Helen is my job,' I said, summoning a smile. I added, 'And I'm afraid you're right. She *can't* do anything to help herself. By now, her habit must be so strong the rest of the world no longer exists for her.'

Thorn's eyes were wet, sparkling. 'It's not a habit,' she wrenched out. 'It's a curse. Needing narcotics is a horrible curse!' She closed her eyes.

'Thorn,' I said, making her look at me again. 'I *do* mean it when I say I'm going to do my job—the job I accepted in the living-room of your home. You must remember that.' I reached out my hand to steady her.

'Yes, I'll remember it, Max Dent,' she said. Her fingers came over mine, warm and soft. She turned my hand over slowly, brought the palm edgewise, and felt the hard, horned ridge developed only by judo. She didn't comment. I'm sure she didn't realize the meaning of the ridge. But she turned my hand over. Now I was holding hers. The left one. On its third finger was a thin silver band.

My eyes asked the obvious question.

Tucking her chin into her slim fingers, she said as if she were inside my mind, 'You want the *Thorn* Ashton story. All right, then. But there isn't too much to tell. You see, in these troublous years, mine's a commonplace female story.'

She hesitated, and distance began growing in her eyes. 'Korea took my man,' she said. 'He was the golden, smiling pilot that never came back. He transferred to Korea a month after we were married in a little Air

Force chapel in British Columbia. He wrote me wonderful letters. Letters from far-off places with fascinating names.' She said the names, very softly. '. . . Pusan . . . Formosa . . . Seoul . . . . It was all very romantic. He was a real Fly-Boy. Bombers. Immense silver ones. I saw them in B.C. They looked too remote, too beautiful to be touched. But they weren't. Because soon it all ended. His letters stopped coming. Then one came from Ottawa. That one told me I'd become a widow. A widow who never really had a chance to get to know her husband. All I had left was a *Thank You* note from the Department of Defence . . . and a little pair of ragged, silver wings.' She smiled, much too determinedly. 'He was a nice boy. Decent and fine. I'm glad I knew him, even a little. But now it seems distant— too long a time ago.'

Thorn's hand stirred abruptly in mine. I squeezed it. The small pressure snapped her attention sharply back.

She said unexpectedly, 'Max, there's another reason I waited for you tonight. I can't get any of this out of my mind. Not any. And even if it sounds silly, I feel that I can be doing something to help Helen. I *want* to do something. Anything.'

I squeezed her hand again. I couldn't tell Thorn Ashton that in my business there is only one yardstick of ability—a *fait accompli*. You must get results—and get them very fast. That is what I had to do now. I had to set up a situation that would leave me with a starting point; a foothold for my first uncertain step inside the drug ring. Then, I would move into a new world where I knew no one, and where no one, not any one, must know me. Obviously, there was no place in such a situation for Thorn Ashton.

I was still shaking my head as I stood up. 'You've already helped me more than you know,' I said seriously. 'And should things work out the way I expect, I'll probably need more of the same sort of help. Perhaps in a hurry. But, right now, I'm going to take you home.'

45

Thorn sat perfectly still, looking at me a moment, then said, equally serious, and not looking quite so much at me. 'Right, Max. When you want me, call me. I have my own telephone at home. I'm written down the number. I did that just in case.' Opening her handbag, she took out a carefully folded slip of paper and handed it to me. 'I'm ready to go now,' she smiled.

At her door, I held Thorn Ashton's hand for a long, extra second. She handed me her key. I opened the door. Beyond me, the hall stretched, dimly illuminated. Thorn turned a little. She looked me directly in the eyes and said, curiously, 'Max, in your work—to do what you are going to do now—a man really has to believe he's immortal, doesn't he?'

'In a way,' I replied, not too comfortably. 'At least, it helps. If a man doesn't believe that, he begins depending on other people. Then he becomes less and less a man.'

Thorn nodded. 'I thought so,' she said gravely, and added, 'I think you *are* immortal, Max. I really do.'

4 When I got back into my car, my watch showed two o'clock. Firefly lights across the city were slowly blinking out. The upper town lay sleep-locked. I drove south to Mountain Street, parked just below Dorchester. Stepping to the sidewalk, had I a stone in my hand, I could have thrown it blind in almost any direction and hit close to a café where liquor and sex were being sold

A doorman with the unhappy, precocious face of a calculating child nodded me indifferently into an all-night café. I moved into the overflow room, shouldered slowly towards a shallow orchestra platform. I found a table with a single empty chair. Noise poured all over me. It was awful. Like an after-hours Bedlam.

Above me, on the orchestra dais, a piano team faced

each other over twin grands. I glanced casually their way. If knowing the right people produced quick results, these two pianists were my dish. The thing was, my strategy would need to be a *tour de force*. A word out of place, and Phil's and Ziggy's addict cunning and caution would shake the lie from it.

The older of the two was a hot-jazz man on his way down. A boogie man with a bad left hand and a misplaced confidence in his ability as a scat-singer. Around town, he was known simply as Ziggy. His piano partner, Phil Chasen, had been a child prodigy. Phil was a bad case of too much too soon. He had skidded until he had become merely a brilliant young pianist with a prostituted talent and an overflow of charm. Phil's talent belonged in a concert-hall. Not here in an all-night dive patronized by cheap women and rounders and drunks. I stared at him until our eyes caught. He signaled with a dreamy nod of his head that he would be along as soon as time came for him to take a break.

The pianos segued smoothly into Latin rhythms. I glanced back at Phil. Beneath his outer contempt, he looked at peace and utterly relaxed; except that sometimes he smiled peculiarly, and the smile was in slow motion. I knew that less than two hours ago Phil had had a needle in his arm. My game, then, would be a waiting one. I would have to juggle Phil and Ziggy very carefully; to keep alert to the uncomfortable fact that my first mistake would be my last. One or the other of these two must be my trail-blazer—the unsuspecting addict who would point my first shaky steps into the fantasy-world of narcotic addiction—and trafficking.

Phil finished his set. He walked without looking to left or right down the narrow space between tables to where I sat; and with careful precision he lighted a dead cigarette he was holding. He said, with his dead-pan expression, 'Since when have you gone in for this kind of slop, Max? What brings you slumming?'

I smiled companionably, answered: 'A friend of mine's in town from Toronto. He's lining up a TV show for one of his accounts. A variety-type thing. I told him I know a top-notch piano team. He liked that. Said he'd talk it over with his partner when they get through burning up the hot spots tonight. He promised to call me at home.' I glanced at my watch. 'His call's almost due, Phil. If you and Ziggy want a chance at an appointment for an audition, it might be a good idea for all of us to get up to my apartment in a hurry.'

Phil's face tightened. 'Count us in!' he said, emphatically. 'Believe me, Max, we could use some of that fancy TV money. My bank account's flatter than a sax with a feathered reed; Ziggy's too.' He stared disgustedly at his tipsy audience. 'We're not due off for twenty minutes. Just the same, we'll break it off fast for a shot at TV. No one in this seedy dump will even know we've left.'

We drove up to Sherbrooke Street to my apartment. The two musicians sat in the back of my car, talking in conversational counterpoint about music, their hands hanging limply between their knees. My mind worked quickly over a plan. I had to stall, to keep these two minds busy, oblivious to everything but the instant, until a now dormant physical need for drugs overtook one of them and pressed the panic button. I had to take the long gamble that both would not feel that belly-clutching narcotic hunger at the same time; that one would be compelled to rush wildly off in search of heroin-relief while the other remained enough at ease physically to stay behind and be pumped for information. *Nasty,* but that was it.

I had the right equipment for keeping Phil and Ziggy oblivious.

The two musicians paused in the doorway of my living-room. They paid little attention to my maroon-papered walls, the armchairs, the long custom-built sofa, the soft white woodwork, the little bar, the laid fire that the touch of a match would send bright and glowing—but their eyes positively goggled at my out-size, multi-dialled, electronic-equipment-laden stereophonic hi-fi cabinet.

This miracle record-player was to be the tool of my trickery. My stalling would be accomplished with it, and some special double-track hi-fi records that even a tone-deaf sleepwalker couldn't resist. My machine is a custom-built Bogan. The cabinet is chambered and packed with sixty pounds of sifted white sand which does amazingly tender things to tone. Add special gadgets like woofer speakers, push-pull oscillators, signal boosters and dampers and you have something tremendous in sound. My machine has all that; it transmits binaural sound through either multiple speakers or individual sensitized headphones.

A stack of collector's item double-track records was ready beside the Bogan when Phil and Ziggy sat down, their eyes still bulging at the elaborate equipment.

'Relax,' I suggested, 'and put on a set of those ear-phones. We'll have a session. Like to hear the Symphony No. 13—the "Madras"? I've a cut of it that'll make your hair curl. No tubas, no trumpets, no trombones. Instead, an orchestra that uses Indian talbas and jalatarang. Apart from entrance cues, the Indian instruments improvise, and the mood they create is as soft as twilight.'

'Some rig! I'd say,' Ziggy ejaculated. 'In fact, wow! Looks to me like this session could be a real bash.'

'Well,' I said modestly, 'it'll keep us happy until I get that call from my TV friend.'

I put the 'Madras' on the turntable, adjusted dials, set the binaural stylus needle, and brought in music softly, grinning in spite of myself as the two waiting faces stiffened. Ziggy and Phil sat suddenly straight-up, rigid, as if their bones were made of glass. 'Oh my God!' Phil breathed. 'Just listen! It's live. Listen to those louds and softs. Those harmonics. I've never, never heard tone so sharp and clean. Never!'

As quickly as the record ended, I slipped on another binaural—Ravel's *Daphnis and Chloe*, the flip side, where the music describes dawn rising over the sheep pasture. Binaural sound thrummed through our sensitized ear-phones. Flutes became wakening birds; violins became soft, caressing morning winds. Brass wailed, bringing in *Daphnis*'s lament at finding *Chloe* gone. Ziggy and Phil sat as though hypnotized, transcended.

Ziggy hunched suddenly forward. His stubby fingers pressed the ear-phones tightly against his head. 'Man, oh, man,' he murmured.

My skin crawled at using the machine for this present purpose. But I kept putting on records—one after another, for an hour, two hours. Another record ... Some hairline adjustments ... The music hovering over us in remote, expanding waves ... No one stirring ... No one ... Then, at last, beads of sweat began to break slowly in bright, wet lines across Ziggy's forehead. Still another record, the flip side, then still another on the turntable. The rapturous expression faded a degree at a time from Ziggy's haggard face ... The sparks in his eyes slowly died into dirty ashes ... The insatiable heroin monkey was stirring on Ziggy's shoulder, beginning to gnaw hungrily, to tear. I reached to a new stack of binaurals. Everything was working precisely, according to my plan.

'Time out for a drink?' I suggested casually. 'Whisky. Anyone care to join me?'

Ziggy shot nervous eyes to the street window, where a square of sky had started to grey. His breath was spurting erratically from his lungs, betraying a mounting pain. 'No-no,' he gasped. 'Not for me. I don't want any whisky.'

I tapped Phil's arm. He brushed off my fingers. 'Unh-unh,' he said, still ecstatic. 'Be gone, Max. No drink for me, nothing. I don't even want to breathe while this music's on.'

I poured Scotch over ice, sipped slowly. I knew the weaker of the two men—Ziggy. Phil either stood closer to his last heroin shot, or he had a smaller habit and survived longer. I cautioned myself to be patient. But I was confident now that soon I would have Phil alone.

So, sitting hunched in a tight semicircle, resembling a trio of head-phoned wire-trappers we listened to the Bogan for another twenty minutes. And sweat gathered on Ziggy's glistening forehead. He looked at least six long agonizing hours from his last session with the needle.

I met his eyes, said casually, 'Warm, Ziggy?'

Abruptly, he lunged to his feet. He ripped off the ear-phones. His voice broke harshly: 'Look! Look at the window! See? It's light out. Bright daylight. We've been here all night. Your TV pal must have got lost in the Bellevue Casino chorus line. Max, I can't wait. Not one minute more. I've—I've got to go. Got to. To . . . to look up a guy.' He chewed viciously at his lip. 'Well, what about it?' he cried, his eyes on Phil. 'You coming down, too?'

Phil waved him off. 'Go yourself, Zig. Hustle on down. I'll be right here with this music until Max tosses me out.'

Ziggy's eyes were desperate in a haggard bony frame that once must have been a round and healthy, fat and smiling face. His emaciated body stirred, shuddered. He tried three times to light a cigarette and each time lost control of his hands and failed. A stream of mucus ran from his nostrils down his long, blue-shadowed upper lip. He brushed impatiently at the clotting filth. 'Money, then!' he gasped. 'Money, man. By Gad, I'm broke, flat. Lend me, Phil?'

'You kidding?' Phil retorted. '*Me*, with money?'

Quickly I took twenty dollars from my wallet. 'This should do you,' I said. 'Use what you need of it, Ziggy. Find a taxi and go wherever it is you must go. Take your time. I've a vocal I want Phil to hear.'

Ziggy snatched the money from my hands. And was gone!

51

For another hour, I listened with Phil. When a second Ravel double-track faded off into whispering woodwinds, I flicked off the Bogan and began faking control adjustments. If my trick didn't work now, it never would. I didn't have even a prayer left to offer. Out of a corner of my eye I studied Phil. He looked like a college boy. Like I had looked seven or eight years ago. Except that my pupils had never dilated to huge, narcotic-bright circles and I'd never needed to hide purple-scarred veins on my arms when I went swimming.

Phil felt my frank, disgusted stare. He misinterpreted its meaning, and began an uneasy squirming. 'Ziggy'll be back,' he said. 'Could be he had to sit around and wait. There's no way he could know for sure what time his guy will show up.'

'Well—the devil!' I growled. 'If Ziggy got stalled, the least he could do is telephone. After all, he has my money. I don't think I like this. Not at all. In fact, I think it's pretty damned second-rate of you two.'

'Maybe he had to wait for a cab,' Phil muttered, after a grinding silence.

'A cab? That's a laugh. He could have made it downtown by pogostick by now. With time to give away.'

Phil laughed, that ridiculous way people do when they feel they have to laugh at something they don't think at all funny. 'D-don't g-go on like t-this, Max,' he stuttered. 'Ziggy'll make it back. Y-you have the d-damndest look on your f-face!'

Now. It had to be now. Now was the moment for me to reach for the information I must have. I heard the crash of a door down the hall—and over that far distant sound, the hard thumping of my heart. I forced cold anger into my face, thinking grimly of how helpless I would be left if Phil didn't rise to my bait. 'Time!' I shouted. 'Curse it, Ziggy's had time. You two are working me for a fool. You must think I'm really easy. Ziggy couldn't care less about coming back. He won't be back tonight. Or ever!'

Phil stiffened, edged away from me. He was smiling and his smile was a sick thing. 'Please, p-please, Max, be reasonable. The fellow Ziggy has to see hangs out a long way from here.'

I reached for Phil's shoulder, drew him to me. 'A long way!' I roared into his frightened face. 'I guess so. A hell of a long way. Siberia? Mozambique? Is that where Ziggy had to go with my money?'

And Phil, his lips white and less than an eighth of an inch apart—as if delivering a fatal verdict—said clearly and distinctly: 'Max, he had to go all the way down to Clarke and St. Catherine. How can you expect him to get there and back in an hour?'

I had my information—I began breathing again. All that remained now was to get rid of Phil.

I stamped about the room, muttering and grumbling. 'One hour!' I said cuttingly. 'That's good. You're quite the comic, Phil. It takes an hour, you say. Well, it's been well over an hour, and I've taken about enough. From both you jokers. I'm going to bed.' Striding stiffly to the door, I jerked it wide. 'Now, get out!' I bellowed. 'Get out of my apartment. But fast. And forget about that TV audition. Far as I'm concerned, it's kaput. But when you sit opposite Ziggy tonight, you'd better tell him I'll be dropping in. That he'd be wise to have twenty dollars waiting for me. You tell him that, Phil!'

Phil swallowed hard. He needed drugs desperately now. His face had the common look of the addict on it— the look of fright, of hungry, drawn, emptiness. Muttering something inaudible, he ran past me—out of my open door in a wild, arm-flapping rush.

Clarke and St. Catherine Streets. Somewhere near that corner—in a café or a club, a store, a rooming-house, a tavern, a restaurant—the city's lost battalion of addicts met drug-ring pushers and bought black-market heroin.

Somewhere in that overflowing area, waited another Phil—another panic-crazed addict who could be deceived into guiding me a step deeper inside. The stage was set, the play was on. Now, I would have to step into character.

5 St. Catherine Street at Clarke looked dirty and old. I stood beside a corner tavern, studying names on storefronts and cheap hotels. Ordinary, unimaginative names that offered me no clue. I was growing more nervous by the minute. The pits of my arms felt wet. A drop of sweat slid down my back. In my trouser pocket there was an addict's hypo and two capsules of heroin I had begged from a doctor friend. The needle and drugs I intended to make available as proof that I could be trusted as a member of the lost battalion.

I moved slowly down the street, only my finger-tips showing below the sleeves of an old, faded trench-coat I'd bought in a pawnshop less than an hour ago. I began wishing to God I were psychic, or that Phil had been a little more specific. I walked on, scanning storefronts for a hint. Two uniformed police paced past me, turned to eye me coldly. I turned back to the corner tavern, the chill wind and the world's eyes on me and my throat choked with dust, and I was finding out too abruptly how it felt to be the hunted rather than the hunter.

The cold wind slid around the corner of Clarke, whipped up the skirts of my trench-coat. The two police paced slowly back towards me. Desperation began tying hard, cramping knots in my stomach. My eyes leaped across the street to a dirt-crusted all-night restaurant. The place had a dejected, hang-out look. I stared through its steam-streaked windows. A dozen or so shabby men and women sat in white table-chairs. No one was eating— only sipping coffee, and waiting, leaning forward.

Muttering a prayer, I crossed the street. I pushed open the restaurant door and stepped inside. To my right, just beyond the entrance, stood a cashier's desk. I stopped to buy matches. An overgrown kid with a pair of shifty eyes slapped two books to the counter and held his hands out for the pennies. I began my act. An act that *must* be convincing enough, utterly realistic enough to deceive a group trained to always doubt, to always double-check. I yawned elaborately, yawned again and pulled out a thick, untidy wad of thirty one-dollar bills. I treated myself to still another vacant yawn. The roll of bills hung loosely from my hand. I scooped up my silver change, and with the expansive, over-careful clumsiness of the drugged man, pushed it and the bills into the pocket where the addict's hypo and heroin caps were burning holes. I bought coffee at a self-service counter, helped myself sloppily to sugar. Then, under a dozen pairs of intent, staring eyes, I stumbled to an empty chair and flopped into it loosely. Again, I managed an elaborate yawn. This time, the addicts in the table-chairs exchanged quick, conspiratorial glances.

Between sloppy sips of coffee and a studied appearance of being drugged and drowsy, I got a smoke lighted. I kept my eyes blinking, closing. My head nodded. The cigarette burned slowly down and singed my hanging fingers. The cigarette fell, spiraled smoke up from the floor. My chin dropped unheeded to the faded lapels of my trench-coat. Feeling with every nerve the electric atmosphere of the restaurant, I feigned drugged sleep.

A voice close by me whispered in coarse French: 'A new one ... Watch 'im. He could be a plant. He's pretty big. Maybe a snooper ... a damn Mountie!'

An English female voice replied from so close the words pinged in my ear: 'No. Loaded. Full of heroin. Carrying a roll, too.'

The French voice laughed mockingly. 'Aha! We weel see. Yes, you bet. Look! Frankie gets ready. 'e saw that roll, him. 'e weel find out sometheeng!'

For a full two minutes not a finger stirred, nothing stirred in that drum of silence and steamy wet heat.

Directly before me, before my hooded eyes, a small, nervous, sharp-eyed man began to fidget. He stared at me so intently I could feel the heat of his burning gaze. Finally, he stood up. He slicked his grey-shot hair, and pressed a thin hand against his side. Like a cautious ferret he edged to the table-chair beside mine, sat down. My eyes remained clamped shut. They stayed so while an inexpert hand slid under cover of a spread newspaper into my pocket. I slumped, limp as a dish-rag.

Little sharp-eyes worked forefinger and thumb around my wad of dollar bills. I felt his thin fingers move deeper to the planted hypo and capsules. I could tell by the quickening of his breathing that he knew what they were. Slowly, cautiously, he began emptying my pocket.

This was the world now. A world of silence where the tiny whispering of flesh against fabric was all that mattered. That, and a tremendous bluff.

Too intent on keeping my body relaxed, I barely re-strained a sudden impulse to wet my lips. I clamped my teeth. Somehow, I got through the lifetime of a few seconds without moving. I sensed, rather than saw, Frankie move away.

A thousand impressions shone before my closed eyes. Everything going on in the restaurant, every small sound, each rattle of cup or plate pointed to me. Every leaning body faced me. I could feel scores of appraising eyes, like floodlights, upon me; feel the mockery of them. In the heavy darkness behind my closed eyes an awareness that was hypersensitive gave me a crazy sensation of sitting straight up and staring back at the intent addicts.

A deep voice across the room suddenly said, 'Son of a—! Me, I don't kick. But always when there is something good, Frankie winds up with the gravy! *Comprenez-vous?*'

A stranger before my lidded eyes cautioned: 'Quiet!

Are you a fool? Don't say a stinking word. You know how easy Frankie can cut us off—well, shut up!'

My head had been down nearly an hour. I couldn't stand it any more. The tension in the rendezvous was reaching out to me, pouring all over me. I raised my head, looked confused. Then I began a convincing impression of a narcotic hangover. I shuddered all over, rubbed violently at my eyes and nose as though they itched, grimaced as though wracked by sudden cramps. As if for reassurance, I thrust my hand into my pants pocket. I forced a look of apprehension on to my face. I dug with frantic haste through every pocket of my clothes. A full dozen addicts edged farther forward in their chairs.

I came to my feet in a rush, whirled furiously to face the silent room. . . .

'I've been rolled . . . Rolled, y'hear me?' I roared at the top of my lungs. 'Some crud of a lightfinger cannoned me while I was on the nod!'

No one moved. I watched the expressionless faces, acutely aware of my own vulnerability. I could hear the sound of my own heartbeat thumping in crazy counterpoint to the ticking of the fly-specked clock on the wall. Then paper rustled loudly as Frank shook out a copy of a show-business newspaper and began reading. Behind his paper, he was singing softly, mockingly.

I lunged forward, slapped the paper aside, grabbed hold of Frankie's lapels. I jerked him to his feet and drove him squealing backward on his heels until his head cracked against a far wall. My arms inched him up—up slowly, until he stood on the very tips of his toes.

I hissed into his fear-white face. 'Some dirty dip picked my pocket!' I lifted him again, shook him like a puppy, held him, and shook him harder. 'You like singing, sing my way! Who did it? Go on, talk . . . Who did it?'

His face pinched with agony, and his eyes glowed like two huge and bright sparks from far, far back in their dark, sunken sockets. Phlegm bubbled nastily in his throat. I shook him again, dribbled his head hard against the white-tiled wall. 'Who got into my pockets?' I shouted.

'Let-me-be!' he gasped. 'I didn't s-see a thing. Not a thing. I been r-reading my p-paper.' His right hand pawed awkwardly at me. 'Thass all—just reading. Lemme go. God-Jesus! You're taking my throat out.'

My fingers relaxed suddenly. Frankie fell in a foolish, untidy heap. A silly desire to laugh stirred in me as he scrambled to his feet, clutching at his throat, flicking resentful eyes at the amused, motionless addicts. Quickly, he circled around me, put a table between us.

'Stay away!' he bellowed, still backing off. 'Hey—you crazy or something? You bloody near choked me. And all the time, I'm telling you the living truth ... the gospel! I didn't see nothin'.' He swept a greying strand of hair from his eyes, and sidled back a little towards me. He looked suddenly ridiculously bland and honest and convincing. 'Why pick on me?' he complained. 'You made a big mistake there. Not that you got much of a case for belly-aching, anyway—' a hint of self-satisfied grin crept over his lips, then crept off '—not after you come wandering into a dead-end dump like this and fall asleep. But maybe you're the type of big guy that likes pushing around little guys, like me.'

I pursed my lips, made a contemptuous sound. But I was thinking furiously, handling each impression as carefully as glass. I heard stiff, sliding footsteps approaching. I turned slightly to one side, and saw a girl coming towards me. Her face was ghastly white, her mouth so bloodlessly tight it might have been a half-healed scar. She passed me, and went on towards the john. 'I'm sick,' she said in a sad, empty voice. 'I need a fix. A fix, a fix.'

Frankie slid into the nearest chair, flicked his eyes to the watchful addicts, slid them back to me. 'So you got robbed,' he said, with returning confidence. 'Well, it doesn't worry me any. I don't even know you. You a local guy?'

I sent a glare around the addict's rendezvous—but I was smiling to myself. 'No,' I lied. 'Vancouver's my town. Be sure of one thing, little man; if I was local I'd be wise to this two-bit clipjoint.'

Frankie had grown completely calm, cautious. 'Who sent you in here?' he demanded with sudden sharpness. 'You didn't just wander in off the drag to buy coffee.'

I stared at him coldly. 'A guy I pal with out west steered me here. Told me the place is—friendly? So he was wrong. D'you care? You a cop or something?'

Frankie didn't hurry to answer. His face had closed in a curious, tight, animal wariness. He dug out a crumpled pack of cigarettes, lit one, blew out deliberate spurts of smoke. He fingered the twisted package, turned it absently over and back, over and back. My eyes were drawn to his twitching fingers. They were nicotined, those fingers, raw with open blisters that come from falling asleep smoking after using heavy doses of drugs. He caught me eyeing his burns. 'That's a crazy crack, pal,' he scowled. 'That copper bit, I mean. You know I'm not a copper. Just like I know you're not the kind of guy that brings his beefs to the law.'

I rode him a little—thrust him back on the defensive. 'For a guy hanging out in a two-bit hashhouse,' I grunted, 'you talk a lot. In fact, you're the granddaddy of all the goofball windbags.'

'Have it your own way,' Frankie said softly. 'In the meantime, let's get factual. You came here and you got rolled. Okay. What did you lose?'

'A pocketful. Enough to give me a few ideas. Ideas about the dream-merchants that sit around this dump, and don't eat.'

That remark won me an odd look, then a surprising wink. For a moment, Frankie concentrated on the smoke trailing from his cigarette. He was thinking about the addict's hypo, the two caps of heroin he had dug out of my pocket. Then, suddenly, he said exactly what I wanted

59

him to say. He said, 'Maybe you heard about me—maybe not. I'm Frankie Seven. In person. I footz around this joint most of the day. I hang out here—and not because of my appetite, either.' He hesitated, then made a decision and added pointedly, 'Pal you should be glad to know me. I'm a guy that can do things for certain people. I'm a guy you can ask questions. I just might answer them. Likewise, I might not. Just ask me.'

Just ask me!

My mouth was too dry. I wanted a drink of cold water. A weakness that had been building in the pit of my stomach was turning to nausea. I edged back to my chair, thinking furiously, wondering if my bluff had really worked on Frankie, as it seemed to have, or if, instead, Frankie, with all his back-alley wisdom and caution, was simply playing a bluffing game of his own.

Just ask me! I hadn't propositioned Franke; he'd propositioned me. That mitigated the possibility of a counter-bluff. So, again, I must gamble. Now that I had established Frankie as a drug-ring pusher, I must work at filling him so full of confidence that he, too, could be used as a pawn.

I played it cautiously—got away from Frankie without uttering another word. I simply got up and walked out. I dared not rush things. I knew that before being fully accepted at the rendezvous I would be manœuvered into further test and attack. When that time came, I wanted to be fully prepared. In fact, I intended to stay at all times a jump ahead, to be always on the offensive.

Still feeling eyes burning against my back, I caught a taxi five full blocks away from the restaurant. No one was behind me. I gave the driver some devious directions, and then checked behind me again. Still nothing. Yet, I had the feeling there were eyes on me. I rode uneasily uptown to Stanley Street, where I stopped for a breather.

Out of nowhere, a sidewalk panhandler sidled up to me, pressed close. The man stank, and the hand he held out was grimy and shaking. He looked as though he'd risen from the ultimate depth of Purgatory. 'Subscribe, my friend,' he wheezed. 'Donate to my utter disaster. Not at all an ordinary bum, me. I imbibe only Pernod. Pernod makes one float. So I float.' He spread his arms, flapped them gently. Made a ludicrous and bleary-eyed wink. I gave him a dollar. Tried to walk around him. He grabbed my arm. 'I tell you, the Lord looks after the fall of every little sparrow!' he said with drunken solemnity. 'Every little sparrow. But you watch yourself. Watch yourself.'

I shook off his arm. His hand came up in a mock half-salute. With a wordless grin, he turned and scurried off into the morning quietness of a deserted side street.

I turned towards a private gym located a block east. For over an hour, I practiced bar-jitsu and judo chops. Gradually, I was getting my mind and body tuned to the ruthless situation I was immersed in. I was hardening my protective covering until it would be as tough as that of the people with whom I was dealing.

For the next ten days I played crazy but cautious games of mental hide-the-button with Frankie. I sat in the same table-chair in the rendezvous-restaurant hour after hour, until my nerves thrummed with tension. Always, there was the same rancid smell of cooking fat, always the same cloying stink of human desperation— desperation radiated by people forced by the cost of their drug habit into daily crime, into becoming shoplifters, confidence-men, safecrackers, hotel-prowlers and house-prowlers, pickpockets and, saddest of all, into prostitutes who worked the streets and shabby hotel rooms, renting their bodies out like lending library books. I became as familiar with Canadian addicts and their habits as I was with the blue haze of smoke layering over the filthy, yellowing walls of the rendezvous.

Each day became like suffering through a tragic play I had suffered through before. It was like watching

61

people resign one by one from the human race. It was my world. Often, I thought of Kipling's words 'To the legion of the lost ones, To the cohort of the damned—'

I kept on top of Frankie. I continued to answer his sly questions, to build up his reluctant confidence, always believing that he would be the one to lead me on towards the centre of the trafficking ring. Slowly, he grew more sure of me. Time came to add strength to his confidence. I left a smoke-blackened spoon on the cracked sink in the restaurant john—a suggestion that, like the bonafide addicts hanging about, I cooked-up and injected heroin there. I knew Frankie would check the washroom after I used it. He always did. Frankie checked everything.

He found the spoon, of course, and came hurrying from the john, blinking excitedly. He stepped directly, purposefully, to my chair. His lips curled upwards in scorn. 'You're so smart,' he sneered, sounding completely disappointed. 'So damn smart, wise guy from Vancouver. Well, you haven't fooled me. You're on Route Zero. You're a user—an addict. A careless one. You left your cooking spoon in the john!'

To angle him a little closer, I acted innocent. 'Dream on!' I said with a laugh. 'What tells you *I* ever had a cooking spoon?'

'This!' With a triumphant flourish, Frankie handed me my planted spoon. 'It's yours—all yours! I know because I checked the john just before you went in, then right after you came out.' Cockily, he blew smoke into my face. 'You know what that proves, pal? It proves that I figured you right. That you're hooked. That you shoot joy into your arms, same as me. But it proves something else, too. That you're dumb, careless. Real careless. Like a booster that don't watch his back. That's bad. You've goofed twice, pal. Lost two out of two falls. Once when you blew into this joint. Again when you forgot this spoon.'

'Okay. I'm careless, so what? It's my skin.' I stared at

him resentfully, and I lied indignantly: 'And I'm a user, too. I take a joy-pop once in a while when I'm feeling low. This round I needed a fast shot. So I took a chance on a quick cook-up in the john. So what?'

Frankie smiled coldly, edged closer to me. 'God, you're perfect!' he said with heavy sarcasm. 'Once in a while you take a small fix! I know what that means to a junker.' He stared away to the steamy-wet street window, to the firmly closed door of the john, then, not looking at me, said casually over his shoulder, 'This pal of yours in Vancouver. Did he tip you off to anywhere else you could buy heroin in Montreal?'

I swept my eyes quickly about the restaurant. Two men stood silently watching Frankie and me from a corner. Watching with hard, glacier-cold eyes. Things were developing fast. Much too uncomfortably fast.

Desperately, I picked a pair of names out of my memory: two small-time drug operators who had some time ago made brief local headlines by stumbling awkwardly into an R.C.M.P. trap and had subsequently sweated out two years of prison time. 'My pal in Van gave me a local lead in, sure,' I growled. 'He told me to contact Socio and Delude. He even tipped me off to the address of the café they run as a blind.'

Frankie stared at me in amazement. Then he burst into a spasm of violent laughter that left him clutching his stomach, his face the colour of greasy cream. 'Those jerks!' he roared. 'Your pal gave you those jerks, he must have been peddling memories. Socio and Delude aren't hustling heroin any more, pal. They're out of circulation. Kaput—have been for a long time. They're ancient history, like.'

I changed my tactics immediately, came in for a frontal attack.

'Okay, my pal tipped me wrong. Should he know those two got pinched? It's three thousand miles to the

63

coast. Besides, he left a little heat in this town and wouldn't be keeping up close contact. All he told me was about this place—and Socio and Delude. Anyway, forget the quiz-biz. I don't go for it. Let's just skip what I was told. Suppose I just plain and simple ask *you* where to connect for H.'

It was a fishing expedition, but Frankie was still circling too cautiously to rise to the bait.

He was laughing. A smug, irritating laughter. His eyes slid to the two watching men. Pinching my sleeve between his finger and thumb, he pulled me close enough to whisper slyly in my ear: 'I'd say, see me in the morning pal. But that's all I'd say. Just that. No more.'

He gave my sleeve a final, sharp tug, then got up and scurried away.

I sat there, thinking. Before going on to the next manœuvre with Frankie, I wanted the mysterious element in Helen Ashton's past cleared up, I wanted to know her present condition. I wanted to visit Helen's hide-out apartment because I was convinced it would tell me something. But I had to be positive Helen would be out, the apartment empty.

I finally paid my bill at the cashier's and stepped out-side.

The streets were afternoon bright, the sky an endless tent of washed blue. Drawing a cool, grateful breath, I stepped along briskly for the West End.

I realized almost at once I'd picked up a tail. The two shadowing me, their shoulders hunched against the October wind, their footsteps moving with a driving intentness of purpose, were equally as obvious now as they had been watching from their corner in the addicts' rendezvous. They were overdue. For a full week, I'd been waiting for the drug ring to set a tail on me.

I walked steadily on along St. Catherine. The side-walks were overflowing. Small groups of shoppers hud-dled in doorways out of the wind. Waiting for street-cars.

Other groups stood in front of store windows. Ahead of me loomed a massive, grey-faced cathedral sided by a narrow, decorous alley. As I reached the alley, the drug-ring musclemen, one big and square, the other short and rapier-thin, pressed along twenty short feet behind. Before they came pounding up, I had a few seconds to turn and run half-way into the alley and step inside a deep cathedral doorway.

I pulled off my gloves.

Footsteps sounded hollowly. I set myself. Big and Square lunged into the alley, his head thrust forward belligerently, breath floating like frozen gauze from his broken nose. He saw me too late, got only a quick glimpse of my raised hand. A flash of blind fear widened his eyes. I smashed the side of my left hand, extended poker-stiff, bar-jitsu style, against the thin, shell-like side of his skull.

Big and Square dropped as though he had been pole-axed. The Pepe le Moko type running too close behind him let out a sudden shrill squeal and tripped headlong over his sprawled body. I jumped over Big and Square, thrust my hand quickly under his playmate's collar. I pumped him up, up until I breathed into his face.

I had to use every counter-trick. I had to eliminate every wispy breath of doubt. I had to pretend I thought this tail was Narcotic Squad—not drug ring—and that I was an addict who lived his daily life fearing tails and official frisking for drugs. I spat at the man I held in my two hands. I spat into his face. 'You Mountie flatfoot . . . Lousy cop,' I ground out. 'Trying to suck me in for a heroin search . . . Trying to grab me in possession. Trying to nail me. I knew you two were Horsemen—figured it as soon as I saw you!'

The little drug-ring thug gaped at me in amazement. I pushed his body off a little, smashed my knee up into the soft spot just under his belly button. The force of the cruel stomach blow set him off into a kind of ballet; his right knee drew up, his left hand pressed into his middle.

65

Another gentle push sent him teetering off. He danced crazily in short mincing steps right across the alley. Then his eyes slid whitely up into his forehead and collapsed like a punctured balloon.

Two priests stepped from the side door of the cathedral, stood utterly still with wide unbelieving eyes. The tableau lasted only a fraction of a second. Then the priests suddenly summoned enough breath and began to holler. I broke for the end of the alley, running with long clown strides that brought me quickly into the thrusting sidewalk crowds.

I stood for a moment in my dusty, library-quiet office, my hand on the telephone, thinking about what I had to do, about what had already been done. A sense of horror and alarm began ding-donging inside me. A picture of the situation as it now existed formed slowly before my eyes . . . an impressionist painting of horror that was a series of faces; Frankie's, the musclemen's, the addict's, as they leaned forward in their table-chairs, all hovering over the city.

I fought down the anger that bubbled inside me, and reached out for the telephone directory. Helen Ashton had no listing. I dialled Information, wheedled an unlisted number. After twenty rings allowed in case Helen was in the tub or in a drugged stupor, the shrill ringing persisted without pause for breath.

I hung up, checked my watch.

In fifteen minutes, I dialled again. Still no answer. I leaned back, thinking; measuring possibilities. Helen could be gone for the afternoon—she could also be at the corner and due back in ten minutes.

Danger there. If I were surprised in the middle of a search, my life could suddenly get very uncomfortable. Still, the apartment had to be checked—if only for stray bits of information that might be gleaned from pawn-tickets for stolen jewels, from forgotten letters, or perhaps from a woman's address book, anything that might help to bring Helen's mysterious past into better focus.

I tried the number a third time. Still no answer. I shrugged into my topcoat—camel's hair, this time, not faded trench—then hurried out to flag down a cab.

6 I sat back in the cab, hoping Helen was not the type to ignore persistently ringing telephones.

I paid off the cab at Cote des Neiges, walked around the corner. Well back from the sidewalk, a large, ultra-modern apartment house sat snobbishly, its windows golden in the slanting afternoon sun. I followed a crescent-shaped walk to a terrace entrance. An aged major-domo told me that Miss Helen Ashton had suite 212.

The hallway on the second floor smelled of good cigars and a hint of scented disinfectant. I went on my toes down a long ribbon of carpet to the end door. I pressed the bell button.

Chimes sounded dully from inside. I glanced at my watch. I had a feeling that the next half-hour could be crucial as far as Maxwell Dent was concerned. Breaking and entering is an extremely serious offence for a private operative. It's almost equally serious to withhold any evidence of criminal knowledge or activity that may be found on the entered premises.

My finger grew numb on the bell button. I put an ear to the door and all I heard was the pounding of my own heart. I took out a thin strip of celluloid and worked it carefully between the jamb and the door, sliding it down until it touched the spring catch lock. I manipulated the celluloid gently around the catch and the door swung smoothly open to reveal a large living-room.

I stepped inside. Soft slats of sunshine slanted through half-closed Venetian blinds. A clock on the white mantle loudly ticked away a full minute. The smell of a woman and the things she lived with teased my nostrils.

Much about the way a person lives is told by the smell of their rooms. The perfume odour clinging to Helen Ashton's chintzed furniture and floor-length monk's-cloth drapes told me she had taste—and access to grandfather's legacy. The lack of food smell told me she seldom ate at home and that her entertaining was limited. The acrid tang of stale cigarette butts in the cloisonné ashtrays and—less obvious—dust told me her housework was done by a casual cleaning-woman.

Two doors led off this main room. One would be a bedroom; the other a bathroom. I tiptoed to the bathroom; nothing, only jars, tubes, vials and the musky smell of a woman's body.

I padded across the carpet to the opposite door. I twisted the glass knob, let it roll silently under my hand. I pushed open the door, smelling the dull, heavy air of the bedroom sweep out into my face.

I caught my breath. Began cursing softly. My feet rooted in the floor, lifeless, petrified.

From the very beginning, I had been utterly wrong. Helen Ashton was not out, not gone down to the corner, not anywhere. The reason her ringing telephone had been ignored was because Helen was incapable of answering it. Nevertheless, there was no turning back now, I had to go inside. Into the bedroom where Helen waited.

It was like nothing I had ever seen before in my life. Beyond the open bedroom door, a thin afternoon light shimmered in a misty pool on the bed. The scene was a fantastic one; it looked exactly as though it were happening on a stage, a nightmare stage.

Helen had left this world. She had gone into the shadows, slugged herself insensible with a terrific overdose of heroin. She lay in a loose, ugly sprawl on the bedspread. A filmy negligee crawled negligently over her thighs. One sleeve of the negligee was rolled tightly up to the shoulder

and that arm extended, white and limp. A doctor's hypodermic syringe hung from the blood-encrusted main-line
vein like an antenna beaming in waves of death.

I stood completely still at the side of the bed. My two
eyes were held nailed to the protruding hypo. The blood
it had let was a crusted smear almost to Helen's wrist. I
reached down to touch her forehead. Her skin felt as
though it held fire. Her broken breathing rasped silently in
my mind. I touched the white flesh on her thigh, pinched
it. She didn't move.

Stepping back I stood just looking at her. Helen was
blonde where Thorn was dark and before drugs had
torn her apart she might have been almost as beautiful.
Now, Helen had no beauty. Only a wasted body barely
breathing under a ruined death-mask of a face.

I tore my eyes from the bed and went deliberately
to work on drawers and on books and under rugs and
on everything in and beyond sight. It was slow work
because everything had to be checked twice to make sure
no trace remained of a search. But nothing turned up.
No pawn-ticket for a missing ring, no letters, no address
book. Nothing. Only an odd feeling of incompleteness,
as though the apartment had something more to tell me
if I dared take more time and knew where to look.

There was still the living-room. I worked down the
walls, lifting a series of framed Bellow originals one by
one until they led me to a third corner and three more
paintings; landscapes by Thor Junger, the mad German
painter. I stepped back unconsciously, my mind drawn
away from my purpose by the almost animate human
quality Junger had invested in the three scenes. Finally, I
moved to the fourth corner of the room and an expensive
Dumont record-player.

I started to pass up the machine, then was pulled back
my curiosity. I lifted a record from a small pile, glanced
at the credit—Gershwin. Another—Revel and Gordon.

Another—Rodgers and Hammerstein. Another—Chopin piano solo played by Levant. I reached again and a ragged slip of pink paper fluttered brightly to the carpet. I bent for it. A telephone number leaped from the pink scrap into my consciousness.

I stared at the penciled number and all the quietness in the room built slowly up around me. Convulsively, my fingers tightened over the bit of paper. I found Helen's directory and checked the number in my memory against the number penciled on the scrap. My memory had been right. I pulled out a handkerchief, wiped perspiration from my face. The number scrawled on the pink scrap corresponded with the telephone listing of the club where Phil Chasen worked. Another point was proven; the drug ring held as small, as tight, and as closely-knit as I had expected. One thing demanded to be done. I hurried back to the bedroom.

Helen hadn't moved. For a long time, she wouldn't even flutter an eyelid. I stared down at her. I could feel a dull throb of pain behind my eyes. All the emotions a man knows when he looks at a woman who has been ruined stirred in me. I don't know what made me want to cover her properly. Perhaps because she looked forgotten and helpless and indecent. Anyway, I reached to the hem of her negligee, lifted it to draw over her naked thighs. Being human, being male, my eyes fell. I felt my face tighten in a grimace that bared my teeth. I was staring at Helen's abdomen, at the naked frightfulness of it. My brain kept rushing signals that should have snapped my locked eyes from the puckered flesh, the cruel incision scars, and the livid criss-crossing weals, but the motor nerves were paralysed and my gaze held.

. . . and I had come looking for causes. Sweet God! I had never bargained for this. Not for this. Not this.

At last, something broke inside me and let a signal through. My hand opened limply and the negligee fell. I backed stiff-legged from the bed.

A voice inside me kept screaming, Get out! Get out before you use ice and steel on her, before you revive her and force her to admit what mad devil of a doctor butchered her that way. Get out before you make her tell you who left her to suffer alone after that criminal brutality was done. . . . Then my mind cleared enough for me to remember my purpose in coming back to the bedroom.

I bent over, and with a handkerchief wrapped around my hand, pulled gently on the hypo until it left the limp arm and lay free in my fingers. I laid the hypo on the dressing-table. Left it there, blood-crusted and vile. Then, in a hurry, I got out into the fresh air.

Anger made me want to smash holes in walls—or go looking for an argument. Instead, I went home and broke out a fresh bottle of Scotch. The whisky tasted horrible. My living-room seemed strange and unreal. The long afternoon shadows seemed to be pushing into my mind and heart.

I set aside my glass—and staring straight ahead, I began thinking, began tightening my plan, preparing for another cautious move.

I decided that early the next morning, on my way to the addicts' rendezvous, I would buy a pair of pretty Royal Doulton china dolls.

7 'Scum! That's what pushers are!' The woman kept buttoning and unbuttoning her shabby coat. 'They're all scum!'

The rendezvous throbbed with tension. Scattered among the white table-chairs were a score or more of addicts—all hungover. Their eyes streamed, their fingers trembled, their limp bodies shook from sneaking spasms of pain. A tall, narrow-faced man rubbed the stubble on his chin impatiently. He turned to a dark, brittle-looking woman at his side, muttered angrily: 'Late, late—always late! Once they get you hooked, the pushers know you'll wait if it takes for ever.'

The street door opened, letting in a blast of icy air. Everyone leaned forward.

A platinum-haired girl with a long-limbed, thin and taut body stood in the doorway. She was looking the restaurant and its inhabitants over . . . hunter-fashion. She glanced quickly from side to side, and went to the food bar to buy coffee, nodding in a semi-hostile way to acquaintances along the aisles.

Said one, 'Well, well, look who's back in circulation. Dream Street Fay!'

Said another, 'Huh! Bad news for the department store dicks. They'll be losing plenty sleep now!'

Fay brought her coffee to the table-chair beside mine. She drank off half her cup in a quick gulp then, as the damp warmth of the restaurant hit her, flung her coat open.

On each inside of the coat's skirts was stitched a foot-square shoplifter's stash pocket.

She watched me light up, and when my cigarette was going, pinched her nostrils suggestively. 'Got an extra one, honey?'

I shook out a cigarette. 'You on an economy binge?' I said coldly. 'Or just fresh out?'

'Yeah—fresh out,' she retorted, her upper limp trembling. 'That's good. Real good. I'm fresh out, all right. Fresh out of the poky!'

I glanced at her with fresh interest.

'Sure,' she said matter-of-factly. 'Didn't you hear the ribbing I got from the bunch here? I just hit the street an hour ago.' She puffed slowly, but with savage gestures, then grabbed my arm and held it like something she'd captured in the woods. 'Say, honey,' she said. 'do you happen t'know little Frankie Seven?'

I said casually, remembering that I was still on sufferance, 'In a way. Fact is, I'm waiting for Frankie myself.'

Fay had sharp, winter-cold eyes, and she jabbed them at me, stared me up and down. Her lips parted in a weary-wise smile. 'You too, eh?' she said, 'Hooked, eh, honey? You must be if you're here waiting for Frankie. Well, I hope the little rounder hurries up.' She snickered and there was something obscene about her snicker. 'I'm dragged,' she said. 'Real dragged. Those Headquarters dicks booked me for vag then held me three days for a blood test. The lice. Three days in the Fullum Street women's poky. Some dump!'

'Aren't they all!' I said sympathetically. 'Just the same, three measly days shouldn't throw you.'

Her lip curled. 'You kidding? With my habit? Buster, I was shooting ten caps a day—more if I could get enough money. I'd be screaming my head off right now if it wasn't for some seconols I smuggled into my cell. What a laugh that was! Say, honey, those dopey jail matrons didn't even search me. Mostly, they're so suspicious they'll skin-frisk a bubble dancer. Not these last few days, though. Reform shake-up nerves, I guess. Anyway, when I went in they didn't even ask for peekings.'

I didn't ask Fay to describe how she had smuggled her barbiturates into the women's jail. Jail-wise women the world over have always secreted their small treasures in the same ultimate female hiding-place. I nodded and smoked, waiting for nerves to prompt more conversation from her.

She muttered irritably: 'That Frankie! I hope the little vulture'll go for a couple of caps on the cuff. I'm broke—tapped, and I'm too for God's-sakes hungover to begin operating before I get a fix.'

'So you're sick,' I retorted. 'Well, who isn't? You'll manage to survive. Ever think that Frankie might be dodging Horsemen this minute? The Mounties must know about this joint. By now, they're damned sure to know. Ever think of that?'

Fay stared at me as though I were a moron. 'Look who's giving advice,' she said testily. 'Talk like that, you must still be wet around the ears. Know about the rendezvous? Sure the Mounties know. It's number one on their hit-parade! But they still can't make pinches without evidence.'

'So? This place smells like herring in the sun. Crawls with evidence.'

Fay's pained expression didn't alter. 'Oh, my God!' she groaned. 'You're not just wet around the ears—you're soaked through. You're a real dish, whoever you are. If you're connecting from Frankie, he should have told you the Horsemen have sneaked plants, undercovers, right inside her. One of them worked right behind that food bar as a hash-slinger for three months last winter. He fingered a few users and they went bye-bye up the river.'

At that point, the street door opened. Frankie Seven stepped quickly inside. His face showed about as much expression as a poker-chip. The little pusher's mind was on business. He stalled by the cashier's desk and studied the waiting addicts as intently as a keeper appraising a cage of hungry animals. His bright eyes jumped from table to table, then took in each of the room's four corners. He stood absolutely still for another moment, then his eyes took off again, went back over each face. Finally satisfied the room held no suspicious strangers, he nodded his head curtly to the expensively dressed girl who was waiting by the door, her two gloved fists striking with savage impatience against her knees. Before the door clicked shut behind him, she was off after him as though released from a launching pad.

For over an hour, Frankie kept coming and going, checking and nodding out and servicing the impatient addicts one by one. Then he stepped back inside to stay, settled down to eat his addict's breakfast of sweets and coffee.

Fay got up quickly, and without a glance at me, hurried across the aisle. She bent to touch Frankie's shoulder, began whispering hoarsely. A look of astonishment came into Frankie's face. Frankie laughed, as I knew he would. His laughter had a slight but tolerant note of contempt that made my hands clench hard against the table sides. Fay caught at his wrists, pulled at him. 'Not ever!' he said sharply. 'Not ever. You know that. Not matter how sick you are, no cuff!'

Fay turned away. I could see her eyes glistening, the gleam of teeth between parted lips. She slipped quietly away, like a whipped dog, pausing at the door to adjust her coat. I got up. Frankie's copy of *Variety* stood like a white wall between us. I knocked it down, and before he could rise, touched him on the shoulder, pushing him back in the seat. I said, edgily, 'It breaks me all up to have to bother you—but I've a question that needs quick answering.'

'So? Why the pushing bit, pal? Ask. That's all you need to do. Why don't you ask?'

'Okay! You're supposed to be little Mr. Answers himself. The little man that knows everything. Well, tell me this: Where can a stranger around here get rid of a little fancy loot?'

'Loot?' Frankie sat up needle-straight. 'Well, well,' he said, 'so you're handling a bit of hot stuff as well as joy-popping? Now how about that! What have you got, pal?'

'Doulton dolls,' I said. 'A pair. The McCoy. Fresh from the counter of a ritzy giftshop on Peel Street.'

Frankie laughed. 'So *that's* how you pay for your heroin,' he said. 'By shoplifting—the addict's old standby.' He got up, wearing a smug, pleased expression. 'Okay, pal. You came to the right man. Come with me to my office—the john. If your dolls're okay, I'll buy.'

Frankie watched me with his elbow on a urinal while I dug out the pair of figurines I had ready in my pocket. He glanced once at the beautiful china dolls, said promptly, 'They're standards. Nothing special about them. I bet every junkie booster in town hits the department stores at least once a week for those Doultons. I'll give you ten bucks for each.'

'Ten bucks! Frankie, you're crazy. The price tags are still on them. Fifty bucks for the pair. I want at least thirty.'

A white line gathered about Frankie's lips. His eyes narrowed into slits that told me I'd fouled out, failed another test.

'Thirty, eh?' he retorted suspiciously. 'You expect thirty, then you're no booster—no shoplifter at all. If you were, you'd know I'm giving you a break. A regular fence'd offer you less than a third—maybe a real big twelve bucks tops for the two.'

And that said all there was to say. I'd simply forgotten for the moment the ridiculously low prices fences pay.

Somehow, I managed a sheepish grin, managed to bluff. 'So—' I said, '—so a guy's entitled to try, isn't he?'

Frankie's uncertainty was so apparent it was as though his mind were laid bare. He perched stiffly on top of the washroom radiator, his legs swinging slowly, far different in attitude from his amused indolence of a moment ago. He was again balancing my ignorance against a needle and two caps of heroin he'd stolen from my pocket, against a blackened spoon, and the razzle-dazzle I had handed the two drug-ring musclemen. He lined a nicotined finger thoughtfully across his chin. 'You're a hard guy, pal,' he muttered. 'Hard to figure. Maybe you're one of them split personalities. But I guess you're okay. Yeah, you must be—the way you clobbered them two goons.'

I feigned surprise, looked startled. 'Two goons? What two goons?'

In spite of himself, Frankie grinned. 'The hoods my boss uses to check on new faces. The muscles that were sent to bruise you up a bit. To see if you're the kind that likes to shoot off your mouth under pressure.'

'Hoods? Holy God!' I gasped. 'Those two were drug-ring muscles? Brother! I thought they were Horsemen.'

Frankie was still chuckling. 'Yeah, yeah—so they said. They said it real loud, too. But it don't make them feel any better. They got a raking themselves, over goofing. They were sent to check—on what your racket is and for proof you're a user. They were going to strip you to your pelt to look for needle scars. To see if you'd stool pigeon the name of the guy in Vancouver that steered you to the rendezvous.'

I shook my head indignantly. 'Not me,' I growled. 'I know better. Besides, I don't ride the stoolie train.'

But while Frankie produced a roll of bills and began peeling dirty fives from it, I made a mental note of the needle-scar item.

Frankie thrust out four five-dollar bills. 'Okay,' he said. 'If you're peddling the hot dollies, I'll buy. And count yourself lucky I'm no regular fence—only a pusher that likes to give a user a break. I'll give you a choice. Settle for this twenty or, if you like it the sweet way, I'll beat it over to my cap plant and bring you bring you back four caps. Suit yourself.'

Frankie's words came as a tremendous thrill to me. They meant that I *was in*. That I was accepted.

We stood in silence for a moment, each trying to outstare the other. Then I played independent, and told another lie, gave him something new to nibble on.

'Give me the twenty,' I said. 'I *have drugs*.'

'You've got drugs?' Frankie's head snapped up. 'What do you mean, you've got drugs? Where the hell without me did you buy drugs in this town?'

I grinned. 'What's the matter? Afraid competition's still trying to muscle in on your boss? Forget it, Frankie. I've got drugs, but I didn't buy them here. Before I left Vancouver, a guy contrabanded in a few kilos of Mexican heroin. Yellow stuff—almost pure. I bought enough to last me here until I get settled.'

And Frankie couldn't argue with that.

'You won't get Mex stuff in Montreal,' he scowled. 'Anyway, you'll fly just as high on ours.' He touched a match to his cigarette, added with sly casualness. 'You making out all right here, pal? Getting organized okay?'

I replied carelessly. 'Sure—why not? This's a good town. I like the set-up. But you know how it works with

77

a new guy. The cops are cold-eyed and the racket guys go all out to set you up as a sucker.' I leaned against the washroom wall. 'I'll make out, though,' I said, with a wise wink. 'There's still plenty of action here for an operator with a few gimmicks—even if this high-flying new City Hall you've got *is* keeping the rounders on the quick jump.'

Frankie made a clown face. 'Screw them hoosiers!' he said roundly. 'They're not breaking any records. All they've done so far is blow a lot of bugles and heave out a few old-time opposition cops. The whole deal is a big smell. What I was saying—about you—you don't act like you really know where to wheel-and-deal yet.'

I thought carefully for a moment, then I made a crucial decision: To begin my major offensive. An offensive based on a bold and outright lie that would either bring me eventually to the very core of the trafficking ring or—but I didn't want to think about that *or.* I said, with a deliberate shrug, 'Maybe I *could* use some information.'

'Here's my grief,' I said. 'I need a knock-down. An introduction. In a few days, a week, say, I might be wanting to do some big-time business with a fence. A high-sailing fence. One of the big boys. Someone solid that deals fast with the blue chips. I've got some real hot swag put away and I'm getting ready to dig it out and drop it.'

'I'm your boy! Hear me?' Frankie's voice was high, completely altered. 'I can steer you. Easy. How big is this stuff? And what is it?'

'Jewellery,' I said coolly. 'Top stuff. No slum. All fine stones, real gems. But don't ask what it's worth or to see it, or where it's planted. I'm not ready yet. I'm telling you enough. That the loot is jewels. And that the jewels are hot.'

'Ah-hah!' Frankie's ejaculation came out with a snap. 'So it's hot jewels, eh? Then, believe me, pal. I know just the place to drop them! All you have to do is say the word.'

'Oh no,' I retorted, with a short laugh. 'No middlemen for me! When I'm ready, I'll do my own talking.'

'Yeah? Your own talking, eh? That's where you're dead wrong, pal. Nobody talks to this particular guy—but nobody! He's too far back. So far, you don't even *want* to talk to him. Just say a prayer that you won't get real unlucky and wind up talking to one of his specialists instead.'

'Some specialists,' I mocked. 'Cretins. One with a black and blue complexion, the other with knee bruises on his belly.'

The curtain of fear fell across Frankie's eyes. 'Pal,' he said, a shudder rippling his skinny shoulders, 'I admit you sure flattened those two goons. But they don't take it so good. Better for you not to be alone when they catch up with you. You could have an accident real easy. They're poison, pal—but poison.'

'Maybe. But I still do my own talking.'

'No.' There was a grim finality in the word.

I shrugged and went to the door, pushed it abruptly open. 'This place stinks,' I complained. 'You need a new office, Frankie. Air conditioned. Anyway, this boy has to get on the ball. But I'll remember every word you said about this far-back guy that likes jewellery. I'm going to be thinking about him. Plenty. Also about his two hard-rock musclemen.'

The look on Frankie's pale face was that of an old and cynical cat looking down at a familiar mouse hole. 'Sure,' he said, 'think about it. But I'll bet a doctor's needle you'll be coming around. That nice yellow Mex you brought from Vancouver won't last for ever. When it's gone, you'll be screaming for a fix. You know, jumping all over, like. You'll be crying for Frankie.'

'Could be,' I said. 'But not to do my talking for me.'

I left Frankie there, smiling his sly, confident smile. All right, Frankie, I thought, but I'm getting through to you and you're beginning to be my boy.

I knew that because gems are easily portable and easy to sell anywhere in an emergency, traffickers grab at

79

every opportunity to acquire them, especially at fences' prices. Frankie wouldn't overlook a chance to prove useful to his boss. I was ready to gamble my hat on the little pusher hurrying a message through the grapevine to the trafficker; a message stating that the addict from Vancouver had arrived in town carrying a pocketful of hot jewels. Frankie just might make the story so convincing it would spring open another door for me.

I walked uptown, keeping in the thin watery warmth of the fall sunshine. After a dozen blocks, I ducked into a side street and went into a small bar frequented by French writers and TV actors. I dawdled over a whisky, losing my tension in the hum of conversation and the bright tinkle of ice in shakers. Then abruptly there was another sound, a muted shriek of laughter as a woman stepped out of the bar telephone booth. The empty booth reminded me of something I should have done before now. I went to it and called Helen Ashton's unlisted number.

After a dozen shrill rings, a voice mumbled in my ear. I listened until the voice became irritable, then thickly indignant. I hung up softly. A quick sense of relief washed over me. The savage overdose that had knocked Helen insensible too fast for her to withdraw the needle had not put her permanently to sleep—not this time.

I walked home with a winy October wind pressing against my back. After a needle-blast shower, I laid out a blue flannel suit and took an extra minute choosing a contrasting but blending tie. Holding a weak whisky in my hand, I set the Bogan to spinning a recording of Franck's *Psyche*. I used the multiple speakers instead of head-phones, and wandered about the apartment in my birthday suit while the music soared. Just as the symphonic poem ended, when the Bogan began whirring another record into place, my telephone shrilled.

8 I picked up the telephone receiver, and said 'Hello.'
Thorn replied. She told me she must see me at
once. She'd meet me at Louis's at two, she said, and
I could buy her a drink. Her voice had the same rich,
throaty quality that had sounded so exciting the last time
we'd talked. I said that I wanted to see her, too.

She hung up and I padded gratefully into the bedroom to get dressed.

When Thorn stepped into the little café she smiled.

It wasn't a gay smile—nothing like it. It was the
worried smile of a fine but despairing person trying to
smile at a nightmare. She sat down. Leaning forward, she
asked anxiously, 'Have you any news at all, Max?'

I replied, cautiously. 'Thorn, I can tell you only that
doors are slowly opening. Doors that lead into a dark,
crooked alley. And that I'm moving a little closer. Closer
to where I can begin action that may be really useful.'

She turned her purse over in her hands. Moments
wasted before she spoke again. Then she said, sighing, 'I
know. I read the progress note you posted to Dad, all three
lines of it. Let that be a lesson to me. It was about as non-
committal as a doctor's report: Things are going as well as
can be expected—words to that effect.' Her eyes sparkled
like wet topazes. 'Max,' she pleaded. 'I'm not an idiot or a
child. Won't you let me do something to help? Anything.
Anything at all. I don't mind what it is. Just something to
let me feel that I'm trying, too.'

After thinking for a moment, I said doubtfully, 'I
don't know. Perhaps there is something you could do to
help. First, I'd like you to answer some more questions.
Then maybe I can put you on a real job—if you're willing
to play girl-detective, that is.'

Thorn said seriously, 'Let's begin with the questions,
then.'

'Well—Helen,' I began. 'I want to know if she ever
married. If not, what men she's been serious about within
the last year or so.'

Thorn paused while she set her thoughts in order. 'No, Helen has never been married,' she said. 'In spite of all this, she's just twenty-two. As for the other, about the men, it would take me hours to give you a satisfactory answer. Helen—well, Max, let's face it. Helen's been quite a girl ... gay ... irresponsible ... crazy for excitement. She wanted what she calls a full life. She often said she intended to try everything. She—darn it, Max, I just don't know. We hardly ever went out together. Sisters often don't, you know. So I really can't say if there was one man in Helen's life, or a dozen. She has had her own interests. Her own circle of friends. Her tastes have always seemed odd. Wild and pointless. But she kept insisting she was having fun.'

Those bad minutes while I had stood holding a wisp of negligee in Helen's bedroom came rushing back at me. ... 'Something stopped being fun,' I said grimly. 'Stopped being fun too hard and too fast.'

Thorn drew in breath so sharply her nostrils flattened. Tilting her dark head back farther, she looked self-consciously away from me. Her cheeks were flushed, and there was a porcelain look about her. 'About the other,' she said quickly. 'The girl-detective part. May we talk about that now?'

'Of course. The thing is, I need more information. Need it urgently. Here is the idea. I believe now that the ring Helen stole from your father's safe has a special significance. I want very much to locate that ring. I want to know if Helen sold it personally, or through a friend, to a legitimate dealer, claiming it was her own. Or if she exchanged it for drugs. If she did that last and we can get a name, it's really important. Because it will be the name of someone high in the drug ring.

'I want you to search the rooms Helen lived in before she left home. Look for anything you'd be surprised to find in your own rooms ... addresses you can't identify ... strange telephone numbers ... or a ticket from a pawnshop, perhaps.'

Thorn smiled. 'No!' she said positively. 'Not pawn-tickets, Max. Helen wouldn't go to a pawnshop.'

'Perhaps not, but look anyway. Drugs force people into situations that aren't ordinary. The thing is, search thoroughly. And remember, the smallest thing you find could easily turn out to be vitally important.'

Thorn glanced off, around the bar, at the straggle of afternoon drinkers, and finally back to me. 'All right, Max,' she said, sounding doubtful. 'I'll look. Perhaps I'll even be able to find something. One thing for sure, Helen has always been terribly, terribly careless.'

That was Thorn's exit line. I put her into a taxi at Louis's door and headed for my office. I walked with aimless strides, thinking about Frankie and the mythical jewels I was using as bait.

At the edge of one of the walks I spotted the Pernod-loving derelict who had stopped me outside the Stanley Street *caffé espresso*. The man was sitting drunkenly, at least his posture seemed drunken from a distance, yet there seemed to be an odd alertness about him for a drunk, an atmosphere of tension and readiness. He was staring directly at me and I couldn't help but think of his strange words 'The Lord looks after the fall of every little sparrow!'

Something about the man began bothering me, bothered me more because I couldn't identify it. Then it became just curious guessing and, anyway, at that point, the watching man got up and ambled drunkenly away.

I didn't see the philosophical drunk again. Not for a while.

In my office, I began deliberately considering Thorn, but my thoughts kept tangenting off to her sister. Before long, I went to the telephone and dialled a familiar number—Police Headquarters.

A gravel-throated switchboard cop connected me with the Detective Muster Room. I asked for a squad man who not too long ago had been sweating beside me on missions over flack-spitting mudlogged hills in Korea.

I heard a sharp click, then a crisp, familiar voice.

'Hello Pierre. Max Dent here,' I replied; and added with a bit of a chuckle, 'how's the Police Department surviving under reform.'

Pierre chuckled back. 'We're all holding our breaths,' he said. 'Wondering whose badge is due to be called next. How about you, *mon ami*? How's the cloak and dagger racket?'

'Bustling. Listen, Pierre; I'm stuck for some case information . . . strictly off-beat stuff.' I hesitated, asked in a low voice, 'The telephone there, is it okay?'

'Safe. Go ahead and talk.'

I asked quickly: 'Still on Robbery and Bunco?'

'Sure. Always.'

'Good. This'll be a cinch, then. But—like me—it's strictly unofficial, off the record.'

'Shoot, Max.'

'If a local thief—or anybody—had a hot ring, diamonds in an old-fashioned setting, where would they bring it for a quick sale? Remember—this ring is hot and extremely valuable.'

Pierre demanded: 'How valuable?'

'It's insured for ten thousand. So it must be worth at least twelve, maybe fifteen.'

Without pause for thought, Pierre said, 'Ruby Marlin. Ruby's the only known fence in town handling that kind of loot. But I dunno, Max. I think even Ruby would draw the line on a ring worth that kind of money. He would for sure if the ring's really hot.'

I went the rest of the way—'If I wanted to find Ruby,' I said, 'where do you think I should go look for him?'

Pierre's laughed pinged in my ear. 'Just step over here,' he invited. 'Ruby's sweating it out right now in a suspect's cell. We picked him up last night. On spec. Like to talk your problem out with him?'

'No thanks,' I chuckled. 'I'll see Ruby my own way. Do you fellows have anything on him?'

'Not this time, Max. We're just coaxing a little info out of the boy. Ruby's as clean as a bird—and singing twice as loud.'

'What would the police do without their stoolies! What will you do with him?'

Pierre snorted. 'Bah! Hold him forty-eight hours until his squeal value runs out, then turn him loose. What else can we do?'

I said my thanks and hung up. It was close in my office and hot. Nevertheless, I sat at my desk for a long time, thinking. Ruby could wait. The outcome of my case now hinged on Frankie Seven and the addicts connecting at the rendezvous. Unless Mr. Big proved a lot less tough than I expected I would eventually be forced underground. I would be forced to move right in with the addicts and pushers. My entrance card would be Frankie.

So I spent a long time at my desk, tying up loose ends, writing letters, notifying regular clients that Maxwell Dent would be out of circulation for a while at least. Finally, I taxied home for a change of clothes.

When I stepped back outside, I wore again the crummy flannel suit and my faded blue trench-coat.

The late afternoon had grown bitter. Thunder grumbled above. Swirling black clouds pressed low over the city's reaching cathedral spires. A cold, slashing rain had started to fall.

9 For three days it rained. Rain swept the glowering skyline in great icy sheets driven hard by a stinging wind. Then at last the sun burnt holes in the swollen cloud-deck and things began getting warmer all around. Because drug addicts are hypersensitive to cold, I got my first real break.

Dream Street Fay came reeling out of the dark back door of the storm, wet and cold. Her eyes were walled in panic, flaming with hangover pain. 'Have you seen that little stinker, Frankie?' she demanded hoarsely.

I shook my head, No.

She moaned, jerked cigarettes from a crushed pack and thrust one to me, producing a match. My head went down to meet the flame. Fay noticed my eyes flick instinctively to her wet, scuffed shoes, to where a long ladder ran ugligly down her stocking. She tossed away the curled match, muttered waspishly: 'All right, I look hellish, I know. No wonder. I've been on the street all night. Dodging in and out of every store I could find open. I finally boosted enough to raise money for a couple of caps.' She brushed a chapped hand over her brimming eyes. 'I'm s-sick,' she said in a rising voice. 'So awful sick. Nobody in the whole world should be allowed to get this sick. Where—oh where is that devil Frankie?'

Suddenly, I remembered once remarking to a U.N. police officer that addicts have no small talk. Not any. That all they ever discuss is the one important thing in their lives—drugs. Now, looking at Fay, it was easy to understand why this was so.

She had fallen back in her chair, her eyes concentrated stupidly on nothing. Fiery patches mottled her cheeks, as though brutal slaps had placed permanent marks. She was struggling vainly to focus her gaze, but her head slowly began a loose, disjointed, side-to-side swaying. Her teeth gritted, she spat out venomously: 'One sure, sold bet— Frankie didn't miss *his* morning fix! God, I hate pushers. I hate everyone in the whole set-up—'

I forced a false yawn. My coffee was cold, but I reached for the cup. I swallowed a mouthful. It tasted rancid, horrible. Using my butt, I lighted a fresh cigarette, deliberately making every small gesture lax and dreamy. Fay's sick eyes burned into mine. She jerked erect. 'You big, blond lout,' she rasped, her voice hard and bitter and snarling with envy, 'you're yawning your head off. No wonder you're sitting there so smug and relaxed. You fixed this morning. You're floating!'

Her eyes were like hot rivets on mine. Blinking drowsily, I leaned back and murmured softly: 'So let me float, Fay. You go for a walk for a while. You talk too much—much too much.'

Her face distorted. It grew old and ugly, violent. She began sobbing with rage. Her hand shot out, clutched my wrist with terrific, animalistic strength. 'Gimme a cap!' she shrilled. 'God! can't you have a little heart? Can't you? Look at me. I'm dying. Little Dream Street Fay's dying. One cap, *please*. I'll square it with you, honest I will. The minute I get set with Frankie. Come on, please. Let me go to the john and shoot up.'

My stomach turned slowly over. Fay's ragged nails dug like claws into my wrist. 'I just used my last cap,' I lied, as calmly as I could, 'What makes you think you're alone waiting it out for Frankie?'

She began a steady, monotonous swearing. 'A curse on that pusher,' she said. 'Curse him all to hell. Curse the guy that got me started. It's his fault—all his rotten fault. Because of him, I'll die in hangover-convulsions in the john, yes, I will!' She flung herself passionately from side to side in her chair, a scream waiting on the rim of her lips.

'Listen, listen!' she cried. 'Do me a favour. Run across to the tavern and see if Frankie's there. Sometimes he stalls in the back. Reading those damned showbiz papers of his until he's ready to serve us.'

'Sure,' I said sarcastically. 'And what do you suggest I tell him? That you're lonesome? You had a real bad night? That should rush him straight over.'

'No, no, you fool. Tell him I'm waiting. That I have money. Tell him Dream Street Fay's so sick she'll pay him extra for a cap. Tell him I'll pay double. Hurry it, please.

87

I'll make it up to you. You'll see. I'll give you something. Anything—anything you want.'

She began to sob again.

The sound of that sobbing was so painful, so sickening, I knew that I wouldn't forget it for a long, long time. 'All right,' I muttered. 'All right, all right, I'll go.'

I went outside feeling weak. The street seemed like another world, filled with people that were strange because they were normal. I walked to the corner and stood there for a few minutes, staring at the reassuring reality of pushing traffic and hurrying people, drinking it in with my eyes and ears and nose, my whole body. Finally, I crossed over and went into the crowded, beery blare of the tavern.

He sat hunched in a pool of loneliness at a back table. His face was set in an expression of utter misery. He stared sullenly up at me.

'Sit down, Vancouver,' he growled. 'You draw plenty of attention standing there. You're so big, you look like a copper.' His lips compressed into a tight, bitter line. 'If you're still peddling china Doultons,' he advised me, 'I got news for you. Bad, bad news. You're talking to the wrong guy. I'm on the skids. For good, it looks like. I'm celebrating my own wake.'

I stared at him. At the crushed look on his face. 'On the skids? You mean you took a pinch?'

Frankie cradled his face in his hands. 'A pinch? Nah! I'm used to that. Worse, pal, worse. I goofed up and let some addict bloodhound tail me to my plant. So now someone knows where the connection was planting the caps for me to pick up and push. The hide's not a hide any more. It'll have to be changed. My boss don't go for guys that goof like that. So he bounced me fast. I'm through pushing!'

'My God, Frankie! how did you ever slip up like that?' I asked the question sharply. The possible effect of Frankie's blunder could be serious beyond description to me. If the little pusher chose to button up now, I would be left helpless, would have to start all over again. If on the other hand, he had been knocked enough off-guard to talk freely, he might drop a hint concerning the identity of his successor, he might even in bitterness and chagrin go a step further and mention a name. 'Yes,' I repeated with desperate swiftness, 'how the devil did you ever get caught flat-footed like that?'

Frankie wanted a friendly ear. He let out his breath in a blast. 'It was crazy!' he said. 'One of those screwy flukes. No tail in the world could have stayed on me if it wasn't for that damn rain storm. Just walking, I got so cold I must have gone half blind.'

I gave him an understanding nod. Waited.

'I still can't figure it,' he continued. 'It doesn't add up. God—I'm a guy that watches everybody and his shadow. I protected the plant every time I moved.' He shook his head in apparent amazement. 'Like when I was serving the users in the hash-joint across the street,' he explained. 'Pal, I played that double-safe. I always locked up at my plant first, then carried the caps under my tongue in a finger-stall. I did that, then I nodded the rendezvous bunch out one by one and steered them to a safe spot before I served them. When I sold out, I got lost for a while to shake off any Horsemen that might be tailing, then worked my way back to the plant, loaded my finger-stall again, and started all over.'

I nodded wisely. 'That's cagey pushing. That finger-stall's a real smart dodge. If the Mounties jump you, all you have to do is swallow the finger-stall.

'Yeah. And if I did get jumped by Horsemen, or even smelled them around, I'd stall it out all day before I started to serve again. But I wasn't serving the rendezvous. Not when my plant got snatched.'

'No?'

Frankie shook his head. 'I'd already served there. I was

out making special meets across town. You know—high-class addicts that won't come down here and mix with the deadbeats and thieves. I had some pretty fancy stuff on my route. But it's pretty tough serving that class trade. A guy's gotta be extra smart. But it evened off, though, pal. I charged 'em all an extra buck. Six bucks a cap.'

'So? Maybe that's where you got sloppy—careless.'

'Not a chance!' Frankie retorted. 'No sir! I played it even safer with those uptown Square Johns. When I served them, I always set up an extra plant—right handy in the West End. And I never planted in the same spot for two trips running. Careful? Man, I was as careful as an odd maid at a Legion picnic.

'Yes, sir! I'd plant the caps I needed for my run in a lane, see? Maybe in a garbage can I knew wasn't due to be emptied soon. Or sometimes, this time of the year, I'd use one of those Street Department sand boxes—they're real kosher, no one ever goes near them. I'd plant the caps already packaged to serve, hide them in the sand in peanut sacks or candy-bar wrappings. But I'd never take no more than one delivery from the plant at a time. And I'd hold that package in my hand or in my mouth in case I got jumped by Horsemen before I sold and had to swallow or throw away fast.

'I'd serve one customer at a time. I'd telephone that customer to get ready, the I'd make the meet some place, nod out the customer, and collect. Then I'd walk away and drop the package careless-like on the curb or in the gutter.' Frankie threw up his hands in sudden disgust. 'Well! that's how shrewd I played it,' he said. 'That much—and more! I even stopped at a bank every few hours and changed all the pay-off money. That way, even if I made a sale to a stoolie I had it beat. There were no marked bills that could be used against me as evidence, see?'

'Can you beat that!' I said, with elaborate sympathy. 'You played it as safe as a country church all the way, but you still get tailed and beat. It looks to me like you must have been set up even before you started out on your deliveries.'

'Right!' Frankie scowled. 'Or I was picked up in the West End and tailed back through that stinking storm. I dunno. I don't know one thing but that I got beat for two hundred caps. God-Jesus! I'm lucky the goon-squad haven't back-handed me into a lane and kicked me to death already.'

I tried to think as an addict would think. I said nervously, 'Sure. You're lucky, that way. But what about me? What about service at the rendezvous?'

Frankie's eyes grew dark and bitter, and his returning anger was like added venom rising inside him. 'The connection finds another pusher,' he growled. 'Meantime, I'm out. You produce the cash or the drugs or fade away. Okay, so I fade. I don't hold no grudge against the connection. The guy holding down this district ain't too bad. It's not his fault. He can't pay off in excuses to the Back Man.'

'*The Back Man?*' The three words rolled softly off my lips—although blood was pounding through me, warming my stomach and throat with a singing excitement. I thought a prayer of thanks for that magnificent three days' rain, and I waited for Frankie to say more.

But Frankie didn't co-operate. He left my question hanging.

The tension had to be gotten over with. I felt like someone digging into an old trunk, trying to hang on to patience so as not to let go and start heedlessly ripping things out to uncover what lay hidden on the bottom. I said, again, 'The Back Man?'

Frankie stared at me suspiciously. 'Sure! Sure, the Back Man. The Big Boy. Mister One. The trafficker. What do you call him on the coast? Goldilocks?'

I made a laugh come. I hoped it didn't sound as sickly to Frankie as it did to me. 'Man, no!' I said. 'On the coast,

91

we don't call the trafficker Goldilocks. We just don't *call him*—period! In Vancouver, no one at all knows whether the Big Shot is male or female, animal or reptile.' Having managed a recovery, I changed the subject in a hurry, and I decided to settle for half a loaf. 'All right,' I said, 'you got beat. I admit that's tough. Real tough. But this morning I shot my last cap of Mex heroin. I'm stuck with an empty needle. Okay, what's the next move, then?'

Frankie grew infuriatingly cagey again. 'How do I know who'll fill my spot?' he hedged. 'That's up to the Back Man. I'm just Frankie Seven—the dead one.'

My fingers closed over his arm, squeezing harder and harder. 'Hear me, Frankie,' I said through clenched teeth. 'It's too late now for any more double-talk between you and me. That yellow Mex junk I had is all gone. Kaput, see? I'm fixed for this morning—I'm steady enough to go out and steal. But later on today I'll be needing heroin—I'll have to have it. You're the only user in this town that knows me well enough to trust me. I'll be looking for you, Frankie. But not for any more left-handed double-talk.'

'Let go!' Frankie yelled, wrenching free. 'For God-sakes take it easy with the arm! I know you're okay. Soon as things get straightened out I'll steer you to the new pusher fast.'

I slapped the table so hard that bottles jumped. 'All right,' I said, hoping I wasn't overdoing it. 'But see that you level with me about the new pusher.' I got up, started away, then turned back and faced him less belligerently. 'If you've any caps hidden away,' I said, 'you'd better break down and sell a couple to Fay. She's over at the rendez-vous and she's screaming.'

Frankie said flatly, 'Nuts to Fay! Suppose I'm wrong about the connection taking over right away? So I get stuck and start screaming myself. No dice. I'm gonna look out for number one. Let Fay go snatch a doctor's bag somewhere. That's what we'll all be doing if service stays off and there's a real panic.'

'If there's an all-out panic, I'll choke the Back Man's name out of you,' I grated. 'I'm not going to wind up shaking myself to pieces waiting for some guy I don't even know to take my money.'

Frankie's face stiffened. His lips moved, but he didn't answer right away. At last, he said, 'Not me, pal. You don't get the Back Man's name from me. I'd commit myself first.'

He turned deliberately away from me, began polishing an immaculate shoe on his trouser leg.

My floppy trench-coat on my arm, I walked downtown to the Sûreté-Police Headquarters. Once inside I hurried through a maze of shabby corridors that led to the Record Room.

I went inside, and there was an old man, a thin old man with an unbuttoned tunic and an eyeshade, sitting at a desk back of a partition that consisted of a row of olive-green filing cabinets stacked shoulder-high. I rapped with my knuckles on the cabinets; it made a hollow, sound-effects kind of noise. The old man jerked his head up and I said, 'A-ha! Fast asleep! Reform squads are out tearing the city apart, and I find my old pal Sergeant LeClerc asleep at his post.'

The old sergeant and I are good pals. The Confidential File Section, also known as the *Lousy File Section*, is always at my disposal if I'm looking for a known criminal to fit to a particular situation. LeClerc stared in astonishment at my shabby clothes. I grinned, and pointed suggestively towards the long metal wall of secret files. 'How about it, *mon ami?*' I suggested. 'I need about ten minutes in there. Alone.'

LeClerc shoved back his chair. He moistened his lips and said gravely in his unpardonable English, 'You say *mon ami?* You name old LeClerc your *friend? Mon dieu!*' He threw up a pair of gnarled hands that resembled twisted roots. 'No, my Max,' he protested in a theatrically

93

dramatic voice. 'I am afraid for to be your friend, to do you favours. You, Monsieur Private Police, 'ave the sad look of the bad luck. For you, business is no damn good, hey? What clothes you wear! Ha! But a beeg disgrace.'

'I need this favour very much. Very much.' I said emphatically.

LeClerc lurched stiffly to his feet. His leathery face contorted into a comical ferocity. 'I am a *vieux!*' he shouted angrily. 'For thirty year I am the cop—servant of all the people. The fat old poppa 'oo is our mayor 'e geeves to us the good city. Naughty, per'aps, but eet is good to be naughty. Then eet all change damn queeck—we 'ave reform an' an old wan lak me doan understan' those 'oo weesh us to remember every rule.' His shoulders heaved in an elaborate Gallic shrug. 'Ah—well! What can an old one do? I go now, my Max, for my *café-au-lait.* I am gone ten minutes—but no more. You mus' not answer any knock on these door.'

Turning quickly to the olive-green cabinets, I began searching for a special drawer dealing with peculiarities of criminal behaviour, personality, and method. The drawer was in the last cabinet at the end of the second row. I dug feverishly for a folder marked *N.* A thick section bulged with N's—N for nyctophobia; N for nympholepsy; N for nymphomania; and so on to N for narcomania. Reaching into that one, I pulled out a handful of Police Record Cards.

I went to work, glancing at each card, tossing the ones bearing unfamiliar photos willy-nilly back into the drawer. My ten minutes began to wear thin. Suddenly, a card showed a familiar face. My eyes slid quickly to the data typed under Remarks: Chasen, Thomas Phillip; Suspected Drug Addict. Age: 25. Weight: 150. Complexion: Fair. Eyes: Blue. Hair: Brown. Scars and Tattoos: None. Occupation: Musician, Pianist. Additional Information: Regular bookings as pianist in Montreal clubs. Pupil Conservatory of

Music, McGill University. Concert at Moyse Hall, 1954. Afternoon recitials of sacred music, organ, Notre Dame Cathedral. Known to associate drug pushers—other narcotic addicts. No arrests. Presently employed: Aldo's Café, city, Mountain Street.

On that, my ten minutes ran out. Old LeClerc's flat feet were slapping heavily back along the corridor. By the time he opened the Record Room door, N for narcomania was back in its place and I was ready to leave.

I went home, and feeling ridiculously like a quick-change artist, again peeled off my shabby clothes. Bed claimed me for the next seven hours. But at three in the morning, my clock-radio blasted me wide awake. I used the shower for a long time then stepped out, shaved, and dressed in a brown, three-button lounge suit.

Loose threads were accumulating in my case, and needed to be tied up. They were important threads. Threads that connected Helen's horrible scars, a missing ring, drugs, and a crumpled scrap of pink paper showing a pencilled telephone number. Again, my problem involved collecting a hatful of information without giving any away.

Addicts are notorious for their intuition. A few minutes later when I sat down in the all-night club on Mountain Street Ziggy's back was to me. But when he turned suddenly from the piano, his eyes instantly locked with mine. He smiled a sheepish smile, stepped down from the piano platform, and walked stiff-legged through noise and layered smoke to my table.

'. . . well, about that twenty bucks, Max. . . .'

Smiling, I said magnanimously, 'Oh, forget the twenty, Ziggy. It's not important. Anyway, the TV audition I promised you two blew up into bubbles.'

'Yeah, but I guess it was kind of drippy, me not coming back. . . .'

I shut him off, abruptly. 'You're playing solo tonight, Ziggy. What happened? Where's Phil?'

Ziggy shook his head as though he would not admit to knowing anything, even his own name. 'Phil went out' he said, his eyes not quite on mine. 'He knocked off about two.'

I blew a smoke ring. 'Expecting him back?'

Ziggy shrugged his shoulders unco-operatively. We weren't making any progress. I started off on a new tack. I said, 'Well it's not really important. I just wanted his advice about some records.'

'At four a.m., Max?'

I winked conspiratorially. 'I just said good night to a brand-new divorcee that was trying to thank me for getting her back into circulation,' I lied. 'On my way home I began thinking about some records I need to complete my collection. I'm a little hazy about the best labels on them. Phil would know. So I dropped in to ask him.'

The lie was weak and Ziggy began tightening up with suspicion, getting away.

I changed tactics abruptly, and said, 'Perhaps you'd like to do me a favour, Ziggy. We'll call it a receipt for the twenty. Get your chef to make me some ham and eggs. I'm starving.'

Ziggy stared, his sparkling pupils rimmed with uncertainty. No doubt he thought I was crazy. He said, hesitantly, 'Well, the chef—he knocks off at two. But I guess maybe it'd be okay. He's a lush and he's still in the kitchen sneaking a few free drinks. You'd have to eat there. There's no food served in here after two.'

I grinned. 'I'd love to eat in the kitchen. I'd even love to buy your alcoholic chef a nightcap.'

Ziggy's smile was so forced it must have hurt his lips. His thin face was flushed and embarrassed-looking and angry. But he led the way past the crowded tables to the kitchen. He stood with his back to a huge refrigerator watching sulkily while I ate. When I crossed my legs and sat back to enjoy a second cup of coffee, he apparently decided there was only one way to get Maxwell Dent moving.

'Look here, Max,' he said, his voice sounding frankly irritable over the sharp kitchen noises, 'there's no use you stalling around for Phil. I might as well tell you. He won't be coming back tonight.'

I said easily, annoyingly, 'Oh, you never know. Phil's a strange person. Unpredictable. He might begin worrying whether the drunks are missing him.'

Ziggy's patience collapsed. He gave up with a disgusted sigh. 'Not Phil,' he said. 'Not that cat. You see, I do know where he's at.'

I smiled. 'Of course, you do. Now tell me.'

Flicking his butt toward a trash can, Ziggy sad shortly, 'Well, I'm only guessing. But I know where he cuts to when he wants to be alone. I figure that's where he is now. At the Waiters' Mass.'

Come again, please?

Ziggy shrugged. 'The Waiters' Mass. It's a special mass they celebrate every morning at four o'clock. It's for taxi-drivers, waiters, musicians—people that work nights. They call it the Waiters' Mass.'

'Well, I'll be darned! Where does this take place?'

'At the cathedral in Place d'Armes.'

I pushed a two-dollar bill under my plate. I got up, saying, 'Well, you took long enough coming out with it. You're positive Phil went down there? A moment ago, you were only guessing.'

From half-way to the door, Ziggy scowled over his shoulder. 'I'm sure, all right. The cat's gone queer about that place. He's strictly from Looneyville!'

10 The cathedral doors yawned invitingly open. A steady murmur of voices reached out into the great nave where strips of light from the street fell in dim yellow patterns on to a spread of red carpet.

97

Inside, the massive church was sodden with sanctity. Ceiling candelabra cast a soft, winking glow.

I stood behind the last of an endless marching row of pews. An odour of incense was sharp in my nostrils. Votive candles fluttered before me over the white and gold altar. The thin, lisping chant of an old, stooped priest rose and fell. He was saying Mass.

I tiptoed quietly past a red vigil light and into a deep, crypt-like alcove. I waited there, beside a holy water stoup, listening to the priest chant the old fine words, but with my eyes held resolutely on the high archway leading to the street door.

Phil left the cathedral on the heels of a laughing trio in waiters' tuxedos. Pausing at the bottom of the stone steps to light a cigarette, he began dejectedly off across the Square. He had never looked more alone.

I caught up with him in a dozen strides. He whirled to face me. Fright filled his face, then slowly drained away. 'You, Max!' he exclaimed incredulously. 'What the devil are you doing down here?'

I stepped up beside him. 'What are you afraid of, Phil? You jumped like a rabbit when I touched you.'

He said guiltily, 'Me? No. No, what's there to be afraid of down here? I'm just out to get some air. Walking around. The club stinks like a slaughterhouse this time of morning.'

I agreed. 'It certainly does. I've just left there. It was poisonous. How about some coffee?'

Phil's stride broke, picked up. We walked in a stiff silence to an all-night restaurant near the Central Station. As soon as coffee was put before us, Phil began fidgeting, talking nervously: 'Listen, Max—if all this has to do with that mess the other night . . .'

I shook my head. 'No, not that. This is something new, Phil. Something new and much more important. For you.'

For a moment, I let it stand at that. Phil stared at me.

'That horse's butt! Ziggy gave me my first reefer. Ever since, I've been stuck with him, carrying him.' Phil stood up abruptly. 'Look, Max,' he said shrilly. 'You're a good guy, square, and you have a heart. But don't keep picking at me. I don't know anything about anything—women, jewels, even what time it is. Let me be.' His voice tilted out of control. 'Let me be, let me be,' he cried. 'Can't you see I'm so damned mixed-up even the canal's beginning to look good?'

I snatched at his arm. 'Wait!' I cried urgently. 'Phil! the woman I'm talking about keeps the telephone number of the clubs where you play marked down—your number! It means enough to her to want to keep. It's not *even possible* she could know anyone at Aldo's but you.'

My words seemed to set off little explosions of fear within Phil. He jumped back, his eyes as wary as a cat's. 'I don't know anything,' he yelled. 'Nothing! Leave me be. Oh, God, Max! Please leave me be!'

His face grey and his mouth making a croaking sound that wasn't words, he twisted about. He turned and plunged, knocking a table flying in a wild rush to the street. Behind him, the door swung in the wind.

I let him go; no threads connected. My only gain had been additional proof of something well established before I'd started: addicts simply never talk.

Then something occurred to me.

Obviously, Phil had drugs. 'Enough heroin,' I said thoughtfully aloud, 'so that he doesn't even care about protecting his job at Aldo's. Somehow, Phil had gotten himself a white nest-egg. Now, how the devil could a half-broke addict-musician have swung that?'

Shrugging into my faded trench-coat, getting ready to leave for the rendezvous, I prayed the Back Man would take a long time choosing a new pusher; prayed that he'd take so long Frankie and the other addicts would suffer enough agony to get desperate, really desperate, careless.

Then he dropped his gaze while I sugared his coffee. He stirred vigorously, not raising his head. 'Funny, you know, meeting you down there on the Square. I was really startled. I thought I was in for a mugging.'

'You should do something for your nerves,' I replied coolly.

'My nerves are all right,' he retorted.

'No. You're jumpy, Phil. Very jumpy. It's starting to show in your music. You're hitting flats. That's bad.'

He was glaring at me. 'You didn't drag me in here at this hour to lecture me about my playing,' he said edgily. 'No more than you met me by accident tonight. What d'you want, Max?'

I folded my arms across the table. 'I want to talk about a couple of things,' I said, leaning closer. 'But mostly about one of my clients.' I stared directly into his eyes. 'Take your choice about this, Phil. Tell the truth, and make things easy for both of us—or play clever. If you decide to do it that way, you'll force me to do things I'll feel bad about.'

Phil altered his gaze. 'What is it about your client?'

I pushed aside my coffee cup. 'My client's a woman,' I said. 'I don't need to mention her name. Either you'll recognize her without it, or you simply don't know her.'

'If that's the way you want it.'

'That's the way. The point is, she's taken some jewellery that doesn't belong to her. Stole it. An expensive solitaire in an old-fashioned setting. She's either borrowed money on it or sold it—' I let a pause become weighted— 'or,' I went on, 'perhaps she gave it to someone involved in trouble with her and he sold or borrowed on it *for* her.'

Phil's fingers no longer shot out and back; they plucked nervously at his sleeve. Clearing his throat noisily, he demanded in a voice either sly or curious: 'Is this an insurance thing? I mean, is some company mixed up in it?'

'That doesn't concern you, Phil. Just try giving me an answer.'

His voice was falsely indignant. 'What do I know about rings?' he protested. 'Or about women thieves? Or any thieves? Where did you ever dream up this insane idea?'

Reaching without warning across the table, I thrust my hand under his collar. I twisted until the face above my hand turned blood red; until the hidden agony in Phil's drugged eyes leaped out at me. 'Talk Phil!' I grated. 'Talk before I twist your had off. Talk!'

Gagging, he clutched wildly at my balled fist. 'M-Max! For—for God's sake! A cop's standing by the door. He sees us. Take it easy!'

'Easy by damned. Cops don't bother me. You had better start talking, Phil. You don't fool me, not at all. I know the score on you. The bright boy you were supposed to be—and the way you've wound up. With a drug habit. A junkie.'

A blue vein in Phil's forehead jumped. I relaxed my grip and he began shaking violently from head to foot. 'You know!' he muttered, his voice flat, thin with shame. 'All along, you've know. I've wondered about that. When Ziggy ran out on us the other night, I was sure you knew.'

'No, Phil,' I said grimly. 'I knew before that. The police have a full dossier on you, Phil. It's not very pretty. It deals with all the things you are—and the things you might have been. You read like the local boy that made bad.'

'Oh—the cops! Sure. They'd gladly tell you about me. They'd like to pin a sign on a junkie's back.'

'Why not? People like you aren't exactly an asset to society.'

Phil's left hand slid into his pocket. He pulled out a worn tennis ball, and began rolling it between his palm and the table.'

He looked at me numbly, and his voice fell into a bewildered whisper. 'It all starts with nothing—nothing!'

he said. 'You're going along great, your music's improving. You start getting better dates. People talk about you. You hear whispers that say, Some day you'll pay $6.00 a seat to hear that kid. Talk like that does things to you . . . fills you with fire and ambition. You discover there's a soul in your instrument, and you want to give it to the world. You begin carrying the tennis ball in your pocket. You keep squeezing on it so your fingers will grow stronger and more supple—so you'll be ready and brilliant when the great day comes. The day you've always dreamed about. The day when you sit before the grand in a concert hall and the audience settles down waiting for you to strike the opening chord.'

Phil's bitter voice cracked. 'But you never do strike the opening chord. Somehow, you're detoured into hell. A so-called friend invites you down the hill to a coloured joint—to ball it u for a night. It's a new kick—so you go. The music's way out, wild and crazy . . . and everybody's blazing reefers. They're high—up with the bluebirds—on marijuana. You can't refuse to smoke, because you're just a kid and smoking marijuana's the big thing to do. So you light up. It's just a short bang. But you're always on the merry-go-round. You get to like smoking—to want it. Then one night there are no reefers around. But there's a drug pusher there—*waiting*. He's so anxious to own your soul, he even shows you how to take a joy-pop. It's a big night in your life.'

'Then?'

Phil clutched at his chest. 'Then you die!' he said. 'Your heart breaks up because you know you're lost. Your dreams are gone. Your ambitions with them. There's nothing left—nothing. Only junk—drugs and a hellish rat race to keep the pusher paid off so he'll keep you from going crazy.'

'You're not suffering now! Nor was Ziggy when I left him an hour ago.'

11

Frankie hadn't turned up at the rendezvous.

I found him in the tavern. He sat slumped at his usual rear table—and he was now spectacularly sick. When he raised his head, I noticed that the whites of his eyes were stained a horrible dirty yellow.

He whispered: 'Pal, pal, I'm falling apart. Almost twenty-four hours now since I've had had a fix. I'm dying, dying, pal. By inches!'

I sat down beside him. 'Are you the only one?' I demanded. 'You forget I use, too. How long will this bloody Back Man stall around?'

Frankie's head rolled crazily. 'There *is* a new pusher,' he whispered. 'Service went on again last night. With a new price. Six bucks a cap. It's the Back Man's way of making up for the plant I lost. He cuts off the supply across town, starts a small panic, then when everybody's going nuts he begins to let drugs out. But the street price jumps up.'

'What about your job? Who's the new pusher?'

Frankie rubbed a finger under his nose and wiped away a hanging loop of mucus. 'The connection,' he said thickly, 'took over. Like I figured he would. But he knows I'm broke and he won't give me credit. He laughed at me when I asked him for cuff. A year ago, he was a two-bit street-mugger. Now he's a connection, a big-shot. He laughs at me. At Frankie.'

I shook my head, but I was secretly pleased, thinking of how Frankie had similarly turned down Fay. I said, 'Face up to it, Frankie. You're not a pusher now. You're just a sick addict. Addicts have to steal. You've got to hustle out and promote the price.'

'Think I haven't tried?' Frankie moaned. 'It's no use, pal. I'm even too sick to steal.'

His head sank into his hands. I studied him carefully, trying to determine how close he stood to the breaking point. He raised harassed eyes, told the answer himself. 'Withdrawal's started,' he croaked. 'Now the heroin's wearing off, everything inside me's loosening up. If I don't get a fix, I'll go nuts.' His fear became stark, pitiful. 'I'll vomit myself to death,' he whimpered. 'I'll get those crazy cramps. And diarrhœa. Every drop of juice that's been asleep in me will come pouring out. God-Jesus, pal, this guy just can't take it. I don't even want to try. I made one cold-turkey cure and it near killed me.'

I stalled over a cigarette; I walked to the distant front of the tavern for matches, then went unhurriedly to the washroom; finally, I stepped into the telephone booth and faked a long-drawn-out call. When I came back to the table, Frankie was blubbering.

I slammed my palm hard on his shoulder. 'Listen to me! I was prowling the stores yesterday. I did a little stealing. Not much—just a couple more dolls. I got thirty bucks for them from a Square John in an uptown tavern. So I'll buy heroin for both of us. But only if I know who I'm dealing with. You'll have to give me the connection's name.'

'Money! Why didn't you say you've got money? Why?' Words spilled from Frankie in a frantic, thoughtless stream . . . 'The connection's name is Leger. The guy's a Frenchy. He serves again at the rendezvous at ten, right on the dot. It's nearly that now. If I hurry and catch Leger we can have a charge in our arms in less than fifteen minutes.'

I didn't move a muscle. Not an eyelash.

'Not so fast, Frankie. *We* go. Not you, *We*. Okay me to this Leger. I'll be needing the guy. Later.'

Frankie's face was already greasy with sweat. He made a hard gesture with one hand, swayed to his feet. 'Let's go! Let's go!' he cried.

Frankie made it groggily out to the street, through traffic to the restaurant.

At the door, he shook off my arm. After a quick, sweeping glance, he hurried over to a nodding addict. The two exchanged a dozen words. I heard Frankie curse in a low, savage voice. Defeat came as a tide back into his face. He dragged his feet back to where I waited. 'I'm jinxed. No fix. All blew up.'

'Leger didn't show up?'

'He showed, pal, he showed. Right on the dot. He served over sixty of the bunch and was still nodding out. Then what d'you think happens?'

'Well?' I was becoming exasperated.

'Fay blows in,' Frankie grated. 'Loaded to the teeth with a bankroll she got for a tray of watches she boosted. So what does she do? She slaps down the whole bankroll and buys out Leger's plant. That kills us, pal. The Froggie won't serve again 'til morning—and by then I hope little Frankie Seven is dead!'

I wiped my face, which had suddenly begun to stream with perspiration. My thoughts were swirling. What now? I thought desperately. Frankie jumped. A quick stain of colour touched his pale face. 'You said something,' I demanded.

'Yeah! got it,' he shrilled. 'Got the answer. Why didn't I think of it before? We'll crash Fay's room, that's what. I know where little Miss Dream Street holes up. Come on, pal.'

Frankie pulled my arm impatiently, held it until we were on the street. Without looking back, he led me past the crummy theatres and cheap clubs on St. Lawrence, until we ducked off into a narrow street that stretched deserted and filth-strewn.

A dozen more steps, then he grabbed my arm. 'Wait!' he gasped. 'I think this is it.' He checked the door number, nodded abruptly, and began to struggle groggily ahead of me up a flight of crumbling stairs. He shoved open an unlocked front door, and together we hurried down a dark, linoleumed hallway.

Frankie stopped abruptly. He began kicking at the door, shouting at the top of his lungs. 'Hey, Fay! Wake up, Fay. It's Frankie Seven. You open up. For God's sakes, let me in!'

For a moment, not a thing happened. Nothing. Frankie and I just stood there and looked at each other.

The door cracked open two inches. It held there on a stout chain. Eyes and a section of face appeared fleetingly. Then the door was flung wide. Beyond it, the room was mean—bed-bug mean. Its furniture was a chair, a lopsided dresser, a tumbled bed.

Fay stepped back.

She tightened the belt of her skirt. 'You two!' she said, plainly disgusted. 'I might have guessed! Well, you're just as welcome as a rusty needle.' Her eyes slid brightly away from Frankie's, rested on mine. She scratched absently. Dreamily, at a tear under the armpit of her blouse through which a bit of skin showed. She shrugged. 'Oh—come on in and shut the door,' she said, with a hard sigh. 'Don't think I'm not wise to what brought you two running. Same old story—nobody's a looser spender than a woman thief. Little Dream Street scores big, she gets real popular.' She sighed again, then smiled a little in spite of herself. 'Okay— okay, flop anywhere. On the bed, the floor, anywhere you can find. The old hag that runs this flea-bag is sorta stingy with chairs.'

Frankie blasted out a hard, ragged breath. 'Fay! I'm dying!'

She tossed her hips. Picking up a mirror, she began patting her hair, which had been freshly dressed and dyed and now fell long and absolutely silver-white, like an albino's. 'I'm gorgeous,' she said. 'Loaded and gorgeous.' Still using the mirror, she pirouetted gayly, winked and began a soft crooning. 'Little Faysy's got no blues, no shakes, no aches. Little Faysy bought her private cloud this lucky morning—her white little, soft little, private little cloud to coast on.'

I barked her back to earth. 'Frankie's not kidding, Fay!

It happens he really is sick!'

Completing her pirouette, Fay waved her mirror gayly towards the door. 'Don't rush a lady,' she said coquettishly. 'In a minute, I'll take a little drift down the hall. When I come sailing back, you two can take turns going where I did—to the johnny-john.'

She opened the door gently, and swished airily into the hall.

The room seemed suddenly empty. My eyes swung to Frankie. I said conversationally, 'Nice little homestead Fay has here.'

'Be happy anywhere with a needle and a cap,' Frankie grunted. His foot began an impatient slapping on the floor. 'She's gone to dig out from her plant,' he muttered. 'Gals like Fay are plenty smart. You can't top a shoplifter for being cagey. Fay's a real pro. She uses thirty to forty dollars worth of heroin a day. She's a Dream Street Faysy, all right, but she don't give no one a chance to nab her in possession.'

Fay opened the door. She was smiling peculiarly and her face was flushed. With a hypnotic gesture, she tossed four heroin caps on the dresser top. They lay there like bombs in an arsenal. 'Everything's set,' she said, all business. 'You cook those caps up in the john—not there. The hypo's stuck under the sink with scotch tape. When you use it—whichever's last—wash it in case of a quick pinch and needle test, then stick it back.' She stepped aside, hands on hips, glaring. 'Well—get moving, one of you. I don't want caps in my room. Not for a hot minute. That women's jail is no playhouse!'

Two heroin caps stuck in his cheek, Frankie tottered out. Fay crossed to the bed, plumped herself down beside me. 'Sick, honey?'

I hesitated, then shook my head, smiled. I was caught in a situation now that I wasn't quite familiar with, and I had to keep thinking twice before knowing how to act.

'That's funny,' Fay said. 'I thought you would be. The supply being bought out, and all.'

I stretched, forced myself to feign drowsiness. 'No, I'm not sick. In fact, I'm almost nodding. I had a few seconds this morning. Enough to keep me alive for a while. But as long as you're giving joy away, just steer me to it. I'll find a place for your needle.'

Frankie stepped back into the room. He had combed his hair, slicked it down, and he wore a huge smile. 'Pal,' he said, 'it belongs to you—the john, I mean.' He blew Fay extravagant finger-tip kisses. 'Thanks, baby-doll. You fixed daddy real good. Man! That white stuff's real gone medicine. I'm on now. Go on, pal, get yourself on, too.'

I went into the hall, turned toward the washroom, I slammed the door shut, then bolted it carefully. In one corner, separated from the rest of the room by a grimy curtain, was a shower. Opposite it, a sink and an open toilet which bubbled constantly. The odour in the room was a mixture of damp plaster and unwashed feet.

Using a forgotten towel, I carefully blocked off the keyhole. Then I flushed the two caps of heroin down the bubbling bowl. I worked Fay's makeshift shoot apparatus loose from the underside of the sink. It was a typical addict's hypo—a #26 half-inch insulin needle secured into an eyedropper by a tight wrapping of silver foil. I held it between my fingers and shuddered. It wasn't pleasant even thinking about using it. I sat on the edge of the window sill. And I breathed fervent thanks that Fay had suggested Frankie and I take our heroin shots separately. I used Fay's cooking match to light a cigarette. After stalling five full minutes, I returned the needle and spoon to their place, carefully replaced the soiled towel, and hurried back down the shadowy hall.

'Remember this is a common pattern,' I cautioned myself, pausing before Fay's door to set myself. 'Remember to keep acting as though you've experienced a heroin-

108

party often enough for it to have become commonplace.'

I turned the knob and stepped back inside.

Frankie and Fay were already high—high in a narcotic ecstasy almost too exquisite to be endured. Fay broke into a soft trill of laughter. Smiled softly at me. 'A real party, darlings,' she said. "Little Faysy's tossing a really smooth dream-party.' Pouring black coffee into cups, she nodded in a vague sort of way towards a collection of sweets on the dresser. 'All a junkie wants is close enough to reach,' she said. 'Just help yourselves, then sit back and let the junkie-wunkie do its magic. Drift into the inner chamber and coast. It's so great, it curls you.'

She sipped at sugar-thick coffee, turned to Frankie and said with a pout, 'Now, shiny shoes, how about letting little Faysy in on how you got so sloppy the connection had to blow you off?'

'Right now,' Frankie replied indolently, 'I feel so dead-on I say nuts to Mr. Connection Leger, nuts to the guy that sniffed me out. I'm high, pals—high like an eagle. Do I care about pushers and connections? Who ever heard of such common people?'

Sinking cross-legged to the floor, Fay said with rancour, 'You moocher, you—don't you respect a lady's natural curiosity? Be nice to me. After all, I'm paying for this party. I likee know wha' happen.'

'Sure, sure. Anything for you, baby.' Frankie said with an easy smile. 'M-m, I was tailed, see. Maybe going in to the West End—maybe after. If it was going in, whoever beat me was smart. He didn't settle for the small plant I worked with in the West End. He hung on until I bird-doged him back to the important one.'

I had no intention of listening twice to the story. '—and he beat you,' I filled in. 'Then all hell broke loose. Including a pretty rough little panic.'

Frankie sighed. 'Right,' he agreed.

'Well, it's a drag, Frankie honey. A real drag. Still, it

could be worse. Service is on again, and you never know—the Frenchy might goof, too. Then maybe you'll get back on the beat. And—as the evangelist said—at least it's not raining here in the tent.'

Carefully, I began to steer conversation. 'Fay's right about the Frenchy,' I said. 'Leger might fall. We all know the rendezvous is hot. In fact, it's all primed to explode.'

Frankie lit a cigarette. He blew feathers of smoke into the still air. 'So what if the rendezvous is hot?' he snickered. 'Suppose the trafficker dropped the word to the connection to set up a new spot. Okay, all that means is that we have a new meet. Nothing else. Inside an hour, it'd be just as hot as the old one and we'd all still be using the same dodges. You gotta play this game like a pro—the hard way. Those damn Horsemen don't ever miss a trick.'

I began to laugh. My laughter filled the room. I laughed wildly until the two addicts began exchanging worried glances.

'Hey! what's breaking you up?' Frankie broke in irritably. 'Tell me what's so funny.'

Another peal of laugher rang from my lips. 'You!' I guffawed. I laughed again. 'Ha, ha, ha . . . you're so damned funny, both of you. From the day I first met you you've both trembled in your socks every time anyone mentions the R.C.M.P.' Slapping my knee, I went off into another wild spasm. 'Ha, ha, ha,' I choked. 'You two sure are dopes!'

Frankie's back was poker-stiff. 'What d'you mean—dope?' he roared. 'I'm no dope. Not Frankie Seven. It's just plain smart to be scared of Horsemen. What d'you think those guys are—boy scouts? Those Mounties cook with gas. With gas, brother—they're murder.'

'Murder, are they?' I roared. 'No kidding? You say they're murder. Then tell me something. Tell me just one little thing, Frankie.'

Thoroughly aroused, Frankie's chin jutted forward. 'What?' he yelled. 'You damn fool, you. Tell you what?'

I sucked in a sharp breath—and I gambled my scanty accumulated winnings on a single whirl of fortune's wheel. 'If those Mounties are really so damned clever,' I taunted, 'tell me why they don't catch up with the Back Man. Tell me that, Frankie!'

Frankie's mouth fell. Words gathered in a rush on his lips, then fear sealed them solidly shut. He looked into my eyes, his again brimming with caution. 'Well, why *don't* they catch him?' I antagonized. 'Why not? It's not so tough to jump one guy if you really grind at it.'

Frankie began an uneasy fidgeting. 'So—s-so the Back man's a brain,' he stuttered. 'Not only t-that, he—well, he's lucky. Just a big lucky balloon of a slob. One of them fall-in-a-sewer-come-up-with-a-fistful-of-loot guys. Besides, no wonder he don't get caught. He don't play it that way. He never carries a cap.'

Oh, no!' I said disgustedly. 'He never carries a cap. He does it all with mirrors. He traffics by remote control.'

Frankie's bright eyes shot out a crackling glance. 'I tell you the Back Man never carries a cap,' he insisted. 'He keeps a kid—a little urchin kid he picked up off the streets. The kid takes all the chances. . . . No one ever puts the Back Man away. He's too cagey for the Horsemen, the devil, or anyone else!' Fay began an abrupt, toneless muttering. Rebellion flamed brightly in her eyes. Rebellion against fear and pain and slavery. Prudence wavered, crashed. Whirling, she faced Frankie. Her voice was contemptuous: 'If all this Back Man mystery is for my benefit,' she said stiffly, 'you can stuff it. It's no mystery to me. I know who the Back Man is. In fact, little Faysy could tell you plenty about the Back Man.'

Sometimes silence can be felt. Nothing moved in Fay's room. She began speaking.

My body came forward under the pull of her words.

12 'I'm not just whistlin' Dixie!' Fay said brittlely. She hesitated a moment, and she gave off little waves of tense, pent-up hostility, her eyes angry and hard, her mouth tight and thin. 'I know plenty about Mr. Fatso Back Man,' she repeated. 'You bet I do!'

Frankie held his hands clasped tightly over one knee. His eyes showed a hot and dangerous light. 'Go ahead, Fay. Go ahead. Talk your crazy head off. But I hope you're the kind that heals quick—real quick.'

Fay sat fiercely straight-up. 'Aw—let it go!' she grimaced. 'I don't have to shut up just because you say so, Mr. Fancy Shoes. This guy's safe—aren't you, honey?'

'Ask the monkey curled up on my shoulder,' I suggested, adding with an impatient shrug, 'Frankie knows damned well I'm all right. So do you. You can talk. *If* you really do know the Back Man.'

Fay's eyes flashed. The challenge affected her like an electric charge. She stared at Frankie, scowling anxiously from his broken chair; at me, now full-length on her tumbled bed. She said with anger and defiance, 'The Back Man's a filthy, fat pig. I know. A guy I used to be real cosy with worked for him.'

I pushed up on an elbow. Suspense had filled me with a strange illusion that this bed hung high in the air, that I lay on its edge looking down, down so far that soon panic would take over and make me jump. I knew the man I wanted would be identified now—or never identified at all. Forcing calmness into my eyes, I said, 'Well, that proves nothing. Who is the Back Man?'

'Jack Moss!' Fay spat the name out as though she were announcing the Marquis de Sade. She made an obscene gesture that brought her arm high enough to part the frayed material at her armpit like a zipper under too much pressure. 'He's the Back Man, Mr. Jack Moss,' she repeated distinctly. 'Aah—I used to believe moss was something that grew on a rock. I changed my mind when I got the low-down on the Back Man. He makes you think of a thing that crawls out from underneath.'

Tension had pulled Frankie well forward on his chair. He no longer rocked. Eyes that had held too much caution were no longer cautious. The possibility of a scene like this had never occurred to the little pusher before; but now that it was being played, he wanted a part in it. He said, quickly, 'Fay's telling the truth. Jack Moss wins all the prizes for being a big-league monster. I'm talking from experience. I know him better than any addict in town.' Frankie's ravaged body shuddered involuntarily. 'I've even been to Moss's house,' he said. 'Seen the crazy room where he keeps his animals—his playroom, he calls it. One time, he even told me the story of how he came to be head trafficker.'

Fay gave a derisive laugh. 'Don't kid little Faysy,' she scoffed. 'You've never even got within a block of Moss's place.'

Frankie swung to his feet. Picking up my cigarette package, he turned it rapidly over and over in his thin, scarred fingers. His lips curled in a quick, superior smile. 'No?' he laughed. 'Okay, I'll prove it to you two. But, first, let's get beamed in all the way. I'm wilting. Suppose we get this dream-party really on the road. Shoot up a little more junk. Then I'll tell you a story that'll start you screaming. The life story of the Back Man.'

'Was there ever a junkie,' Fay complained, getting up, 'that was too pooped to pop? Or one that could stay put until all the junk in the world was in his arm?' She brushed her albino hair back with soft motions. 'Okay,' she nodded. 'We'll shoot up plenty. Only, first I look out for number one, little Faysy. I'm setting up an extra plant so's I'll be sure of a quick fix in the morning.'

Fay drifted out, came back into the room smiling smugly. Frankie and I went into the now familiar bedroom-to-bathroom routine again.

Again, my share of Fay's heroin went into the bubbling toilet bowl. This time, three caps. Now Frankie and Fay were dangerously high. Another three-cap injection and they would drift completely away from me into the phantom half-world of narcotic stupor. If a story were to be told, the time for telling was now.

Frankie slid to the floor, assuming a sitting position. He hadn't bothered to put his coat back on. He rubbed at a smear of blood clotting on his arm, then rolled down his sleeve in slow motion. Lighting a cigarette, he handed the flaming match up to me, and smiled. He was on mountain-tops. Hunkering deeper into his private pink haze, he began speaking with delicate softness.

'The Back Man,' he said. 'Everything about him is weird . . . It's all so damned weird. Fantastic—like his animal room, his private arena room. Two sets of cages, see? Specially built cages. One set filled with rats that he feeds until they're big enough to harness and drive. Then'—Frankie lifted brilliant eyes to drill them like rivets into mine—'then Moss leaves the rats go without food for a few days. Not long enough for them to get weak—only enough to turn them mean and vicious.'

A dropped needle would have struck like a clap of thunder. Fay cleared her throat noisily, cleared it again. I caught myself cracking my knuckles. Frankie slid his tongue across his lips. 'You see,' he went on, 'in the second set of cages, Moss keeps cats. Alley cats. Big and strong as pumas. Understand?'

I sat up stiffly on the bed, looking at nothing, thinking we all were out of our minds.

Frankie took a single, very deep breath. 'The animal battles, that's only part,' he said. 'Like I told you, one night Moss really let down his hair to me and howled. He told me the way he climbed up from the gutters . . . the story of his life.'

I said, 'Keep talking, Frankie.'

114

Frankie paused, struggled to organize his story. 'Moss claims he don't remember too much about being a kid. He don't remember his parents at all. Says he raised himself on the streets. That he was a gutter-brat, running with street-gangs, stealing from stores and cars, like that. Later on, when he got a little older, he began driving a cab. Also being a wheel-man for the mobs. Not for long, though. Even then, Moss didn't like taking risks. Besides, he wasn't satisfied with the percentage. Like now, he wanted money fast—and plenty of it.'

I suggested, softly, 'So he started pushing drugs.'

Frankie scowled. 'I'll tell it,' he said. 'Let me get it in order. No, Moss didn't start pushing drugs, not then. Drugs were tied up solid by some mighty powerful boys at that time. Moss got into another racket. A racket that paid big money those days. Smuggling aliens. Chinese that could get to Canada but couldn't make the U.S. quota.

'Moss's part of that deal was sneaking the Chinese from here across the line. He bought himself a fast boat and shipped from point to point on Lake Champlain. He still gets big kicks boasting how he couldn't lose on that deal. Says he collected his price first from the Chinese and then if the patrols or coastguard gave him a chase dumped them overboard, sink or swim. But he finally out-foxed himself. He hated to deadhead back an empty boat. So he made contacts and worked out a deal for his return trips. Smuggling American lamsters into Canada. But one of those fugitives talked in time and Moss took a pinch over it and wound up doing time—for his first and last time.

'After he got out,' Frankie continued, 'he hung around corners, making a quick buck peddling reefers and pornographic stuff. In time, he worked up a fat bankroll. He claims he never spent a dime. Says he lived in a three-dollar-a-week room and ate what he could steal from fruit stands and open markets. He lived like that until his bankroll was king size. Then he went right back to the district where he ran as a kid and opened up a table-stakes gambling-joint. He went right back where he started—only this time as a Big-Shot.'

Frankie smiled a humourless smile. 'According to Moss, that gambling-room went like a tent on fire for a while. But Moss couldn't stomach paying off for protection. You know what that means. The boys in blue and brass got fed up and raided him until they forced him to close. But Moss was way ahead of the game. As well as his profit, he had the protection pay-off snug in his pocket. He had enough piled up to buy in on the big, cushy deal he'd been drooling over for a long time.'

Frankie concluded: 'The local head-trafficker had just been shot dead over a delivery-protection beef with one of his suppliers. Moss stepped in fast and grabbed control. He told me drug control in Montreal was the plum he'd always planned to pick for his own.'

Fay nibbled on her lip. 'Does Moss really talk like a preacher?' she asked in an awed voice. 'That's what my friend said.'

'Rolls it off like a Methodist deacon!' Frankie replied emphatically. 'He's a real bug about learning stuff. Kinda wacky about it. Dig this: Soon as he got settled solid, he began going to night-school. Never missed a single night for two whole years.' Frankie slapped his knee gleefully. 'How about that!' he roared, suddenly wide awake. 'That teacher sure won herself a prize when she drew Moss! And books! Say, that crazy house of his is full of them. He tells me he's read over a thousand books. All kinds. But specially history. He's loopy about history.'

'You, Frankie, how did you ever meet up with him?' I prompted.

Frankie's eyes fell to his shoes—to his beautifully polished shoes—And some of the fire in those eyes seemed to die. He said with a sort of reluctant pride, 'I'm showpeople. Well, anyway, I was once. I headlined in vaudeville for fifteen years: Frankie Seven's Seven Steps to Happiness. That's how I come by these special kicks. They're what's left of twenty pairs I owned when I took my first joy-pop.'

Fay's hate boiled over. 'From Moss!'

'That's right, from Moss. He'd just taken over the racket. Didn't even have pushers out yet. He was hustling himself, trying to keep service up so the ushers wouldn't spread out like the Twelve Tribes of Israel, leave town for Toronto or Windsor or Calgary or anywhere else service was good. At the time, I was playing the old Gayety down the street. Doing a soft-shoe and song routine. Moss used to come backstage every night to deliver caps to a junkie singer. One night, he bust into my dressing-room and talked me into sampling a bang. That did it. I lasted about six months more, then I got too weak to hoof. The old pins just wouldn't take it. And I was flat broke—I didn't have a dime. Nothing.'

Fay snorted. 'Huh! That's for sure!'

Frankie stared off into space. 'I tried stealing then,' he said bitterly. 'I went out on the boost to get dough for my habit. But I was always half sick and half crazy—running in circles for fix money. I kept going back to the stores. So one day the dicks got fed up. I wound up doing time in the city poky at Bordeaux.

'When I sprung,' Frankie said tonelessly, 'Moss was standing by the prison door. He was organized, rolling. What he needed was a pusher. Someone to work the central rendezvous. That meet was giving him nightmares. He'd had grief with every pusher he'd set up there.'

Fay said, 'Then along came Frankie Shiny-Shoes. Right on cue. Set to be number one engineer on the Snowdrift Special.'

Frankie turned his head away, so that Fay couldn't see the naked bitterness on his face. 'Moss was screaming for a pusher,' he repeated. 'He offered me a buck a cap commission and extras. It meant being close to the supply.

I jumped at the chance. For six months I'd been lying in a prison cell fighting my habit. Soon as I pushed a few caps, I bought one for myself. Then I started hitting it like crazy. All I could get. I was right back leading in the rat race.'

I said, significantly, 'Yes, right back. Until you blew your plant. Moss's plant, that is.'

Frankie merely grunted. 'I'm in a mess, bad,' he said with a short nod. 'Sure. But I wouldn't switch places with whoever scooped that plant—not for all the heroin in the world.' He shuddered.

And that was all.

Fay shattered the mood by rearing up with an abrupt jerk.

She started at Frankie and me as though seeing us for the first time. She swayed to her feet. 'Wow and wow,' she cried disgustedly. 'How about this turning out to be a real screwball dream-party! You two free-loaders bust in here and talk about nothing but trouble. I was on—but I'm not on so much now. The world's coming too close. I'm going to shoot myself back to cloud nine. I've had enough of you two. You get one more cap each—then off you go. Little Faysy wants to go dream-streeting single-o.'

I stood up. I wanted to get out—to take my information and leave.

'I'm sailing high for the rest of the day,' I grinned. 'Another cap will hold me up there until tonight. Got to go, anyway. I've a couple of important things on the fire.'

Frankie's eyes slid shrewdly up to mine. Moving spasmodically, he sat himself up straight. 'Things like fencing that hot ice you talked about?' His voice was light, and mocking, but it carried an undertone of hard challenge.

I glanced at Fay. She was staring at me oddly. 'Crazy Frankie,' I said. 'He talks and talks. No wonder he lost his plant.' I hesitated, then suddenly decided to use Fay's promised extra capsule for a precaution that, had she known, would have sent her at me like a tigress. 'Well, how

118

about it?' I said. 'Do I get that extra cap?'

'You get,' Fay said, still wearing her odd expression. 'Come with me.'

Insisting I wait in the hall, Fay cat-footed out of sight. A minute later, she stood swaying before me again, belly flattened a little now as if she were holding it in, one hand on a stuck-out hip, her eyes brash with invitation, her out-size breasts brushing suggestively against my chest. Pressing a heroin cap into my hand, she threw the hook I expected. 'This cap's just a little sample,' she said in a whisper. 'I was only kidding about dream-streeting single-o. Come back, honey. Get rid of Frankie first, then come back alone. You and me'll have a dream-party that'll be a real dream.'

I shook my head.

'Wish I could,' I said, hoping the lie sounded convincing. 'But sometimes you just can't. You know how it is. A guy has to get out and hustle.'

Fay pressed closer. 'Jewels, honey? You're going to sell some hot jewels, aren't you? You can tell little Faysy. I know better than to talk. I'm the original clam. That's me.'

I didn't answer. I just smiled, and winked.

Fay stepped abruptly back as though she had discovered something nasty hanging under her nose. 'All right, dummy up, then, if that's the way you want it,' she said waspishly. 'I have my pride. You don't need to spell it out for me. I know I'm not much of a bargain any more.'

'Now, Fay . . .'

'All right, all right, I know. You've got plenty of class, for a junkie. I'm not for a guy like you. Not any more. Go ahead, then. Take off. Go peddle your pencils.' She gave me a resentful little push. 'Well, go on. Just go, that's all!'

I hurried out into bright November sunshine. The air, snapping with cold, smelled sweet and untouched. The houses on the reeling street were a blur. My body and mind felt filthy; as though part of my addict disguise had rubbed in too deep; as though my mental make-up had penetrated too far inside my brain. I half ran along the block, fighting a mad desire to shout.

Fay's cap of heroin burned like a murder-weapon in my pocket.

A drugstore at the corner caught my attention. I ducked inside and paid a dime for a plain white envelope. Standing with my back to a scattering of customers, I peered over the tops of display-racks and through the window. Nothing suspicious or extraordinary moved on the street. I slid my hand into my pocket, pinned the red-hot heroin cap between my fingers. Two seconds later, the cap was sealed inside the envelope. Returning to the counter, and using it as a desk, I addressed the envelope blindly to R.C.M.P. Headquarters.

When the envelope lay safely on the bottom of a corner mailbox, I stood for a few minutes listening to the sweetly solemn music of distant cathedral bells until I managed to wave down a passing cab.

13 Leaning back on the leather seat of the cab, I felt the beginning of a snarling rage.

I was thinking of Frankie and Fay, the story they had told. Of the facts that shrieked out against the Back Man—Jack Moss.

Waves of disgust washed over me. Soon, I promised myself, soon. Soon, I will smash through the wall of caution and end this. But the hoarse, accented voice of my French taxi-driver slid into my consciousness as he carefully ticked off street numbers. I fell back against the seat; let the chill drain out of my spine. As my driver did, I would do also, working towards my destination, slowly and precisely: one—and two—and three—so on, to the end.

Paying off the cab, I had a cold shower on my mind, and my hall door key held in my hand.

I turned the door handle slowly, then stepped inside the opening door.

My living-room tingled with a tantalizing odour of perfume. In spite of the closed Venetian blinds, it was light enough to see her lying there.

My eyes adjusting to the half-light, I moved closer.

On my sofa, fast asleep, lay Thorn. Dark coiled hair framed the white blur of her face. In her sleep she was smiling—but frowning a little, too, as though worry stood too close to be pushed entirely away.

Stirring, she drew a deep shuddery breath. The rhythmical lift and fall of her blouse halted. Then she moved again, restlessly, as though aware of being watched. Her hand lifted with female instinctiveness to brush at her hair.

I touched her gently on the shoulder.

She awakened instantly.

I said, astonished, 'How ever did you manage to get in here?'

Long, slender legs swung to the floor. Standing, Thorn flicked her skirt into fit with a fascinating twitch of her hips. Her smile was faint and wry. 'I started trying to reach you early this morning,' she explained. 'By telephone from home. That didn't work at all. So I decided to come down here and wait. Well—I could hardly sit outside in my car until you decided to come home. So I gave your janitor five dollars to open your door and let me in. After I told him I'm your sister from Toronto.'

I chuckled. 'Clever girl! It makes a nice surprise for me. But why, Thorn? I mean, it's not exactly your sort of thing to do. Has something gone wrong?' And I flicked on the wall light.

Thorn didn't reply. Her eyes were wide, and growing wider. 'Good Lord, Max,' she gasped. 'Your clothes! Max—that suit! For heaven's sake!'

I crossed to my living-room bar, not smiling, too concerned to smile, repeating over my shoulder: 'Has something gone wrong?'

Over splashings of Scotch into glasses, Thorn's voice came to me: 'You weren't very serious in Louis's little café when you spoke of my helping you. I realized you were simply trying to be kind. And I thought it very nice of you. Just the same, since then, I've been checking every inch of the rooms Helen had at home. I've been looking for anything that might be useful to you.'

Glasses in hand, I spun slowly to face her. 'Thorn, are you telling me you *did* find something?'

'Not exactly, Max. Not by searching her rooms. I mean, there was nothing *in* the rooms. But, yesterday, a telephone call came for Helen. She wasn't at the house, of course, so I took it. The call was from an automobile dealer who bought her car last week. She'd forgotten some personal things in the glove compartment. He wanted to know what should be done with them.'

'You picked them up, of course.'

'Of course.'

Opening her handsome reptile bag, Thorn produced a tight cylinder of musician's manuscript paper and an embossed leather address book. She handed both to me.

Laying the address book aside, I rolled the elastic band from the cylinder which burst out of my hands. Music sheets fluttered like white leaves over my carpet. I picked up a sheet, glanced at it curiously: a Bach cantata. I reached down for another: a Bach prelude. Another: a Bach fugue. But mostly sacred music. Each sheet initialed P.C. P.C. for Phil Chasen?

Thorn stared curiously over my shoulder. 'Music! Whatever does it mean, Max? Helen's not a musician. She can't read a note.'

I gathered the scattered sheets. Carefully evading Thorn's eyes, I said, 'For now, let's forget the music. It has a meaning, all right, but we can talk about it later. Have you gone through this address book?'

'Page by page. There's something funny about that

book, Max. I recognized almost every name and telephone number. They were all commonplace—you know, family friends, dressmaker, hairdresser, dentist, so on. Then I came to a barely discernible scribbled number. It has an East End exchange—Falkirk. That seemed odd. There was no name with the number, but I'm sure Helen doesn't know anyone in that east end section of the city. Anyway, I tried to call the number. The operator told me it has been disconnected. I couldn't think of anything else to do, so I circled it in the book in case you might want to check it.'

I leafed through small, mostly blank pages. The pencilled number, when I found it, was just a number. Shutting the book, I slipped it into my pocket. 'Naturally, I'll check this,' I said. 'It's just possible it might be something.'

Thorn picked up her glass, cupped it in both hands, stared unseeingly into it.

'Right now,' I said, 'I have enough information gathered to make it possible for me to do several things. Things like handing over to the R.C.M.P. names and descriptions of dozens of users and at least one pusher—all of whom have probably been on the narcotic-squad suspect or conviction lists for years. I could go even a step farther. I could give them the name of the psychopathic devil who is top character in this nightmare.'

I threw up my hands. 'It wouldn't do the least good, Thorn. The Mounties would still be helpless. The old story: No possession—no evidence; no evidence—no conviction. At best, it would mean only a new name added to their list. A special list, perhaps, because it's the number one man's name. But there would still be no real profit.' My voice hardened. 'Nothing tangible *can* be gained until that number one man is tricked into pulling a bad boner. Meanwhile, the hell of it all goes on and on—with the real victims, the addicts, dying by inches each day while I sit by and watch.'

Thorn's eyebrows arched with a sudden distinctness

123

that gave her face a look of excitement. 'Max! The helpless ones—the ones using drugs . . . you really feel for them. They've become important to you now, haven't they?

'I know newspapers never print any real facts about addiction,' Thorn said. 'Not about the psychological or medical side of it. Only little snatches of police information. A paragraph about some addict or other being arrested. Or a raid where a supply of drugs was seized. Never any of the real trafficking story. I know, because I've been watching. And there's never anything at all about where or when or why addiction begins. What it actually means.'

'Here are facts to think on,' I said. 'Last year, eighteen tons—tons, mind you—of barbiturates were sold in this country. Kids all over are going ga-ga over them. They call them goof-balls and bombers—and they hold bomber parties. Thrill-mad youngsters out for a new kick—they're the ones helping to burn up those tons of barbiturates. They don't realize what they're getting into. Don't realize they're the addicts of tomorrow. And this *isn't* happening in some remote, fictional place, Thorn. It's happening here. In our country and our city. Now!'

Thorn came towards me. Her eyes were too bright. After two steps, her arms raised impulsively, reached out to me. She looked up at me, then, her face contorted terribly, the reaching fingers of both hands opening and closing, her shoulders shaking rendingly. I caught her hands and pulled her to me. 'I hate it all,' she said, her voice a desperate sob. 'All of it, every bit. It's evil, wretched.' She looked up at me miserably. 'Oh—Max! Sometimes it's as though the whole world were growing dim and shadowy.'

'But it's not,' I said, as gently as I could. 'It never really will.' My hand moved along the soft column of her throat, found the pulse thudding there, and then I held on, feeling the anguish move in her.

'Oh, Max!' she cried. 'The time is all wrong. For us, for—for everything.'

Moving away from me, she went back to the sofa, her face held whitely between her hands, a single curl fallen dark and shining over her temple.

I poured two drinks and brought one to her and looked down into the small, pale oval of her face. 'Don't nurse this—drink it!' I said. She gulped the straight whisky gratefully, then at last the ice in the bottom of her glass stopped rattling and she became calm. The errant curl bothered her and she swept it into place made herself smile. 'That drink won't do my driving any good,' she said. 'I didn't have any breakfast.' And then suddenly, she added in her own completely charming way, 'Max, I'm sorry I went all to pieces that way. I know tears won't solve a thing. But it's done now, and can't be helped. I should go and fix my face. I will. But—'

For a moment, she studied me with darkening eyes, as if she were trying to make up her mind about something. Finally, she decided and her eyes cleared.

She said, 'I'd like to ask a question. It may sound silly. Female-silly. I hope not. It's been on my mind for days and if I don't ask I won't have any peace.'

'Fire away,' I said.

'Well'—she bit her lip, went on uncertainly—'police *do* arrest addicts. The ones you describe as being small-fry.'

I nodded encouragingly.

'Then, when they arrest them, Max, why—why couldn't they give them lie-detectors tests and find out about the drug ring and traffickers that way? One hears every day about these tests. They *are* supposed to work.'

I began to smile, then stopped myself. To this decent girl, criminals of the addict type would be incomprehensible; the quirks and defences of their weird minds beyond her credulity.

'Well, for one thing,' I explained, 'the results of lie-detector tests aren't admissible in court as evidence. But, anyway, even should they be, the sad fact is: that sort of test is utterly useless on addicts.'

Thorn was sitting straight up on the edge of the sofa. 'But why? What is it about addicts that's so different?'

'The test isn't any good on a pathological liar,' I said simply. 'And addicts invariably are pathological liars. The furtive lives they lead make them so. They lie and cheat so much for survival their responses harden. The lie comes out like the truth. Doesn't even cause a twitch on a lie-detector needle.'

'I see,' Thorn said, adding thoughtfully, 'Then that means their emotions are dead—doesn't it?'

Nodding, I was again aware of whom Thorn's thoughts were centred on. We went down to the street together.

She surprised me by pulling down my head, brushing her lips against mine. 'In case your janitor's nosy,' she smiled. 'He thinks I'm your sister from Toronto, you know. And sisters rate a good-bye kiss.' She brushed another kiss against my ear, whispered softly: 'Max, I'm glad, so damned glad, I'm not really your sister.'

'Amen,' I replied fervently. 'Amen and amen!'

Her legs flashed attractively down the street. Gracefully, she slipped behind the wheel of a blue and shining M.G. She turned and waved.

After a moment of just standing there and thinking, I hurried back upstairs. I dialled the Falkirk number circled in pencil in Helen's forgotten address book. The operator cut in, confirmed that the number had been disconnected. I spoke to Information. No information. I called Supervisor. After two minutes under pressure, she finally informed me that the listing had been a private hospital, and that the telephone office did not under any condition release information regarding cancellations of service.

I hung up. The disconnected Falkirk number added another link to the chain. The new link was as vital evidence as were Helen's tattle-tale scars. As vital as the sheet-music cylinder of fugues, preludes, and cantatas that stared whitely at me from my living-room table.

14

My eyes opened to a room that was swaying from side-to-side like a huge hammock. It swayed and stopped and swung back, and voices kept mumbling, running words together in a meaningless rising stream of speech. The voices became louder and united in a beautiful singing and, as they did, I grew aware of a hint of exotic perfume. Suddenly, the voices stopped, and the music behind them died away.

I heard instead a steady, monotonous scratching.

I came instantly, fully awake.

My arm lifted automatically to switch off the Bogan, which had run out a new record of Weill's *Three-penny Opera* while I drowsed. For a moment, I remained motionless, and a little thoughtful in the hollow of my sofa where five hours before Thorn had lain.

The present and its problems swung suddenly back into sharp focus. I got up and padded across the room. A crumpled silk handkerchief lay on a small Chinese ceramic pillow beside the telephone. Wrapping a fold of handkerchief silk around the mouthpiece of the telephone I dialled, and when I had an answer, asked to speak with Phil Chasen. The same answer I'd had earlier in the day was repeated: 'Chasen's not around yet. He hasn't checked in. No, we don't know when he'll be here. Try later.'

I dressed in crummy flannel and my shiny trench-coat. Phil could wait—but not Frankie. By now Frankie should be out of Fay's room. By now, he should be vulnerable again.

Minutes later, I located Frankie in his familiar corner at the tavern. His eyes sparkled like stars on a clear, sharp night. His blood stream still held a liberal share of Fay's windfall of heroin.

'Man, you're blazing!' I said, slipping into the vernacular.

Frankie concentrated on the thought. When my words got through to him, he grinned lopsidedly. 'That cagey Fay,' he said. 'We banged twice more after you left. Three caps both times. Then, when all my lights are on, and I figure I'm all set, she puts on the clamps and gives me the quick heave-ho.'

'So? You're still a high-flying kite.'

Frankie grimaced. 'The morning, doll man! What happens then? When I go into the shake and shudder routine? Pal, I got to get action some place.'

Nodding understandingly, I said, 'Action is the magic word. At six bucks a cap, ten caps a day, a guy has to hustle some.'

'Hustle? You've got to fly, pal. I already tried to line myself up a spot. A guy I know runs a horse-book on University. I figured he might put me on as a runner. No go. So I tried a friend has a barbotte game going in the north end— up on Bernard. No dice. The reform clowns are knocking off one joint after another all across town.' Frankie spat disgustedly. 'Reform! Those jerks should have their heads read. Why don't they smarten up and grab off a potful of protection money while they can. Reform can't last. It better not last! It's getting so a guy like me can't even find a place to work.'

I started to bear down. 'Let's skip the City Hall,' I suggested. 'It's morning, not reform, that has me worried. You know, pale dawn and the shakes. We've got to set up a meet. Now!'

Frankie swung around. 'Well? I can set up a meet. But I can't pay for the caps.'

Opening my hand, I revealed two folded bills. 'My last twelve dollars,' I told Frankie. 'All the money I have. Good for two caps—one cap each. Providing I go with you to connect.'

'Say, what's with this twelve-buck routine?' Frankie demanded, and flashed me a hurt look. 'A few hours ago, before we went to Fay's room, you had thirty. That's what you said. From the Doultons you sold. So now you only have twelve left. What gives?'

'I paid room rent,' I retorted. 'It's twelve, take or leave. If you want a cap for free, let's go. I want action,' I growled.

'So? Slip me the twelve. We'll go across to the rendezvous together. I'll set up with the Frenchy. He's due there now.'

I waited by the cashier's desk while Frankie made arrangements to connect for the drugs. The transaction was set up with apparent ease. The little ex-pusher nodded his successor off to a corner, jerked his head in my direction, spoke a few rapid words, then came back winking a stage-wink. 'Everything's moving,' he announced. 'I gave Leger the cash and we connect in a few minutes. And you're in, pal. But proper. Frenchy says he'll sell you all you can pay for.'

'Not so fast,' I hedged, thinking sudden uncomfortable thoughts about a Mountie guilt-by-proximity charge. 'How does Leger work?'

'Smart, pal, smart and easy,' Frankie said grudgingly. 'We just drift into the meet naturally. His service is better than Eaton's. Personalized: know what I mean? But first, we stall a little—about ten minutes. Long enough for him to get to his plant. He's already left.'

'I noticed that. What comes next?'

'In ten minutes by that clock over the food-bar, you and me ease out. On the street, we turn west and walk one block. Leger'll be waiting on the opposite corner. He'll drop a red cough-drop package. The two caps'll be inside. Then Leger'll drift away, and I'll move over and stand there for a minute. I'll pick up the package like I'd dropped it myself by mistake. Then, pal, we'll both do a fade, knowing we'll wake up tomorrow a.m. with what we need to start the birdies singing.'

No backing out now. This time we would follow through. I would have to accompany Frankie while he made an illegal purchase of heroin.

Outside, the afternoon had darkened into early evening. An earlier rain had settled into a steady drizzle, and a thousand neon signs tinted it all the colours of the rainbow. Small depressions in the pavement held shallow pools of water that danced and shimmered in the light and exploded under the busy feet of pedestrians. Automobile traffic was heavy, and cars were parked bumper-to-bumper at the curbs. I stepped along briskly with Frankie; past crowds waiting to cross the street during a break in the thrusting traffic; across the street itself until we were standing in a tight knot of people waiting at a street-car stop.

A queer uneasiness grew in me; as though something unreal were going on. An odd movement in the streaming pedestrians sent me a quick warning. A moment later, I noticed a corresponding movement in a group half-circling a news-stand.

Leger took up his position. Frankie spotted him, touched my arm, then edged eagerly forward. I moved with him.

I sensed, rather than saw, a quick eruption of movement in the crowd at the news-stand.

Whirling, I was just in time to see someone hurtling through the dusk and drizzle at me. It was pure reflex action which made me plunge towards him rather than away. But, even then, I was not nearly quick enough. The wet pavement seemed to lift under my feet as shoulders slammed me expertly and violently against a storefront, spun me around. Fingers and a thumb—tight and squeezing cruelly tighter—dug into my throat. My arm, the right arm that had automatically cocked, grew into a burning mass of pain high behind my shoulder. I writhed in agony, staring stupidly into a display-window while unseen hands riffled quickly through my pockets, ran down my trouser legs, under my collar.

'Okay, this one's clean,' the searcher grunted. 'Nothing in his clothes.'

Abruptly, pressure relaxed on my throat. Before I could suck breath into my straining lungs, the man gripping my arm spun me back to face him and closed in fast. I saw his balled fist go back—then my stomach seemed to burst wide open.

I heard a voice that was faint and growing fainter say, 'And no caps in his throat.'

The neons along St. Catherine swung and dipped. They went out suddenly, as if someone had smothered them with a dark curtain.

When my eyes cleared, I was alone in the back of a car that was leaning into a curve. I gulped quick mouthfuls of air. I sat erect with an effort and my linked fingers tightened convulsively over my stomach. One of two men in the front seat turned to face me. 'You don't really feel too bad,' he advised me pleasantly. 'You should see your two pals. In the car up front.'

'Hey! what the devil,' I gasped. 'Why the Gestapo treatment?'

The man showed me his back. 'You'll find out,' he said with a short laugh. 'This ride's on the government—Federal. You're on your way to Headquarters. R.C.M.P.'

That was it. An answer to my question. I sat back wondering if I'd ever stop sweating again.

The car pulled up before a huge, barracks-like building. Wordlessly, the two constables escorted me through a narrow hall and down a steep narrow staircase to a basement detention room.

Leger was already seated stolidly in one corner, giving his finger-nails an earnest going over. Frankie stood doubled-over near the door. He rubbed tenderly at his stomach, nodded to me, then blinked up at the grilled windows. 'Hell's bells!' he groaned. 'Home again!'

131

I sat on a narrow bench. I felt fatigue-weary; not up to this. Frankie slid close. He looked like a walking disaster as he whispered tonelessly into my ear, 'Clam up! Don't say nothing that can be used. Dictaphones! The Horsemen are hip to every angle.' He began worriedly dry-washing his hands. 'But they'll have to let you and me go,' he muttered hoarsely. 'They only jumped us all because they weren't sure which one had the caps.'

I glanced at Leger; now sitting poker-stiff in his corner, wiping his face nervously with a dirty handkerchief he could not hold still. 'What about him?' I asked.

'He's done!' Frankie shuddered. 'He's dead stinking fish. Those two caps were his one-way-ticket to the penitentiary. But that's not all. Man, no! He's going to have to kick his habit cold-turkey. Jesus-God! A miracle is what he'll need to help him live through that.'

Sitting still was impossible. I rose, began a restless pacing. I paced the room, back again, debating what to say. Leger swore at me. He stretched out flat on the bench, clasped his hands behind his head and stared fixedly at the ceiling.

A key rattled, made a sudden gash of sound. The door swung wide.

A constable stepped into the detention room. His face was as cold as a pebble. He glanced at each of us with keen eyes, finally stabbed a finger at me. 'You!' he said curtly. 'The inspector wants you.'

Frankie jumped as if he'd bitten a nerve. He took a full step towards me, yelled: 'They're gonna grill you. Don't admit a thing. Nothing. Don't even listen. Tell 'em we was on our way someplace innocent—to Evening Mass.'

The constable glanced at Frankie once, without interest, then tapped my arm. 'Come this way,' he said.

I was guided quickly down a narrow hall to an elevator. We went up two floors. The constable tapped my arm again. 'Come this way.' He marched me down another hall, past rows of oblong bulletin boards covered with tacked-up police flyers to a long block of offices with anonymous, closed doors. In front of the last door, a solitary, empty chair waited. 'Sit!' the constable said brusquely. 'The inspector will see you when he finds time.'

The inspector's door opened. A scarlet-jacket Mountie stepped out, nodded curtly to me. 'Step in,' he said. 'The inspector will talk to you now.'

The inspector's office was small. It had the cold, hygienic smell of all places where police work is done. The hard-used little room looked familiar; identical to a dozen such rooms I had known across the face of the globe from Tokyo to Toronto. Metal filing cabinets lined one wall. A thin carpet, worn in a circle around a chair, faced a desk. The desk itself was severe, small, and piled with papers and criminal dossiers.

A tall man, grey-haired and lean, rose to meet me. He looked as I had expected he would look—aggressive, tireless, fanatic about detail, and severely determined to arrest and punish criminals. Dedication is rare, and when you meet it you can see the mark it leaves. This police officer had that mark.

He spoke coldly, precisely. 'I am Inspector Welch,' he said. 'I am not pleased that you had to be brought here.'

I shifted uncomfortably. 'Say the word, Inspector. I'm prepared to leave at once.'

My joke wasn't good. It provoked only a wrinkled brow and a piercing glance. The inspector pushed cigarettes and a lighter across his desk. 'Perhaps you will be permitted to leave later,' he said grimly. 'But, first, we'll have a talk. Incidentally, to economize on time, I'll tell you at once that I know who you are—also, what you've been attempting to do . . . However, just as a matter of routine, would you mind telling me where you were in August of 1952?'

My cigarette stalled unlighted in mid-air. It took a full thirty seconds for me to grasp the significance of Welch's words.

I leaned back, sighed. 'Just where you think I was, Inspector,' I answered. 'Shuffling back and forth between Tokyo and various spots in Korea.'

'I see,' Welch nodded. 'Would you by any chance know anything about a Korean communist called Dr. Live-Again?'

I shrugged. 'Dr. Live-Again was convicted by a U.N. police court of supplying U.N. troops with pipe opium. His real name was Chang Yen. That is the name he used when he went to a communist leadership school. He was shot in a *hsien*—a small village—near Seoul.'

'Yes,' Welch said.

'Look here, Inspector,' I said lamely, 'not a day has passed that I haven't thought of coming in here to get things straightened out. In fact, I've been more than worried about stepping beyond the orbit of my present licence privilege.'

Welch smalled his hands against his desk. 'Damn it, Dent! You know you should have called me five minutes after you left Ashton. You know bloody well you've extended yourself far beyond your privilege. No one should know better than you that we are the police agency in this country in the matter of drugs.'

I said, awkwardly, 'I—I, ah, suppose you've been behind me right from the beginning?'

'From the moment you first spoke with Frankie Seven until today. When we finally decided to bring you in.'

I was dumbfounded. My hand fell to pat the raw bruises on my stomach. 'You've a damned impolite way of delivering invitations,' I muttered.

Welch smiled. Not a huge smile, but a smile. He said briskly, 'Our men are trained to be effective. And *we* didn't think up that swallowed finger-stall trick, don't forget— only a way to defeat it. As well, I intended your arrest to look convincing.'

Welch pulled a desk drawer, produced a constable's duty sheet, leaned forward. 'Dent,' he said, his words clipped, 'we know a lot about you and your case. Things we're not certain of, we are able to guess. For instance, the type of agreement you must have with Huntley Ashton. Also, why Ashton is so completely determined to get a dangerous job done without identifying himself to the authorities.'

'You know why Ashton hired me instead of seeking official help?'

'Naturally,' Welch replied impatiently. 'And I'm willing to respect your client to the extent of not asking you to discuss either him or his daughter.' He stared pointedly at me, then flipped papers until he found the one he needed. 'Now,' he said forcibly, 'we'll have that talk! We know you are out to smash the top man in the local drug ring. The trafficker for this particular section of the country. A man known to the underworld as the Back Man.'

'Jack Moss,' I said. My voice had a diminishing quality.

'Exactly!' retorted Welch. 'Jack Moss. Understand, Dent, that we have had a raw file on Moss for a long time. He's clever—a calculating schemer—but he's not nearly clever enough to remain completely unknown to us. For a long time, he's been under special surveillance. Surveillance, but that is all.'

I began to speak, hotly. 'Sure—'

Welch glared. He continued in a monotone, his cold eyes never leaving mine. 'We could have picked up Moss a dozen times. On suspicion. But never when we knew for sure he had drugs on his person. Never when we knew for sure he had drugs on his person. Never when we had proof enough for a conviction.'

I edged forward on my chair. 'Okay!' I retorted. 'But meanwhile this damned trafficking and addiction goes on and on. The Narcotic Law is so precise—'

'As you well know, Dent,' Welch snapped, 'the law

demands proof positive. Suspicion, even certain knowledge, isn't enough. *Proof.* That's what judges convict on, Dent.'

The dam inside me burst. Sudden, unreasonable rebellion leaped in me—revolt. I came to my feet, shouting . . . 'Proof! You received an envelope in the mail the other day. A plain white envelope with a cap of heroin in it. I mailed that envelope. That cap came from me. I had just been given it by a pair of addicts that between them use twenty or thirty caps a day. Jack Moss supplies those caps. But that's nothing. Nothing, d'you hear?'

My words rushed on. Hate choked my voice: 'For an entire heart-breaking month, I've been watching the drug ring operate. Night and day I've been doing just that. I've by God seen all of it—with the dirty blanket ripped off. It's going on now—this minute. Whole-sale trafficking—all over the city. I know it, and you know it! And we're both sitting here on our butts chatting about technicalities.'

Welch said, ominously, 'Dent.'

'What are we coming to,' I roared, not able to stop, 'what kind of society is this when a mad beast like Jack Moss can keep operating—adding victims to his list every week—getting fatter and richer laughing at the law and the people trying to enforce it?'

Welch's hand lifted threateningly over his desk. Instead of smashing it down again, he reached for and began stuffing tobacco into a bulldog briar. 'Precisely,' he said, with determined calm. 'Precisely. Nevertheless, Dent, I'm glad you mailed us that capsule. It puts you in a much better light. It proves to me you were aware that before long you would have to work with us.'

Welch struck a wooden match, fanned it gently across the bowl of his pipe. Smoke poured out, drifted aromatically across the office. Welch sat back and smiled a little, obviously not dissatisfied with the way things were developing. He said gently, almost soothingly, 'You could get in a few real hard licks for our team, Dent. That's the profit I see in this. You see, single-handed, you've accomplished bloody wonders.

'*But,*' Welch continued, clamping his teeth hard over the stem of his pipe, 'fantastic as that is, you and I aren't actually helping each other. In fact, we're working at cross purposes. Your contract is to stop Moss. Your intention is to manœuvre him into a spot where he can be arrested supplying drugs to some pusher or connection. Then you intend to let Ashton get to work applying hidden pressure for a maximum sentence.'

I sat down. 'Well?' I demanded. 'Wouldn't that wash out Moss? Smash his organization?'

Welch smiled, 'Would it?'

'Why not?' I glanced curiously at him. 'Suppose Moss, his pushers, his runners and district connections all went down together. Suppose that happened. Then what?'

'We get rid of our problem for a while,' Welch grunted. 'Moss and a few of his underlings go to prison to serve short sentences for possession. Possession only, because they support each other's perjured testimony that they are users, not traffickers.' Welch shook his grey head. 'That's not nearly good enough. We have other plans for Moss.'

'Plans, yes,' I retorted. 'Police always have plans. No matter how long it takes, you people are content to wait. You'll wait until you can get Moss for trafficking—until you can convict him for the limit—fourteen years.'

Welch's face grew cold, severe. The lines calipering his thin lips suddenly seemed more distinct, deeper. 'The Criminal Code,' he said curtly, 'has recently been revised. That revision gave the courts authority to put traffickers and distributors behind bars for life—on indefinite sentences. That's why I am content to wait.

'It's why we have avoided alarming Moss. Avoided putting pressure on him that will frighten him into hiding. Naturally, we keep arresting common addicts. Sometimes we even get a pusher—like Leger. As you know, we keep trying without much success to wring information from them. Our eye, however, remains always alert on the main target, Moss—and what lies beyond Moss.'

I was finding it impossible to hold respect from Welch. There was a confidence of command about the man that could not be ignored. I waited for him to reach his point. 'We'll finish Moss,' he said forcibly. 'Wipe him out. You can help us do that. But that's not all we want. The link in the chain that connects to Moss must be smashed with him. We intend to completely cut off the supply of heroin that has been pouring into the city—to eliminate it by locking Moss's supplier fast in the cell next to his. Then our job of work is done. Perhaps—with addicts forced to disperse or take cures—illegal drug sales can be reduced to a negligible minimum.'

Staring at me, he said exactly as though he were addressing a squad that had the duty: 'Now, I have enough data on you, Dent, to know you are the type of private operative that keeps his client as his first consideration. That's as it should be. Otherwise, you wouldn't be worth your salt. But I'm going to ask you to think a lot farther. Beyond your client, even beyond the addicts and the hell on earth they exist in. I want you to consider for a minute a completely different sort of drug-trafficking victim. We have a file on them, too. We call in the T.S.V. file.'

The initials conveyed nothing to me. I told Welch so.

'Trafficking's Secondary Victims,' Welch explained crisply.

Swivelling his chair to an open file drawer, he pulled out a bulging correspondence. 'Look, Dent!' he rasped. 'Look at this! Letters! From stores, wholesale display-houses, and business men's associations all over the city. These people complain they're being robbed out of business. They go so far as to compare addicts to a swarm of locusts attacking a grain field. They plead with me to do something. But I

138

can't. And the result is, I feel and look like a fool.

'Shoplifting appeals to addicts because it is easy and quick, not too dangerous. They've made a science of it and they depend on it for their incomes—men and women. Except that the women usually resort as well to prostitution. Now, normally, those two offences don't come under our jurisdiction. But storekeepers know that drugs do. So we get their most bitter complaints. One can't blame the stores. Not at all. Not after considering their losses.'

I made a hazy guess. 'A few hundred thousand a year in merchandise—throughout the city, I mean.'

Welch's face distorted. 'Millions!' he snapped. 'Here, Dent—just listen to this breakdown.' Picking up a sheet, he began quoting from it: 'The average addict in Canada spends at least eight thousand dollars a year for drugs. If he or she shoplifts for this money, as most addicts do, that means twenty-five thousand dollars worth of merchandise must be stolen. This amount, because few merchandise fences pay in excess of a third of the value for stolen goods.'

Welch put down the sheet. He continued talking, with a rising inflexion in his voice: 'Montreal has something over two hundred known drug addicts. Now, suppose only half of those are shoplifting—which would be an absolute minimum. It's still a staggering thing. Because when you multiply the twenty-five thousand dollars worth of merchandise stolen each year by each of that minimum total of addict-shoplifters, you find that local business is being robbed annually of about two and one half million dollars.'

'Whew!' I gasped.

'Yes—whew!' Welch echoed roundly. 'Some evening, when you've time to spare, compute the losses across the country—with approximately five thousand active addicts on the loose. Then consider the other facets of the drug problem. The continual break-ins of drug-stores, small hospitals, doctors' and dentists' offices and homes, everywhere drugs are kept. The maiming and crippling and killing that goes on during ring wars. The suicides.' Welch threw up his hands in despair. 'Add to that the bloody awful fact that each day we discover new addicts.' Glancing at his desk clock, the inspector banged shut the correspondence file.

'Because of deliberate violation of privilege, your license could be cancelled,' he said. 'Or you could be forced to turn over every scrap of information you have gathered on the young woman you are indirectly representing, and on the rendezvous addicts. I will not recommend either, Dent. Not now—not since you've managed to ferret your way inside. Go ahead. Go through with your investigation to its end. But heed my warning. You will get no official tolerance. None. Information you may need, yes. Help, if it is necessary, yes. Tolerance or protection? Absolutely not! If you go on, you go on alone!'

For a silent moment, I stared at the worn carpet. A hot flush rose along my neck. 'You mean the Narcotic Squad won't be alerted. That if I'm caught handling drugs while I'm working my way in to where I can set Moss up, you'll still prosecute.'

'It will have to be that way,' Welch said. 'You can't expect it to be otherwise. You're on our sure list, but you're not actually one of us. Therefore, while I can tell you unofficially to go on, I must also warn you that you do so at your own risk. And another thing,' Welch said forcefully, 'I insist that regardless of how the wind blows you contact me within one hour of the time you first meet Moss. That is, assuming you ever do.'

Realizing what Welch had in mind, I nevertheless demanded: 'Why?'

Welch smiled. 'Then *we'll* move in behind your play. Ready to make the arrest once you have Moss set up to contact for his trafficking supply. That way, we nab two instead of one—Moss and his presently unknown supplier. Otherwise,' Welch stated flatly, 'neither you nor anyone else makes a move.'

I nodded agreement. 'From what I've learned about supply methods,' I said, 'I picture it this way: Moss gets his drugs in bulk lots—no doubt several kilos at a time. My guess is that he line-connects—that is, reduces his own risk element by having the drug package juggled about fast, shifted from waiting accomplice to waiting accomplice before it finally reaches him. He probably handles it for only a few minutes. During that time, he cuts the heroin personally. Then he gets it out of his possession in jig-time. Shoots it on to his district distributors. What I must establish then, is exactly where and when and with whom Jack Moss connects for those kilos of heroin.'

'That's it!' Welch nodded emphatically. 'We have to catch Moss in *flagrante delicto*. We have to reach him and his supplier during the split-second it takes them to deal—

'A split-second' he rasped. 'Good Lord! it's like trying to catch a handful of fireflies. Everything surrounding Moss is enigmatic, baffling. We aren't really sure of a thing. Not even that he deals himself with his district con- nection. Our stool pigeons tell us he lives with a young street waif. A boy called Shadow. The story is that Moss completely dominates the boy. That the boy takes all his risks. An unthinkable thing!

'But I don't know.' His lips curved upward in exasper- ation. 'We have no dossier on the boy—nor have the City or Provincial police. Sometimes I begin to wonder if this Back Man really exists at all.'

My thoughts had gone swinging off. I was thinking of Frankie, his shabby cigarette-holed clothes, the funny pride that kept him clinging to his dancing shoes; of Fay, her emaciated, shrunken body, her bright, furtive eyes, her pathetic loneliness; of Phil, his prostituted talent, his confused life, his wild fear; of Helen Ashton, her drug- shot, insensible body, her ghastly scars, the needle hanging

141

from her bruised arm. Then my thoughts took wing again, went out to the Back Man, to a perverted, sadistic game he played with starved animals.

I said, looking squarely at Welch, 'The Back Man exists. I'll trap him by using a lure even he can't resist. And when I've done that, I'll lay him right plump in your lap.'

'Be careful, Dent,' Welch warned, flatly. 'Lure, or no lure, you be careful. Moss is a schemer in the old tradition. That, we know. Fancy him using that boy!'

The inspector got up to walk around his desk. 'You know, Dent,' he said with a warmth that surprised me, 'it's rather a pity you prefer being on your own. I'd like to see you carrying our credentials. Ah—well,' he smiled ruefully. 'I suppose twenty-five hundred a year, squad duties, and plenty of no-pay overtime don't add up to much of an attraction to a man with your background.'

He reached to open his office door. 'I'll just walk along as far as the elevator with you,' he said, and added, 'Remember, now, Dent—you are completely on your own. We have no official recognition of either you or your case.'

I pressed the elevator signal button. 'One thing, Inspector,' I said. 'You can help me tremendously simply by holding Frankie Seven in cells until he gets thoroughly sick.'

Welch smiled, a wise smile. 'We'll give Seven time to cool out,' he agreed at once. 'Leger, of course, will be held for trial—and, you may bet your hat, for conviction.'

I held out my hand. I don't know just why I did so; but I was glad I did. Welch gripped it firmly, and came desperately close to grinning.

'Good hunting, Dent,' he said.

At the street door, I stopped and squared off the block, wondering about a tail. Instead, a corner light silhouetted a spare, ragged figure standing arms-akimbo before a heavy-set man loaded with a shopper's parcels. '. . . watches over the fall of every little sparrow,' I heard a voice say. Then the ragged one whirled abruptly and trotted past me, ignoring me completely as he shrank into a dim alley beyond the barracks. Vaguely, I heard an eerie, diminishing chuckle.

15 I sat at a crowded snack-bar in a small delicatessen for a half-hour, smoking over a cup of coffee, immersed in the pleasant smell of kosher food—zemmel, chalahs, lox, halva. It was warm and my eyes kept falling shut.

The last few days had wrung me out completely. I sat trying to assemble my thoughts; wondering whether it would be wise to hit now at Phil Chasen and wring from him information I desperately needed, or to go home and rest until Frankie staggered sickly back to be used again.

I caught myself staring blindly in front of me. This was ridiculous—sitting here deliberating the next move. What had to be done was patently clear; just as obvious as was the disturbing fact that doing it would be unpleasant and perhaps a little sad.

I went to the telephone booth, dialled a number. I asked a question through a fold of handkerchief I had wrapped around the mouthpiece. This time, my question was answered. An irritated voice said: 'Phil Chasen is through here. The piano team broke up—don't ask me why. The last I saw of them they were screaming at each other. But, if you're interested, Chasen opens tonight in another club. The Melody on Sherbrooke Street. In a solo act.'

The Club Melody stood back from the street—from inside came a sound of music, loud now over a sudden lull in traffic. As I stepped in the door, the music became recognizable as the intense vibrato of a single piano.

I sat at the bar. Facing me, on the wall over a triple tier of glistening bottles, hung an emormous mirror. The mirror reflected the entire lounge. The orchestra dais was clearly visible. Also the baby grand, the pianist bent low over it.

143

A soft wall light behind Phil laid patterns of shadows across his white hands. The ice melted in my glass while he fingered through selection after selection. Then suddenly the music stopped, forgotten at once under a quick rush of conversation.

Standing up, I moved stiffly across the room to tap him lightly on the arm. He turned slowly, blinked. His brow wrinkled in puzzlement. He looked as if he were trying very hard to remember where he had been. I felt as though I were doing something unclean. I said, 'Take a break, now, Phil. We're going to have another talk.'

He stumbled from the dais, turned towards a side door. 'Dressing-room,' he mumbled. 'Let me get my coat. I need some fresh air.'

I followed him to a mean, shabby dressing-room. 'Why not talk here,' I suggested. 'All you need do is answer one or two simple questions.'

Phil made an embarrassed gesture. 'No. I—well, you understand, Max, I—I took a little too much. I've got to walk it off.'

'If you want, Phil. Let's go.'

We walked side by side to the corner, crossed the street. Phil moved beside me in a sort of drunken half-stagger, his head deep in his upturned collar, hands thrust into his pockets. He spoke only once. 'Walk,' he muttered. 'Walk. God, I think I've walked a million miles this way.'

My eyes studied him. He was a sleep-walker. No hint or flicker of expression showed on his face. We turned into a side street leading up to Pine Avenue and the eastern slope of the mountain. 'All right, Phil,' I said grimly. 'No more stalling . . . This time, we're going to get a few things settled.'

Phil halted. He stood stiffly. 'Now, listen; stop acting like a cop,' he grated. 'You can't make me do anything. Nothing at all.' He dug his hands stubbornly deep in his pockets. 'And I'm not moving,' he said. 'Not one inch until you tell me exactly what you want.'

Nothing could be gained now by subtlety. The question I wanted an answer to would have much more impact coming unexpectedly 'Your Bach sheet music,' I said bluntly, 'what was it doing in Helen Ashton's car?'

'The Bach! Helen!' Phil shrank back. He flung a hand out as if to ward off a blow. Then control flew, leaving his voice wild and shrill: 'Helen! Max—if you've mixed Helen up in my troubles, I'll kill you. So help me, I'll kill you!' Convulsions of fear twisted his face, made it grotesque. 'Curse you,' he screamed. 'Curse you, Max, I warned you to leave me alone, to stay out of my life.' He drove his hand up, hard, struck me on the shoulder, spun me off balance.

Whirling, he sprinted away from me down a dark lane.

Night blackness sucked up his fleeing body. I almost lost him, then, at a turning at the inner end of the alley, caught up and reached out to his shoulder, jerked him to a stumbling stop.

My hand went under his shirt collar. 'By God, Phil, you'll talk now—plenty. Before I bang you around until your teeth rattle.' I exerted fierce pressure on my fistful of collar and neck. 'Tell me about Helen Ashton. Did you start her on drugs? Did you?'

Phil was ballet dancing, on his toes, utterly helpless. I relaxed my grip. He swung his head violently from side-to-side; the negative gesture. His face was rigid from an intensity of concentration. He was attempting to fix Maxwell Dent into place; trying to decide if he were caught in something more serious than an unofficial talk about jewels and a girl and drugs. Struggling to get back control, he managed to pant out: 'See here, Max. You've no right to do this to me. No right at all!'

I twisted his collar, snapped: 'I want this information, Phil. I'm going to have it. Please don't make me force you to talk. Don't. Or you will regret it every hour of every day for months.'

'You've no right—' Phil retorted.

145

The rebuttal came from between my teeth. 'But I have. Yes, I have. And to enforce it, I have this . . .' Drawing back my hands, fingers extended rod-stiff, I judo-chopped him smartly across the bridge of his nose. 'I am going to make you talk. Go on, tell me where you met Helen Ashton.'

Blood was a bright glistening over Phil's upper lip. 'Smash me to bits,' he screamed. 'Kill me. I don't care. I'm half dead anyway.'

I chopped upward, where his swelling nose met with his lips. 'You fool!' I cried. 'You've no choice but to tell me now. What made Helen the way she is? Who carved her up?'

'No, no. I can't. I'm afraid. Why? Tell me why you want to know.'

I chopped three times more. Once down against Phil's bobbing Adam's-apple, twice against his lips. He slumped, then threw his head back, kept bouncing it back against the end of his spine. 'No, no—no!' he screamed. 'I can't. I can't tell you anything. You don't understand. They'd kill me.'

I twisted until his back was exposed. Then I chopped hard over each shoulder. He let out a wild, animal scream. 'Who operated on Helen?' I insisted. 'Tell me. Don't make me keep on. I know twenty more places to hit. If I have to, I'll start working on the neural centres.'

Phil's head was a bloody, wig-wagging pendulum. His nose had already ballooned into red agony. 'L-let go-go,' he pleaded. 'Let go my collar. Please s-set me down.'

Steps opposite where we stood ran down into a deep cellar entrance. I pushed Phil ahead of me, helped him down the stairs, propped him against a grilled door. His phrenetic trembling quieted. There was only the sound of his broken breathing. It was horrible. In a shrunken, resist-less sobbing whisper, he asked: 'You haven't—gone with—the cops?'

'I'm still on my own, Phil. All I'm asking for is the truth about Helen Ashton.'

Phil began crying. 'I kn-know you'll make me t-tell you.'

Pressing his handkerchief softly to his dripping lips, he peered in fascination at the thick, darkening blood that stained it. He groaned. 'Max, I—Max, I d-don't know what to say.' He groaned again, horribly. 'It was all . . . awful.' He sank to his knees as though he were standing in quicksand. 'You did wrong to hit . . so much,' he gasped. 'I . . . I peed myself.'

Taking out two cigarettes, I lighted them and put one smoke between Phil's lips. 'Puff!' I told him. 'Draw on it. Puff.'

He drew heavily, then gagged and spit out the cigarette. His voice vibrating with pain, he began talking: 'Helen's . . . a funny kid. Met her at a deb ball . . . mad about excitement. I was playing . . . She asked me to do . . . solo number. I remember it . . . the Polonaise, Chopin. She asked me . . . for more. I joked . . . said, Come to club . . . Promised I'd play for her all night . . . if she would. Helen was . . . lovely then . . . lovely.'

I filled in, quickly: 'So Helen came to the club. And you played for her. Then you began meeting her away from the club, after you were off. You took her around to places.'

'That's how it all started. Then she asked me . . . bring her to jam session . . . said she's never been. I brought her. A couple of us . . . the bass player and I . . . we were shooting junk. Helen was saw us and I . . . honest, I couldn't stop her. Honest to God, Max . . . swear it. She was curious . . . Said she wanted to try it . . . That if I didn't give her a shot . . . she would find one . . . somewhere else. Honest, Max . . . honest . . .'

I ground my teeth. 'All right, all right. So Helen got started.'

'She started taking joy-pops . . . Not too bad, Max. Just once in a while. Then we . . . we sort of . . . of paired up. You know . . . together. It just happened. Sometimes she couldn't go home. She was afraid to. Because . . . because she'd got a little too high.'

147

Breath blasted through my lips. 'Go on,' I urged. 'Tell me about Helen's scars.'

Phil's eyes showed whitely. 'I didn't know about that,' he said in a horrified whisper. 'Not until . . . after. Helen had told me she was . . . pregnant. She wanted to get married. Said she wanted the baby. But there . . . there were . . . oh, God'—his hands clutched vice-like on mine—'how . . . how *could we* get married? How, Max? How?'

'Why not, you damned fool? You're both over twenty-one. What could possibly stop you?'

I don't think Phil even heard the question. His head was thrown back. His eyes were staring wildly. 'Look!' he screamed. 'Look behind you, Max. Between the gaps in those buildings. See it there. See it! That's what stands between Helen and me. You can see it . . . see it even from here!'

My head turned instinctively. Instantly, my eyes were blinded by a blaze of light that poured down from the crest of the mountain through the gaps in freakishly-positioned buildings. The meaning behind Phil's words became instantly clear and it staggered me. My eyes still dazzled by the intensity of light, I said, my voice struck with awe, 'The Cross! The Cross on the mountain. My God, Phil, I think you've gone crazy. What about the Cross?'

He was still on his knees, his voice a tortured plea for understanding: 'I'm Roman Catholic, Max. I was brought up in the Church. I—I can't marry out of my religion. I can't . . . and Helen won't convert. She says her father wouldn't stand for it. So she told me . . . it was all over between us . . .' He began blubbering again, aghast with horror. 'She said she'd commit a real sin . . . That she'd have the child taken from her . . . That she'd find someone to do it. She did find someone . . . She called me after. She'd just been released from . . . phony nursing home. She . . . she showed me her stomach. She was screaming. She'd waited too long. They . . . they'd had to open her up

'...and the doctor was drunk. She told me they had nearly killed her. She said they'd made a monster of her ... that they should have let her die. That all she wanted from me was an okay to the pusher. I—I fixed that, Max. I had to.'

'The doctor,' I grated, 'the doctor that aborted her. Who is he? I want his name, Phil.'

'It doesn't matter,' Phil screamed, racked between spasms of pain and fear. 'It doesn't matter. The doctor's in the penitentiary. For life. He was tried for murder, then commuted. A week after he butchered Helen ... he killed a girl.'

'Oh my God! What about the ring, then? The ring Helen stole and sold.'

In a grotesque, weaving lurch, Phil came to his feet. 'I don't know,' he moaned. 'I don't know. Please, don't hit me and keep asking. I just don't know. I don't, I don't. It must have been after we ... split up.'

'Who delivers drugs to Helen?'

'Frankie the pusher. Little Frankie. Please, Max, don't question me about drugs. Please don't make me talk about that.'

Suddenly, two and two clicked together—added up to the answer to who tailed Frankie through the storm and raided his plant. 'When did you last connect for drugs, Phil?'

Phil wiped blood off his face. His voice tilted to a high, almost comic falsetto: 'I got a lucky break. About a week ago. I got enough ... enough heroin to last me a long time. A whole month. That's why I split up with Ziggy. I was afraid he'd find out I have all that heroin ... and make me share it.'

He swayed, and I grabbed at his shoulders. Emaciated, panting, his shoulders skeletal beneath the padding of his tuxedo, blood flowing, as from a spout, from his nose, Phil seemed no longer human. A full ten minutes fled before his rubbery legs could support him. Filled with a great

149

weariness, I asked him where he was living. He groaned out an address.

I half carried him out of the alley and down the street to a cab rank. I got him into the back seat of the first cab. He collapsed there, his face buried in his hands. Tears streamed through his blood-crusted fingers.

I told the driver to take Phil home.

When I got home, I went into the bedroom to stare at myself in the mirror. Something told me my face must be changed, that on it there must be hints and shadows of violence. But the fact was another thing; my face looked the same—even though deep inside me was a hard knot of disgust.

Pouring a huge drink, I went to the window. The dark street, its pavement a mantilla of moon lace, stretched momentarily deserted except for a boy and a girl sauntering along. I stood there, forcing myself to resume thinking about my case, reminding myself that each small point now held paramount significance. If the Back Man did as I expected and, because of the arrests of Frankie and Leger, shrank deeper into his shell, if he decided to wait until Leger's case was disposed of before resuming service at the rendezvous, there could be but one result. Panic! A total drug panic—the addicts' constant nightmare; the time when addicts grow increasingly desperate and much, much easier to influence. Should that panic occur, as experience told me it must, then Frankie would again be my bird-dog. Frankie would flush out the man I wanted. The trafficker—Jack Moss.

Looked at logically, then, my course was plain. Get back on Frankie. Be ready for anything.

But the logic was all fouled up with grimly whirling disobedient thoughts; thoughts about the endless don't-dare-to-spit precautions I had to keep taking; thoughts about the dire consequences of any mistaken act; thoughts about the things I had to do that hurt so much while I was doing them. I thought that merely to lie down and breathe freely again would be a full and complete life.

I looked out the window at nothing, whistling soundlessly. Then the disobedient thoughts, that had spoken so eloquently, ceased, left my mind clear. I put my left hand forward so I could see my watch. Instead, my eye was caught by the ring gleaming on my little finger. I began wondering again where Helen Ashton had sold the ring she had stolen. Somehow, from someone, I was determined to recover that ring. To make use of the information that would come with it.

That thought sent me away from the window. I paced about the room. Memory refused to give up the name Pierre, my friend in Robbery and Bunco, had obligingly dropped into my ear. Ruby—something. Ruby . . . Macklin? No, no. Ruby Marlin!

An informer. A stool pigeon. Pierre had said plainly that Ruby was an informer. Time again to be careful. Even a doting mother wouldn't dare trust an informer.

Shrugging into a dark coat, I started towards the hall door. Half way, I stopped. The punishment Phil had absorbed was still tugging at my conscience. I swore softly and growled at myself for being a prize brand of softie. But I turned back to the telephone. I dialled the night number of a private nursing home. A nursing home operated by an old white bear of a nurse who had given me my first slapping a few seconds after I had come into the world.

The phone droned unanswered for minutes. Finally, a clipped, irritated voice answered: 'Yes.'

'Max Dent here,' I said, and added, not too brilliantly, 'That you, Miss Kelly?'

The efficient voice crackled now, like starch: 'What do you mean by calling here after midnight? Are you sick, Max Dent? Or in trouble? Yes, trouble is much more likely!'

I said quickly, 'I'm just fine. Now listen, Miss Kelly; I have a patient for you. A friend of mine. He's in pretty bad condition. From a—an accident. He badly needs a week or two of your special care.'

Miss Kelly snorted. 'Ha! never mind that blarney. If your friend is sick, there's room here for him. Providing, of course, the accident has been reported to the police.'

Miss Kelly, night-watchman of illness and pain for uncounted years! The thought of her plump, plain, pink face and short, curly white hair and fine blue eyes was warmly comforting

'God bless you, darling!' I sighed, then, with my fingers crossed, I added, 'The accident this chap had isn't the sort that needs reporting. I'd better tell you, though, that your new patient's a drug addict. He will have to be put on a reduction cure.'

Miss Kelly's answer came flat and automatic: 'No, Max Dent! No, no, no! I will not have an addict in this home. Not even for you. The better-equipped hospitals refuse them, why shouldn't I? When addicts start coming off, they're strait-jacket cases. This isn't that kind of nursing home. Besides, my nurses won't take addict duty. No—'

'Wait!' I protested. 'I said this fellow's hurt. That he's a friend of mine. What kind of nurse are you? Will you let him die?'

Miss Kelly bridled. 'Don't you dare talk to me like that, Max Dent! Addicts are worse than paranoiacs. I'm thinking of my other patients.' I heard her sigh a soft sigh of resignation. 'Oh, well—bring him up. I'll put him in the cellar and bar the door.' Her voice sharpened up a little. 'But I don't think much of the friends you keep, Max Dent. And addicts never have a penny to call their own. You'll be held responsible for the bill!'

I taxied at once to the address Phil had mumbled while I held him in my arms in the alley.

The place turned out to be a tumbledown tourist lodge a block from the mid-town bus depot.

I climbed to a room that was as bare as a monk's

152

cell. I helped Phil out of the narrow bed, bathed his face with a towel I found on the sink, and patted it dry. 'I'm sorry,' he said, no longer quite sure what it was he was sorry for, but just saying it exhaustedly. He was again half-unconscious when I carried him out in my arms. All the long climb up the mountain to Cedar Avenue, he babbled madly about Helen Ashton and the Cross.

Miss Kelly gave me a very bad five minutes. Then she tucked Phil between crisp white sheets in a private room and gave him a sedative. 'He is a danger to the other patients,' she said in an indignant voice. 'I am not equipped to handle people that are in a mess emotionally.'

'Just take care of him, please,' I said. 'I'll figure out something for him.'

Outside, my driver waited patiently beside his cab. 'Well, where now?' he demanded.

'The Chez Paree. If it's still going after hours.'

In the Chez Paree lounge, a barman poured my Scotch over an ice cube. The drink at my elbow, I took out a five-dollar bill, folded it, and placed it under my glass. The barman stared unblinkingly at me. I smiled, then said conversationally, 'Ruby Marlin. If you wanted to find Ruby, where would you look?'

The barman leaned against his hygienic sink. He stared through a glass partition at the white flashing legs of a show-girl line going through a standard routine on the club stage. To no one in particular, he said, 'This is a nice night for gambling. Swell. That's exactly what I'd do if I didn't have to work. Yep! I'd scram over to the all-night restaurant behind the Sheraton Hotel and use the free chauffeur-service out to the barbotte game. Be okay out there tonight. All kinds of interesting people around. Plenty, but I mean plenty, of action.'

'Action? City Hall has been sending out bulletins all week—'

The barman began a bored humming. 'You asked me

a question,' he reminded me, 'so I answered it. Shuttle-service leaves the Metcalfe Street restaurant every hour— on the half-hour.' He pulled the bill from beneath my glass, folded it once more. His eyes flicked again to the inner area of the club. 'That floor-show's not so hot,' he said, like a lawyer resting an unassailable case, 'and the time's only twenty after three. You want to meet people. Why not take a nice free ride out to the barbotte game?'

I pulled deeply at my drink, set it back on the gleaming bar. 'That,' I said, 'sounds like a really fine idea.'

I walked two well-lighted blocks, then up a dark one to a small restaurant. Two seven-passenger limousines were parked suggestively in front at the curb. I opened the rear door of the first limousine, and got in.

At the first throughway, we spun sharply east, con-tinued on to the outskirts of the city, then made time past the sprawling grounds of the Municipal Golf Club. The driver swung the limousine into a side road, angled it cautiously past gaping potholes, avoiding the grassy soft shoulder and the drainage ditches that ran along each side. He braked slightly, his eyes scanning a frame house set apart in a grove of trees. He pulled into the gravel driveway, parked the limousine quietly, stepped out and flung open the rear door. 'We 'ave arrive!' he announced dramatically. 'And pouff! to the reform.'

The entire lower floor of the house was converted into one huge room. Along its centre, spaced thirty feet apart, stood three baize-covered tables, each ringed now by a hundred or more players.

Under brilliant lights, the gamblers were intent, silent. Their eyes followed with quick, mechanical motion each white bounce of the dice; their hands, clamped over damp bills, were held poised to place bets.

A sudden hush seemed to circle the room, breaking from the crowded tables, as though searching for a way to escape. Then play on the no-limit table was completed

154

and a feverish, excited mass sigh ballooned into the hot air.

In one corner, the house had set up a self-service bar. I stood to one side for a moment, then moved over to the bar and poured myself a drink. In my hand I held an unlighted cigarette. A thin-faced little man with a ragged copy of the *Racing Form* protruding from his pocket snapped the lighter at me.

I nodded, said casually, 'Thanks. Seen Ruby around? Ruby Marlin?'

'Seen Ruby around? Well—I guess so!' The little man smiled expansively. 'You think I haven't? Ruby's over there, for Godsakes. At the no-limit table. Making a killing.'

I glanced to the centre table. It's always easy to spot a big winner. I found Ruby at once.

Ruby Marlin was small and thin with sleek black hair streaked grey over his narrow temples. His suit was over-tailored, pin-striped, and worn over a loud, open-throated sports-shirt. In each hand he held a huge fold of bills.

A crushed-looking player moved away from the table with short, jerky steps. He left room enough for me to squeeze in beside Ruby. When Ruby bet again, I threw three twenties on top of his money.

'A thousand on the point!' the speaker was a tall, flamboyantly beautiful woman wearing a blue mink stole slung carelessly over one shoulder.

Ruby threw the dice.

'Ah-h-h-h!' The sigh unwound like a steel coil as the dice bounced to a natural.

'Let it ride,' Ruby said coolly.

'Ride. Right again,' the woman said.

'Ride,' I said.

Ruby's dice exploded from his fist, capered across the green felt, pirouetted, and came to rest showing a pair of fives—a winning point at barbotte. A boxman raked in the stakes, deducted the house percentage in a matter of seconds, then paid off the winners. Ruby counted his winnings, peeled off a hundred and thirteen dollars, and handed it to me as my share. 'Ride with Ruby and you wind up living high,' he said stuntishly.

'Pass the dice, Ruby,' I said. 'It's time for you to open your office.'

Ruby grunted in surprise. 'What the—!'

My fist was tight over his elbow. 'Don't sell my offer short,' I smiled, still pressing his elbow. 'It's the best offer you'll get all night. Let me be your friend, Ruby. The kind of a friend that rides a bet with you, then steps out for a little talk with you because you do business with funny people. I can save you a boxcar full of headaches, Ruby. Come along, we'll have a drink together at the bar.'

The boxman's voice drawled out 'One thousand open.'

Ruby's eyes shifted. Scowling impatiently at me, he stepped beyond the ring of player. 'Forget the drink,' he snapped. 'What's the big idea of bugging me when I'm hot? Who are you?'

I steered him determinedly towards the bar. 'You can come out a winner with me by just answering a question,' I said. 'You can also save yourself a night's trouble.'

Ruby's narrow face was watchfully sullen. 'You could be muscled out,' he retorted. 'I'm big enough here to fix that. But why should I? You just might have something worth listening to.' He jabbed a freshly-manicured nail into my lapel. 'But I don't know a thing, and I don't say a thing until you prove who you are—and that's for positive!'

'This is more like it,' I said, and began lying. 'I'm an in-surance investigator,' I said. Ruby's eyes bugged. He took a fast sideways step. I went on hurriedly: 'Now, wait a minute. This isn't official. Information is all I'm looking for. Information about a ring—an expensive solitaire in an

156

old-fashioned setting. If the ring is available, a deal can be made to buy back with no questions asked. Fair enough?'

Ruby came back a step. 'Sounds like the old, sad story,' he said, making his voice gruff. 'One of those lovers-fall-out deals. Before, I've heard it. Some young dope swipes the family rocks to make big time with a high-stepping gal. When he cools out and smartens up, he learns that she's peddled the pretty baubles. Right?'

'Not quite right, Ruby. But you're within fading distance of the general idea—that so far no one has made a claim. All my company is interested in is recovering the ring before someone does.'

'What's with this ring? What's it worth?'

'Ten thousand. Maybe a little up on that.'

I felt Ruby's back muscles tighten under my restraining hand. 'Listen, amigo,' he said. 'I wouldn't touch a single stone worth that kind of money. Not on your life. To begin with, it's too easy identified. Also, it would be too hot. That's not all. It might take me two, three years to find a buyer. Longer, unless some fancy dame or showbiz character turned up looking for investment ice.' He shook his head. 'Unh-unh! If you want to find that ring, don't look in town. Stones worth that much go out of the country fast. Either that, or they get sold to some private buyer—a non-professional.' Ruby jabbed the same finger into my chest. 'I know, friend,' he said confidently. 'Believe me, I know!'

That ended it.

Giving me a curt nod, Ruby wedged back in among the no-limit players.

Dawn had just started to show in the darkness as a faint line to the east. No shuttle cars waited. I trampled through damp grass to the roadhouse to pick up a taxi. No longer was there any doubt in my mind as to who had the stolen solitaire.

Slowly, the vicious circle was closing, drawing in its own loose ends. The waiting game was over. I was ready to make my first definite step into the centre of the drug ring. I would be propelled there by the vicious force of a major drug panic.

16

'I can't do it,' Frankie kept moaning. 'Believe me, pal, I just can't. The Back Man would turn his gorillas on me. I'd end up wringing blood outa my hair.'

Easing back in my chair, I stared curiously about the rendezvous.

Panic had been on all day, mounting in intensity minute by minute as a replacement for Leger failed to appear. Addicts waited in tight clusters; some dumb with pain; some still coherent. In one corner, a savage argument raged between a pale, furtive-eyed fiftyish man and a down-at-heel woman half his age. Near the food-counter, a teenage girl sat staring wildly into nothing, her legs rigidly extended before her, her arms clasped tightly and twitched over her abdomen. I had seen that stare and twitching frequently enough now in other addicts to be able to tag it as an indication of the degree of withdrawal sickness, a kind of barometric reading of the internal storm. I flicked my eyes to the chair next to hers where an old man with dark, cracked skin leaned forward intently, his watering eyes fixed madly on the door.

It was like watching a psychodrama staged by asylum inmates acting out their own psychoses.

Beside me, Frankie sniffled, then shuddered horribly. 'No use,' he mumbled. 'No use at all. I can't take it no more. Gotta have something. A goofball, anything. Gotta go find a shot. I'm blowing my top.'

I said sarcastically, 'Stop killing yourself. We've been sitting here all day and nothing's happened. This rendezvous is a deadfall. Service is kaput until Leger gets sentenced and the pressure blows off.' I repeated, for the twentieth time since morning: 'You refuse to try connecting direct. To try contacting Moss for a fix. All right, so what do we do? We sit around here like zombies, and we watch each other die.'

Frankie pressed his lips together. Eloquently.

I kept digging at him. 'Not even a barbiturate in here now,' I said pessimistically. 'The supply's all sold, swallowed. There's only Moss. He's all that's left for us. Nothing else. Just Jack Moss.'

Frankie swore like a Spaniard. 'No, no. Don't bug me. I'm game for anything. But not that. And if you must keep talking about you know who, don't use his name. Say the Back Man.'

I needled him, kept rubbing him raw. 'Okay, you damned fool!' I retorted. 'Go on being careful. But you're so weak now you can't even go out on the prowl looking for a loose doctor's satchel. You're an inch from doing flips.'

His face was stiff with stubbornness. 'Oh, my bleeding heart!' I rasped. 'You can't see anything, Frankie. You're so blind that you can't even see that he must be expecting to hear from us.'

As though he were moving a ton weight, Frankie lifted his head. He brushed bubbles of spittle from his white lips. 'W-what's that?' he demanded stupidly. 'Expecting to hear from us? The Back Man? You crazy? How d'you figure that?'

I began marshalling arguments. 'Why not? He knows we were knocked off with Leger. That the Mounties interrogated us and then let us go. Don't you guess he's curious about that? That he wants to know what was said? His curiosity alone should be worth a fix.'

'No, no, not him. Curiosity or no curiosity, the Back Man won't spring for no fix. He plays it too cagey.'

'For God's sake, Frankie,' I said bluntly. 'When are you going to learn that the Back Man doesn't happen to be God?'

'Not God, eh?' Frankie retorted. 'Huh! Take another look around you.'

I sighed wearily. My eyes roamed, as Frankie had suggested, over the slumped addicts. It seemed incredible that a single man, Moss, could hold such power of pain over so many people; still more incredible that at this moment across the city other addicts squirmed and sweated out the agonizing hours, waiting for that same man to start the wicked machinery that would wash away their pain.

A woman, her eyelids swollen and her hair tangled about her head, started a constant giggling. Suddenly, she jerked to her feet and fell like a board to the floor. The man sitting beside her wordlessly picked up the limp body and dragged it to the washroom. In passing, one of the woman's shoes scuffed against my leg.

I leaned forward, circled Frankie's shoulders with my arm. I started my campaign all over again. 'In another hour you'll be as sick as that woman,' I told him. 'I'd be, too, if I was stupid enough to wait with you for a pusher that won't show up.' I stared into his dripping eyes. 'Make up your mind, Frankie. Now! Either bring me to the Back Man, or I leave you and find myself a doctor. I'll dig up a phoney somewhere that'll sell me heroin. In my book, that's smarter than waiting here until I start throwing up all over my shirt.'

Frankie had to swallow twice before he was able to speak, and then his voice came out brittle as glass. 'I know a doctor,' he said. 'He'll sell us both a shot—all we want. I've been to him before. So's Fay. Some of the others, too. He stings you twenty bucks for a half-grain cap.'

'Don't be a dunce,' I retorted irritably, 'I haven't got the forty bucks it would cost to get both of us fixed that way. Neither have you. If I have to, I can pay for myself, and that's what I will do. But it's a last resort. The smart thing to do now is give your boss a whirl. His curiosity, remember?'

I watched a teenage girl totter across the room. She had a pitiful double-jointed look. She was talking rapidly to herself in a raw, throat-tearing whisper. I turned away from her, looked directly into the pools of misery that were Frankie's eyes. 'See that girl!' I cried 'That's the way we're going to look. Like gibbering idiots. Listen to me; I still have my big ace in the hole. The jewellery I brought from Vancouver. Rather than get the way these others are—' I lifted a shoulder expressively, let it stretch out, made it sound as though I had said something that had a terribly important meaning. 'You claim the Back Man is a real eager beaver for diamonds. Specially hot ones. Well, let's talk to him about mine. If he wants them bad enough, who knows? Who knows, Frankie?'

A sixth sense told me Frankie was on the verge of cracking. Watching tautly from the other side of the table, I thought: He's going to break. He can't hold out much longer.

I said aloud, 'Have it your own way. Sit here with the rest of the fools and shake yourself to death. But not me! I'm leaving before this place gets so hot it explodes. There's a doctor somewhere that'll fix me. I'm going out to find that doctor. I can pay for one fix. For me!'

Frankie reeled to his feet. 'Wait!' he screamed. 'Oh my God, don't leave me here. You know that even if a pusher does show up I have no money. Wait! We'll try him. It's crazier than playing Russian roulette, but we'll try. We'll go see the Back Man.'

'Then quiet, you fool,' I hissed. 'Do you want this whole place on our tails? You're shouting loud enough for the addicts in Toronto to hear you.'

Frankie sank back. When he didn't reply, I said quickly, 'Well, now that we've made up our minds, let's get the show on the road. Exactly where does the Back Man live?'

Momentarily, Frankie did not say a world, but merely stared at me as if I had spoken in Icelandic or Cree. Then the expression of his eyes seemed to withdraw inward, leaving them veiled. He said as if chanting a sick refrain: 'You don't understand. We don't go to his house. We never go to his house. We don't even think of going to his house unless he okays it in advance.'

'Then where *do* we see him?'

Frankie sniffled, nervously. 'Well, it's this way,' he explained. 'This is Friday. On Friday nights he always takes in the floor-show at the upstairs club across the street. You know the place—the Pink Cloud. It's an awful fleabag—a goon's hangout. But to the Back Man it's strictly the Normandie Room at the Sheraton.'

Now that it actually had happened, the relief I had anticipated didn't come. Instead, a voice called out in warning and I felt doubt, doubt and dark uncertainty. 'I don't know about this,' I said. 'It sounds like a real long shot to me. What guarantee have we he'll be at the Pink Cloud on this particular night?'

'Floor-show change,' Frankie said, trying to focus his brimming eyes on mine. 'Every time the show changes, him and his foundling kid turn up over there to take in the new acts. That's once a week. Fridays. I think he's part owner of the place. It could be one of his fronts,' Frankie gagged, then he plucked a cigarette from my pack, dropped it, bent, dropped it again, bent, then tore the wrapper off with shaking fingers and stuffed the tobacco under his lower lips like snuff. 'The best time to catch him over there is at nine,' he gasped. 'In about an hour. But remember one thing; this was your idea.'

Each one of the next sixty minutes drew itself out and magnified itself and filled itself with tension. Crazy or not, now came my crucial test. If Moss himself accepted me as a narcotic addict on the strength of yesterday's Drug Squad pick-up, I could start concentrating on the final action. It all seemed logical, to add up to a workable situation: the Back Man's informers *must* by now have carried to him every detail of the R.C.M.P. street arrest; Moss *must* believe me to be an addict; Frankie *must* have reported to Moss that I had in my possession stolen jewellery worth a huge sum. Those *musts* would be underlined items in the Back Man's book.

The mere thought of Moss turning up casually for a night's entertainment at a club like the Pink Cloud was staggering, part owner or not. I stared at Frankie. I said, 'So help me, Frankie, I still can't see him going to the Pink Cloud. It doesn't make sense. Not for a big operator like him. Showing himself at a cheap hangout less than a block from this rendezvous.'

'So who knows him? Me—Dream Street Fay—Leger— the connections he has out in other districts. So what? He goes to a club like anyone else does. Mi Gawd! let's not talk any more about it. We're going up there, that's bad enough. Already, I can smell the embalming fluid. Target for tonight, that's me—Frankie. Born for bruises.'

I glanced at the clock.

'Frankie,' I said sharply. 'Nine. It's now or never. The Back Man must be at the club by now. Let's go.'

We crossed Clarke Street and began along the next block, passed a dollar-a-night hotel and came under a neon sign that simulated a pink cloud.

Paint long ago had worn from the surface of the stairs leading from the street up to the Pink Cloud. The steps were splintered and cracked and creaked under our feet. As we neared the top, with Frankie pulling himself upward as though he were breasting a gale, I could hear the noise of a small jazz band playing with plenty of volume and using a great deal of brass. At the rear of the second-floor landing, a bouncer leaned against the wall and talked to an unshaven man with his arm in a cast.

Small eyes gelid, the bouncer examined us. I shrugged my shoulders and waited for him to finish his thinking. Finally, he nodded silently, first at me, then at Frankie.

With me hugging his elbow, Frankie staggered inside the club to its bar, stood there gasping for breath.

'God-Jesus!' he gasped. 'I didn't think we'd make it!'

He clutched my arm and pointed to a corner table. His hand was trembling like a leaf.

I looked closely at the table which had been placed just outside a circle of light which fell on a tiny dance floor. It was impossible not to recognize the Back Man.

Moss was obese, massive. His soft, flaccid features melted into a profileless blob of a face. Some time during the evening, he had thrown off his coat. His shirt, yellow and tent-like in proportion, was plastered wetly by body humidity to his huge, shapeless torso, bulging now over the rim of a table it reduced to toy size. His shoulders were heavy and rounded and sloped in the peculiar manner that is distinctly simian. Over and about him hung an atmosphere of unhealthy dirtiness. His pale eyes were restlessly active.

I forced my gaze from Moss. I checked the features of the little street waif sitting beside him, memorized them.

Frankie's elbow dug into me. 'The Back Man—he's seen us. My God, pal, he don't look too happy. Neither do his two musclemen. They're back of him and the kid.'

'Let's go,' I said tersely. 'Remember, we cool Moss out right off—fast. Get him thinking. That way we have a chance to angle for drugs. You better tell him I'm ready to deal for the hot jewellery.'

I moved away from the bar, and with Frankie at my side, approached the circle of light, Moss's table. I was prepared to make rash promises about the mythical jewellery. The floor-show was starting, featuring strippers. The blare from the orchestra and the enthusiasm of the audience made talking safe. Frankie hunkered down to talk. I hunkered with him.

I caught a whiff of Moss. It staggered me.

He stank. He smelled sick; sick with the evil within himself. On a hot night you could probably smell that evil sickness half a mile downwind. It made my stomach feel queasy. It brought a foul taste rushing to my mouth, tightened my fists into knots.

Moss straightened his back. His shoulders hunched up and he inclined his big head forward in a way that gave him a bull-like appearance. He was furious, but with an ominous, restrained force and his eyes remained cold and active and intelligent.

'So, once again, it's little Frankie Seven,' he said, and for some reason he laughed. His laughter was brittle, like the sound made by two pieces of broken glass being rubbed together. 'Well—did somebody by God send for you? Not that I know! And you don't even come alone. No, you bring another addict—a total stranger to me. Have I succeeded in teaching you exactly nothing? By God, Seven. Another cursed mistake.'

Frankie's cheeks were quivering. '—not a mistake— not this time, boss, just wait while I—' his lips shook out frantic words, but they had no meaning.

Behind fat slits, Moss's eyes were as bleak as grimy sleet. 'Sit down!' he said, with an awful, soft emphasis. 'Both of you, sit down! You're here and you're not wanted, but I'll listen while you tell me about Leger. Another blunder.'

Sweat was beginning to slide uncomfortably down my spine. I couldn't take much more. Not of this. Bending forward, I brought my lips to within an inch of Moss's ear. 'Leger didn't take that R.C.M.P. fall alone,' I hissed. 'There were three of us. All with heroin habits, remember? Leger's not the only one that's sick. Look at Frankie and me. We're half dead.'

Moss smiled. An almost triumphant smile. 'But of course you are sick,' he granted coolly. 'You poor addicts suffer so when you are deprived of drugs. But I have no

165

intention at all of doing anything about that!' He grunted noisily, working his chair closer to the table. 'Now, tell me about the arrest,' he commanded, his eyes taking on a curious and hateful glint of anticipation. 'I understand the Horsemen beat you. Was it painful? A bad beating?'

I described the street grab and roughing to the ultimate detail, elaborated. Moss's eyes gleamed sadistically. He said, tart and vehement, 'Ha, police are all brutes. You two were innocent—you carried no drugs. Yet those Mounties deliberately abused you. Came at you like hussars. Now, I want the rest of it—every detail.'

I said, with a stuntish shrug, 'Same old story! Naturally, I was steered inside. To an inspector's office. A hard-rock by the name of Welch.'

Angrily, Moss snarled: 'Yes, Welch. I by God know him! Clever policeman—very clever. Welch used to be head of the Counterfeit Currency Squad. He's new on Narcotics. He must have been furious. Ha! Well—they brought you to Welch, did they? And what did you tell Welch?'

Frankie blurted out in a voice shaken with fear, 'Nothing! Me, I warned him, boss. This guy didn't talk. Honest, boss, he didn't say—'

Moss silenced Frankie with a glare. 'Some day you'll get shot, Seven,' he said cuttingly. 'Shut up!'

'What do you suppose I told Welch?' I retorted, in answer to Moss's question. 'I gave him the same goofy story I always hand prying cops. I said I was just passing by the restaurant and happened to drop in for a cup of coffee. That I didn't know Seven, Leger, or anyone else in the dump. I said I was amazed by such high-handed police treatment. I made a big noise about contacting my alderman to complain about it.'

Moss studied me suspiciously for a moment, then said grudgingly, 'Umm, good—if true. In fact, excellent. The police hate indignant attitudes. That's the sort of thing that shows them up as fools. Which they are.'

I stared at him deliberately. Never before had I seen a face look so unpleasant or so dangerous. 'Maybe so,' I granted him. 'The police may be fools. But right now that doesn't help me. I'm sick of pussy-footing around that bloody hashhouse waiting for a little fix-man that's not going to turn up. Do you intend us all to go nuts stalling out this panic? Waiting for action?'

Moss slumped in a huge, brooding silence. His breathing made wet, bubbling sounds. His eyes flicked from side-to-side like a snake's seeing everything while they actually appeared to see nothing at all. Meanwhile, the boy beside him sat staring numbly at his dirty hands. The two thugs kept cold eyes riveted on Frankie, on me.

A few seconds ticked by. No one spoke. The noise about us seemed to increase. We stared at each other with mute, fixed expressions. 'I'm not getting any better,' I said in a harsh voice that brought Frankie up rigidly. 'In fact, I'm getting even sicker. How about it, Moss?'

Moss laughed. He looked from one to the other of us, his huge head rolling back and forth, laughing, spilling laughter from his thick lips in a violently fluttering streamer of derision. Picking up a paper napkin, he pressed it against his bubbling mouth and coughed, then put down the damp napkin and, still laughing, said, 'I—I don't know. By God, I really don't know. It all strikes me as being so damned funny!'

My temper leaped. Reaching out, I banged a glass hard on the table. 'Maybe I belong back in Vancouver,' I cried. 'I can understand the humour there. This goes over my head.'

Moss ignored me. He turned the other way. Leaning over, he draped a massive paw over the boy's thin shoulder. 'They look funny, eh, Shadow?' he roared. 'Don't they look ridiculous? Standing there, both of them, wanting something they can't get. Whining to me. Telling me all their piddling troubles.'

The floor-show was concluding. Soon the protective

167

conversational cover of its noise would end. Moss thrust forward so suddenly his belly hit the table, sent it rocking. Wetting his lips, he said in a low, furious voice, 'Careless! Great God, but you've both been fantastically careless. I don't stand for that. You shouldn't even have thought of coming here. Never dare to contact me in a public place!' He heaved awkwardly to his feet, glared balefully at Frankie. 'You are an idiot, Seven—a double idiot. It doesn't surprise me you couldn't attend properly to business. But you'll get a chance to make up for the trouble you've caused.' Moss's face grew pale with contained fury. He said in a way that was a threat and a promise and a simple declaration, all at the same time, 'Yes. You will get your chance. Come to me in the morning. With your reckless chum. We'll talk more about this pinch. And maybe about the jewels your friend claims to have. But remember! It will go very bad for you if you've lied about your session with the Mounties.'

With that, Moss turned about. After a single venomous, backward glance, he lumbered towards some anonymous rear exit of the café, the boy following him like an obedient puppy, the two goons hulking behind the boy.

Frankie's voice was all pain now. It sounded like an untuned violin.

'See,' he whined, 'Moss is gone. We took a screwball risk like this without even coming close to scoring a fix. We don't even get close to talking a deal on your hot jewellery until tomorrow.' He used the table to help himself to his feet. 'Gotta go dip up Fay,' he moaned, in a surrendering way. 'Fay's my last chance.'

Frankie shuffled off through his grey tunnel of pain. I let him go, knowing that if he were alive in the morning he would be back waiting at the tavern or the rendezvous. The floor-show ended, I walked hurriedly uptown to where it would be safe to call down a cab.

Later, warm in bed, the days tension slowly unwinding,

I listened to a cold rain drum against my window, thinking with utter sobriety about Jack Moss. Three separate problems now stood up like pins at the distant end of a dark alley, waiting to be bowled over. First, when would Moss need to replenish his own ever-diminishing supply of drugs? Next, when would that all-important meeting of supplier and trafficker take place? And, finally, would Moss transact himself? Or, would he chain-connect? perhaps trusting the boy, Shadow, to collect the priceless parcel at the end of the chain. That last alternative seemed highly improbable. The drugs involved in that transaction would be worth a black-market fortune. Yet, was it reasonable to assume that a man of Moss's ingrained caution would take such a fantastic risk himself? Or would he trust a boy? Just wait and hope that you can make Moss walk into the net somewhere, I told myself.

I fell asleep with dawn, murky and cold, prodding grey fingers over my bed. But, in the jumble and confusion that comes on the verge of sleep, there was a warm, bright light shining through the haziness of my confused thoughts and plans. Thorn—lovely Thorn. She came towards me through that haziness—a flash of long, slender legs, hips moving ever so slightly, a smile touching the corners of her lips. Then sleep pressed down on me like an avalanche, and Thorn disappeared like a sun-touched shadow.

Less than three hours later I got up and set on coffee, showered and shook into a robe. I walked about in the dimness of the kitchen, picking things up, putting them down again until I felt I could reasonably call Welch at his office.

I reached the inspector at a few minutes past eight.

'I've made personal contact with Moss,' I told him, in a carefully contained voice. 'I talked with him last night in a St. Catherine Street club called the Pink Cloud. The conversation lasted for about ten minutes—was mostly about Leger. Frankie Seven beamed me in. I bluffed Seven

169

completely, but Moss wasn't at all happy to see us. Just the same, I made plenty of time. Seven and I will see Moss again. This morning. It might be bad for Seven, but I've got Moss nibbling on a line. I've made it, Inspector,' I said, almost in surprise. 'Now I'm *completely* inside!'

Welch said quickly, his voice a shade too high to hide his excitement, 'Remarkable, Dent! An excellent piece of work. But the situation will get very tricky now. Now you will need help. Exactly what do you want?'

'Background, Inspector. Seven has told Moss I drifted in from the West Coast—Vancouver. I expect Moss to make an issue of that. I'll need an addict's knowledge of the illegal drug set-up out there. I want names, places, right off the hot list. That's what I need. Give me pushers' names, addicts' names, the name of a connection, if you have one, a couple of hangouts. Enough for me to be able to bluff out a tough questioning.'

Welch barked a short laugh into the phone. 'Great Scott, Dent! Vancouver has over two thousand addicts. However, as you realize, our file offices exchange information. We have a complete reference here on West Coast drug activities.'

Snatching up a pencil and paper, I copied names, descriptions, and addresses furiously while the inspector dictated crisply from secret police records. When he was done, Welch insisted I read the compilation back to him. Then he wished me luck, cautioned me over and over, and let me hang up to get to work committing the data to memory.

An hour later, I taxied downtown to make a hurried call on my doctor friend. When I left his office, an envelope containing two harmless capsules that resembled heroin caps but held only sugar milk waited ready in my pocket.

I was expecting the final test; I intended to be fully prepared for it.

I headed at once for the addicts' rendezvous.

'Well, did you make out with Fay?' I demanded bluntly of Frankie, as soon as I reached the table where he was sitting.

He stood up, rubber-legged at my side. 'Help me to a cab,' he said thickly, then added, 'Fay's sicker than me. She—all she had was some hemorrhoid ointment. That stuff that's made up of gall and opium. She tear-jerked it from a drugstore without a prescription. We wrapped the ointment in tissue paper and swallowed it. It lifts you back for a while. It don't last, though, pal. It don't last.'

I got him out to the street, and into a taxi. 'Better not be broke,' he warned. 'It's gonna be a rough morning. Before we get to the street where Moss lives, we'll burn up plenty of cab fare.'

From that point, Frankie took over. Drug-sick as he was, the little addict put on a display of zealous, disciplined caution that flabbergasted me. For two hours, obviously following a preconceived and well-tested pattern, we dodged about the city in a series of stops, starts, and switches master-designed to throw off the most alert of R.C.M.P. tails.

Starting from near the rendezvous, we taxied straight east across town to the wide-open area of the city's public Botanical Gardens, then, after a stop while Frankie pretended to study dying flowers, straight south to the traffic-jammed waterfront—seven miles.

Frankie instructed this first driver to pull up.

Together, Frankie and I hurried across the street and back a block to another cab rank. This time, after mumbled instructions to a new driver from Frankie, we taxied west through a small, dirty industrial district and then north past lines of bright storefronts to the rutted streets of an incompleted housing project, then back west.

'Turn!' Frankie grated out the order at the mouth of a busy intersection.

Cursing, our driver swung south. He picked a wide boulevard and stayed on it until abruptly instructed to head down into the centre of the mid-town shopping district.

Frankie waited until we were in a snarl of cars. 'Stop!' he shouted. The driver ducked into the curb. We got out.

'Jesus!' the driver howled.

'Jesus!' I echoed.

Gritting my teeth, I paid the fare. With me dogging his heels, Frankie swayed drunkenly through the crowded lobby of a hotel to its side entrance. We stood in a booming wind until an empty cab drew up. Frankie ordered the driver to circle the block then, at the completion of the circle, re-routed him, telling him to carry on past Windsor Station, then cut down through the lower-town section.

Finally, two blocks beyond a bare, open area of sprawling railway yards, Frankie mumbled a final command to our current driver. 'Pull up, pal.'

We stood on a lonely sidewalk. Frankie grinned weakly at me. I stared at him, standing there, sick and disreputable, and much, much tougher than ever I would have believed. In spite of myself, I grinned back. 'What now? Helicopter?' I demanded.

Frankie dug cigarettes from his pocket. 'We smoke,' he replied, with an involuntary shudder. 'We smoke and we look around once more for a Horseman tail.'

We smoked a complete cigarette. Frankie threw his butt in the gutter, and shivered out an extra minute. He swung his head from side-to-side and, appearing at last fully satisfied, croaked out: 'Help me, pal. Let me lean on you. We start walking now!'

With Frankie leaning heavily on me, we circled the block and came back somewhat foolishly to our starting point. Frankie grinned grotesquely and jerked his head towards a narrow side street connecting two east-west throughways. 'Down here,' he grunted. 'We can do the rest in a soft-shoe-shuffle. We're safe now.'

I supported him, as a man supports a drunken friend,

'So,' Moss growled. 'So! You must have a reputation [h]ouse-prowling, eh? Or a police record. Exactly what [is] taken from this room?'

'Diamonds,' I said, very, very softly. 'Diamonds. Ice. [J]ellery valued at more than thirty grand.'

Moss's eyes blazed with greed. 'The gems,' he de[ma]nded. 'Where are they now?'

'There's a silly question,' I retorted. 'Real corny. If [yo]u really expect me to answer it, that is. How could you [da]re me to tell *you* where the diamonds are?'

Moss flung himself angrily against the back of the [so]fa. A trickle of sweat ran down his huge cheek. His eyes [me]t mine with the force of a blow. 'Here, now, be sensible,' [he] said in a thick, soupy voice. 'You will need to sell those [je]wels. You know it. You can't buy heroin without money, [e]y? Well, I'll deal right for your diamonds—right! Open [an]d above board. Money is only a means to an end to an [a]ddict. No one knows that better than Jack Moss.'

'So?'

'So I'll make part payment for the stones in drugs—[u]ncut heroin. Fair enough? Think of it. Your troubles [w]ill be ended. You'll have enough heroin to keep you in [e]cstasy for a long time. You'll be God on top of the world [f]or months.' His eyes wavered a little, shifted, wavered again. 'I'd not handle the drugs myself, of course,' he said clearly. 'I never do that. But I might arrange a meeting between you and someone that does.'

My collar was tightening. I undid the button, put contempt in my voice. 'What do I care about deals with other addicts?' I retorted. 'You'd pay peanuts to start with, then you'd shuffle me through middle-men that would sluff off half the heroin by chopping it three or four times before it got to me.' Edging closer to him, I added forcibly, hoping that I would sound convincing. 'Ah-no, Moss! No rush tactics and no third or fourth-hand payoffs for me. I don't do business so. When I deal, I deal direct and save the sam-

half-way down the block to a spic-and-span two-storey house. We climbed short steps to a low, wooden porch. Frankie swabbed at the glisten of sweat shining on his face.

He jabbed a trembling finger at a brass bell.

Waiting, I conceded one unshakeable fact. The Back Man's pushers were indeed scrupulously trained—well conditioned to every precaution and every trick of evasion!

Pulling out a handkerchief, I wiped off my own dripping forehead.

17

We waited at Moss's door for an agonizing ten minutes.

Suddenly, from the sidewalk behind us, came a quick, deliberate shuffling of feet and a bright ripple of laughter.

Shadow stood there, dangling a key, looking up at us irritatingly.

Moss's waif-boy either had picked up our trail at some distant point or, at the sound of the doorbell, had simply circled around from the rear of the house. Gamin-faced, he grinned at us. When he was ready, he skipped wordlessly up to the porch, inserted the key, and pushed open the door. Still without a word, he slid quickly inside, twitching his bottom as he passed by me, as though he expected it to be kicked.

I left Frankie to stumble along by himself.

Shadow led me swiftly down a narrow, brilliantly lighted hallway. We came into a room obviously intended as a kitchen. Its furnishings consisted of two straight-backed chairs, a surgically clean sink, and an old leather sofa. In one corner lay an expensive equipment case on which a tripod was strapped; on the closed roof of the case was a Rolleiflex camera, the electronic flash unit, the auxiliary lights and reflectors. Addicts' loot that had reached Moss in a roundabout way? Or, I wondered fleetingly, did Moss take photographs of his heroin drops before meeting there with his suppliers? And was this the elaborate equipment he used?

Nodding to me, Shadow disappeared like a puff of smoke.

I was not alone. Stretched across the leather sofa, his bloated body almost obscuring it, lay the glowering Back Man.

Moss pointed impatiently to a chair. As he did, my eyes were drawn to his little finger. A large, very dirty diamond glittered there.

'Sit down!' he growled.

Frankie came stumbling wild-eyed through the doorway.

Moss grunted himself erect in a series of short, awkward heaves. When he had recovered his breath, he swung his trunk-like legs almost daintily to the floor. Then, he folded his arms slowly, almost dramatically, across his belly.

He sat there like a gross symbol of evil. His small eyes flicked palely and restlessly from me to Frankie, from Frankie to me. While he studied us so, he kept rubbing his sweaty-wet hand across his thigh, agitating the grimy jewel on his finger to a dull, uneasy winking. His eyes finally held, resting on me. His voice came as a venom-filled whisper— 'You both must be desperately ill. Damned sick. That doesn't concern me. You two choose to be addicts. Your suffering and your ecstasy is of your own making.' He slid his eyes away from me, to Frankie, back to me. 'I want to know how you managed to meet this shaking fool, Seven,' he said to me, coldly. 'Also, I want to know why you came here, to Montreal.'

'The coast set-up was smouldering—getting much too hot for me,' I said, equally coldly. 'I left while the going was

good. Naturally, I asked around to find a drug meet here. A user pal tipped me o on Clarke—told me it was a big Montrea there, I met Frankie. I was trying to cont

'Whom do you know in the drug bu ver,' he growled.

Words poured out. I spoke calmly, too glib, parrot-like. I mentioned name an addict-pusher; Archie Walton, an add Govini, a lesser connection; Gizmo Lee, a pushed to the street-girls; Leo Tessier, a one dealing only with touring show-people; J user with trafficking ambitions who pushed trade. I gave a brief, completely factual recita the data made available to me from Welch's e

Moss pursed his lips. His expression re while he nodded recognition of names, places. with a stream of coarse, bitter complaints rocketing heroin prices in Vancouver.

Moss's next question came like a bullet you wanted by the Vancouver police?'

I smiled, thinking that Frankie had embro jewel-story a little. 'Theft,' I answered. 'Suspici heat, but no real evidence. I didn't stick arou picked up and held while the cops made sure.'

'Surely you were intelligent enough not evidence—Only idiots and amateurs do that.'

'Well, figure it out; all I said is that the po suspicious.'

'How did this remarkable theft occur?'

'An American big shot's wife stayed a few d Vancouver after holidaying in the Rockies. She was w for heavy fog to lift so she could fly back to Californ the papers said. Anyway, she took a suite in the Ge Hotel.' I paused, smiled. 'Someone hot-prowled that r The police out there figure it was me.'

pling. Or I don't deal at all.'

Moss laughed, abruptly, almost explosively. 'By God, you are a wise one,' he said. 'Not only that, you're not nearly so sick as you pretend. Don't think I haven't heard about the Mexican heroin you carried with you from Vancouver. My guess is, in spite of what you've told Seven here, you still have some of that heroin cached. All right. Be independent while you can. But be independent long enough and you might regret it.'

'Not independent,' I retorted. 'I'll deal when—'

Frankie sprang suddenly out of his chair, head flung high. In a wild, wobbling rush, he made it across the room. Jack-knifed over Moss's shining sink, he began to retch violently. He was ill again and again, vomiting in hard spasms until his stomach was wrung dry. Slowly, he turned to face Moss. A shivering mouse facing a steam-roller. His teared eyes pleaded for a saving shot of heroin.

'Whew!' Moss said. 'Whew!' He filled his lungs and blew out his huge cheeks. Sitting back, and looking more than ever like the epitome of evil, he said, grinning, 'Well, now, Seven, you are one sick addict. You're sick as a pig, and poor foolish Leger's locked-up in jail. What are things coming to? So much trouble and suffering. And service temporarily off, too. Why? All because you made one stupid mistake.' Moss chucked nastily. 'Ah-well, Seven,' he said, 'in time you might feel happier. Leger might even live to serve out his sentence and get busy pushing heroin again. Shall we write Leger a little letter and tell him what the poet says, Seven? Shall we? You know the line I'm thinking of. The one that says, Stone walls do not a prison make!'

'The bloody hell they don't!' Frankie screamed, and his rubbery legs buckled to topple him in an untidy heap at Moss's feet. He fell and lay there on an elbow and a thigh, staring insanely up at Moss.

'Damn you, Moss, give him a cap!' I shouted furiously. 'Do you want him to die here? Do you want to have to explain a corpse? Don't you see he's on the verge of spasms? Do something for him!'

'Do something?' Moss said. His voice was rancorous and frigid. 'Ah-yes! perhaps I should do something. I believe the loss of a finger-nail is quite painful. Which nail should I start on? I can give him a manicure he'll never forget. That's what I should do for Seven. *What he deserves.*'

'Add that kind of agony to his withdrawal pains, and you'll kill him,' I said evenly.

Moss studied Frankie critically, smiled calmly. 'Seven and the other addicts will be able to buy drugs again in one hour—at the usual place,' he said cuttingly. 'Service will start then. But not one minute before. No narcotics are kept in this house. Not now. Not ever!' His smile suddenly grew sour, curdled on his face. 'Don't expect me to feel sympathy for Seven,' he hissed. 'Or for you, if you ever manage to get that sick. I'm a business man. Not a psalm-singing humanitarian.' Thrusting out a tremendous foot, he booted Frankie into a corner. 'Now get this ridiculous weasel-hearted fool off my floor!' he roared.

Frankie struggled to his hands and knees. I lifted him to his feet and sat him in a chair.

Two drops of sweat moved with the tantalizing slow-ness of bugs down Moss's face, then fell to his shirt and left two widening spots.

'Nobody!' he shouted in a sudden, grinding voice. His mouth twisted. 'Nobody!' he shouted again. 'By God! I have nobody I can trust. Not one human soul. Skill and intelligence and bull-strength are needed for this business. Can you have skill or intelligence when you are forced to depend on idiots like this puking wretch? And muscles—' he looked venomously at me 'muscles are easy to outsmart, eh?'

'Some muscles,' I agreed, meeting his gaze.

He banged the arm of the sofa, repeatedly, until the dust rose in clouds. He ground his buttocks into the leather in anguish, and in another of his lightning rages, he barked out: 'You out-smarted my bodyguards. Don't for a minute think you'll hoodwink me. Remember that I know addicts. Remember also that I despise stool pigeons. I hate double-crossers. I spit on them. I blow snot on them. Be a thief, or be police. But don't be a rotten Judas!'

Shock ran through me. No certain meaning could be made from his rushing words. Was he up to another of his endless tests? If so, I had to react as the person he thought me to be would react. 'Just who the hell do you figure you're needling?' I yelled, stepping in on him fast. 'What do you think I am? Some two-bit purse-snatcher? You don't need to lecture me on that thieves honour bit!'

For a moment then Moss and I eyed each other, neither moving.

'How, now, let's not get excited,' he said, grinning and waving a placating paw. 'No need at all to get excited.'

'Excited! Damned right I'm excited. I have a right to be—'

Moss stepped back. For a moment, he stamped about the small kitchen, looking strangely like a great bear doing its clumsy best to walk on two legs. 'Now, this is all very good!' he said with satisfaction.

'What?' I shouted.

'Very good!' he repeated roundly. 'Yes, your reaction pleases me. You resent being called stool pigeon. That's exactly the way every good thief should feel. All right, then. You can come back here tonight—*alone*. I'll be pleased to talk further about your hot jewels with you.' He rubbed his hands over his mountainous hips, sent them down his thighs, leaving wet stains on his trouser legs. 'Yes, yes, come back. I'll expect you promptly at eight. In the meantime, ah, Seven will stay. I'm not quite through with him. You—you leave now!'

He clapped his beefy hands, making a sound like a rubber tyre exploding.

As if by magic, Shadow appeared. His fingers touched my shoulder almost before Moss stopped speaking.

'Check the street up and down before he goes,' Moss roared at the boy. 'Now move. Get him out of here. I've a few things to say to his snivelling friend!'

Sobbing and moaning again, Frankie asked to be forgiven.

'This way, monsieur,' Shadow said abruptly.

I followed the boy down the hall. At the door he turned, made a small, impudent smile. 'Monsieur must remember—eight on the clock. Monsieur Moss, he get mad like the bull if he have to wait. Now me, Shadow, I tell you. You check the damn street yourself!'

I had to grin. 'Eight o'clock, little man,' I agreed. 'And I'll remember to check the street, too.'

A taxi took me back to Clarke and St. Catherine. I went into the rendezvous, bought coffee, settled down patiently to wait.

18 Frankie came dancing through the rendezvous door. Seeing me, his face broke into a huge grin. He did a fast, heel-and-toe dance between tables.

'What's going on?' I demanded.

Frankie's thumb and index finger struck a confident circle. 'What do you know, pal?' he cried, his voice again a living thing. 'I'm way up there. I'm fixed—and I'm operating again. Frankie's back in town!'

'What?'

'Sure as red poppies grow thick in Paradise! Pal, I just blasted two caps. Cooked them up in one of those public johns the city kindly built.'

'Well, hello, hello, hello!' I said, feigning surprised delight. 'But what's all this about operating again? Don't shock me by saying that Uncle Bulgy decided to forgive and forget.'

'He put me on trial,' Frankie admitted. 'None of the other pushers know the West-End route like me. But I'm gonna have to be one careful little Frankie. No more goofs. Anyway, I'm pushing again. This's the life for me.'

'You can have it,' I said, and waited. Obviously, Frankie had something on his mind.

He grinned all over. 'You beat it across the street to the tavern,' he said with a sly wink. 'I will be right behind with a fix for you. *I'm going to cook up for you.* In fact, I'll even tie your arm for you so that the vein sticks out and says, Hello.' He glanced quickly around the restaurant, barked out a short laugh. 'Well, how about it? I gotta come back here and start fixing up this bunch. Betcha there's not a dry stomach among them. But you're first, pal. Like I said, I'm holding your arm while you stick in the spike.'

I stood beside my table-chair. Willed myself to relax; deliberately killed the anxiety and revulsion welling inside me. Now came the final test, the ultimate test. I thanked God I had prepared for it; prayed that I would be adroit and alert enough to fool even vigilant Frankie Seven. 'Come on, then, Witch Doctor,' I said. 'You know your way across the street, don't you? But watch the buses crossing, I don't want anything to happen to you before I get that free cap.'

I had Frankie on my heels until we were inside the tavern. Side-by-side we went into a washroom that was ice cold and seemed to be more dismal and deserted than any place I had ever been. A dim glow seeped in through a wide open window and sent grey unfriendly shadows moving across the broken tile floor. The drip, drip, drip of water in a yellowed urinal was alarmingly loud in the dead silence.

Flicking the door catch with furtive swiftness, Frankie bobbed his head to the single booth. 'We cook up there,' he said abruptly. 'Come on, we can both push in.'

I slid my hand into my pocket. Closed my fingers over

181

the harmless sugar-milk capsule I had wheedled from my doctor friend. 'Get inside, then,' I ordered. 'I took a spoon from the restaurant. Here it is. Let's have that heroin.'

Frankie tongued a finger-stall from inside his cheek, spit it into his hand, rolled off the elastic that sealed it, then shook out a single heroin capsule. 'For you! Compliments of the House of Moss,' he said in a dramatic whisper.

First, I palmed Moss's heroin in my left hand. Then I bent low over the toilet bowl to scoop a few drops of water into my spoon. Frankie pushed in until I could feel his bony knees against my rump, but when I straightened up, the heroin cap had been switched with the harmless sugar-milk cap I had been holding ready in my other hand.

Frankie struck a match and I watched it burn, the charred wood curling slowly like a dying thing. The spooned water began heating. When it bubbled, I dropped in the drugless sugar-milk cap, which dissolved completely in less than twenty seconds. I held the spoon while, with the concentration of a high priest performing a ritual of tremendous significance, Frankie fitted and attached an eye-dropper to an insulin needle.

'I'm your doctor,' he said, grinning across the bowl. 'Your get-well man.'

The handkerchief bit into my arm until veins slowly began swelling. I took the hypo from Frankie's cold fingers, squeezed it, sucked up the milky fluid from the blackened spoon.

Then I pressed the needle determinedly into a bulging vein.

I squeezed the rubber bulb on the dropper until it flattened emptily between my thumb and finger. At last, I withdrew the needle from my arm and swabbed away a bright, glistening balloon of blood.

I rolled down my sleeve.

Frankie's narrowed eyes had followed each move with cold, unblinking suspicion. He stared at me steadily for what seemed to be a minute. I could see the doubt jell in his eyes, the lines of his mouth tighten.'

'Man!' I said, loudly. 'That stuff's manna. Milk and honey. I'm high, high as a kite. I mean it. That one cap shot me right back to cloud nine.'

'What's the gimmick, wise guy? You got clean wings—not a single needle mark!'

'Not on your life,' I agreed easily, trying to be as patronizing as possible. 'No arm shots for me. Usually, I shoot in the cheek, the fanny. Your way, you get so many puncture holes your arms look like embroidery. No thanks! scarred veins are for meatballs—they're quick-frisk evidence for the Horsemen. The first thing they look for when they make a grab. This time, it was different, though—emergency. I needed this bang too bad to wait for a skin shot to take effect.'

Frankie's eyes and mouth made little round circles of surprise.

'How about that!' he howled, doubt vanishing. 'In the cheek. Joy-pops! I made you all along for not having much of a habit. Know why? You hardly get sick. You don't hunger enough. Not nearly enough.' Shaking his head, he added emphatically: 'But you will, pal, you will! You'll hunger and you'll get sick, and you'll start hitting the veins. Your habit'll get so big, you'll wish you could punch needles into your brain.'

'Well, I'm trying to control it. That's another reason for the skin shots. I'm trying to keep where I can afford it.'

Frankie smiled. 'Let me be the first to wish you luck, pal,' he said dryly. 'Now I really gotta skiddoo. Customers waiting.'

When I got home, I switched on the Bogan, listened to records until I discovered I was hungry.

Lunch and a change of clothes used up an hour. Afterwards, I taxied downtown to my office for mail.

183

There was a cheque and hand-written note from Huntley Ashton. The cheque, a surprisingly large one, went into my wallet; the note required more thoughtful and immediate attention.

I spoke carefully and non-commitally over the phone with Ashton for several minutes. I made no promises, gave no information a frantic father could hang too much hope on. That uncomfortable duty accomplished, I walked to the bank, then came slowly back through the crowds on Notre Dame Street as far as Louis's.

That Frenchman showed his surprise at seeing me in the jerk his shoulders gave as he turned towards his opening door. 'My friend the big detective!' he cried. 'Well, how nice. I think for a while you have forget old Louis. I am desolate,' he waved me grandly past a cluster of arguing customers. '*Voila!*' he said importantly, when I had joined him at the rear elbow of the bar. 'Today I have the veree nice inquiry for you. Where is the eye-private, Monsieur Dent? I am asked. Alas, it is not Louis that can tell the answer. Non! I must tell the so chic ma'amselle I do not know!'

Louis winked broadly. He pressed his round belly tight against the bar, leaned closer. 'But *la petite ma'amselle* she waits,' he confided. 'She sits alone in the corner there. Sometime she make the smile at me. Me, I make the smile back,' Louis made a theatrically ferocious scowl. '*Oui*—but it is not the old Louis she desire. Pah, *non!* Eet is the eye-private who can nevair be found—Monsieur Max Dent!'

'Tell me, when was Miss Ashton here?'

'She depart one hour past.' Louis dug with great solemnity into a pocket in his bar apron. '*Oui,* one hour past. But before she go, she leave in my private safekeeping one small message. On one leetle paper, she mark her telephone.'

I thrust unchecked into my pocket the slip of paper he handed me.

'Thank you, Louis,' I said, and shrugged with elaborate unconcern.'

I took out two five-dollar bills, pushed them across the shining counter. 'Can you let me have a roll of quarters for these bills?'

Louis stood in silence.

He stared at me bleakly. After a moment, he reached without lifting his eyes from mine into the cash-register for the paper-wrapped silver. He weighed the heavy roll thoughtfully in his hand. Finally, in a voice as solemn as a tolling cathedral bell, he said, 'Ahh-*mon* Max, *mon* Max! This trick, Louis knows. In the closed fist of a man, this roll of twenty-five cent piece is like the blackjack. Eet is veree dangerous. Perhaps enough dangerous even to kill a man.' He balanced the roll on its end on the bar. 'You have the trouble, *mon ami?*' he inquired in a soft, sad voice.

Automatically, I shook my head. 'Forget it, Louis. Just pour me a fresh drink and smile and try to look like the happy man you really are.'

I worked slowly on that fresh drink. My mind kept sliding ahead to my appointment with Moss. The lure of my mythical jewels had worked much more effectively than I'd ever dared hope. Was greed, then, the Back Man's weakness? His Achilles' heel? The hole in his rock-hard armour? If so, greed could swing wide the ultimate door. The scene in which two principals joined covertly to exchange money for drugs—to traffic.

It was like hanging a cause on a single thread.

'But it *has* to work,' I kept telling myself. 'It *has* to. I'm committed to that plan now. *It has to work!*'

Louis advanced in a steady waddle down the bar. He freshened my glass, his black old eyes studying me frankly. '*Vraiment, mon ami,*' he said in a troubled voice. 'Tonight I weel light a candle to Sainte Thérèse for you. I will go early to the Waiters' Mass. I will pray for my friend, Max. Because he has the look of one who is being torn into the small pieces.'

That little spot of friendly concern dissipated the

185

tension I'd been building up during the day. I felt better, able to grin and mean it. I chatted with Louis about reform politics until a woman down the bar cried in a loud, resentful voice 'I dropped my stupid drink' and Louis hurried off to fix her a refill. Restlessly, I wedged into the telephone booth to call Thorn. The saucy maid answered to tell me Miss Thorn had gone out for lunch and had not yet returned.

I went back to my drink, drummed restless fingers on the bar, staring straight ahead of me, watching shifting images in the bar mirror. Turning away, I glanced distractedly out the window to the noisy, sun-splashed street where a tight, horn-honking traffic jam was forming. An urgency to be doing something—anything—began again, grew overpowering.

I let Louis pour me a final drink then, without appearing anxious about it, said goodbye. I went to a near-by garage and picked up my car. It was a good forty blocks, most of it through midday snarls of traffic, to the semi-residential district where Moss lived. By the time I reached there, almost an hour had fled.

I whipped around that narrow, somewhat depressing corner and, quickly, driving at slightly more than moderate speed, passed the drawn shades of the Back Man's house. Then, in ever-widening circles, I cruised every street and alley spoking out from that block.

That done, I parked my car at the mouth of a side street and step-by-step scouted every inch of the district on foot. At last, completely confident of my ability to navigate the area, its every small avenue of escape or evasion, without danger of being confused by its geography or thrown off by anyone I had on tail, I returned to my parked car.

Leaving the car to be winterized, I taxied back home. I thought, longingly, about a tub full of water, a pot full of steaming coffee, a quick nap. But think was all I did do. I put on my shabby grey suit and dug out a worn Air Force duffel bag just large enough to hold the things I needed: fresh socks and underwear, a wrinkled, unlaundered shirt, toilet articles.

The duffel bag in my hand, I walked quiet streets until I was well away from my apartment. Then I flagged down a cruising cab. I told the driver to take me to Chinatown.

I paid off the cab at the intersection of Lagauchetiere and George; the heart of the Chinese district.

I mixed with chattering, shuffling Chinese until I came to a lopsided eating-house. Inside, I found an empty booth and ordered tea from a plump, grinning Chinese. On his return with a steaming pot and small cup, I asked with proper formality: 'Ling Tan? Does the great elder still spend his afternoons playing fan-tan with his friends?'

The plump one bowed. 'It is so!' he said, still grinning. 'One with old bones does not change his habits.'

Once my tea was finished, I followed a short, crooked street to an old building that leaned slightly over the sidewalk. Furrowed steps fell to a basement door. I went through that door to a small anteroom.

An elderly Chinese stepped silently from a small office counting-room, waited without expression for me to speak. I mentioned Ling Tan's name. The old man bowed, and shuffled away. A moment later, Ling Tan, his almond eyes already warming, walked sedately into the anteroom. 'Welcome, my son,' he said in his soft, beautiful voice. 'Do you come again with your belly roaring like a hungry lion for our food? If so, I shall leave my childish playing and we shall eat together.'

'A pleasure I must deny myself,' I said. 'Today, I have another favour I must ask of you.'

'As you will,' Ling Tan said graciously. 'We shall sit for a moment in the small room, then. One of our young men will bring the hottest tea you can drink. Then you may talk as much as you think is wise.'

We sat on a silk-covered couch before a low, teak-wood

187

table. A teenage Chinese boy brought tea in thin, transparent cups. Ling Tan sipped his tea, belched his approval politely, and returned his cup to the table. I sipped and my fingers brushed Ling Tan's lightly as I put down my cup. I made the customary comment on the exquisite flavour of the tea, then said without further preamble, 'It is possible that very soon a certain person or persons will become curious about where I am living. It is also possible these people will take desperate steps to find out. Should they do so, it would help me greatly if they discover I live in this area. That I came here alone as a stranger a few weeks ago, looking for a room. That is all I would wish these people to learn about me.'

Ling Tan opened his heavy old eyes. 'It will be arranged,' he said quietly.

I smiled. 'Without questions? Even from you?'

'If such a thing is asked, it is because you have a need. Your problem would not be eased if you tell an old man its cause.'

I said, 'I might require the room for just a few days—or perhaps for as long as a month. Perhaps the precaution will be wasted entirely. That is something I don't know.'

Ling Tan spread his thin hands, palms upward. 'A wise man,' he smiled, 'prepares always for the unexpected.' He clapped his two hands, Chinese fashion. The same boy appeared like the genie out of the bottle. Ling Tan pointed to my duffel bag, spoke in rapid Cantonese. Both bag and young Chinese quickly disappeared.

'You will walk one block down the street. The house where you will live is the one beside the eating-house at the corner,' Ling Tan directed me. 'My son, you will be the only white there. If they see you, much amusement will be had by the other boarders. They will call you *Mr. Round Eyes*. And they will laugh delightedly to themselves. But no one will trouble you. The building is one of my properties. It is attended to by one of my tong.'

An enigmatic old Chinese woman let me into the rooming house. She led me to the second floor and down a short hall to an end room. Handing me a Yale key she turned, and her heelless slippers slapped back down the dim hall. She had not uttered a word.

The key let me into a tiny, surgically clean bedroom. My duffel bag yawned emptily at me from the floor; my shaving things lay in a precise line on a shelf over the shining sink. My wrinkled shirt hung neatly over the radiator. Warming for me to slip into. On the bedtable, a copy of the *Saturday Evening Post* lay beside a folded Chinese newspaper.

I lifted my head and gave a long, suspicious sniff. Musk threaded the still air as a light mist. Perfume, musky perfume. Pansiao! Umm, the honey-skinned daughter of Ling Tan—Pansiao!

The bed had been tucked invitingly down. Late sunlight lay ripely across the crisp sheets. I stripped off my trench-coat, jacket and shoes. Two hours remained before my appointment with Moss.

Common sense told me to spend that two hours resting.

19 The street on which Moss lived stretched dark and shadowed, alive with muffled noises and a sighing of the wind brushing along its dirt-choked gutters.

My fingers wavered over the bell button, then fell.

The door swung instantly wide open.

Moss gestured impatiently to me. 'Quick, quick. Don't you know better than to stand there? Come inside.'

I stepped past him into the unlighted hall, and he pushed me a little.

In the kitchen, I stopped with my back to a shaded window. Moss pounded past me to the rear of the room.

Unlocking a stout door, he shouted, without turning: 'Come along!'

He began up an enclosed flight of straight-up stairs built snugly against the outside building wall and leading to its second story. After each two or three of the short steps he paused, blew out great blasts of air. Before he reached the top landing, his shirt was darkening and stuck wetly to his back and a sickening odour of sweat hung over him like a cloud.

Crossing the landing, he produced a large key-ring, selected and used a key. 'Come in, come in,' he gasped. 'This is where I live. Well, come inside and look.'

I wasn't listening to him. I had moved past him and I was standing in a living-room that came to me as a page out of the Arabian Nights.

The room was huge. Two walls were bright red and there were black slave statues standing in deep niches. A lavender carpet stretched from wall to wall, the long sofa was pale blue and the two lovers' seats cerise and Chinese red, all finished in blond wood. The two other walls were mostly book-shelves, filled with heavy volumes, except for two spaces on which hung reproductions of Goya's etchings of war atrocities, the violated women, spread-legged and bloody-breasted, the hulking violators, moustachioed, lascivious, sated, and a third space over which hung a large tapestry, a flamboyant design, after Goya, of boys playing at bull-fighting. In one corner, stood a little white bar and close to it a huge Capehart record-player sided by stacks of albums. Scattered about the carpeting, convenient for lounging or other basic pleasures, were white bearskins and violently coloured out-size hassocks.

There was also, strange and ominous and evil-looking, a high-backed, throne-like chair made of king ebony, brilliantly polished and reflecting light almost as though it were illuminated from inside.

Moss heard the startled blast of my breath. He must

have misunderstood it. He couldn't know that I was think-ing his room should have been painted solid yellow: the colour of madness.

Pounding across the violent carpeting, he sat on the throne chair with his heavy arms on the rests and his body flung back. 'Those bloody stairs,' he gasped. 'Too much for a big man—too by God much. Well, damn you, don't stand there gaping. Pour me some wine.'

Still fighting for breath, he gestured towards the little white bar. 'That bottle on the shelf to your left. Pour me a glass from it. A rare Cyprian wine—very expensive. Try some yourself. It won't dull the effect of the drug you use, as spirits do.' He gestured impatiently. 'Now, hurry! We'll drink a glass of wine, then we'll talk. Yes. And later, I might even show you my animals.'

Still numb from the effect of the nightmare room, I went to the bar and found the bottle of Cyprian. I poured the blood-red wine into goblets as bright and fragile as tear-drops.

Moss took the goblet I handed him and he gulped greedily, ignoring the crimson trickles that coursed over the slack flap of soft flesh that hung below his chin. His belly alternately swelled and sank with a hollow, rumbling sound.

I drifted across the room, found a flaming-red hassock and sat. My wine remained untouched in the tear-drop goblet in my hand.

'What do they call you?' Moss demanded. 'Seven didn't say. I don't often talk with people I don't know.'

'Does it matter?' I parried. 'Would it make any differ-ence? My name could mean nothing to you.'

'Don't count on it. But, no matter. I know if you gave me a name it would be false.' He drank noisily, belched as he jack-knifed to place his beautiful goblet at the foot of his throne chair. When he lifted his head, it was to bestow a proud look on his monstrous room. 'My deep respect,' he

191

said in a growling voice, 'goes always to a thief who makes a lot of money. Small crime is senseless,' he said emphatically. 'Ridiculous. But a good haul—something of great value, great beauty—ah-hah! Now there is a real theft!'

His fingers crawled up and down his belly like fat white worms: 'Yes! beauty and value. Like the jewels you recently stole. A real nice theft, that—daring and profitable.' His chuckle was silky, all ugliness. 'There's a satisfaction to that type of theft that only a good thief can appreciate,' he said. 'Just think of the look on that fool of a woman's face when she woke up to discover her precious diamonds gone. Think of it!'

'Think of the police heat,' I retorted. 'I told you the cops were so anxious to make a pinch they were grilling each other.'

'Of course!' Moss cried triumphantly. 'My point to a T. You have taken the words right out of my mouth. Jewels are a satisfying and profitable theft, yes. But they are extremely dangerous to hold, risky to sell. Oh my— but how quickly they can get a poor thief into a bad mess!'

I looked away from him to the little white bar, which stood strangely like an altar in that mad room. 'Don't break up and cry,' I said, a deliberate edge to my voice. 'A smart thief can always peddle ice. The thing is, big ice— like this is—takes a little longer. But it can always be sold. For a price, too. You know that.'

'A price! Ah, but consider the risks. You're an utter stranger here in Montreal. You know no one. No fences. None of the non-professionals who buy hot stones with hidden business profits. There, my friend, is point number one against you. Number two, the R.C.M.P. already have you under surveillance. Number three, as an addict, you are subject to street and house search, even arrest, at any moment.' Closing his eyes tightly, he shook his head sadly. 'Your position,' he said with stage-comic concern, 'is bad—yes, very bad. There is also point number four.

Jewels are very easy for police to trace.'

I found his eyes, held them with mine. 'Ah, but I do know the odds, and the risks,' I retorted. 'I knew them long before I frisked that hotel room in Van. So your three points don't add up to a thing. Specially the point about fences. By the time I was sweet sixteen, I knew you can always find a fence in any town that has a pool-room or a tavern. And fences are always boiling-hot to deal. Besides, my stuff is right, made to order for a fence. Don't forget this jewellery is all top stuff, in fairly small pieces.'

'Fences—thieves!' Moss threw back his head and shouted angrily: 'You damn fool, you can't trust fences. They rob thieves blind. Pay less than a third value. Much less, with valuable stones. Ha! sometimes they even squeal on thieves if they refuse their piddling prices.'

I said, invitingly, 'Well, perhaps. Okay, you say you buy expensive jewels. You say you pay better prices than ordinary drops do. In cash, you say—*and other things.*'

'Why not? Money is nothing to me.' Moss said this with a great air. 'I have plenty of money—plenty. I am a very rich man and I have already bought many splendid gems. Buying yours would be a mere nothing to me. I'll pay generously. The way you want payment most. In uncut heroin. There! There's a bloody great concession. It's no small matter to get together the amount of heroin that will require. And dangerous. I am very sure *you* know *that.*'

I looked thoughtful; as though on the verge of giving in.

'Well—?' Moss demanded harshly, his pig-eyes gleaming. 'When can you produce the stones? I must see them before we can get down to discussing price.'

I considered quickly. On the surface, Moss's offer to deal was genuine. What last moment trickery he intended was another matter. He certainly wouldn't sit still and let me pick all his feathers. But, in fairness to Welch's purpose, I had to stall, to delay trying to set up Moss until

193

the inspector's Narcotic Squad was alerted and stood ready to nab both Moss and his as yet unknown supplier. For certainly Moss would have to make contact and re-new his black-market stock if he *actually* intended to pay partly in heroin for my mythical jewels.

'No!' I said, feigning anger. 'Nothing doing. We've been over all this before. That jewellery doesn't move one inch until I see exactly what I'm getting. Until I *see* the heroin.'

Moss nibbled at his purplish lips, wet them. He paused, and slowly, his impatience gave way to a quiet slyness, brightening his eyes and narrowing them. He said, with awkward caution, 'Now, now. Don't think for a minute I'm trying to rush you. Pour some wine. Yes, fill the goblets. And, by God, we'll have some music. Let me tell you, my record collection is priceless. I'm a great collector, you might even say a connoisseur.

'Ha!' he said with a fantastic smirk, 'I collect many things. You would drool over my collection of porno-graphic art. Believe me, I possess one of the best and most esoteric collections extant. But back to the music. You've noticed my machine there in the corner. A Capehart, very expensive. I obtained it indirectly from an addict that had robbed a warehouse. Actually, it is more of an instrument than a machine. Right now, there's a recording of Bartok on it. Play it! You'll enjoy Bartok. A great composer.'

As the Bartok began, Moss heaved his bulk into a more comfortable position. He smiled a ghastly smile, and started off again, now on a benevolent tack: 'Really, I do feel sorry for you. Being an addict and a stranger in town, as well. Where are you living? Did you manage to find a nice, safe place? Addicts must be so terribly careful.'

I glanced at him sharply. The weakness of his new thrust surprised me. With a short smile, I said, 'Chinatown. I'm living there.'

He blinked.

'Chinatown!' he cried incredulously. 'Clever, by God—very, very clever. Police seldom bother even trying to investigate anyone living in Chinatown. They know it's useless, ha! Orientals know how to keep a close mouth. Yes, very clever.'

Silence jelled and set. There was nothing to do but sit it out; to let Moss scowl and mutter and brood. He sat a long time, motionless. I sat expressionless. Rolling the beautiful wine goblet slowly between my hands.

Suddenly, Moss threw back his head. Peals of laughter shrilled from his wet mouth—laughter ringing with frustration, with grudging respect, laughter completely without joy. 'By the Gods of Gomorrha!' he screamed, 'But you're a wise one. You've wound that fool Seven around your little finger, and now you're trying the same game on the Back Man. You—you're trying to make me so hot for those jewels that I'll pay any price.'

He was on his feet. And his laughter still piped out in wild, hysterical blasts. 'Ha, ha, ha!' he roared. 'So smart. So utterly damned clever. I like you—by God, I do.'

Like a vice, his clammy-wet hand closed over my arm. 'By the Great Satyr,' he screamed, 'I'll show you something now. You'll be entertained here like few people ever have. Come! Come with me, my clever bait-dangler from Vancouver. The Back Man will show you his performing pets.'

He pitched across the room and threw wide a side door. Bowing with ludicrous ceremonial grace, he bellowed: 'Come! Come into the arena-room. Come inside and see my beauties!'

His eyes showed a hot and dangerous light. They dared me to refuse his invitation. I joined him, and found myself in a brilliantly lighted room. The back of my neck began to prickle. Small animal voices reached my ears. Scratchings and scramblings. From meshed cages lined along opposite walls, bright and furtive eyes flashed over hideously slavering mouths.

I had stepped straight into the antechamber of Gehenna.

Moss reached out for a metal prodding-stick and thrust it forward.

The room went mad with a horrible, shrill, animal squealing.

I left Moss there.

I felt hot and dirty. My whole body shook, and one-handed, using the other to hold on to the little white bar, I splashed liquor into a glass. The entire fabulous, sordid scene had affected me too deeply, rocked my sense of balance and proportion.

Ten minutes passed. Twenty agonizing minutes.

Moss came reeling out of his animal room. His eyes looked red, as if they would glow in the dark. He snatched up the bottle of Cyprian. There was only a heel left in it. He drained it and hurled it. The bottle struck the now firmly-sealed animal room door, shattering, spinning chunks of glass across the violent carpeting.

The chunks of glass, glistening bright blood-red with droplets of wine, crunched under Moss's feet as he pounded across the room to fling himself into his throne chair.

'Go on and believe I'm mad!' he called out to me in a depraved, twisted voice. 'Be too self-righteous to admit there is gratification in witnessing bloody death. Laugh, if you will. But you are laughing at something superior to you. Were not animal battles like those I enjoy staged to entertain kings and emperors in an age far more splendid than this? Now—in this puking civilization of sham and hypocrisy our modern arena is much more elaborate, more grandiosely stage-set for viciousness and deliberate, calculated ruthlessness!'

Shock washed over me. Shock and disgust that cut off speech.

'War is our modern arena,' he shouted. 'Are you a fool

that believes wars are fought for ideals? That is nonsense. The need to kill was born in man with the need to eat! So it has always been. Since the dawn of time! What is war but calculated and regimented violence?' He shook his huge fist at me. 'History books?' he howled. 'Have you ever read history books? Gibbons, Macaulay—the medieval writers?'

'I have,' I retorted. 'Does that prove anything?'

Moss bristled. 'Prove anything? I once spent six months in prison. Every cursed hour of it in solitary. Only educational literature was permitted by the discipline guards. I studied history. The medieval records. Page by page, text by text. Now, what do you think those records reveal?' He burst into a mad, triumphant, ringing laughter. 'I'll by God tell you what they reveal. They reveal the imperious voice of murder that snarls in every man.

'They describe war, those records, and intrigue leading up to war. They describe endless chains of war, battles, antagonism, punishment and death. That's the story of the days of our world. A chronicle of hate. That's the story of mankind. Mankind saddled with violence and dripping red with human blood. It's what the world is, has been, and always will be. Human animal at human animal.'

Laughing nervously, I protested: 'Here, now. Yours is a vicious opinion. You didn't read history in an objective sense. You read it as a moral sceptic, anxious to find roots for criticism—'

I should have known better.

'A-moral-sceptic!' he gasped. 'Oh, poor man—poor man—poor, insignificant addict man. You call me a moral sceptic.' His face bright red with amusement, he roared his contempt to the ceiling. Then, suddenly, his expression changed. Now, all at once, he was ice-calm, strangely subdued.

'At least you speak like a man who can think,' he said. 'Not like the usual lame-brained addict. You're an

197

exception, then. Now, I am wondering just how much of an exception you really are.'

Again, it was impossible to tell exactly what he meant. He took me in intently as he went on: 'You are my guest, here, of course. So I suppose I shouldn't protest your opinions. Just let me say this; I have absolutely no moral qualms over enjoying my animal battles. None at all. Believe me, most people that would jump to condemn me have worse vices. The interesting thing to *me* is that *they* believe they are moral.'

The record-player, which had never let up playing Bartok, was driving me silly. I started towards it to turn it off, but Moss reached the machine before me. Tapping the switch, he came back to stand midway between me and the door. His fists clenched and sweat broke again on his face. 'All right!' he grated. 'We've had some pleasure, a little talk. Now, back to cases. With no more damn nonsense. You'll tell me right now what you intend to do with those stolen diamonds.'

I shook the dizziness out of my head. I didn't think I could stand much more. 'No, not yet,' I said, and I forced a smile. 'You've offered me drugs. Let's talk about them. I have my own plans to consider. My idea is to pick up a kilo or so of heroin here and sneak it back to the coast. I've thought it all out.'

I elaborated, quickly built up an imaginary plan. 'I figure I could stop off at a few spots along the way and unload as I go,' I explained. 'There's a gold mine in drug peddling on the prairies. Cities like the Hat, Regina, Moose Jaw. A few spots in Alberta. A guy can con those yokels into paying telephone number prices for junk. Then I'd drop what I had left in Vancouver. Out there, prices are really booming. With a few kilos pure, I'd clean up big— once things cool off, of course.'

'Don't waste my time telling me about your plans,' Moss snapped. 'I know the western market. And I know all about the headaches Horsemen are causing the traffickers out there, too. That's not my worry. You tell me what kind of deal you have in mind. Maybe it will be acceptable to me. How do I know I'll still want these jewels after I see them?'

'Oh, you'll want them. You'll drool for them. They're gem-quality stones. Didn't you hear me say they're valued at thirty thousand?'

'Well, go on!' Moss pressed.

I went on in a careful, almost robot manner. Desperately, I was trying to remember the precise plan I had decided on for setting up a phony sale. 'I want the same price a good fence would pay,' I told him. 'That's half value. Fifteen thousand. But I want half that in heroin—uncut. And I might as well tell you now, there's no use trying to angle with the heroin. I'll test it, in my arm, before I accept it.'

'By God!' Moss roared, puffing up to a new hugeness. 'By God, but you have big ideas. Big gall. Let you get loose in this business and there'll be little enough room for the rest of us. Well, keep talking. Where do you expect to make this test of the heroin?'

I heard my own voice, astonished at its control. 'That's for you to decide,' I was saying. 'I don't have a damn one way or the other. Just so long as I don't get double-crossed.'

'You talk of a few kilos. With that quantity of heroin, you could go back west and set up in business.' Moss's expression was thoughtful. 'A smart man would forget about making those stops on the prairies. He would wait until there's a bad panic in Vancouver, *then* shoot the heroin out on the market. That way, he might win control out there. Be the Man. Providing, of course, he could keep getting fresh supplies of drugs. Is that what's running around in your cruddy mind?'

'I might think about it,' I retorted. 'Everybody else at the coast is having a crack at control, why not me?'

Moss snarled. His snarl was animal-like, blood-curdling. 'Control! You prattle about control,' he said, puffing up. 'A man has to be a giant! Always, the wolves circle. Every addict and connection is for ever scheming to slide his hand into your pocket. Every damned Horseman is out to punch the key that will open you wide for prosecution.'

'Part of the game,' I shrugged. I stuck a dead cigarette in the corner of my mouth, let it dangle. I felt exactly like a character from a B movie.

'The wolves are always circling,' he repeated, sighing gigantically as if to tell the world it was all beyond him. 'You've got to be as tough as any of the thugs that get ideas. When I started, I had to put hooks in plenty of thugs. More than a dozen times I've been earmarked for a quick, bloody death, or a stool-pigeon pinch. I've beat them all. All my enemies. Every damned one of them.'

Moss stared vaguely about his hideous room. 'This business would make a liar out of George Washington,' he said. He stared me sneeringly up and down, totalling my crummy clothes, my two day's growth of beard. 'You by God don't look like much,' he said. 'I don't know what you have in your scheming mind, and this might all be a trick. You show nothing—prove nothing you say. Yet, you're young, and you're strong. And, in spite of being an addict, you're alert. It's possible, barely possible, you believe you could go back west to traffic. There's always somebody that thinks a bigger man's shoes will fit them.'

'That's how I figure it,' I said, breathing more freely. 'I've told you that. So let's you and I get down to the talking part of a deal.'

Moss's eyes again grew sly. 'Delivery of such a large quantity would take time to arrange, a week at least,' he said. 'Meanwhile, you still don't show me the jewels. You still act as though you expect me to buy a pig in a poke.'

'You can see the jewels—any time,' I said carelessly. 'Any time. As soon as you prove you have the heroin available.'

Somewhere in the room, a telephone began an insistent ringing. Moss opened his mouth, then clamped it irritably shut. Struggling to his feet, he stamped to the little white bar. He lifted a plug-in house phone from a hidden shelf, grumbling angrily to me over his shoulder: 'Wait, wait. Wait until I see who's calling me. Some fool, no doubt, at this cursed hour. You can see I never get a minute's peace.'

He barked a greeting into the phone. For a moment, as he listened, everything grew silent in the room. Then he began slamming his fist hard against the bar, rocking it. His face grew white, congested, and he seemed to stop breathing. A sudden, bestial harshness welled into his eyes. 'So you have the double-crosser!' he howled triumphantly into the phone. 'You found him, eh? Bring him here to me, then. I want him. Oh, my God! how I want him. Don't touch him. Just get him here at once!'

Smashing down the receiver, he spun, and pointed imperiously to the hall. 'You will leave at once!' he commanded in a quivering voice. 'By God, I'm going to be busy for the next hour. I don't want you in my way. So, out. Out of here, at once. This way. Not the way we came in.'

He half pushed me into the dark hallway, bulldozing me with butts from his huge belly. Throwing open a narrow door at the hall's end, he shoved me on to an outside porch standing high over a sharp fall of stairs that led down to the street. 'Get down there,' he barked. 'Get to the street and out of the district at once. But you by God be back here at the same time tomorrow. We'll make our deal then, for drugs and jewels both. Now, go. Get out of sight as fast as you can.'

The street had a strange, abandoned look. The shadows lay long and black. A gentle melancholy seemed to fill the still night air. I went hurriedly to the near corner, rounded it, then glanced quickly over my shoulder.

Moss's porch was clear, empty. On the street there

was no car, no hurrying person. I sprinted in hard, loose strides completely around the block, came back opposite the Back Man's house to a leaning, abandoned-looking building. Rusted iron stairs rose under a litter of dirt to the top storey. Climbing hurriedly, I stepped into a cramped porch where the shadows hung blackest.

I began waiting.

Exhaust echoes made lonesome pistol shots along the street, then died abruptly away. A black Buick sedan came to a lurching stop before Moss's door. Two men got out. The larger of the two stood on the curb-side and reached inside the car. From the rear seat, he pulled out an unconscious man. With a curt nod to his companion, he slung the unconscious form over his shoulder and ran lightly up Moss's stairs.

Beside the parked car, a street-lamp flickered. Under its light, the unconscious man had been easily recognizable.

Long after Moss's door was sealed, I stood staring into the soft darkness, searching for an answer to a new puzzle.

I couldn't even begin to understand how the Back Man's musclemen had managed to catch up with Phil Chasen.

20 The night phone at the Cedar Avenue nursing home rang and rang. At last, Miss Kelly's voice sounded, sleepy and annoyed: 'Hello! Hello! Who is it, please?'

'Maxwell Dent. Miss Kelly, in Heaven's name, what happened to Phil?'

First, came a stiff, crackling silence. Then, a bristling rush of indignation. 'Th-that m-man left, Max Dent,' Miss Kelly spluttered. 'He simply climbed out of b-bed, p-put on his clothes, and left. But—mind you—not before he tried to break into my drug cabinet. Not before he screamed for drugs until he had the entire home in an uproar. Max, if you ever, ever dare—'

'Please, never mind that. Just tell me when Phil left. What condition he left in.'

'He left about six this morning. Just as the nurse was going in with his breakfast. As for his condition, it's bad. That is, his physical condition, from what you claim was an accident. Apart from that, he has a temperature and he's in the usual severe pain and discomfort of early reduction cure. He had an injection of morphine at ten last night.'

'What dosage?'

'Why, the usual, of course! A quarter-grain.'

'Oh, Sweet Mother of God! Didn't he tell you? Didn't you know? Phil's been using twenty quarter grains a day—maybe more. He has a fantastic habit. That's why he crashed out. You were bringing him down too fast. He's going crazy for drugs.'

'Then Phil Chasen belongs in an asylum,' Miss Kelly said, and there was a distinct snap to her voice. 'At any rate, he sounds crazy enough. In coma, he kept continually raving about some girl. Some Helen, or other. When he wasn't doing that, he kept asking the nurses if the Cross on the mountain showed from his window. I don't know what it all means, but it doesn't sound sane to me. Don't you dare ever bring me another addict, Max.' Her voice softened a little. 'Yes, well, Phil's bill is seventy dollars up to today. There's no hurry for it but, please, Max, if you telephone here again, try to do it in the daytime. It's past midnight again.'

'I'm sorry,' I said, 'Sorry.' And I hung up.

I stood in the telephone booth, my head in my hands. Piecing together what had happened to Phil was no problem. After breaking away from Miss Kelly, he had discovered that for some reason or other his supply of stolen drugs wasn't immediately available. So he had taken the long chance of not being suspect of raiding Frankie's plant, and he had gone to the rendezvous to buy drugs. And he had walked straight into the arms of Moss's musclemen. Exactly as Moss had known that some day he must do.

I went outside to the street.

A cold, sleety-wet rain had started to fall. This time, the first in weeks, there was no need to worry about being followed. At this precise moment, Moss's two tailmen would be busy with brutality.

I walked until worry drove me across the city, back downtown.

Finally, I found myself on an unfamiliar side-street, realizing that I had forgotten the hours, feeling how my ankles had gotten wet from the cold rain, feeling the dampness on my bone-chilled shoulders. My eyes lifted from the streaming pavement to see the lonely grey unfolding of dawn. To see rain clouds, dark and swollen, slowly moving away.

Around me, the city began noisily shaking itself back to life. Car tyres made silk sounds on smooth, wet asphalt. Street lights were dimming. Milkmen's bottles clinked Good Morning. Still, Moss's face swam before my eyes. My ears remained numb with his brutal words. 'I want him. Leave him for me!' And, because of my obligation to Ashton, my responsibility to Welch, I had to fail Phil. Right now, Moss's door was shut, bolted, and barred against me by Ashton and Welch themselves. I had to stand impatiently apart while Moss took what I knew would be a terrible revenge.

I went back to Chinatown. Stretching on my hard, narrow bed, watching daylight flow across the windowsill I swore a solemn and considered oath. I swore that soon, somehow soon, my entire case would be manœuvred to a head. I swore that I would bring to its end this nightmare state of malice and anguish and brutality. I would end it all. Soon.

Outside, in the hallway, near my door, a soft, slurring step had sounded.

I catapulted to my feet. My fist closed over the rolled quarters weighting my pocket.

I wrenched open the door.

'Hi, Max!' Pansiao smiled prettily up at me.

'Wow!' I said. I stared foolishly at her. Her eyes, long, with pupils black as onyx against the clear whites, glittered with amusement. A honey-yellow hand protruding from her brocaded kimono sleeve held a cup of steaming tea. 'In this house,' she said in her lilting voice, 'tea is always served to an honoured guest. May I put this cup beside your bed?'

I felt light with giddiness as tension slipped away. 'If you'll sit down and talk for a minute,' I bargained.

Putting down her tray, Pansiao turned, reached her arms behind my head, pulled it close to hers, and shyly kissed me full on the lips. 'Such a thing only comes from foreign learning,' she smiled. 'Hello-kiss for a friend who never drops by to see me any more.'

The kiss left me with a queer, high sensation.

Stepping back, Pansiao closed the door firmly. As she moved, her ankle-length gown spoke in sibilant, silky whispers. Coming back, she sat beside me on the bed, tucking her tiny feet daintily beneath her. She thrust her hand into her sleeve, brought out a book of matches and lit a cigarette for me. 'Smoke!' she smiled. 'The tea was just my excuse. Men always need to smoke when they are worried.'

Smiling back at her, I said, 'What heathen sorcery tells you that I am worried?'

'Chinese always know when a person worries.' Aware of a creeping pinkness under her cheeks, Pansiao hesitated. 'White people can't hide their emotions as well as we,' she explained. 'As well, you wouldn't be staying here unless you had a problem.'

205

'How clever you are,' I teased.

Pansiao pressed my shoulder gently until I lay on my back. Her soft fingers smoothed my forehead. 'An old Chinese philosophy,' she said, her teeth gleaming under the cherry of her lips, 'teaches that keeping ill news in one's belly spoils the liver and dries the gall. That sounds much better when my father says it,' she laughed, 'but it still makes sense. It means that anger and sorrow and trouble all must come out. Or one will grow ill.'

Her soft fingers fluttered, then went back to their smoothing. She wrinkled her nose. 'Chinese say that fear and worry are psychological viruses. That they distress the heart and soul as well as the body.'

I smiled up at her. 'Did you come to hear my troubles, Pan?'

She shook her head. 'No, Max—not I. Before you slipped out last night, I heard you speaking on the telephone in the hall. You were talking with a girl. But trying to hide from her the things your heart wanted to say. It was as though you were afraid to let her know the way you feel about her.' Pansiao hesitated, then went on stubbornly: 'I didn't need to break a fortune-cookie to know about her. Your voice told me she is a very special girl. The one you should hurry to when you are tired and worried and bad company for yourself.'

I grinned. 'Aha! Now you're the ancient philosopher. Not a pretty Chinese student of physics.'

'Women of my race are born older than men,' Pansiao said, smiling gravely. 'I think perhaps all women are. Perhaps that is why immediately from the beginning we know what we want. Why we know, too, that no one, not any one, can do anything really capably if they insist on doing it alone.'

My little Chinese philosopher became silent. Only her fingers moved, soft as feathers. Then, somewhere in the house a chime sounded. Pansiao stood up at once, hurried to the door. Opening it, she turned back to smile a lovely smile at me. 'Yes, Max,' she said, 'That is exactly what you should do. Go talk things over with your girl. Soon.'

A rustle of silk, and the door clicked softly, and I was alone again. Undressing, I slid between the cool sheets.

I slept until four o'clock. Then I shaved, dressed, and went out.

I found a public telephone booth and called Welch. He listened without comment while I spoke of Moss's kidnapping of Phil, of Phil's involvement with Helen Ashton. But his voice tilted off-key over my unproved belief that Moss was now sliding closer to the danger line.

We made quick, tentative plans with Welch continually interrupting to say: 'Yes, if you can buffalo him into contracting to buy that quantity of heroin, if you can establish *when* he's going to buy it there's a good, a really good chance we can throw a net over him. *And* his supplier. But be careful, Dent. You know how to play it safe. Play it safe, then.'

'I will, I will,' I told him over and over again, until he at last hung up and let me go.

Massive and glowering, Moss sprawled on his throne chair. His fingers were curled like white ropes around one of his beautiful wing goblets. 'So you're back, by God!' he roared, by way of a greeting. 'Well, sit. Last night we were interrupted, but this time we'll complete our business. Tonight will be the showdown.'

Thinking of Welch's words, I hurried to take the offensive. I retorted: 'Showdown nothing! The showdown comes when you produce the drugs you're offering to trade. That's a lot of heroin. How long will it take you to get it?'

Moss hunched forward. 'You reckless, bait-dangling idiot!' he snarled. 'Do you think you'll leave here tonight before I know where you've hidden those gems?'

I couldn't speak. I was stunned. This crisis had come too fast.

'Name of an idiot!' he cried, lurching to his feet. 'Come, come with me. Come, I say. I'll show you what happens to people that try to outsmart the Back Man.'

Thrusting out a hand, he grasped my shoulder. He half dragged me across the room, moved me as easily as if I were a dummy filled with straw, sent me reeling against the wall. At once, he was behind me, his body holding me helpless, his fingers fumbling with a key. He got a door open, and backed through it, still holding me.

'Come in,' he invited, screaming. 'Come in, you reckless idiot—and learn!'

I shook him off, stepped around him. A sweet, cloying smell of blood came at me from a crimson puddle that glistened on the floor.

I moved towards the puddle, and horror slapped me so hard it stung me back into self-control.

Phil lay in a corner in a twisted heap. His chest was smooth, still, only a page vein at the base of his throat showing any throb of life. Phil wasn't suffering. He was unconscious, indifferent to the agony waiting in the ripped flesh and smashed bones of his utterly ruined left hand.

'See him' Moss ground out. 'That boy is a trained pianist—he was, that is. What is he now? He's nothing. Just an addict thief with a crippled hand. He was brought here unconscious. To be punished. Later, he'll be thrown in a lane somewhere. Still unconscious. Punished.

'He imagined he was being very smart, very clever,' Moss gloated. 'He thought he was being clever enough to outwit my organization, me. But his cleverness ended differently from what he expected. Not only is he through as a pianist, but that left hand of his is so completely lifeless he won't even be able to use it to stick needles into himself with. He'll remember me. By God, yes! He's not likely ever to forget trying to outsmart Jack Moss.' Moss wheeled, said harshly, 'Now you've seen. Come. We'll finish our talking in the other room.'

Choosing a hassock, he sat. 'You have exactly one minute,' he stated. 'I have been amused listening to your prattle about Vancouver and your cross-eyed schemes for making money. But now you have exactly sixty seconds to tell me about the gems.'

He extracted an old turnip watch from some inner recess of his shiny suit, checked off the time. When the full minute had expired, he glanced up from the watch. He read the unblinking No in my eyes.

Without comment, he reached out to a table for a tiny silver bell, shook it violently.

His two musclemen stepped abruptly into the room.

They stared at me with cold, expressionless faces.

It was too much. So very much too much that I didn't move or make a sound.

I let pent-up rage run wild along my veins, enjoying its feel after weeks of submission and careful control. This anger was right, just—it was cleansing and cool and it let a man think, and because of that it was all the more deadly.

I stared wordlessly back at Moss's now scowling and fidgeting bullies.

'That's the right idea, look at them!' Moss roared. 'You've met them both before. In an alley beside a cathedral, wasn't it? You took them by surprise. They remember that incident. It reflected on their ability, you see. They are anxious now to correct their first, stupid mistake.'

I could afford to give these two no chance.

I knew I lacked time to separate them so, before either could move, my hand flashed out to the bar. Tightly, that hand closed over Moss's bottle of Cyprian. I hurled the wine bottle into the smaller hoodlum's pale, sneering face.

The bigger man blinked once, then charged at me. He came at me as solid and thickly-built as a bridge piling. His expression was gluey, turtle-slow, but his charge was like the charge of a mad rhino. I'd felt his strength in the cathedral alley when I'd had him at a disadvantage. I knew better now than to contest it.

I let myself be butted across the room by his rush. I fell. I did so deliberately. I landed on my back, legs doubled. Then I straightened my legs bar-jitsu style with all the uncoiling power of my body.

The bar-jitsu kick stunned the big hoodlum to a ludicrous stop. He hung momentarily as though suspended by ropes, then fell backwards all arms and legs into a bookshelf. He was dazed, he was helpless and vile. I knocked him unconscious with a chop from the side of my hand.

Moss was on his feet. A small, vicious-looking Italian pistol was almost invisible in his huge hand.

He stood a yard from me, struggling desperately to squeeze his finger into the pistol's tiny trigger-guard.

Thrusting out my hands, I grasped his massive shoulders. With my last ounce of strength, I twisted him, began to spin him. His pistol swung inch by inch away from me. I lifted my hands suddenly. He whirled back to face me. Hate boiled inside me, bubbling over. I braced myself.

I smashed my knee upwards under the soft inner fat of his exposed groin.

He dropped like a flour sack. He got up and fell again. His savage will brought him back to his knees. His eyes kept rolling back into his head and the expression on his face was a ghastly thing to see. He crawled across the lavender carpeting, words dribbling from his drawn, colourless lips, 'You wouldn't hit a man—when he's down. You wouldn't—hit a man—when—he's down. Too fat— too—by God fat—my heart will stop. You wouldn't hit an injured man—down.' With a superhuman effort, he got back to his feet and went half-way across the room, jack-knifed, half running, half reeling. 'Don't hit,' he managed to gasp again in a dying voice, and weaving, he made another supreme effort to stay up on his feet. Then he was down again, out completely, insensible.

Scooping up the Italian pistol, I went back to the room where Phil lay. Phil hadn't stirred. I looked at him again, touched his cold, waxy skin. Turning back towards the living-room, my steps were short and halting, like those of an old man. I staggered from room to room until I found a heavy blanket. A mass of words had begun to ferment inside me, and now they bubbled forth. 'Curse Moss. Curse him for the butcher he is. Damn him. This is horrible. My God, it's ghastly. God made an awful error in allowing this.'

I went back and wrapped Phil up like a mummy, carried him as I would have carried a child up to the front of the house.

A sudden blur of movement flattened me against the hall wall.

Shadow slid from behind a chair. It startled me to see his dark eyes dancing with joy. 'Ah-h—*monsieur!*' he cried. 'Me, I shall see all from outside the door. One, two, three. Bang! they fall. *Mon Dieu!* you are so strong, and, truly, so veree clever. Monsieur Moss makes the beeg bluff, *non?* You are so right. Nevair would Monsieur Moss have paid for your diamonds. Nevair. Always he hope to steal them!'

Shadow stepped smartly aside. 'Now go queeckly,' he said. 'Run before Moss and his bodyguard are again awake. Me, I will wait until you are gone many miles before I help them.'

Cold air was like pellets against my face as the door was flung open. I cradled Phil in my arms. A hysterical urge to cry bubbled in my throat. Now I had a community of victims of pain and violence; the three lying helpless on the carpet behind me; Helen and her ravaged body; Phil lying broken against my chest.

Before my eyes, the stairs weaved, falling down, far down, in a long iron curve.

Tightening my hold on Phil, I forced my feet, one-two, one-two, across the landing. The long stairs fell away into nothing. I took a halting step, down. I began wondering if I would be able to find a willing taxi-driver, wondering what I could possibly tell Miss Kelly, wondering if this was the last step, wondering what all those people who kept screaming about the basic goodness of the human being were doing at this awful moment.

Night hung around me in a thick, dark shroud. I reeled crazily down the street.

21 My crumpled grey suit and faded trench-coat smouldered and stank at the bottom of the incinerator shute outside my apartment door.

A cigarette smoking in my hand, I listened over my telephone while Inspector Welch protested indignantly: 'Complete failure, Dent? Utter nonsense. Ridiculous. Regardless of what happened last night at Moss's house, you're still inside. Wait until you're feeling fit again, then come along to my office. I want to see you. In fact, I insist on it.'

Two days passed. I fidgeted around the apartment. I tried desperately to push away thoughts of Helen, and Phil, and Thorn. It simply wouldn't work. I realized my mistake in underestimating Moss: realized how I had underrated his total capacity for degeneracy and raw brutality.

I reconciled myself to agreeing with Welch that it would be senseless to influence the City to arrest Moss on the only charge we could at this point make stick—an E.C.A. count (Extreme Cruelty to Animals) that at best would keep him behind bars for a couple of years.

An obsession again began growing within me, demanding that somehow the Back Man's evil power be exposed. I could still see his face, contorted in spasms of hate, his pig-eyes glittering with triumphant revenge. 'See!

That is what happens to people that try to outwit the Back Man!'

The third morning I awoke feeling better. My sense of defeat diminished and left only a stirring stubbornness to end my case the only decent way it could be ended. Room for suspenseful waiting for the miracle break no longer existed. I had to plan like the devil.

First, I had to bring my client up to date. I called Ashton to explain there had been a serious setback. He surprised me by not being annoyed; only typically urgent. I promised to call in to see him. Then I spoke long enough with Thorn to arrange a meeting with her for later in the afternoon.

Dressed, for a pleasant change, in presentable clothes, I went down to the street. The first call on my list was a duty call on Phil. I repressed an aggressive impulse to skip it, walked uneasily up and down, back and forth in front of my door.

A taxi drew up before the apartment entrance. Getting in, I gave the driver the address of Miss Kelly's nursing home.

The nursing home foyer was a shell of deadly, shining quiet. I went upstairs and found Phil's door open. At his bed, Miss Kelly stood holding up a thermometer.

After a few minutes Miss Kelly bustled out of Phil's room with a faint crackling of starch. 'Heaven knows what actually happened to Phil this time! And if *you* know, I'm sure you won't tell me. Well—you'd better arrange to have him moved at once. It's not just his hand, Max. It's something psychological. Phil knows now that his hand is finished.'

'No!' I said, feeling the colour rise in my cheeks. 'Moving Phil is out. He'll go berserk if you even mention a regular hospital. He'll be scared stiff of being forced into a cold-turkey cure.'

Miss Kelly glared at me. 'Cold-turkey cure, indeed!'

213

she retorted. 'Let Phil start worrying about his hand. In another ten hours the swelling will be down. He'll need a surgeon and a bone specialist then to work on that mess. All we can do here is ice-pack the hand to reduce it.'

'Then what? Is there any hope at all?'

'No chance, Max.' Miss Kelly's old eyes were soft with pity. 'My house doctor tells me the hand will be permanently useless. Will you go in now and visit with Phil?'

I went inside. My eyes moved uncomfortably to the white island that was Phil's bed. He lay completely still. Then, violently, he shook himself from a deep, drugged stupor. His head swung up, bringing his eyes forward, on mine. 'So she told you!' he cried. 'Miss Kelly told you, didn't she? I can see it in your face.'

I nodded. My eyes grew strained trying to avoid staring at the huge ice pack on Phil's crippled hand. My heart faltered over a beat, then dropped back into the pit of my stomach; I felt as though a fine instrument I had known and enjoyed had been smashed by vandals and the pieces scattered about my feet.

Phil kept staring at me. Tight with bitterness, his voice came: 'In a few minutes,' he said, 'a nurse will come into this room. She'll slop alcohol over my arm. The good one. Then she'll find a vein and shoot a half-grain of morphine into me.

'Imagine that!' he said, the fever in his eyes looking like madness. 'Imagine anyone bothering to put alcohol on a junkie's arm. Imagine anyone being that hygenic. My God! I've scratched my veins open with knitting needles when I needed a fix badly and had no hypo.' He propped himself up on one elbow. 'Max, do you know what I'm praying will happen when the nurse comes in with that shot?'

'No. No, Phil. God help us, I don't know.'

Phil told me: 'I'm hoping the nurse will make a mistake. That she'll leave an air bubble in the hypo that will

214

hit my heart and stop it. If that doesn't happen, I hope they goof-up in the dispensary. That I wind up dead from an overdose.'

'Wait, wait!' I protested. 'Phil, this isn't an absolute end. A man can do so many things—'

His voice flailed at me like a whip. 'Are you going to snow-job me about finding substitutes?' he retorted. 'Well, I've already had all that. From that doctor. I shut *him* up by asking him how he'd like to flush his fifteen years of study and practice down the drain and start juggling bedpans again. He didn't answer me. He backed away from my bed, stuttering stupid apologies.'

Reaching his good hand under his blanket, Phil brought out his tennis ball. 'Take it,' he said bitterly, sinking back against the pillows. 'Take it, Max. You're the guy who loves music. Give it to some kid you see on the street carrying a music case. There are no one-handed pianists. None, Max. I'm dead, I'm dead!'

I breathed deeply, got a good taste of the room air. It smelled hot and humid, sick. Dropping the magazines I'd brought on Phil's bedtable, I got out of the room.

I still had the tennis ball in my hand. I didn't know what to do with it. I put it in my pocket.

All the way through the city to the addicts' rendezvous, curses fell from my lips.

Inside the rendezvous, trouble was ready, waiting.

Service was completely halted. The situation was becoming violent. For the second time in a week the city's addicts were caught in the turmoil of a major drug panic.

Fay offered me information. Her platinum hair a hopeless tangle, her eyes darkly circled, she nevertheless appeared to be in reasonably good shape. With a jerky gesture, she pointed to the empty table-chair beside hers.

'Knock me down and call me Toots!' she said, incredulously. 'Take a look at dressed-up you! What did you do to get those glad rags. Prowl a suite in the Ritz?'

After a quick look about her, she began slipping her words furtively out of the side of her mouth. 'Listen, honey,' she said, 'I'm taking a screwball chance even talking to you. The Back Man's kid was in here last night. The kid spilled it to Frankie that you'd worked over Moss and his Charles Atlas boys. I think you must be a little loose between the ears, doing a crazy thing like that.'

'Maybe, Fay, maybe not. Tell me about Moss's pushers. Are any of them working? Any at all?'

'Dead stop! Service's been off for three days. Not only at this meet, but all over the city. Can't you tell? Look around. Everybody has the screaming-meemies. Big Red—the east-end pusher—came in an hour ago. Red had a pocketful of nembutals he stole someplace. He got two bucks apiece for them. Sold out the lot in less than five minutes.' Fay squirmed nervously about in her chair. 'There's a character hanging around the corner,' she said. 'A guy I don't think you know. A guy by the name of Nadeau. He's one of Moss's connections. Right now, he's on his own and he's peddling laudanum. Shoot it in your arm or try it in your coffee. That's what everybody else is doing. I've kept alive on it all day. Cost me twenty dollars so far.'

'What about Shadow's story? Do the addicts believe it? They don't look too hot at me. Only a little leery.'

'Leery, maybe. But not mad,' Fay said, patting my arm. 'Relax, hon. Don't forget there's no one in this place, or in any other rendezvous, that doesn't really hate Moss. Anyway,' she said, her voice tired and listless now, 'who knows if it was really you that did the clobbering? Moss's brat could be telling stories. Some of the bunch think the Horsemen finally caught up with Fatso. Who cares?' she cried. 'Who cares what happens so long as someone, anyone, starts pushing again?'

I studied the slumped addicts. 'This bunch are sick,' I said. 'And they are getting sicker. But they haven't been three days without drugs.'

'Hey, monk, where have you been cloistered?' Fay's face was stiff with surprise. 'Haven't you read the papers? Things are really popping, honey. Even that goofy reform clean-up has been knocked off page one by drug news.'

'Well, tell me. I haven't looked at a paper for three days.'

'Well, the heat's on, but good! I'll bet there's Horsemen undercovers in here right now. See, after Shadow told us service was staying off for a while everybody got real desperate. Last night, three drugstores and a doctor's suite were crashed open. Then, early this morning, it was, a guy and his girl sneaked into the Women's General on Tupper Street. They hit the jack-pot. They got out with all there was in the emergency cabinet.'

My God! I thought. Welch must be climbing the walls!

I got up, adjusted my topcoat, and said goodbye to Fay. But she hooked her hand under my arm, held on tightly. 'Wait, honey,' she said, as if struck by a sudden thought. 'You might be able to do all of us a little good. Why don't you look up that kid of Moss's and pump him? The kid really thinks you're quite the guy. He just might sing pretty-pretty and tell you exactly what's cooking in Moss's fat head.'

Shadow?

Thoughtfully, I walked back towards the West End. For the first time since the disastrous battle in Moss's house, I began to feel myself coming really alive. Fay's remark about Shadow kept nudging me like a friend trying to turn me in a new right direction—and the feeling of aliveness lingered to build into a small, warm area of comfort.

I stopped to telephone Welch from a street booth. The inspector listened without comment while I told him I'd stumbled on a completely new angle which I intended to put to work at once. This time, Welch didn't refer at all to my lack of official authority. That convinced me he was under serious pressure from higher up. To cement that conviction, he ran off to me in a blistering voice a long

217

list of burglaries and break-ins, mostly of wholesale drug supply-houses, that even Fay had not yet heard of.

Still an hour ahead of my date with Thorn, I went to an alcove in the La Salle Hotel lobby to enjoy a smoke.

In sudden, startling detachment, I became able to look down upon my entire case as if I were now standing apart, no longer involved in it.

I began to attack the basic problem—drug addiction. To attack it with fact and logic. First, I had to admit the un-happy truth that addicts, as such, are completely incurable. That was a big, shining fact. So long as drugs remained available, regardless of price or penalty, addicts would ob-tain and abuse them. Next, I had to admit that addiction is a progressive habit which leaps abruptly into compulsive need.

But what if there were no black-market drugs? What then? *What if addicts simply could not obtain drugs?* Is it possible psychologically, for a person to remain obsessed with a need for something that a person knows is unob-tainable? Will an addict, under that knowledge, and after being completely withdrawn, still retain a mental need? Will an addict retain that need *after the body has been released from its physical hunger for drugs?* Here was the vital question. The question that, while a black-market in drugs flourished, must remain unanswered.

But memory suddenly swirled me back and back. Before me stood a Korean Chinese officer. An enemy officer who had become addicted while smuggling opium to Canadian ranks and G-I's. Questioned after hovering close to hell during a cold-turkey cure, the imprisoned Korean had smiled. 'Opium?' he said. 'When it is no longer obtainable, one quickly forgets. Provided, of course, one is again physically well and strong.' His long eyes had slid to the barbed wire of the prison compound. 'There is no opium here,' he had shrugged. 'No, Captain. I no longer think about using opium.'

Granting that to be a normal reaction, my position became strikingly clear. I had become, in a sense, a symbol for freedom. Freedom for Helen, for Frankie, for Fay, for all others of the local lost battalion of drug addicts. Therefore, my problem and its only possible solution swung me directly back to Moss.

I stirred, quickened in my lobby chair with sudden energy. I blinked. I realized that while I'd been lost in thought my gaze had unconsciously held on a slender chain that suspened a chandelier over the lobby entrance; that each time the street door opened a blast of air swayed the chandelier, set the chain to quivering. It was a slender chain. Slender but strong. Like a chain of circumstances, a series of small, related facts, that met and formed into links that, joining, added up almost to a solution. I had so many loose links now. Actually, I needed only one more. Could it be possible that the last connecting link could be supplied, as Dream Street Fay had unwittingly led me to believe, by Moss's boy, the street waif, Shadow?

Shadow?

It was long after I went out to the street that I grew aware of the early afternoon all about me. I walked unhurriedly back along St. Catherine, then turned off down Windsor Street, past the dead garden of Dutch tulips on the square above the station.

Walking across the deserted square, its silence hung all about me. Except for a single person, I was alone. A familiar figure, ragged and square, sat twisted forward on one of the wooden benches.

My philosophical panhandler.

My eyes followed the man as he came off the bench in a fluid twist, moved towards me. His eyes were red-rimmed, bright from the wind, giving a Satanic turn to his dark, unshaven face. Reaching me, he thrust out the same grimy paw, paused like that, his fingers twitching. 'For Pernod and my glorious ruin.'

219

I handed him a dollar, staring at him speculatively.

He stood his ground. Clutching my dollar possessively, he bowed in a mockery of politeness. 'The Lord looks after the fall of every little sparrow,' he said in his familiar rote. 'He also helps those who help themselves. Be one of those who do, my friend. Be cautious-prudent. Be cautious-prudent.'

I reached out in sudden suspicion to grab at his arm but, surprisingly nimble, he evaded me. 'Wait!' I cried. 'Wait, I want to talk to you!'

Whirling, he strode off across the square, past the dead tulip beds. A wind whipped his loose, ragged coat—and that wind carried back to me a sound I was beginning to dislike. A low, soft chuckle.

I shivered and I didn't know whether I shivered from the wind or because of a sense of uneasiness left from this crazy, recurring scene in which I had again unexpectedly played a part.

I stood pondering it all over a cup of coffee in the lobby at Windsor Station until, at five, I caught a taxi at the lower-street entrance and was on my way to Louis's.

I walked down the bar to the end booth and said hello to Thorn. 'I saw your car outside,' I said. 'That little M.G. is hard to miss. As soon as I saw it, I felt sorry about all the minutes with you I've lost by not getting here sooner.'

Before Thorn could reply, Louis was at the table. He made bright, tinkling noises with ice and bottles.

Finally I was alone with Thorn.

I got cigarettes going. 'You said on the telephone you had something important for me,' I said, suggestively.

Thorn's expression changed abruptly. So abruptly it frightened me. Panic leaped into her eyes and she ran a distracted hand through her hair. 'It's about Helen, of course,' she said. 'Something has gone wrong recently. Terribly wrong. Something that must have frightened her half out of her wits. Max—oh Lord, Max! she's really fixed it this time. I found out yesterday she's been going to see that doctor friend of mine. The one I told you about.'

'She's been bothering him for heroin injections?'

'No. Worse than that. At first, she simply asked him for a prescription for sedatives. Then later she went again to ask for a morphine solution. Both times, he gave her what she wanted. He said he hated to, but that he realized she is an addict and extremely ill. He says he felt disturbed because he was unable to do anything that might really help her. Then—well, the situation got much worse, Max. In fact, dangerous.

'She didn't bother my friend too much. I don't think he would have minded that. What happened is that when he was called out of his office for a minute during her last visit, she stole one of his prescription forms. A blank one. Last night, she filled it in and forged his signature to it and took it to a drugstore. She pretended to be his nurse and bought a huge supply of drugs.'

I felt a quick, hot rush of blood to my face. 'Oh, my God!' I cried. 'Well, that ties it. It ties it for sure if a fraudulent purchase report is made. Do you know if either the druggist or your doctor friend notified the R.C.M.P.? Or the City Police?'

'No, Max. Neither did. As I told you, the doctor is a fine person, kind and very considerate. He told me that shortly after Helen left the drugstore the druggist became suspicious of the signature on the prescription form, and telephoned him. Well, he lied to the druggist. He told him he had cut his finger on a scalpel and was having difficulty writing. That the signature was his.'

'Thank God the man was alert enough to realize what had happened. And that he's human enough to protect someone helpless.' I expelled a long, caught breath.

'He told me he realized as soon as Helen left his office that she had stolen the form,' Thorn said. 'It was the last one on his pad and he missed it when he went to write a prescription for a woman who had come in with a sick baby.'

'Helen's desperate, desperate,' I said, and told Thorn: 'There's a drug panic on. It's a difficult thing to explain to a non-addict. But it's a terrible thing. Not nice to talk about.'

'It seems there are no bounds now to what she will do,' Thorn said sadly. 'None at all.'

'The situation's getting too rough for her, Thorn. She must have known—she did know—that form would be missed. She's desperate, and I . . . oh, damn it all, I'm still not quite ready to set this thing up the way I have to set it up to end it.'

Thorn began speaking. Then her voice twisted with futility and drifted away.

'Look, Thorn,' I said grimly, 'I want you to know I've plans for Helen. Plans to force her into making try at breaking her habit. The whole thing will be a gamble,' I admitted. 'A sort of psychological shock-treatment. I've had it in mind for Helen for a long time. The trouble is, it's so extreme it might even be the end of her. Just the same, I intend to convince your father to let me try it the minute the main issue of my case is on its way to being settled.'

No questions. Not even the ones I had expected. Instead, Thorn made a noticeable effort, and smiled. 'Here I am, doing everything I promised myself not to do,' she said. 'Letting my concern for Helen take selfish precedence. Forgive me, Max, please do.'

'Forgiven!' I smiled. 'And to prove it I'll take the evening off if you'll have dinner with me at Café Martin.'

It was long past midnight when I walked Thorn up the stone steps and across the flagged terrace fronting her home. The silence of the huge, bulking old house fell all around us. I tilted her chin, kissed her. It started gently, then she swayed against me. There was an instant when our bodies fused, joined in a quick, upward, blinding spiral of desire then, like a phantom, the dread image of Helen thrust itself between us. Thorn pushed me with both her hands and turned her head aside and said with something like shock, 'Oh, no, Max! Oh, no, not now.'

'That was a mistake,' I said, stepping guiltily back. 'A—a thing that rushed up on me too suddenly.'

Fumbling with the catch of her handbag, Thorn moved to the door. She got it open, and I heard a soft sigh. She came close again and her lips reached softly to mine. 'Good night, Max. And be careful, please. Now, more than ever. You see, it rushed up on me, too. A long time ago. After I'd known you only a short while.'

22

After parking Thorn's M.G. in the Ashton garage, I began walking.

The snow fell heavily. As I walked, my footsteps struck silently on the sidewalk, and the sounds of passing traffic came muffled from behind the thick white snow curtain. In this quiet world, there existed no earth or sky, only snow slanting from the wind. The white hush was a solemn thing, like the moment of benediction in a church.

At lower Park Avenue, the Cross on the mountain appeared over my shoulder. I tramped on down to St. Catherine, then east through dancing mists of snow sparkle that exploded about the crowns of street-lights all the way to the addicts' rendezvous.

Inside, I stopped to brush off my coat.

I found Shadow.

The boy sat forlornly at a table close to the food-bar. His thin, dirt-streaked face was sunk miserably into his hands. I stepped down the aisle, stood over him. I tapped his slumped shoulder. As his head snapped up, his eyes widened and brightened with recognition. 'Monsieur!' he cried. 'Ah-h—by gosh! Monsieur the beeg fighter! Me, I have been wonder where you are.' Obvious astonishment crept into his eyes as he eyed my clothes. '*Mon Dieu!*'

223

he ejaculated. 'But Monsieur has the look of the swell. The beegshot that live on the mountain. Such clothes! Monsieur stole them, no? Me, someday I also will be the beeg thief. Me, I will steal everything!'

In spite of his cocky front, Shadow looked tired and hungry. Only a child, right now there was much of the child in his eyes, in the grimy channels tears had left on his cheeks. I went to the food-bar, brought a wedge of cake and a glass of milk back to the table.

Sitting down beside the boy, I pointed to the cake. 'Eat it, little man. And drink the milk!'

Shadow bent greedily. He went at the cake like an animal, cramming huge pieces into his mouth.

'Whoa, now, take this easy,' I cautioned him. 'What's the big rush? Worried your boss will whistle for you before you get it all eaten?'

Shadow's eyes flashed, hate-filled. 'Let him whistle all he like!' he cried, his handful of cake stalled in mid air. 'Moss he is *sale cochon*—dirty peeg. Me, I hate him. Tonight, he come home from the hospital and at once he beat me.' Jumping to his feet, Shadow began attacking his buttons furiously. 'Look, Monsieur. See, I show you the mark.'

'Good God! do up your pants,' I protested, alarmed. 'Just tell me what happened. That's all that's needed. And tell it quietly.'

Shadow stabbed at a crumb with a wetted finger. 'Monsieur Moss,' he explained petulantly, 'he is veree mad that I don't give him the help when you make the beeg fight. So he take his whip and he beat me.' The boy stuck his chin out defiantly. 'So now I hurt veree beeg on my—where I sit. But I am glad I don't help. I am glad, yes. Monsieur, you were wonderful to behold. *Mon Dieu,* such force! Such courage! Bam! Bam! Bam! One-two-three, they fall.' He stared up at me, his expression worshipful. 'Ah-h-h-h!' he glowed. 'Three, you take. Three! It was truly wonderful.'

224

I said, 'Look, pardner, let's keep it down. Just finish your story.'

'Feenish? But that is all.' The boy's eyebrows popped up. 'Tonight, the bodyguard breeng Monsieur Moss home. He is still veree painful. Veree—what you call it?—tender? Pah! this beeg cow, it is better you kill him. Me, I am with him since I am eleven. Tonight, after three year, he poosh me out in the street!'

Sighing, Shadow let his head sink forlornly to his chest. Certainly, it was very touching. Except that one of the little monster's eyes remained slyly on me, studying my reaction to his story. While I considered the situation carefully he waited, stabbing hungrily at crumbs.

Finally, making a decision, I told the boy to go out to the street, to walk ten blocks west and up one. He was to wait there ten minutes. I would pick him up in a taxi. He looked at me with a half-frightened, incredulous stare, but when I gave him a slight push he got up at once and started for the street.

For a moment, I waited and then went out the door.

At the first corner, I saw a taxi coming. Hailing it, I gave the driver directions. A moment later, I picked up Shadow.

The minute I had the boy safely inside my living-room, I shot the first question at him. 'You've been living with Moss three years. How did that start?'

Shadow's eyes widened, as though my question were ridiculous.

'But, Monsieur,' he protested. 'What am I to do? Me, I have no one. No mamma, no papa. I am on the street.' Spreading his grimy palms, he grinned hugely. 'You understand, Monsieur? No one want me, only Moss. I am the accident. No momma, no poppa. Me Shadow, I am a mistake.'

'Why do they call you Shadow?'

'Because when Monsieur Moss find me I swipe everything. I am in the store and gone like the shadow. He call me Shadow.'

'All right, Shadow,' I said grimly, reaching for his ear and feeling completely out of my environment, 'You may be an accident, but you're a darned dirty one. Get out of those filthy clothes and into the bathroom for a shower. Scrape all that muck off your face and out of your hair. When you've done that, you and I will talk. Now, go along.'

Shadow's lips snapped tightly together. 'I do not go!' he wailed, planting himself before me like an outraged midget. 'No! It is too much. Monsieur wishes to make of me the sissy. Take the bath! Takes off the clothes! This I will not do!'

But when I raised my hand threateningly over his bottom, he scowled uneasily then trotted off fairly happily to the bathroom.

After ten minutes, the bathroom door slammed.

Shadow barefooted across the kitchen. His face shone, his hair hung down straight and uncombed. He was barely recognizable. He looked like anybody's boy sneaking down for an early peek at Christmas presents.

I cast a surprised glance at him, said in what I hoped was a severe, parental tone, 'Now sit down, I'm going to as you a few questions.'

Perching on a stool, Shadow hooked his feet under the high rung. Eyes bright and attentive, he said simply, '*Eh bien!* What does Monsieur like to know?'

'Everything!' I said, leaning forward. 'Everything you know about Moss. How he connects for his drugs. Whom he connects with. When he connects. You may start with *how.*'

Shadow's eyes grew incredulous. Questions trembled from his lips. 'But Monsieur will be my protector? If I make the stool pigeon you will not send me away? You will not poosh me out on the street? Me, I have no fear if I stay with you. But if Monsieur the Back Man catch me—' the boy's voice became flat, utterly convinced '—I am sure he will kill me. I think perhaps he give me to his rats.'

I assured Shadow he would be protected; a promise that left me with considerable qualms. The amazing thing was, the boy didn't question my motive. He showed no interest at all at this point in why I wanted information. His mind obviously on the beating he'd had from Moss, Shadow simply switched from Moss's side to mine. 'Yes,' I repeated. 'I promise you that. You'll be taken care of, Shadow.'

'*Bon!*' the boy cried. 'Good! Then I will tell you everything of Monsieur Moss.'

A nightmare story poured from the boy's lips. He drew vivid word pictures of drug drop after drug drop, detailed successful trafficking coup after successful trafficking coup until, as clearly as if staring at a great screen, I saw the open, turning machinery of the drug ring. Before my eyes moved the grotesque figure of the Back Man, Moss, pressing his human buttons, keeping in motion the ingenious mechanism of his evil trafficking operation.

Shadow explained delightedly how Moss's original contact system had been his most enduring and successful, yet most simple. Moss had often boasted, the boy said, of confounding the police with this ruse. A ruse which had entailed employing an expensive West End brothel, flourishing at that time under police tolerance, as a heroin drop.

As always, to mystify and mislead had been Moss's cardinal principle. He had succeeded admirably at that by beginning a confusing series of daily visits to the brothel long before each date of rendezvous with his supplier was actually set. Then, once he was completely satisfied the area was clear, that there was no Mountie stake-out, or inside spot, Moss would advise his supplier when to visit the brothel as a casual client. At a pre-set minute during that visit, his supplier would deposit in a clothes-basket in one of the brothel washrooms a package containing uncut heroin. Seconds later, Moss would enter the washroom and

227

pick up the heroin package, leaving in its place an envelope containing currency payment. The two principals, Moss and his mysterious supplier, were never seen together—never did they enter or leave the establishment at the same time. 'This trick it was veree clever,' Shadow said, seriously. 'Only, the lousy cops they spoil it. They put the padlock on the place of the girls.'

What Shadow meant was, a vice clean-up had at last resulted in police pressure being exerted on the premises and Moss had been forced to abandon that drop scheme. But the Back Man had wasted no time devising a new, equally devious method of connecting for his priceless poppy-dust.

His substitute method, according to Shadow's description, had also been ingenious and elaborate. It was also, Shadow said, when Moss first began using him, then a boy of twelve. Shadow became end-man in a four-way-switch the essence of which was timing. Moss began making contact with his anonymous suppliers on the commuter trains that service the suburban towns spreading like a string of pearls along the thirty-mile Lakeshore area west of the city. Contact was made in the crowded aisles as the locals chuff-chuffed erratically along between stations.

Moss's number-one man and the supplier would first covertly exchange money for drugs. The priceless parcel would then be slipped immediately on to Moss's man number-two, who would become instantly lost among the commuters. Number-two would jump off the train as it was pulling away from the next stop, exactly on schedule to catch a city-bound bus. During that short bus ride, the parcel would again change hands—going on this time to man number-three. Number-three would carry the parcel on to a city bus terminal, and there be met by Shadow. Shadow, after quickly becoming lost in a succession of crowds, would hurry the heroin on to the safely waiting Back Man. Identical stations or time schedules were never

228

used twice. Never, Shadow said, with the bare exception of himself, did Moss ever use the same personnel a second time.

To Shadow, apparently, drug trafficking was a fun-filled game.

'You're doing great, son,' I said, encouragingly. 'But tell me, did you ever get near enough to the first switch to get a look at any of Moss's suppliers?'

'Never! No, never did I see that. But it would not help because it is not twice the same man. Many time, I hear Monsieur Moss say: I wish I know who they send this time. Monsieur Moss always worry like hell the next man will not be enough careful.'

I nodded, thoughtfully. 'Well, that takes care of the train trick. So what happened after Moss gave that one up? How did he connect next?'

Moss, Shadow said, had become increasingly cautious, and suspicious. No one was ever really trusted by the Back Man. He checked and re-checked each small detail with scrupulous care. He invariably chain-connected, and the precautions he took throughout the chain and particularly at his end were practically unbeatable. Shadow explained, with evident relish, how in the last year Moss had outfoxed City police and Mountie Narcotic Squads with a dozen different ruses.

The hard, white powder, worth thousands of times its weight in gold, had been tossed to him from passing cars, dropped into his eager grasp from suddenly opened windows as he edged cautiously into position. He had waited in stiff wintry winds, sweated under the blazing summer sun, hunched in wet misery against autumn's rain and sleet waiting for the green light, the green light that cleared the way for his possession of the white dust that gave him wealth, and an awesome, sadistic power.

Dawn was reaching into my living-room at the close of Shadow's fantastic story. Switching off lights, I put on a pot of fresh coffee. Shadow didn't move. His eyes were still intense, but dark-ringed now, giving him an odd, schoolboy-allowed-to-stay-up-late look. Another question, the big one, then I would have to decide what to do with him.

I said abruptly, 'All right, Shadow. So far, you've done fine. Now, what about the next delivery?'

Shadow yawned; then he gave me a frank, intelligent look. 'If you wish to jump Moss when he connect for his next beeg supply, you have the good chance,' he said. 'This time, Moss has no one to make the chain. No Leger. No me. And the other connection they are too sick with the panic. The chain, she is bust. Now Moss must go alone to make the pick-up.'

'Yes. You've made that clear. But when?'

'*Qui sait?*' Shadow spread his hands. 'Who knows? perhaps today Moss connects—perhaps tomorrow. This is something I cannot tell.' He blinked sleepily, then smiled slyly, showing interest in causes for the first time. 'You will swipe from Moss the drugs?' he demanded. 'You will rob him? You are the highjacker, no?'

'I am the highjacker, no!'

I got up to pour two cups of coffee. The brew was strong, black. 'Do you usually drink this stuff?' I inquired.

The boy laughed. 'Pah! Me, I am not the sissy. I drink like the fish. Moss, he give me much wine—sometime whisky. But for you,' he said, making an amiable concession, 'I will drink the coffee.'

I was caught with a pint-sized monster. A four-and-one-half-foot monster who was regarding me with whole-souled confidence. 'Now, listen here,' I told him sharply, 'for the next few days at least I'm going to keep you right here with me. But I'm warning you, you'd better start behaving right now. If not, I'll paddle your bottom until you do.'

The boy's expression was innocent and clear as he turned to look through the kitchen door into my living-room. 'Monsieur must be one damn clever crook,' he said appreciatively, 'to have such a place for living.'

'Never mind what I am,' I retorted. 'Just remember what I said about behaving.'

'Behave!' the boy cried, his voice piping and indignant. 'But of a certainty! Monsieur is my protector, no? Then I am for you, on your side. Not even do I care for what you ask the question about Monsieur Moss. *Voila.*' He clapped his hands excitedly. 'There! I am for you. While you are gone to make your racket I take again the bath. Twice in the same day. How about that!'

Something had to be done at once about the boy. It simply wasn't safe to leave him alone.

I finally called Thorn, of course. Shadow listened, his eyes circles, while I explained that I needed her and asked could she please come at once. When I put down the phone, Shadow was glaring at me. He said in a high, indignant voice, 'Pah! Me, I do not like this. Monsieur did not tell me he has a woman!'

'Look here, you little terror,' I said testily, 'a lady, a very nice lady, is coming to spend the day with you. I expect you to be polite and not ask questions and do exactly as you are told. The nice lady will take you out to buy some decent clothes. Choose what you like—but, whatever else you do, try not to disgrace her. Behave!'

Slowly, resentment washed from Shadow's eyes. In its place, came a bright sparkle of incredulity. It took another few seconds for him to really understand the meaning of what I had said, then he blurted out: 'You do this for me? You buy me the new clothes? Monsieur, me Shadow, I will be so damn good I don't even try to make the leetle shoplift in the store where your woman take me.'

Not long after, Thorn stood in the centre of my living-room, her legs spread, her two hands thrust deep into the pockets of her cashmere wrap-around. She smiled attractively at Shadow. 'Like sports cars?' she demanded. The boy shifted from one foot to the other, plainly puzzled. 'Little fast ones,' Thorn explained. 'You know, whom! a mile a minute. That's the sort of car we are going to go shopping in.'

Shadow stood motionless, undecided. He looked from Thorn to me.

'Well, it's a pretty good car,' I said, with an off-hand gesture. 'It's fast. Real fast.'

Shadow broke into an excited laugh. He was still laughing when he was taken by the hand and led out the door.

I went into my bedroom. In the bottom drawer of my dresser, a Police Positive .38 lay in its slip-pocket shoulder holster. The weight of the pistol sagged in my hand. I worked the trigger rapidly, a half-dozen times. Then I fed a clip into the pistol and pumped one shell into the breech. Putting on the light shoulder harness, I hurried outside in time to hail an empty passing cab.

The cab took me to Place d'Armes. I paid off the driver, and walked a block to my office. I pushed aside a week's accumulation of unimportant mail and reached for my telephone. After a single ring, I was clicked through to the private line of another private operative. 'Work for you, Paul,' I said. 'See how fast you can make it over to my office.'

I broke the connection and sat with the silence around me swallowing my words. I began thinking about Paul.

Paul Dupas had worked for me before now. He had left me with a large respect for his ability. Dupas was French-Canadian, utterly reliably, hard-hitting, and a tireless worker with a few fancy tricks of his own. Born in Montreal, this tall, rangy Dupas knew every twisting street and dead-end alley in the city. He had complete, facile command of both languages. But he possessed another, greater asset; an asset I now intended to use to advantage in my altered case. Dupas read lips. The science was his hobby and his consuming passion.

Paul came in and stood for a moment in the burst

of light that came with the opening of the door. He was carrying his famous doctor's satchel. He moved forward and we shook hands with me grinning at the bulging black bag.

'The Maxwell Dent passion for long bull-sessions is no secret to me,' Paul retorted, grinning broadly. 'So I prepared myself.' Zipping open his black satchel, he took out and thumped emphatically on my desk three quart bottles of ale. 'Ike, Mike, and Spike,' he said with another grin.

Paul opened and poured, handed me a glass. He blew off a beautiful puff of froth, drank, belched politely, then raised a quizzical left eyebrow.

'You have a case, Max?'

I went over it all in precise detail. I omitted only my client's name. At the close of my long story of Montreal drug trafficking, Paul straightened, sucking air into his lungs and swallowing fast. 'Son of a cockeyed gun!' he said, and then he let out a long speculative whistle. 'This one is really weird, Max. Drugs, a society-girl addict, a fat blimp or a trafficker with a yen for Italian pistols, wow!'

'Consider a few other queer sides,' I suggested wryly. 'Like a boy held for three years in what practically amounts to slavery. Scores of addicts filled with fear and agony in rendezvous across the city. Staged animal battles. Mystery and intrigue and a frightful case of out-and-out surgical butchery.'

Paul divided the last of his third bottle of ale, then leaned back. 'One thing for certain,' he said, and sipped thoughtfully. 'After all you've been through, you'll never forgive yourself if you're not in on the finish of this—and what a finish that will be!'

'That's what we're going to talk about now,' I said. 'The finish!'

'Starting perhaps with a wire tap on Moss's phone,' Paul said suggestively.

233

'No. Not a wire tap, Paul,' I said, shaking my head decisively. 'No electronics with Moss. No doubt we could manage to get a line and wire recorder on him without too much trouble. We could certainly slip on a sensitized outside wall mike that would pick up house conversations. Either way, what would we get? Professionals of Moss's caliber don't talk shop carelessly. I have another plan, Paul.'

'Yes?' he said mildly.

'You know the tactic most operatives describe as the fate worse than death?'

'Stake-out!'

'Exactly!' I replied. 'A stake-out and round-the-clock tail backed by R.C.M.P. support.'

Paul lit a cigarette and, when he had his light, tucked one foot under the other and blew smoke at the ceiling; then he eyed me directly, his narrow face otherwise expressionless. 'My God!' he said bluntly. 'This is all mighty big-league for me, Max. I've never been in one quite like this before.'

'The Mounties will cover us, probably with a single man, every time we tail Moss,' I explained. 'Whichever of us is on stake-out watch will alert Welch, using a runner, immediately our tail starts off. If there is even the slightest likelihood of immediate trafficking action, the cover Welch sends out will re-alert him. He will then beam in an entire squad. In the meantime, of course, whichever one of us is on Moss stays on him. Ready to zero in the Narcotic Squad as soon as they approach the trafficking scene.'

'This cover man, will he be working right with us?'

'Not with us, but supporting us. Welch will shoot out the cover every time we notify him Moss is on the move.'

'Then, once our stake-out is set,' Paul said, 'we'll actually be using a three-way contact system. Between whichever of us is on watch, our runner, and Welch. We'll need extra men, then. If we're going on round-the-clock.'

'I've already worked out the contact system,' I said.

234

'I'll map it for you in a minute. First, for our extra men, I want you to try to get those two we used on that showgirl shake-down affair. They were good—fast and tough. And I don't imagine they'll balk at twelve-hour duty.'

Paul's nod was tacit agreement. 'Now,' I said, 'watch this carefully and start memorizing.' Taking out a blank sheet of paper, I sketched a plan of the inside of the old building I had chosen as our stake-out site. 'This window—' I explained, marking an x 'looks out directly on Moss's house. It's where whichever of us two is on watch will sit.' I drew an arrow, then marked another x. 'These stairs lead to the street floor. There's a front door, which naturally we can't use. There is also'—I drew another arrow, another x—'this rear door which leads out to a well-paved alley. Whenever you or I start out on tail, leaving here'—I underlined the window x—'we use these stairs and on our way down we send off our waiting runner to telephone Welch that we've gone off on tail.'

'Hold on a minute, Max,' Paul protested. This is all very fine. But it has a great big hole in it. We notify Welch's office, they shoot out the cover. Good. But how does that cover make contact with our tail? How the devil does he find out where we've got to?'

'That's the risk element,' I admitted. 'But it's not nearly as big a risk as it seems. Think a little. Certainly, which-ever of us is tailing will have opportunities along the way to contact Welch and give him locations. The cover will start from here and pick up our changing locations by phone. Don't worry about time. Remember this: Moss won't simply meet his supplier and exchange money for drugs on the spot. Not if I know traffickers, and I do. If the trafficking is accomplished at the first meeting of the two, which is very improbable, there'll be but plenty of pussyfooting around first. Those two will stall until they believe for sure they're well in the clear.'

'I can see that. Okay, it fits. There will be time for

organizing. Then the rest is up to Welch and his squad.'

'Welch, his squad—and Maxwell Dent.'

'*And* Maxwell Dent,' Paul approved. 'No one, not even the typical rule-bound R.C.M.P. inspector, would expect you to step aside at the final moment. Not now, Max.'

I said that Welch wasn't unreasonable, only filled with Mountie caution and long-drawn patience. I added that the way to break that down was to confront him with a workable situation, and that was what we were about to attempt.

For a last time, we went over the signal system. Paul had it down pat. I wrote him a checque for expenses, warned him to be ready with warm clothes.

As soon as he had gone, I telephoned Welch.

The inspector listened me out, then asked a series of pertinent questions and criticized the risk element in that stiffly official way of his. He huffed and puffed a lot, but he agreed to keep his squad standing alert. He concluded by adding thoughtfully, 'And this man Dupas reads lips, eh? Now, there's an approach the force might well give a little attention to.'

I could feel myself grinning a little, slyly, stiffly, and then, as if aware of my smugness, the inspector hit me with a bit of unexpected news that stole the smugness right out from under me. He said crisply, 'The girl, Fay, the one who first gave you information on Moss—she won't be available for a while. Probably not for quite a while. She being an addict, we are notified each time she's picked up by the City police. They have her now. She was arrested yesterday for shoplifting.'

On that, the inspector hung up. Easing my shoulder holster into position, I hurried out to pick up my car.

23

The vacant building from which I had watched Phil being carried into Moss's house looked gloomy, deserted; a lookout made to order.

I walked a full block away to a small café. Wedging into a telephone booth that smelled like the inside of a wine barrel, I called Paul and told him I was starting the stake-out. 'Okay, I'll be there promptly at six to relieve you,' Paul promised. I broke the connection, jiggled the receiver hook a bit until I heard a new dial tone, then called my own number.

My apartment phone rang unanswered.

I circled back through narrow streets and down the paved alley to the rear of the look-out house. I booted open a door, and stepped inside.

The lower floor lay heaped with debris and dirt. I climbed worn, rickety stairs that creaked with age and sent sharp warnings ahead. On the second floor, cobwebs were dirty veils in every corner. Papers were strewn and a split mattress leaned against a peeling wall. The cold air stank.

I searched around until I found a backless chair. I wiped it off with a cloth I took from my pocket. Puffs of dust rose and sparkled in bright, golden sun rays that slanted in through cracked windows. From somewhere deep in the bowels of the old ruin came a furtive scampering of tiny feet that reminded me of Moss's animal room.

A shudder ran through me.

Sitting down, I snuggled deeper into my coat, seeking, animal-like, for warmth.

I began the first watch.

The long afternoon hours marched past. The house dimmed slowly as day waned and early night crept softly inside. Bitter cold washed through cracked walls. I grew stiff and utterly miserable. Across the street in Moss's house lights, blinked on. Pantomime was staged before my tiring eyes as the Back Man's massive shadow flung itself upon his drawn window shade and made huge, expressive gestures to an unseen companion. Then the silhouette lengthened, faded, and finally disappeared.

The wind mounted and blew away silence. It swept through the old house like a giant sighing in his sleep. The entire building groaned and cracked. And there were other and closer sounds; the window rattled and shook and not far away the dry slapping of an enormous branch against the side of the house was like the distant slamming of an old screen door.

I sat quite still in the dusk, with nothing in my mind save Moss's house and the natural sounds around me. Time flowed on. Under my staring eyes, the doors, the two porches across the way wavered, swam and blurred, disappeared, sucked into the brick walls that held them.

I prepared myself mentally, getting ready for the sound of a whistle. Finally, it came, soft and low.

Paul slid out of the shadows. His face was a white blur. His familiar satchel was tucked under his arm.

He gave me a long distasteful look. 'Max, you sure can pick 'em,' he muttered critically. 'This is the crummiest, dirtiest, shabbiest building I've ever seen.'

I tried to press the ache from my eyes with my fingertips. 'It's safe, very,' I retorted, jerking stiffly to my feet. 'It's good, too. Just as good as if we were Bell-tented on Moss's front porch. No action yet, but when it breaks we'll be on top of it like a blanket. Where's our runner? I haven't heard a peep out of him.'

Paul tapped the floor with his foot. 'Below. Near the bottom of the stairs. Ready to break fast for a phone. He was there less than two minutes after you first sat down on that chair. You'll see him on your way out.' Paul peered at the floor, scuffed his feet over the frost and exclaimed softly: 'Hey! No cigarette butts. Didn't you smoke?'

'No. But if *you* smoke, put the butts in your pocket. Fresh cigarette butts are the first thing anyone suspicious will look for.'

Paul reached for the backless chair and pulled it towards him. He sat down stiffly. He said aggressively, 'Same goes for ale caps, too? All right, a simple precaution. Beat it now, Max. You look like an icicle.'

Downstairs, our runner waved to me from behind a curtain of shadows. I moved out into the alley, now a long tunnel of darkness. The sight of my car, standing alone and oddly vulnerable, made me pause, and I suddenly felt an odd stirring inside me that was apprehensive and uncertain. Shaking it off, a little impatient with myself now, I got into the car and drove hurriedly home.

Thorn and Shadow were listening to records. On the sofa, beside them, was a pile of cardboard boxes of all sizes.

'I see the shopping expedition came off all right,' I said. 'But why is Shadow still wearing his old clothes?'

'Well, he just wouldn't change,' Thorn smiled. 'He insisted on waiting until you came home to say it's all right.'

'But yes! Of course. Only Monsieur can tell Shadow what he must do.' The boy jumped to his feet. He puffed up like a banty-cock. 'And at the store, he said proudly, 'I do not make the disgrace for Ma'mselle or for you. *Non!* Me, I do not make even the small shoplift. I pinch nothing at all.'

'Shadow really behaved well.' Thorn put in. 'Imagine! not a single question out of him. Only if he could know your name. I said he could call you Max.' Getting up, her shoulders began a suspicious shaking. 'Of course,' she added, her voice catching, 'when we were driving along Sherbrooke Street he *did* spit at two policemen.'

'He *what?*'

Shadow's face fell. 'Ma'mselle was not veree happy about that,' he said sadly.

Thorn loaded Shadow with cardboard boxes. She said, 'Max, you look simply terrible. Let me get you a drink. Shadow simply must go to bed. He's been blinking for hours. He'll be staying here, won't he?'

I nodded. 'At least, until I get a few things settled.' I

ruffled the boy's hair a bit, pushed him off towards my single bedroom. 'Get along, Shadow,' I said. 'Get into bed. When you wake up tomorrow, you can show me how smart you look in your new clothes.'

The boy's face altered completely in a sudden, shy, warm smile. 'I am permitted to sleep in Monsieur's bed?' he asked incredulously. 'Surely such a thing is not possible?'

I gave him an extra push. 'I have to stay out here near the phone,' I said. Then a sudden, alarming thought struck me. 'How did you two manage to get back in here?' I demanded. 'The door was locked and I forgot to give you a key.'

Shadow laughed, his own man again. 'It was nothing' he said with elaborate modesty. 'With the small piece of celluloid I make the housebreak. Many time, I make the break-in with the celluloid. This door? Pouff! It was nothing at all!'

'We were inside so quickly,' Thorn said, her face too-serious, 'I thought Shadow did have a key. Yes, it was nothing really.'

'Nothing!' Shadow insisted, deprecatingly. 'Nothing at all!'

'Good night, Shadow!' I said ominously.

The bedroom door closed over Shadow's soft laugh.

Thorn fanned out her dress and leaned back on the sofa. A note of repressed anxiety crept into her voice. 'You're getting very close now. You *are*, aren't you, Max?'

'Close, yes. Very close.'

She shivered. 'How close, Max?'

I couldn't answer. She had come forward and, suddenly, her lovely face was between my hands. Her hands touched my back and held there as my shoulder turned her body to mine. My lips lingered over hers.

She stirred, and again, we fell apart. She drew in her breath sharply, gaspingly, like an exhausted swimmer. Her face was pale.

'Some day,' she said unsteadily, 'A moment will come when all this trouble is over. We'll be together then, Max. I know we will.'

I got up, moved to the arm of the sofa.

'A nice man,' Thorn said softly. 'Yes, you're a nice man, Max Dent.'

'No, not nice,' I said, shaking my head. 'Just trying to be intelligent. Careful not to spoil something that I know will soon be wonderfully good.'

'Then perhaps we had better talk about your case.'

I cleared my throat, said, 'How close I actually am depends on a lot of things that sound too fantastic to be real. The man I want must make a move soon. *The* move. Then someone—his side or mine—will make a mistake. If the mistake isn't ours, the ring will be smashed and the illegal drug supply cut off.'

Thorn looked at me solemnly. 'That's when you'll take that gamble you spoke of. The gamble with Helen. Isn't that so?'

I nodded. I didn't want to tell Thorn my exact plans for Helen. I didn't even analyse my reasons why not—I simply didn't want to. 'About Shadow,' I said, instead. 'Take him places, show him things, if you like. But don't let him out of your sight a single moment. And be sure not to take him east of downtown area. Not anywhere beyond Phillip's Square.'

I took her down to the street, then went back upstairs and called the Cedar Avenue nursing home.

Miss Kelly's glare penetrated miles of wire. 'Phil,' she replied sharply to my question, 'is no longer in this home. When I didn't hear one word from you, Max Dent, I managed to persuade Phil to transfer to the Royal Victoria. He's in one of the wards there. They'll be trying bone surgery.' She paused significantly. 'The ward doctor has taken a keen interest in Phil,' she added. 'Busy as they are, that's a rare bit of luck. Phil will be getting help now that I couldn't possibly give him.'

I asked her to explain.

She said starchily, 'A new drug, methadon, is being used successfully as a reduction treatment. Taken in fifteen milligram doses, it eliminates pain. The patient starts regaining strength—moral and physical strength—almost at once. Phil has agreed to try that treatment. It's just possible he might be prevailed upon to try for complete readjustment.' Miss Kelly's voice grew into a loud crackle in my ear. 'Now you listen to me. You get up there to the ward to visit Phil. That boy needs all the encouragement he can get. Go in the day-time. At night, he'll be under sedation.'

Before I could thank her, the old white bear slammed down the receiver.

I made a makeshift bed on the sofa. Sleep came instantly, lasted the night through.

I woke up barely in time to let in Thorn.

When I left the apartment, she was sitting in the breakfast nook talking to Shadow about sports cars.

24 Paul was standing to one side of the look-out window, rubbing the back of his neck slowly, as if the rubbing believed an aching tension. He shuddered slightly. 'These are a bloody cagey lot, these trafficking characters,' he said bluntly. 'I don't think Moss has any notion he's staked out, but he made a play last night that could have suckered a waiting tail into betraying himself.'

'All right, let's have it,' I snapped. 'What happened?'

'He pulled the empty taxi trick. You know the one. I was scared spitless. I shot the runner out fast to call Welch. It was three in the morning then and I was afraid it would take the Mounties too long. But man! did they move. About an hour later, around four, a Mountie plain-clothes tapped me on the shoulder while I was sitting here at the window. I didn't even hear the guy come in and let me tell you I jumped some.'

'So?'

'So the Mountie told me that they'd picked up the taxi-driver after he'd gone back to Moss's to be paid for his empty run. The cabbie was one puzzled guy. He said he's been given two addresses to call at for parcels. He was told to do that first, then go to the Walton's restaurant on St. Catherine and buy a carton of Buckinghams.'

'The two addresses were duds,' I said.

'Vacant lots. One in the north end. The other way down east near the Imperial Oil refineries. After he drew a blank on the first call, the driver got a little worried but went on to the second just the same. He drew a blank there, too, of course, and he told the Mounties the first thing he thought of was that he was being set up for a way-bill mugging. But when he made it back to downtown he figured it could all be just a dizzy goof-up. So instead of reporting to his dispatcher as he'd intended to do, he bought the cigarettes at Walton's and went back to try and collect his meter fare.'

'Which he did.'

'With a fat tip. And a big smile from Moss.'

'Did the driver notice that he was being spot covered?'

'No. But about five minutes after he left Moss's after collecting his fare, a Buick sedan turned up. It stayed parked down the street for a few minutes, lights off and the motor running. Then two guys got out. Typical goons. They locked the Buick, then went into Moss's house by the lower porch door.'

'Moss's tail-men,' I said. 'Going back to share the laugh. They went ahead of the cab to each of the phony addresses, waited hidden near by watching to see if there would be a Mountie tail on the cab. They probably covered the cab back to Walton's too. As well, Moss no doubt had someone planted in Walton's watching to see if the cigarette girl would be Mountie-checked after the taxi-driver left with the cigarette carton.'

'At three a.m.!' Paul snorted. '*Brother!* these guys sure use some fancy tactics.'

'Moss is an old hand at this game,' I reminded Paul grimly. 'He is preparing now for what he sees as another successful drop. He's trying to sucker the Mounties into revealing if they have him covered at the moment. That's why I told Welch to stay completely off any action unless it is led by Moss himself. Well,' I sighed, and waved at the house across the street, 'it's one for our side, anyway. What Moss *has* done is warn *us* he's getting ready.'

My words seemed to sober Paul. 'He sure goes to a lot of trouble to rig an elaborate sucker scheme, though . . .' he muttered.

'He'll go to still more trouble for what he has at stake,' I said. I floorpushed Paul's empty satchel to him, sliding it across the frost-whitened floor with my foot. 'Go home, Paul,' I said softly. 'I'll stay with Moss until it's your turn again.'

But for four long days, Moss didn't make another move. During those empty stretches of light and darkness, whistling north winds battered at our stake-out house until it snapped and cracked with cold. I checked twice at the rendezvous and each time found that the panic was holding and the situation boiling. Welch gave me a grim bit of news: '—every hour around the clock addicts are being picked up; for loitering about close to hospitals and nursing homes; for breaking and entering of doctors' offices; for uttering and attempting to pass counterfeit drug script; for common crime ranging from shoplifting and prostitution to crimes of violence. Some of the addicts are beginning to drift away to other cities and towns, to anywhere drugs are illegally for sale.'

Paul and I continued our desperate staggering of shifts. We were fighting now to hold off extreme fatigue and a terrible, mounting tension. Cold became a bitter enemy; each succeeding shift a cruel battle to be fought.

'I don't like it any better,' Paul told me at midnight as he came to relieve me on the fourth day, 'But I have something to tell you, Max.'

'Tell it,' I shivered.

'That guy across the street owes me now for so much suffering. I'd stay on this case until spring for free just to see him get clobbered.'

'Watch the two porches,' I growled.

Then, at bright noon of the fifth day, Moss gave us our first false alarm. Monstrous and scowling and pale, ugly smears of darkened skin under his eyes, he lumbered painfully from his lower-porch door to join his two bodyguards in the waiting Buick.

I got on the Buick as it turned off at the lower corner of Moss's street. I tailed from well back during a long, uneventful drive. There wasn't the slightest indication of a cover within miles. Just the same, I could feel an invisible presence, sense it.

False start number two came the next day. Alone, Moss left by the same lower-porch door. He walked, putting forward an uncertain foot and following it with the other, shifting his weight on to it, like an invalid walking for the first time, for a dozen blocks. Then he disappeared abruptly into a doctor's office.

Ahead, and partly visible just inside a corner, was a street telephone booth. I ran frantically, the back of my neck suddenly cold.

I telephoned the inspector. After a ten-minute delay, while one-way traffic whisteled past the booth, Welch called me back to advise me the doctor was a reputable practitioner who reported he had treated Moss in hospital for serious genital injury and was now continuing the treatment in his office. The inspector ground his teeth over the phone. 'Damn it, Dent!' he raged. 'Why the devil

245

couldn't you have kneed the swine somewhere that heals in a hurry? Mark my words, Moss will wait until he's completely fit again before going into action.'

The inspector, too, was getting edgy. But he was right. Moss stalled, waiting until his every last weakness was eliminated.

Three days slid by, a week, another week. Paul and I struggled to forget our frozen bodies and to fight the deadly waiting out of our bones. I grew terribly, terribly tired and worried. A conviction haunted me that, somehow, I had made a ghastly error; that somehow Moss had managed to trick us and make his meet. The thought was like a bucket of cold water in the face.

Paul agreed. 'No stake-out can be effective this long,' he complained. 'It's just not possible. One of us must have goofed. Moss is wise to us. He's either sitting back laughing and waiting us out, or he's gone around us and connected.'

'He can't have!' I retorted, reaching out at the only straw I could see. 'Service is still dead at the rendezvous. At every meet across town. Would it be, if Moss had connected?'

'I don't know,' Paul mumbled, picking up his empty satchel. 'I just don't bloody know, Max.'

But, on the morning of the fifteenth day, Moss suddenly appeared again.

The sunshine was streaming over the sreet and spreading a bright, warm carpet as Moss's black Buick sedan came to a stop before his door. The bodyguards leaped out. After a quick, careful check about the area, they ran back to the car, quartered the street again, then gave a horn signal that brought out the Back Man. The car door clicked shut and the sedan rolled sedately towards the corner, angling gradually to get into position for a turn.

I felt an odd, stomachless sensation as the waiting exploded into quick action.

I was away from my window like a shot.

Our runner caught my frantic wave and, before I slammed out of the rear door, was off ahead of me to alert Welch.

Moss's Buick was again turning a corner as I skidded my car into the lower end of his street. The distance between his corner and the first available side street was too short. Covering it allowed scarcely the time needed for me to signal and get set on tail. Our system would have to be tightened. Three blocks of shifty driving was required before I brought the now speeding Buick into safe shadowing position. On a turn, I saw Moss clearly. The artificial brilliance of a theatre marquee splashed a weird green light through the Buick's window to give me a glimpse of that ghastly face and those huge, simian shoulders, dressed now in a dark suit and coat, an evil man staring straight ahead as he slumped back on the seat cushions. He maintained that slumped position until the Buick turned right at Guy Street.

Then the trickery began.

The Buick climbed quickly to upper town, then was deliberately brought into a line of bumper to bumper traffic. Moss's driver, the hoodlum with the crooked nose and brows warped by scar tissue, stuck to busy throughways now.

At least five cars always between mine and the Buick, I tailed with comparative ease. The Buick continued determinedly on into the West End. I prepared myself for a long driver.

But Moss never did the expected.

Before downtown traffic began to thin, the Buick swerved abruptly north and roared with dangerous speed across and over the wide mountain shoulder and down a long, cemetery-sided road to a traffic-snarled lower-level intersection.

The chase ended there. The Buick made a reeling right-angle turn, skidded to a shuddering stop, and backed into a conveniently empty parking space.

Putting a corner building between the Buick and me,

I slammed into the curb, leaped out and ran back. Moss and his companion pair were still sitting in their car. They were leaning towards each other, and talking very earnestly. Fifty feet off to one side, an empty street telephone booth waited. I rushed to it and dialled through to Paul in a hurry. After repeating my location twice, he slammed down the receiver.

I got back on point.

For a moment a pert little brunette carrying a hat box obscured my vision then, as she moved by, I saw Moss at once. Sided by his bodyguards, he was moving stiffly through a thick crowd on the opposite sidewalk.

I looked, and suddenly, I beheld the cunning of Moss. I saw it laid bare, and I couldn't believe.

For sheer emphasis, Moss's ability for the unusual was stunning. Under my fascinated gaze, he was now raising himself from the third of an endless stretch of cement prayer steps. Steps that mounted in series upon series of broad, gentle flights to what appeared distantly to be a shrine in the clouds.

I spoke my thoughts aloud in a voice that held awe: 'Moss *is* making a meet. And for it, he has chosen the most unlikely place in the world: Brother Andre's Shrine—a faith-healer's shrine perched on a city mountain-top!'

Leaning forward on the balls of my feet, I watched.

Up and up, higher and higher, step by step Moss forced his protesting body. Watching, I fell into the rhythm of his movement. It had a hypnotic effect. Like watching the bobbing of a single fly on a fly-ridden wall. A third-way up the great staircase, he was still five hundred yards from the top landing.

Surrounding Moss, lay the vast, open spread of the cement steps. No single nook or niche within hundreds of square yards offered cover. A bird couldn't flutter a wing and escape detection. Nor could a narcotic agent, almost all of whom Moss knew by sight or description, get even remotely close without both he and his purpose being identified.

Straining against the saffron sunlight, my eyes moved with Moss and his bodyguards. They passed dutifully to kneel on each obligatory prayer-step, bowed their heads, rose, mounted higher and higher towards the great marble terrace of the distant shrine. As they moved they rubbed shoulders with the devout, the day's flock of crippled and diseased petitioners for miracle-cure.

I dropped my eyes to my strap-watch. Lifted them quickly back to the steps.

Twenty minutes since I'd called Paul. The three pilgrims were now better than half-way to the top. My shoulders and the back of my neck felt stiff. I looked at my watch again. Then back at the stairs.

Another minute crawled by, slowly, laboriously, like a candle guttering out.

Paul skidded his car to a stop beside me. One of his front wheels banged against the curb and sent its hubcap spinning crazily off. Then Paul tumbled out to the sidewalk and stood there swaying slightly, as if solid waves were beating at his legs. 'Where's Moss?' he gasped. 'Don't you tell me he's slipped us. I damned near got killed bucking it through traffic to get here.'

'Look!' I said. 'Look, Paul!'

Paul was already staring up at the prayer-steps. I pointed high towards the purple cloud mists above them. 'Start there, from the shrine terrace, and look down,' I instructed. 'Keep checking down until just above half-way. You can make out Moss clearly. He must be dropping blood by now, but he's still right there moving up. The bodyguards, too. See them?'

'Them I see.' The words came out stiff and jerky.

'You'll have to fly, Paul,' I said sharply. 'Skip a few prayers on the steps so you can catch them before they reach the terrace. Watch it inside. They'll probably split up. If they do—for the love of God stay on Moss. Right on him!'

Paul began an excited muttering deep in his throat. 'A maniac spot for a drug meet,' he said. 'I'll never believe I've actually seen this.' He laughed nervously, added, 'Wait until Welch hears about this. I got him. By now, his men will be inside.'

'I'll be waiting by the corner,' I said hurriedly. 'By an outdoor phone there—Dexter 8-7143. Here, I've jotted it down for you. If there's action inside the shrine, find a phone there and call me. If not, abandon Moss and tail whomever he meets. If you don't call me, meet me after you complete your tail on Moss's man. I'll be waiting at Louis's on Notre-Dame. And Paul, keep checking for counter-tail. Watch yourself every inch of the way!' I slapped him on the shoulder, sent him off.

He dodged swiftly across the street. He looked up once, the hurried to the first of the cement steps and kneeled briefly. Moving with quick, economical motions, he spent less than three seconds on each succeeding step. At the outer apron of the shrine terrace, he slipped inconspicuously into a crowd moving slowly behind Moss.

An hour passed. My eyes held on the shrine's haze-softened terrace. Behind me, the street telephone booth remained silent.

The hour lengthened into two. I stalked up and down in front of the booth now. 'What can be keeping them?' I kept repeating to myself.

Suddenly, I saw Moss' driver. The big hoodlum was coming from some place of concealment across the shrine entrance. He pushed through a crowd and began impudently running down the steps, brushing aside several of those coming up, sending a couple of them reeling. I stood in the telephone booth, watched him run, one hand to his heaving chest, across the street to Moss's parked Buick.

He swung the heavy Buick into an abrupt, tyre-squealing U-turn and drove straight past the cement steps to the intersection. He made a complete circling check of the block then drove hard to a side driveway that led to the rear of the shrine.

All the way, I'd been pacing the Buick, keeping its fast-travelling rear in sight from the front seat of my own car. Now, I pulled in behind a truck parked beneath a 'Loading Zone—Trucks Only' sign in front of a large store siding the driveway.

Almost at once, the Buick came swirling down from the shrine. Moss lay spread-eagled in utter exhaustion on its rear seat. Abruptly, I threw off the brake and raced my car around the parked truck back into the street. I roared past the driveway entrance, followed the Buick that was now out of sight. I caught a glimpse of it as it reached the first level of the mountain, back-tracking the route it had taken to the shrine. I tailed it without incident at a sedate pace back to its starting point, Moss's house.

I waited, parked just inside the corner, until Moss's door slammed. Then I ducked low and sped down the street, past the twin porches, past our stake-out. A tiny circle, immediately erased, that appeared on the frosted look-out window told me Paul's man was keeping our watch intact. I turned east towards Louis's. It had begun to snow, hard snow that began a grapeshot noise on my car roof. Soon it would blow up to a real storm.

I left my car at the end of a long line of white lumps behind the City Hall. I crossed the street and stamped gratefully into Louis's. The malty air in the little bar smelled familiar and warm, full of reality.

25

Paul kept me waiting two agonizing hours. When he came in, he banged through the front door, then stopped a moment at the bar. Carrying a quart bottle of ale and an empty glass, he slid in beside me. He rapped the tabletop sharply with his knuckles, grinning. 'A thing happened to me today that I thought was impossible! Wow! Those pain-clothes Mounties sure are the business. The sons of guns rode right on my back all the way through without me ever being really sure they'd turned up!'

I tried to control my excitement. 'Absolutely. The R.C.M.P. are good. Now tell me what happened.'

'Your man made a meet,' he said flatly. 'No drugs changed hands. But it was a trafficking meet and a time was set for a deal.'

'When?' I demanded impatiently.

'Hey, whoa!' Paul protested. 'Let a guy tell this his own way. I had to gumshoe around the shrine until I got dizzy. So much happened so fast, if I try to tell it in a hurry I'll only get confused and forget part.'

I bit my lip. 'Sorry, old man. Go on.'

Paul blinked at me. 'That Moss blueprints a meet like a convention manager,' he said. 'Everything was arranged so that each person concerned knew precisely where he was going, and why. Like you figured, Moss' party split up as soon as they got inside. The two hoods stayed on watch. The little one outside the terrace door. The big one near the side entrance. Moss rolled around for a bit, pecking and poking, then struck off in a hurry to the room where they exhibit Brother Andre's heart.'

I made no sound, only waited for Paul to go on, biting my lips while he did nervous things with his bottle of ale. 'When Moss was in that exhibition room,' he went on, 'he started what appeared to be a casual conversation with another visitor. Just the sort of thing two strangers might do in such a place. But Moss knew this man. Either that, or the guy was waiting there for someone answering Moss's description. Anyway, those two got real buddy-buddy. They visited two testimonial rooms together. They browsed about among the discarded crutches and wheelchairs, braces, and so on, talking casually but obviously keeping their eyes peeled. Then things began getting hot. Moss and his friend drifted off down the main corridor of the shrine. To the chapel.'

'Moss has made rendezvous with suppliers in chapels before. Chapels must be his favourite spot for a meet.'

Paul nodded seriously. 'Maybe he prays for a good growth of poppies. But, this time, nobody did any praying. While Moss was squeezing into a pew beside his man, I moved into sight position away off to one side and a few pews in front. By twisting a bit in my pew, I was able to see both Moss and his meet clearly. Before long, Moss began whispering away like mad.'

'And you were reading his lips!'

Paul grinned. 'Well, I guess! Let me tell you something. An interesting point about lip reading is that whispered words are easier to read than normally-pitched ones. The whispered word is spoken more precisely—so the lips become more visibly expressive. I read Moss like a book with big print. He made an appointment to meet his man again tomorrow. Saturday. That sentence came out as clearly as if it had been written in neon. To clinch it, Moss's pal repeated "Saturday" three times.'

I thought Paul would never come out with it. 'Fine! Great!' I said. 'The two meet tomorrow. But where? Where do they meet?'

Paul's happy expression collapsed. He gave a deep sigh, then looked down into the golden whorl of his ale. He answered in a distressed voice: 'This part, you won't like, Max. Right there, the whole lip-reading deal blew up in my face.'

'Oh, oh God, no!' I protested.

'It blew up *because*' and the word Paul stressed exploded from his lips 'at the precise damned moment Moss's pal got set to name the meeting-place and the time, two old dolls moved in between us. They plumped down in a pew behind me, directly in my line of vision. That bollixed it. Moss and his meet were completely screened off. I couldn't see another bloody word.'

I wanted to cry. Instead, I found a grin somewhere and made good use of it. 'All right, all right, Paul,' I said. 'The breaks, that's all, the unpredictable breaks. What then?'

'Well, in about a minute, before I could risk a seat change, my two got up and left the chapel. Moss rolled down the corridor to a side entrance. He waited there for his car. His meet went the other way, scrammed in a taxi he picked up at a cab rank a block from the shrine.'

'You tailed?'

'Natch, I tailed. I forgot about my car and flagged down a cruising cab. That's all there was time for. But I got a good driver and I tailed Moss's meet straight to the Laurentian Hotel. His cab dropped him at the Dorchester Street side.'

Paul beamed 'And the lurk swung back in our direction, too. While my man waited at the elevator bank, I noticed a house dick I know standing by the cigarette stand. I high-signed him to follow Moss's pal upstairs. The rest was a shoo-in. The house dick nailed the room number, then waltzed down and checked the register. I gave him five of the best and he gave me the name. Our man is registered as Victor C. Garino, Utica, N.Y. He's in room 5001.'

I leaned back, breathed a little. '5001! Paul, that's our pay-off number. What about the Mounties?'

Paul eyed me aslant. 'Oh, my God!' he said. 'Look, I didn't even have a clue they were so tight behind me. The fact is, while I was sweating it out waiting for the house dick to get Garino's room number and come back, I began wondering what the devil had happened to Welch's Narcotic Squad. But no sooner did I step outside the hotel than a guy that looked ike a college kid came up to me, flashed an R.C.M.P. identity card, and said as politely as you please, "Excuse me, but would you care to pass over that name and room number. Inspector Welch is waiting for it."

Paul blew a token kiss. 'They're terrific, terrific!' he concluded with serious respect. 'Matter of fact, I'd forgotten how good they actually are.'

'Good, but cautious,' I said. 'Cautious and very methodical. In fact, that sometimes worries me.' For a moment, I sat in deep thought. Every little detail that might be established now about Garino had top significance. The whole involved issue might depend on this man's next move. Paul waited for me to speak, his angular face set and shiny and his dark eyes steady. 'This supplier, this Garino,' I said, 'what first impression did he make on you? What does he look like? What kind of man does he impress you as?'

'Five-ten. Slender. Grey-black temples under the roll-brim. Personality radiating wealth and assurance. Leisure class. Culture. Ritz for martinis—the Sherbrooke Street museum to fill in an hour.'

I stored into the bar, drumming my fingers, aware that the description was probably perfect. Culture, the Ritz and martinis. Then why does Garino stay at the Laurentian? I mused. Why *not* the Ritz. Or the Windsor? The Sheraton? *Any* of the more fashionable hotels? Then, thinking about it, I didn't wonder any more. I knew why Garino stayed at the Laurentian. For small sacrifices in luxury he might have to make, the Laurentian had many advantages to offer a man in Garino's position. The hotel's central location, its wide, busy lobby, its almost instant elevator service, its double street entrances and exits all added up to valuable assets to a man whose very life might depend on a fast, unexpected move.

My dependable leg-man finished his ale. 'Garino,' he concluded with perspicacity, 'has a frank, intelligent face. Also, a very pleasant personality. He's a type that could fit in anywhere. Looking at him, you would figure the most lethal weapon he ever handles is a Dow-Jones ticker tape.'

'Sure,' I growled. 'That's why he's dangerous.' Then I added, 'Paul, you're not inexhaustible. You look wrung out. You'd better go home right now and get a little sleep. Although we can't reasonably expect a move before morning, you're going back on watch tonight. Another thing. I want an extra point man. I want him ready to go on at six a.m. tomorrow. Have him dressed up as a delivery man of some kind. There's an alley back of Moss's house that leads clear through to Chatham Street and I want someone on spot in that alley. There's one chance in a million Moss will try to make it over the fences behind his house to throw off a tail, but it's a chance we won't take.'

'Right, Max. I'll set it up as soon as I get back to my office. I think I can get Blakely. You remember him. He has the patience of a Franciscan, and he's pretty good at looking like something he's not. Now, when do I see you next?'

'At midnight. I'll relieve you then. That way, you'll be able to get a bit of extra sleep and still make it back to the stake-out again by six tomorrow morning.' I hesitated, and feeling a little uncomfortable, said, 'Now, listen, Paul; Mounties, or no Mounties, we play this safe. Right until we get the bird, or birds, in our hand. You'd better be wearing your pistol. Right?'.

The faint lines on Paul's face deepened. He coughed, then grinned. 'I will be wearing the pistol, Max,' he said, then walked quickly to the door and out to the street without once looking back.

I called Welch. The inspector held me a moment while a receding buzz of voices told me he was clearing his office. Then he said some surprisingly warm words of praise and told me two men had been put on Garino. We used up a minute more discussing Moss's fantastic meet. Crossing my fingers, I broached the risky idea I had so long had in mind as shock-treatment for Helen Ashton. Welch fell into an abrupt, edgy silence. I don't know whether he hesitated because it wasn't politic for him to speak of Helen Ashton, or whether it was the grim plan itself that stopped him. When he did speak, his tone was quietly aggressive as he reminded me I was expected at his office to help set up the tail plan for Moss's final move. Then he added, and now his voice indicated he was hanging on to his patience by a rapidly thinning thread, 'It occurs to me that you might be going much too far out with what you plan for the Ashton girl. I know your first interest is for your client, but it's remarkable that you would even dare try such a thing. The odds are fully a hundred to one for failure. Your experience with addicts must tell you that. However, it's on your own head. No doubt, you'll go at it with your usual utter thoroughness!'

I broke the connection, and went to the bar to buy a drink. The hands on Louis's wall clock pointed to one minute past noon.

I felt as though I'd been brainwashed.

I went back to the telephone booth. I telephoned the Royal Victoria Hospital and asked to be connected with Phil's doctor. The doctor refused politely to answer questions over the phone. He suggested that I come to the hospital and he promised to find a few minutes to talk with me if I did.

I dialled my own number. Thorn answered as though she had been waiting with her hand on the receiver. I asked her if she could leave Shadow somewhere he'd be safe for the rest of the afternoon and then meet me in an hour in the parking area in front of the Royal Vic. I said I would be waiting there.

'And'—her voice tilted a little—'then?'

'When I'm through at the Vic, I want to pick up Helen and take her downtown,' I said. 'I'd like you to be with us.'

Silence. The receiver pressed hard and damp against my ear. Then Thorn replied, quite calmly, 'I think I'll bring Shadow home and leave him with the chauffeur. He'll

257

see Shadow doesn't get into trouble. And I'll have plenty of time then to meet you at the Vic.' There was another silence and I had a feeling that Thorn was shaking all over. I heard a long, shuddering breath, then: 'Max? Max, are you about to try that experiment you've talked of? That psychological shock thing? Is that it?'

'Yes,' I said very quietly. 'In a few hours, I expect my case to be finished—one way or the other. So, if anything conclusive is to be done about Helen, it must be done immediately. Like you, I want Helen to be able to live again as a free human being. I'm going to get a few medical facts straight at the Vic. Then I'm going to call your father. Naturally, I won't make this attempt at all unless I get his permission.'

Thorn said, 'You may expect me at the Vic in exactly one hour.'

And the phone was dead in my hand.

Fifteen minutes later, I stood in the Royal Vic before a desk marked: Information. A nurse sent me by slow-motion elevator to the tenth floor.

I found David Markham, M.D. in a tiny office wedged into a corner outside an emergency ward filled with white mounds of pain. He listened without looking at me while I told him what I intended to attempt with Helen Ashton, what I needed to know.

While I talked, Markham kept running his finger-tip over an open card-index, unconsciously tabling each case.

When I had finished he sat back, stared up at a ceiling ventilator.

'As you know,' he began crisply, 'I don't specialize in drug addiction cases. Actually, I've never heard of a doctor that does. However, that type of compulsive addiction interests me and, from time to time, I've had addicts as patients. But always without spectacular success.'

Markham paused to blow out a tube of smoke.'

'This girl you're interested in,' he continued thoughtfully, 'offers us a number of problems. First—and most immediate—her addiction to heroin. You believe that by showing her the inevitable end result of her abuse of drugs you can shock her into breaking her habit. Shock her into trying for a normal life. Considering her fine background, heredity and traditions of culture and so on, that just might work. Might. But there's a twist here, a curious one. A paradox. The greatest psychologists— Adler, I suggest as an example—teach us that all excesses are motivated by fear. So, in this girl's case, we have an addiction which is motivated by fear and which you hope to destroy by a counter-dose of fear. That is our curious twist. And our major problem. We wish to eliminate an unhealthy fear by creating a sensible, reasonable one.'

Markham was pushing me beyond my depth. 'Can you break that down?'

'Well, it's fairly simple,' the doctor said, with a nod and a smile, 'as long as we stay away from psychiatric terms. Let's start off easily. Why does this girl use drugs as an escape? Because she was aborted clumsily and horribly disfigured. Now, what goes on in her mind? That isn't difficult to guess, is it? She believes that no man who sees her mutilated body will see it as a man is expected to see the body of a woman he desires. Her self-respect and pride are denied. She anticipates neither desire nor love from any man—only disgust. Next comes fear. Fear of being deprived of a normal female life Fear of exposure as a loose woman. Fear of living out her life as a manless woman. It's a sort of atavistic throwback. A fear of being thrown out of the cave on a cold night. Then comes fear of the self-disgust she knows each time she looks at herself. Fear! Fear! Fear! Psychiatry calls it *pantrophobia*— fear of everything. So then drugs as an escape from fear. Finally, fear even of cure—because it means mental sobriety and facing up to reality.'

I nodded. 'Yes, I get it now. But where does that leave us?'

259

'Well, we have a girl with a badly bruised personality,' Dr. Markham said precisely. 'A girl who is hiding to escape from further bruising. That fear must be washed out. This girl must be filled with hope and strength in order that she may face her problem—and life—squarely. Eithr with, or without, the man she loves.' He glanced sharply at me. 'You said something about a religious mix-up? Or did I get that from Phil? Well, I've no patience with such things. The girl and Phil evidently need each other. In such extreme cases, I don't see that creed should be allowed to form a marriage barrier. If those two are to make anything of their lives, they'll do it better together.

'It could save Phil,' Markham said positively. 'As well, it certainly might help the girl. Naturally, it would have a tremendous psychological effect if she knew drugs were no longer illegally available. That's your department, and something to hope for. But, first, she must want to break her habit and still live.'

Markham got up, his grey gaze probing and intent. 'Go ahead with this business of giving her shock,' he said. 'Scare the very devil out of her if you can. Then do your best to get her up here. I'll have a private room waiting, and I'll handle her myself during her withdrawal period. She will be put on methadon and seconal for a start. 'This girl better know where to find a great deal of strength,' he said. 'She's going to need plenty of it.'

There was still Helen's father to convince. Huntley Ashton gave me a gruelling twenty minutes on the telephone. The inquiring worry in the man's voice was pitiful. But, at last, he did give hesitant permission.

Thorn was waiting in the hospital parking area. As always, she looked dark and lovely, but a little worried in spite of a great effort she was making to mask her emotions. 'You're never late,' I complimented her. 'I didn't think there were any women like that left in the world.' She smiled and stared in silence at the road ahead. 'I phoned

Helen,' she said. 'I know you are concerned about being away from your case, so I made sure she'd be in. I told her I was on my way over; asked her to wait until I got there. She said, Yes. But she didn't sound very pleased about it. She doesn't know you'll be with me, of course.'

On the ride across the snow-dappled mountain breast, down the hills from level to level, we sat silently, the wipers still clicking, sweeping scratchily. Thorn swung the M.G. into the driveway before Helen's apartment.

Before going up, we sat for a moment, not saying anything. The building cast a shadow across Thorn's face. It make her skin seem a little tanned and her eyeballs very white. She looked remarkably beautiful.

She bit her lip, then looked at me honestly, directly. 'Whatever it is you are about to do, Max, I know it's for the best and that it will be all right. But I'd better tell you now. Over the phone, Helen sounded as though she were utterly at the end of her rope.'

We got out of the car and went towards the entrance, walking side by side and close together in curious intimacy, like mourners approaching a grave. We took the elevator to the fourth floor. The hallway stretched dark and chapel-quiet. The long runner carpet lay smooth, as though all day no one had walked there.

26 Helen jumped abruptly back from the door and glared at us like a cat suddenly set to pounce.
'Really Thorn!' she fumed. 'You might at least have warned me to expect a visitor.'

I could hardly bring myself to look at her. I was afraid she would see the revulsion I felt. I wished suddenly I could make it easier for her. That I could tell her that perhaps she wouldn't always look this way.

I watched Thorn. She was looking at Helen and I

261

could almost see her heart wrench. Helen was pale and the skin around her brilliantly hostile eyes looked blue, as if bruised by pressing thumbs. The lipstick on her wide, slack mouth contrasted sharply with her pallor. She looked like a person who had been knocked unconscious and couldn't remember what had happened immediately before that. Her slender body had become hard, brittle. Shrunken until her clothes hung on her.

I took her arm and led her across the room to the sofa. 'I want a cigarette,' she said sharply.

She made no move to take my hat and coat, so I laid them across a chair. I was a little shocked because I was sure the omission was more than a lapse in manners; it was an unconscious expression of resentment against anyone outside Helen's chosen circle, the drug ring.

She sat down on the edge of the sofa, legs clamped together, and her two hands on her skirted knees. She said, 'I'll get my own damned cigarette, never mind.' She reached to the coffee-table for a silver box. The box slipped from her fingers and fell clattering to the floor. I picked it up and held it to her while she took a cigarette.

I waited until she was smoking. Then I said with what I knew was crashing frankness, 'This isn't a social call, Helen. Thorn brought me because I insisted. Because she knew I'd have come alone if she hadn't agreed. I'm a detective. Private, but a detective.'

She made an ugly, resentful grimace. I could see her brace herself.

'Then it's about the ring,' she said, tightening her mouth. 'The diamond ring I . . . that I took without permission from home.'

'No,' I said. 'At the moment, I'm not interested in the ring. I have something much more serious on my mind, Helen. I'm going to take you downtown with me. To see someone you know.

'Someone who is indirectly responsible for supplying

you with the black-market heroin you have been using.'

She had pushed up into a semi-sitting position, her weight supported on one stiff arm. Perhaps a second passed. Then she slowly fell forward, twisting as she fell, so that her buttocks and her heels hit the floor in that order. I picked her up and carried her to the bathroom. She came to and leaned over the bowl as unprotesting as a child while I found a washcloth, soaked it, and held it against the back of her neck.

I led her back to the sofa and when she sat down her eyes were dull. Crossing her arms as if holding herself together in readiness for a blow, she turned to Thorn with something like pity in her eyes, 'You told,' she said. 'Oh, you fool, Thorn! You heedless fool.'

'Thorn covered up for you,' I retorted. 'For much longer than she should have.' I stood up purposefully. 'We'll go now,' I said. 'You'll make everything much easier if you'll be reasonable. But one way or another, we're going downtown. Get your coat, please.'

'Please!' the voice was Thorn's. 'Please, Helen. I think Max will carry you if you refuse.'

'Max will,' I said grimly.

Helen was on her feet, shuddering, her hands over her eyes. 'All right,' she said tonelessly.

She went into her bedroom and stayed there a full ten minutes. When she came out her hair was smooth, her face powdered, and her lips freshly rouged. She looked like a tidy, lifeless corpse primed for the funeral service.

'I just took some seconols,' she said. 'I stole them. Are you shocked, Thorn? Don't be. I've done much worse things recently.'

I helped her put on a heavy beaver coat that no longer fitted her. She clasped the ill-fitting coat around her with both hands, as if depending on its thick fur to hold her shrunken body together.

The drive downtown was nightmarish. Helen sat

263

stiffly, not watching the snow-dusted streets, but watching me, her eyes narrowed and anxious. She looked away at last and instead stared out the window until she became aware of herself looking at her own reflection. Then she said—'this is what he sees when he looks at me . . . this, and worse . . .' —and it was as though she were talking to herself. She twisted her hands together and stared at the floor. Not another word was said until I pulled the M.G. into a short street siding the Sûreté—Detective Headquarters. Then, Helen gasped out—'Oh!'

Her sense of communication with Thorn and me seemed to be short-circuited. Still clasping her beaver coat around her with both hands, she walked stiffly between us to a large, first-floor room in the Sûreté.

Sun spilled through windows to lie in rectangular blocks over desks and filing-cabinets and, before us, a long counter. A policeman moved towards us, then turned away. An alert-looking crew-cut type had stepped from a side door into the room. After glancing keenly about, he swung at once towards us. 'Hello, there,' he said. 'You're Maxwell Dent?'

I produced my credentials.

He showed me a thin pliofilm jacket holding an identification card. He said, 'I'm LaFarge. Constable— R.C.M.P.'

Helen gasped. With the braced and desperate nonchalance with which one walks away from savage dogs, she moved as far as possible from LaFarge.

LaFarge appeared not to notice. He turned to me to remark amiably: 'I've been instructed about this visit. My orders are, Take you three all the way. Wherever you care to go.' He nodded towards a bank of elevators. Except for a very busy pair of dark eyes the Mountie looked very much like a successful St. James's Street securities salesman.

'Well, we'll begin with identification,' he suggested. 'A criminal identification line-up goes on stage there in a few minutes.'

A sour-smelling elevator whisked us to the second floor. We went into a huge, square, desk-jammed room overflowing now with both police and civilians. At one end of the room stood a high stage, empty and brilliantly bare under stabbing arc lights. In spite of whirring fans and soap and paint and disinfectant, an odor of fear clung to this room. It trailed up and down and up and down, like the ghosts of a thousand frightened people.

'This is the Detective Office of the C.I.D.' LaFarge said pleasantly. 'But it is best known as the Line-up or, in the vernacular, the "You've Had It" Room.' He pointed towards the stark, white brilliance. 'All suspects appear several times on that stage before either being released or charged with specific crimes. Those arcs you're staring at are adjusted to eye level. They blind the suspects—prevent them from seeing the complainants standing out here attempting to make identification. The purpose, obviously, is to prevent the suspects from recognizing the complainants.'

Her voice shocked, Thorn blurted out: 'But that doesn't seem fair. At all.'

'Fair?' LaFarge smiled. 'Perhaps not, Miss Ashton. It's safe, though. It protects the complainants. Eliminates threats and attempts to bribe witnesses when accused are released on bail before trial.'

The crowd in front of the stage had increased, was now milling noisily. LaFarge gestured towards them. 'Complainants,' he said, 'Waiting for line-ups to start. They've all been had by muggers, conmen, pick-up girls, pickpockets, gunmen. Everything in the book. Often, they have to come here a dozen times before finally making an identification. Sometimes, the criminal charges have been laid against are picked up for an entirely different offence. Or if they have a previous record, merely on suspicion or vagrancy holding counts. But they are put in line-ups, and sometimes the complainants catch up with them that way.

'There!' LaFarge raised his hand. 'Now, watch! You'll

see it all for yourselves. Police are bringing out the first line-up now.'

A plain-clothes man stepped on the stage, and rapped sharply on a steel door. He shouted into a small rectangular peep-hole which had been cut out of the door at eye level. 'Ready! Bring them out!'

Someone inside flung the door open with a crash. Uniformed police paraded out followed by, and following, a struggling line of twenty men. A policeman carrying a clasp-board holding a sheaf of printed dossiers stepped briskly across the stage apron, yelled loudly: 'All right, you suspects! Line up! Line up! Turn about. Face the front.'

Helen's eyes were glistening. 'How awful!' she muttered resentfully. 'How utterly awful. It's ugly—not decent.'

The line of suspects straightened. They stood like targets pinned to the wall by the stabbing arc beams. The groups of waiting victims stared at them as one would at fish in a tank. A bodiless voice in the darkness shouted gruff instructions: 'Turn left ... Right ... Hats off ... Turn side-face ... You, there! lift your head ... Walk ... Stop ... Turn....'

'Oh, my God!' Helen gasped. Her face had taken on a breathless, shot look. She stumbled a few feet towards the stage, stopped. Her breath whistled through the room. Leger was at the end of the line-up, tottering up and down the stage, his feet slapping disjointedly, his voice a rising wail of pain and protest. The ex-pusher-connection was drunk with the ripping agony of withdrawal.

Then a woman at the side of the stage began sobbing with a bobbing shake of her shoulders. Her voice leaped key by key into a thin, hysterical scream: 'That's him! The one beside the screaming man! That's him. That man held up my store! That's the bugger. I'll swear to it in court!'

'Come. We've had enough of this!' a voice said. I was surprised to know the voice was mine.

Outside, we walked through bright sunshine along Notre-Dame Street. Helen's face now had the blank, drawn expression of a horror mask. Her shoulders hung thinly. She was forcing herself to walk, not run, but she seemed to lack muscle sense, moving as though her knees wanted to double back on themselves. She ignored all three of us, Thorn, LaFarge and me right up to the last moment. And then it was no longer possible for her to ignore me because I had her arm and I was leading her up the stone steps of the Criminal Court Building.

LaFarge guided us into a small courtroom, empty except for a seated judge and a tight knot of standing court officials. There was a lot of fussing with papers and quiet conversation and at last a clerk called in a loud, bored voice for the case of the Crown *v.* Georges Leger.

'They whisked him over here by van,' LaFarge said quietly. 'A short ride. His last but one for a long time. The other will be to the penitentiary.'

The trial was over in ten minutes. An R.C.M.P. prosecutor presented two capsules as evidence of illegal possession of narcotics. Next, the R.C.M.P. constables who had street-jumped Leger took the stand in turn and testified that the accused had been carrying a cough-drop package containing the two capsules. An R.C.M.P. laboratory technician was called. He gave sworn testimony that each capsule contained a quantity of powered sugar milk and heroin.

The judge questioned regarding the scientific method of establishing that a portion of the capsuled powder was beyond doubt heroin.

His dark eyes sardonic, and his voice flat, the technician explained how a narrow beam of X-ray was employed to bombard the powder substance and the angles of the bending, or diffraction, of the rays recorded on to photographic plates. Since every crystalline substance bends these rays at known specific angles, the technician testified, the identification was established without the slightest element of doubt.

The accused was proven guilty of illegally possessing drugs.

The prosecutor read the accused's criminal record in detail.

No word was spoken in defence.

Leger stood desperately clutching the dock, too numbly sick to care what became of him. His face held no expression but pain as the voice of the court sounded as cold and ultimate as the clicking of a cell lock . . . 'Six years in the penitentiary at hard labour. Fine of one thousand dollars, or one additional year.'

We filed out. I looked at Thorn. The small, beautiful oval of her face was expressionless. Helen remained wordless, stiff-backed. I drew LaFarge aside. 'I said we would go the whole way,' I reminded him. 'How about the other one? She's the one I really want. Fay.'

LaFarge started in surprise. 'Good Lord, Dent!' he exclaimed. 'Isn't that laying it on a bit thick?' he shuffled his feet a bit, muttered something below his breath about instructions then nodded in a curt way. 'It's your party,' he said. 'But Fay's is a City case, you know. We have no jurisdiction. I'll go and see what I can find out.'

After a quick, silent look at me, and then a hard grimace, he swung out of the courtroom corridor.

'She's upstairs,' he said, returning. 'They have her in the women's detention-cell block. She was shipped here this morning from Fullum Street Jail. For trial. But she's too weak to stand up, or to know what's going on.' LaFarge sucked at his lips. 'I don't know,' he said doubtfully. 'I really don't know. This Fay's a pretty gruesome sight. Maybe you should just describe a cold-turkey cure to your friends. Let it go at that.'

'No!' I protested. 'I can't do that, LaFarge. I'd only be defeating my whole purpose. I've got to go right through with it. There is no other way. Too much hangs on this to drop it now.'

'Bro-*ther*,' LaFarge said.

I said, 'Well, do we go up? Incidentally, I'll take just one of the sisters inside. Helen, the sick-looking one.'

LaFarge didn't look at me. 'Yes,' he said, with a shrug. 'We go up.'

He led us through a narrow door backed by a metal-walled staircase. At the foot of the stairs there was an iron gate. It was locked. LaFarge hit the gate with his palm of his hand, rattled it. 'Let's go!' he shouted. 'I'm taking them up.'

A uniformed policeman came out of a side door and unlocked the gate. He stood aside and with LaFarge leading, we went up the metal-walled staircase. We came out into a narrow, bare corridor. A uniformed matron sat before another steel door, jiggling a ring of keys.

LaFarge spoke a few words to her.

I beckoned to Helen. She pushed one foot towards the matron, slid it back. 'Rubber necks, eh?' the matron said, wearing a smile that sagged like a worn-out dress. 'Okay with me. The thing is, it ain't no rose garden in there.' Helen thrust up her chin, and shivering in her beaver coat, walked shakily to the steel door. The matron unlocked the door and stood slamming her keys viciously against it. 'Go right inside the cell block, dearie,' she smirked. 'No one in there can hurt you. There's just the one, a junkie, and she's kayoed.'

We moved forward, Helen poker-stiff at my side.

The matron slammed the door behind us with a decisive crash. A crash that echoed, and echoed, and echoed.

Inside the confinement block were three small cells. In each, a naked bulb burned dimly. I stepped closer to the iron bars of the first cell, motioned to Helen. With terrible slowness, she turned her death-white face to peer inside.

A yard-wide board covered with a wafer-thin mattress hung on chains from the steel wall. An open toilet bubbled. Lipstick scrawlings of names and addresses, of lewd suggestions, cobwebbed the walls. A line-caked bucket stood in one corner. The heavy, fetid smell of confinement fouled the hot, still air.

269

Helen wheeled around suddenly and, throwing back her head, screamed: 'No! Oh, no, no!' I don't have to look. You can't make me. I want to get *out* of here. I just want to get *out* of here!'

I got an arm around her and restrained her. I brought her to the end of the cell block. On the stained mattress in the last cell there was a heap of twisted clothing. The girl lying in the clothing was Dream Street Fay, and at that precise moment Fay rolled over on her back, her strained, yellowish eyeballs protruding madly.

There was an instant of no motion. Helen was crying. Her eyes were huge as they stared into mine. She seemed to be pleading with me, begging me to understand. Then she covered her eyes with her trembling hands. 'I want to get *out* of here, *please*,' she said frantically.

A sudden stab of withdrawal pain spun Fay from her bunk. With no strength to get back, she lay spread-eagled on the cement floor, jerking in mad, double-jointed spasms. Pain beat like another heart within her. Her heels beat slow, precise tattoos on the cement. As her monstrous torment mounted, she began screaming, screaming that she wanted to die. She lay back on her bony elbows and screamed: 'Wannadie, wannadie, wannadie!'

My fingers tightened determinedly over Helen's shoulder. 'Take a good look at her,' I said with every ounce of firmness I could command. . . . Look at her face, her body. Listen to her screams, her agony. Listen and look well, because what you're seeing and hearing now is the end of the road for every addict. For everyone that thinks there's a thrill or an escape in heroin. For you— Helen Ashton!'

I dropped my hand to Helen's arm steady her. Her arm felt as stiff and cold as a steel bar. I forced myself to go on, to keep her facing Fay's cell. 'Now, hear me,' I said with cold, calculated savagery. 'That could be you in there. Lying in your own filth, as Fay is. In this cell block,

270

there's plenty of room. Because you are Huntley Ashton's daughter doesn't mean a thing to the Mounties. They don't play favourites. Not with people caught in illegal possession of drugs. Not with anyone.' My hand was still tight on that hard, thin arm. I forced Helen still closer to the screaming addict being ripped apart before her eyes. It was a terrifying spectacle, a human being trying to writhe out of her own body because it was paining her so much. 'Well, Helen,' I demanded in a harsh voice, 'do you want to do something about your drug habit? Do you? Do you want to give yourself up for treatment? Or shall I save us all the time and trouble? Shall I call in that beast of a cell block matron now? Shall I hurry things a bit and tell her to shove Fay over to make room for you?'

Helen's breath came out slowly. She slid with a queer gracefulness gently back into my arms. Consciousness oozed out of her like paste from a squeezed tube. I carried her to the steel door, her arms and legs hanging limply. I kicked at the door and a key rasped and it was flung open. The matron stepped back with an ugly little smile that reached only her lips. 'Well, how about that!' she said. 'Little Miss Rich-Bitch passed out cold, eh?'

'Get over to that cooler and bring some water!' I roared, glaring at her. I sat Helen in the matron's chair, and with Thorn's help, began working over her. Twenty minutes later, she stumbled unsupported into the Admitting Office of the Royal Victoria. Dr. Markham took one keen look at her and called for a stretcher.

Helen Ashton had stared down the long, dark, twisting tunnel that led to a possible cure.

A twist to my mouth, I stepped outside. It was too much. I felt above my responsibility; felt like a special, lunatic-type merchant of pain. Tension had my nerves snapping. Nothing guaranteed me that Helen Ashton had strength enough for her coming struggle; that she would respond and heal instead of failing and falling away.

Thorn came across the parking area. She got into the car. She folded her arms, unconsciously bunching her breasts, brooding silently over her thoughts as she looked fixedly into nowhere. Then she said in an odd, high voice, 'It doesn't matter how bad it is. Nothing could be worse than what Helen has been doing to herself. Perhaps the doctors can make her want to live again. Perhaps they can find a way to fill the emptiness in her. To make her accept herself as she is. Maybe they can even make her feel beautiful again.'

Beautiful again!

I gave Thorn a moment of thoughtful appraisal. 'Then you knew!' I said softly, and stared hard at her. 'I haven't been deceiving you at all. All along you've known about what was done to Helen.'

'After Helen moved from home,' Thorn said, her voice keeping its peculiar, gaunt, rising inflexion, 'I kept going to that darned apartment. When Helen was in, sometimes even when I knew she'd be out. I kept trying to find a way to help her. Then one day I almost bumped into you in the lobby. You'd just come out of the elevator. I stepped into an alcove and watched you go by. You looked as though you'd just seen a ghost.

'When you were gone, I went upstairs. Helen was lying on her bed, unconscious. As she must have been while you were there. Anyway, I saw Helen that day. Her body. How she really looks now. The ghastly thing that was done to her. After that, everything somehow became much clearer. Easier to understand.'

My mind whirled back over the scores of times I'd lied, evaded the issue, side-stepped conversations that might lead to the origin of Helen's trouble. And, always, this wise and lovely woman who was so experienced in many considerations had known.

She touched her eyes with her fingers. Stretching out one hand, she waited for me to take it in mine, then said in a low tone, 'My father has told me a lot about you, Max. Of how you studied to be a lawyer. Of how you gave that up to go into the Air Force. Of how you were decorated for special duty. Of how you endured shocking things like voluntary imprisonment in an enemy compound to destroy something you hated. Of what destroying that something did to you. And now you are part of that world again.

'Not because you wanted to be. But because my father spoke convincingly enough of his worry over Helen to make you believe it was your duty to be. And this afternoon, because of that duty, you forced yourself to do a thing that brought tears to your eyes. You, Maxwell Dent, are very, very much a man.'

It was not the sort of statement that could easily be replied to. I said, and I tried to say it lightly, my hand fishing for a cigarette from the pack beside me on the seat, 'And you, Thorn, why would you pump your father for all that history of Maxwell Dent?'

Thorn slowly brought her lighter up to my cigarette. 'Could there be any reason but one?' she asked simply. 'Because I love you.'

We rolled down the hills to the cab rank beside the Ritz. Before getting out of the M.G. and leaving Thorn, I bent over, brushed my lips over hers. 'Again,' she whispered, and moved closer. 'People are looking, but I don't mind at all. Kiss me again. Hard!' This time, her hands pulled at the front of my coat, fumbled over the hard ridge of my shoulder-houlster. There was a tight, awkward moment with me looking at her and she looking at me for some reaction to what I had just given away. And then she shook her head and opened her eyes wide so the dark lashes pressed against her clear skin.

She made a spirited try at humour. She whispered softly, 'Max, if trouble rears its ugly head and things start popping before this is over, please don't forget to duck.

But, if you do forget, wherever you are,' she pointed up, then, with a small whimsical smile, down, 'just you be patient, darling. Because I'll be along shortly.'

27

The hands on Welch's desk clock showed four o'clock when I finally sat down in his office. The inspector didn't notice my unsteadiness, or pretended not to. He got right down to business. He poked a Police Identification photo across his desk to me. 'Victor C. Garino,' he said curtly. 'Moss's supplier. The police record plate number pinned across Garino's lapels indicates that mug-shot was taken in the Receiving Room of the U.S.A. Federal Penitentiary at Terre Haute, Indiana.'

'So Garino has a police record!'

'The man's made a career of crime,' Welch snorted. 'I had his entire record teletyped to me as soon as we made an identification.' A communication strip lay on the desk. Welch tapped it. 'This is the F.B.I. confidential report we received on Garino—or Webb, Charles Schwab, Edward Everest, and so on. The man has used dozens of aliases. Luckily for us, he registered at the Laurentian under a recorded alias instead of using a special accommodation name for this contact job. Otherwise, we'd have had to lift print specimen from his room to get this make.'

The inspector cleared his throat, consulted the teletyped record, and read off—'Garino, Victor C for Claude. Age fifty-three. Born at Butte, Montana. First arrested and printed nineteen-thirty, fraud—mining shares—convicted and served three months Bridewell Prison, Chicago. Nineteen thirty-five, arrested Long Island, Jamaica—passing American counterfeit—served two years at Federal Penitentiary, Terre Haute, Indiana. Nineteen thirty-eight, arrested twice: June, Florida—race-track touting—acquitted: July, Florida—fraudulent real estate manipulation—acquitted. Nineteen forty-five, released from Wormwood Scrubs, deported to U.S. and subsequently released by immigration. Since then, Garino's had a good run. His record's clean from forty-five. Until now, he'd managed to stay clear of the law.'

'But not even a hint of drugs,' I said, surprised. 'Garino's been arrested for every crime in the book but possession and trafficking.'

Welch tapped the communication strip significantly. 'That's right, Dent,' he agreed. 'But remember one thing. Garino has always gone to prison alone. As you know, that's the mark of the gold-medallist among thieves. Whenever Garino falls, no one gets squealed on. He takes his medicine, shuts up, and serves his time. That's one reason why he finally got his chance at the big money— drugs! He got it because the ring operators know they can depend on him not to talk if he runs into trouble and gets arrested.'

I sat up, rigidly. 'The ring operators!' I said. 'The ring operators don't matter to us. Not now. Garino's the link. If we get him, we break the chain. And at the same time, we get Moss.'

'Exactly! Nevertheless, we'll try to pump Garino when we get him. We'll try to dig a few identities out of him that might be helpful to the F.B.I. But that's all we'll try to do as far as his boss-men are concerned. Naturally, our own problem comes first.' Welch paused, and then he said with great emphasis, 'You know, you now have a staggering responsibility, Dent. You're now the lead-in man to a wholesale drug ring clean-up. We've not had a chance like this for years. Be dead sure that if we make these two grabs whoever tries to fill Moss's empty shoes will be given a very rough time. Now,' Welch suggested vigorously, 'we'll go over our plan for tomorrow's action.'

'They say everything comes to him who waits,' I grinned. 'I've always wanted to see one of your picked squads go to work. It looks like I'm about to have that chance.'

Welch made a deprecating gesture. But his eyes grew tattle-tale with pride. He pointed to a foot-high, front-and-rear wooden mock-up of Moss's house that stood on his desk. 'You're to be on point through night to morning. Located here.'—Welch kept pointing to specific locations on the mock-up as he spoke—'Your man, Dupas, joins you if the stake-out still stands at six. He, with one of my squad, waits on the alert downstairs. Here. Others of my squad will be scattered about the district.' The inspector fanned out his hands. 'The instant Moss moves, you will signal Dupas and my man so they can get our full tail into action. All of this, of course, is based on the premise that Moss will not move before morning.'

'He won't,' I said positively. 'He was very definite in the chapel. He said Saturday.'

'Yes.' Welch gave his desk an emphatic thump. 'Then you will be on look-out and you will remember this: You will signal that action is starting *before* you leave the look-out window. *And you will stay at that widow*—here—until you have directed the tail-contact to whatever direction Moss takes when he turns off at the corner.'

I stared at Welch. I couldn't believe what I was hearing. I thought the man had gone suddenly crazy. 'But I'll have to yell my lungs out to be heard,' I protested. 'Suppose Moss leaves a man behind to check him out? He's sure to do that. And my voice will carry clear across the street.'

'You'll make much less noise than a mouse,' Welch replied grimly. He pointed to a box-like contraption on the floor. 'You will use this,' he said. 'The constable waiting downstairs with Dupas in the old house will have similar equipment. As will the point men waiting to alert tail-control.'

I stepped around the desk, picked up the heavy, square, black box. It was a walkie-talkie, sensitized, and fitted with every known device for facilitating communication.

Welch produced an artist's scale-drawing of the district immediately surrounding Moss's house. Indicating certain heavily scored lines on the drawing with the stem of his unlit pipe, Welch said, 'You will note we've divided the district into four separate areas. At the borders of each area, several point men will be posted. Each point man will be equipped with hand-size electronic equipment capable of radio communication with the walkie-talkies. Regardless of which direction Moss assumes when he turns out of his street, regardless of which end of the street he exits from, one of the waiting point men will pick up that intelligence through you and relay it without a moment's delay directly to the tail-control.'

I said, humbly, 'The tail-control, of course, will be you. But how many tail units will you have out?'

Discussion of tactics seemed to stimulate Welch. He leaned forward and smiled distinctly, suddenly animated. 'We'll have five two-men cars working inside the subject's immediate area of road movement,' he informed me. 'Only one of those cars at a time, of course, will actually sit on tail. The others will be cruising near by, always within a block or two, ready to relieve as soon as any tail car gets too hot for safety.

'On the fringe areas, working as spotters, we'll have three trucks. Two light-delivery type, one transport. In each, we'll have a constable dressed as a uniformed company driver. As well, we'll have a constable working as liaison between all units. He'll be wearing a C.P.R. Telegraph uniform and riding a radio-equipped sidecar-motorcycle.' Welch reached out and flipped open one of his endless files. 'There will also be five cars cruising on call,' he said. 'Those will stay well outside the route Moss takes to get to his meet. They'll be called in only if the tail lasts so long we have to substitute units over and over to keep

277

Moss from noticing the same car or truck coming up too often behind him.'

'If necessary, you'll replace even those relief cars with others.'

'That's correct, Dent. If necessary, we'll keep switching cars and personnel all day. Our plan is precise in design, tightly knit, tightly controlled, and highly mobile. It should be foolproof. Except for one element. Who knows? Who can ever foresee what fantastic schemes a drug trafficker will dream up?'

'The advantage is all Moss's I agreed edgily. 'He knows where he's going. We don't. As well, no matter how cautious we are, Moss may spot us. Or, with that damned trafficker's instinct, he might simply sense something's off-key and call off the whole damned meet.'

A queer sensation, a premonition, washed over me as Welch made a thoughtful steeple of his fingers and said, 'Yes, he might. It's like trying to solve the Riddle of the Three Enigmas. I realize that. But, remember, once Garino starts towards the meet, his every move will be under red-alert watch. He'll be out of contact with Moss, so if things go awry and Moss bolts, we still get him, proper. Because he'll be the one carrying drugs to the transfer stop.'

'Here, hold on, Inspector,' I said desperately. 'You want Garino. Fine. I want you to get him. But I've got to get Moss. I've got to get him. Moss has been my whole case. He's been responsible for all the hell and horror I've been living with for the last two months.' I slapped my palm hard on the desk. 'So the devil with Garino. I want Moss.'

The door opened quickly. Just wide enough for a constable to look in. Welch shook his head good-naturedly. As the door clicked shut, a soft chuckle sounded. I twisted slowly, astonished, certain that the chuckle was familiar. 'That man'—I said, and I was associating the chuckle with a spare, ragged, Pernod-drinking destitute—'that man, who is he?'

'Just a duty constable,' Welch said, smiling. 'Now about Moss. It's not necessary to remind me you want him. Believe me, Dent, while we will settle for Garino alone if we have to, we also want Moss. We intend to get him, too.'

Standing up, Welch said something that I missed because I was still trying to make the necessary mental adjustment after hearing that chuckle. I brought my mind to attention, and heard Welch saying kindly, 'Now I'm going to give you a bit of advice, Dent. Go home. Get into bed for a few hours. You'll soon be needing every resource you possess.'

I went home to find my apartment empty. Thorn and Shadow, a note told me, had gone to a movie.

I went to bed.

At eleven o'clock I got up and dressed quickly, bundling up with a thick muffler and heavy, dark coat.

The walkie-talkie was a dark blot on my living-room floor. I picked it up, and hurried off to the stake-out building. I had that feeling again of teetering on the edge of a precipice.

This must be my last watch on the Back Man.

Paul greeted me from the window with his eyes.

He jerked up stiffly, swinging his arms, blowing spumes of frozen breath through the trail of light that seeped in weakly from the street. His thin-lipped face was shadowed with tension and fatigue. 'Just one single minute of action,' he wheezed, pointing to Moss's firmly-closed door. 'Two guys came hot-footing along early this evening and ducked up Moss's stairs to the lower door. There was a bit of snow then. You can still see footprints on the porch. One set large, one small. You know who those belong to!'

Through the window, I peered at the frozen white moulage. 'The musclemen!' I said. 'Is that all? No other movement?'

'That's it. Moss hasn't budged. About ten tonight, a plain-clothes Mountie slipped up here,' he said. 'The guy gave me a sheet of instructions for the tail. Said to memorize them. Said you'd know about it. It's okay?'

'It's religion. Obey those instructions to the letter. The Mounties will be leading the tail. In the morning, do exactly what you're told. Exactly. As long as the tail holds.'

I set the walkie-talkie beside my chair and laid my eyes directly on the splash of light seeping under Moss's lower front door.

Almost at once, snow started falling. Flakes slid down lazily, dropping like furry white-winged insects, muffling sound.

Night wore on. No one entered or left Moss's house. The temperature fell steadily. The snow, dancing now in white whorls, sifted through the cracks in the window onto my knees. My eyes kept switching, like the eyes of a person watching a tennis match, from Moss's door to his window, his window to his door.

The hours slid by. The outside whiteness was beginning to blind my eyes. I got to my feet. I went into a wild, crazy, arm-swinging, leg-throwing dance until charging blood washed away my stiffness.

The sky began to lighten softly. Dawn broke slowly and with dawn the wind died. Distant sounds of City snow removal squads came creeping through the white silence. Across the street, a light shone dimly, then blinked out.

That small spurt of action struck me as a blow.

My eyes were riveted to Moss's lower door.

Then the stake-out ended with a sudden, startling burst of action.

Moss's Buick slewed around the lower corner.

Before the car skidded to a stop before his door, I slapped down the transmitter-switch. In spite of the cold, sweat broke across my forehead. I cleared my throat, cleared it again. 'Alert on Moss!' I called, too loudly. 'Now, Red alert on Moss!'

The downstairs voice replied, calmly: 'Roger. Red alert. Go ahead now. But don't take my ear off.'

'Buick at the door,' I reported, bringing my voice down a key. 'Two bodyguards in the front seat. The same black, four-door passenger sedan. Motor running. Licence, 143-769 Quebec.'

Moss's lower-porch door opened. Moss came out at once. He began a nervous edging down the slippery, white-crusted steps. His huge, bloated face was intent. He was walking with the careful, tilted walk of a pregnant woman.

I spoke again, over a dry throat: 'Moss out, and moving. Slowly. He'll reach the Buick in less than thirty seconds.'

The Buick's rear door slammed and the car sloshed through wet gutter snow and roared to the corner.

The transmitter phone hard and cold against my lips, I began to call urgently: 'The Buick angle-turning. West. West at the corner. West. All clear on this street.'

I dropped the phone, sprinted out of the now empty house.

At the alley entrance, motor running, an R.C.M.P. car waited, inconspicuous and unmarked and commonplace except for an out-size buggy-whip antenna.

I leaped for the car's opening door.

A plain-clothes constable, grin and eager, shot the car forward and did some fancy driving that within two minutes worked us into our position in the moving tail now spreading fan-wise behind Moss.

'We're three hundred yards back of our lead car,' the constable informed me with a slight grunt. 'That car's fifty yards behind Moss. Separated by two cushion cars.'

We began a deadly game of mobile chess with each of our moves triggered by commands radio-telephone from Inspector Welch in the control-car. Even in the first traffic-congested area, the head tail-car never kept that position for more than a few minutes, never did it tail at all after

Moss's Buick made an angle turn. Invariably, following turns, Welch barked out an order. The lead car was sent off and another moved up behind the charging Buick.

My attention hung fast to Welch's droning voice. 'Hey, our cars and trucks are switching like mad!' I said, frowning. 'We're all over the street. Moss is an idiot if he doesn't get wise. In fact, he's a mortal cinch to spot an agent he knows. Whether or not he is already suspicious.'

My constable opened his mouth to speak, clamped it shut as Welch's radioed voice broke in with fresh commands. After easing our car into an inner lane and picking up a block in a hurry, my constable muttered: 'That fat guy's some slippery. Four turns in the last half mile—all right angles.' Then he answered me. 'Don't worry about any of our men being recognized. None of us have worked Montreal Drug Squad before. Inspector Welch brought us together specially for this go.'

Welch continued to pinpoint Moss's Buick from city block to city block.

Headed from the beginning towards the wide quiet avenues on the mountain crests, Moss's driver had reached them and was now running down the hills, playing hide-and-seek along cul-de-sac entrances and residential crescents bordering on the city's wide, neon-blazing Sunset Strip.

Muttering a harsh word under his breath, but obeying orders, my constable swung on to the Strip. Traffic was faster, and the constable did not like this situation at all. Horns were honking now.

'Dangerous,' I said uneasily. 'This damned traffic could foul us up.'

The constable squinched up his eyes. 'Right,' he said. 'This guy's an eel. He's all eel, all right. Listen!'

A radio communication directed to the control-car was coming in on our set: 'Hear this: Twelve to Control. Twelve on Garino. Garino now proceeding on foot east along St. Catherine from Peel towards University Street. Garino covered east from Peel on St. Catherine. Over.'

From his control-car, Welch snapped out a command that went half-way across the city to the squad covering Garino. 'Control to Twelve—to Twelve. Plan holds. Remain on Garino. Cover Garino to destination. Subject One now one mile north on Sunset Strip from Queen Mary Road. I will contact. Over.'

I sweated. 'I hope Moss's radio equipment can't get him in on the wave length were using,' I muttered. 'Surely not. Our radios must all have been pre-set.'

'They were. But, anyway, Moss's equipment couldn't reach us. Moss, or anyone else, can't buy equipment that will. Good thing, too.'

'It is,' I growled. 'If Moss's set could bring him even close, static interference would have warned him by now that something's going on. This is one damned-well-spread-out operation.'

'Take it easy, Dent.'

Welch's voice continued its precise plotting. Fringe cars were being steadily drawn in now. Over-exposed units were being knocked out as the fan-tail was spread or narrowed according to traffic or pace. The lead car was now almost on top of Moss. The Buick was switching traffic lanes fast as it approached a truck-happy industrial area at the end of the Strip.

Suddenly, apparently completely satisfied now, Moss abandoned his evasions. Abruptly, the Buick reversed direction. Driven fast, faster than it or the snow-covered streets were made for, Moss's car headed back downtown, swirling behind it huge white snow clouds.

Welch cracked out commands.

Two cars crammed with picked men moved from the fringe of the tail to assume lead positions.

The change of pace and direction brought the back of the Buick into my sight. I glanced worriedly at my constable. All the constable said was 'Thank God for the snow-cloud that Buick's kicking up. It'll do nicely. It's better than a smoke-screen. Good thing. The fat guy's nose for danger is long.'

The Buick right-angled again, this time directly towards the downtown shopping district. Moss's driver headed straight down Sherbrooke Street. He wheeled the Buick a good twenty blocks, a lot of it over dangerously slippery powder-snow, hitting the signal lights perfectly all the way.

Welch's voice became brittle now, charged with tension as he worked at drawing in our tail.

'Sweet Jesus!' said my constable, and he suddenly stiffened and began mumbling. He stamped the brake and brought our car to a sliding, brake-burning stop. 'Look ahead!' he said, in quick alarm. 'The whole damned street is jammed solid with snow removal equipment. There's miles of it. Surely to God Moss won't try to get into that . . .' He broke off, drew a deep breath, then said in an utterly wooden tone, 'It won't work, it can't. It's a solid block. Moss'll trap himself among those trucks and snow blowers.'

'This is the final precaution!' I said, rasping out the words. 'This is what Moss has been looking for all morning. A jam-up that he can crash through and buy himself cover for long enough to complete the actual trafficking. Don't take your eyes off him!'

The Buick crawled ahead for fifty feet, then was dead-stalled by a truck piled sky-high with snow. Moss's driver waited for the break that could come when the truck turned off towards a near-by open sewer to unload. The break came. I watched Moss through the Buick's rear window while he leaned forward to give orders. I could almost hear the clash of gears as the Buick's tyres began spinning snow. Then the big tyres dug in, and caught, and sent the car charging at a crazy, canted angled along the drifted sidewalk to a cleared street.

Welch's careful pattern of fan-tail collapsed into a jig-saw. The tail lay helpless, spread in a dozen, disqualified, stalled pieces. Moss had, without even being sure the tail existed, released himself adroitly from it.

I slammed my hand furiously down on my constable's shoulder. 'Crash through that snow!' I shouted. 'Forget the rest of the tail. Crash through! Once Moss clears that side street, he'll shake us like a snake shakes its skin.'

I almost went through the windshield as my constable sent us off with a roar. There was a grim, hideous shrieking of metal as we side-swiped a dump truck. In the space of a heart-beat, I saw another truck rush towards us, loom up monstrously, then veer off into the curb and leave us in the clear. We ploughed after the Buick.

Ahead, on the side street, still visible, the Buick began backing with a sideway-sliding motion into a cleared parking space.

Moss got out of the car. He turned confidently towards the entrance of a large department store.

I lost ten seconds giving our location over our now silent radio. I bailed out, shouting instructions to my constable on the go: 'Get into that store after Moss. I can't follow too close or he'll see me and panic. I'll wait here and follow in behind Welch's squad. Hurry, man, this is the meet.'

Inside the department store door, Moss went down three steps that led to an arcade lined with display windows. He stood for a while scanning what later turned out to be a three-weeks-old copy of the *Toronto Globe and Mail*. Then he threw down the paper and went through the wide double-doors admitting to the shopping aisles. He bought a package of gum from the girl at the sweets counter, and he watched, moving his head slowly from side to side as a snake moves its head.

I spotted him there, as did my constable, standing at the sweets-bar, staring about him with snake-like intensity.

Then, with the force of human movement around him, his intensity seemed to lessen. Ahead of him was a booth with a lighted sign over it: Information. He butted his way through a crowd of early shoppers to the information booth.

I waited for a heartbeat, then began jockeying for a better position in a nearer aisle. Around me, the steady clatter of women's high heels was incessant. The hollow, piercing clack of wooden heels, the empty chatter of women's feet. And voices. I stood, waited, watched.

Moss swabbed his face and left the booth. He crossed the store to a broad staircase on the west side. He stood there for a moment running a comb through his hair. Suddenly, he swung, balling his heavy shoulders. He walked determinedly back to the centre of the store.

Fifty feet off to one side, well screened by shoppers, I cautiously followed. Five of Welch's picked squad edged slowly into striking position.

At the book department, Moss came to an abrupt halt. He began browsing idly about, glancing at titles. He picked up a novel, dropped it back to the counter, moved on. Each time he stirred, he came closer to a high pyramid of colourfully dust-jacketed novels on a table near a side exit.

The situation was whirling slowly to its inevitable vortex.

Garino stepped nonchalantly from behind a screen of shoppers.

Outwardly completely at ease, the dapper supplier ambled from a side aisle into the book display area. He reached for a heavy volume, studied it, then laid it down and stepped still closer into the ever-tightening R.C.M.P. circle.

Garino and Moss now stood less than twenty feet apart.

The roar of voices, the chatter of wooden heels, the shifting, anonymous shoppers had somehow fallen away, disappeared. All that was left on that great floor now was the intent, motionless body of Moss. That, and the slender form of his calmly cautious supplier.

From seventy feet off, over a hundred heads, I saw Moss's eyes lock with Garino's.

It was as though two understanding minds had joined with a precise, sharp click.

Moss reached out for one of the colourfully dust-jacketed novels. As he did, it seemed to me that he pantomimed an object with his hands, an object that might be a parcel perhaps four by six inches. Then one busy hand deliberately brushed a novel to the floor.

Garino stepped forward. He picked up the fallen book, smiled pleasantly, politely held it out to Moss. Moss reached with both hands. And Garino moved still closer. He crossed his arms on his chest, as if protecting a vulnerable place. Slowly, one of his hands freed itself and darted ferret-like into his inside breast pocket. When that hand was again visible, it was holding out to Moss a thin, wrapped parcel. I was able to see the blobs of sealing wax on the string knots on the parcel.

It was the moment of trafficking.

My Mountie made a headlong dive across the aisle at Moss . . . and in that precise instant, fate's nightmare shadow took flesh. A clerk, blinded by a huge armful of books, stepped unwittingly between the flying constable and Moss. The constable and the clerk met with a breath-blasting impact. The constable clawed at the air, reeling until the clerk folded and grasping out pulled him down with her. I jumped into brightly showering novels, into a mad tangle of thrashing arms and legs.

Behind me, pounded the Narcotic Squad.

Moss's mouth had fallen wide open. He stood utterly motionless there. His hands hung emptily. Then, as if his brain had suddenly cleared of fog, he erupted into violent, determined action.

Stepping back, he thrust his massive arms under the book-laden table. He put his weight to it, and with a bull-elephant bellow of rage, sent table and books crashing over us.

I crawled helplessly about on my hands and knees, slipping and sliding on books, fighting to regain my feet. A whistle blasted. Voices slammed against my ears: 'Get him! Go that way! Get Moss. Oh . . . get him!'

I scrambled to my feet.

Moss was nowhere in sight.

I heard a voice shouting 'No!' and realized that it was my own. It seemed futile and far away, lost in the screams of the crowding shoppers.

I felt a column of emotions rise thick in my throat, disbelief and then anger and then sadness. The department manager pushed insistently at me. He had thick, protruding lips and a shrill, irritable voice. His nose quivered when he spoke.

My hands were shaking. My head still spinning. 'What? What is it? What did you say?' I cried.

The manager glared indignantly at me, his nose quivering. 'Really, sir! Really! While you keep kneeling there what do you expect me to do with that table?'

I hadn't even realized that I'd slipped on the book-littered floor, fallen again. But the manager's pomposity outraged me.

'Shut up!' I yelled from my knees. 'Shut up, you stunned idiot, or I'll tell you exactly what I would like you to do with that cursed table!'

28

We were sitting side by side on my sofa. Thorn stared intently at nothing. She brushed her hair back and gave me a wry grin. 'Damn,' she said. 'It seems I'm not good at waiting, either.'

I grinned back at her, no longer quite so tired. I got up and swung a chair around and straddled it, arms folded on its back. For a moment, I studied her, intrigued more by her spirit and optimism than by the ever-fresh loveliness of her face. She inclined her dark head. 'Can't you try the inspector again?' she asked. 'By now, there surely must be news.'

'Not yet,' I said, reaching for my coffee cup then forgetting it. 'Welch promised he'd call me. He's doing his job. Every outlet is blocked off—bus and train stations, air terminals. Every bridge in every area is under R.C.M.P. surveillance. Welch is sitting tight, waiting.'

Deliberately, I took time out to get a cigarette, to offer Thorn one, and provide a light. 'I wish I shared Welch's confidence,' I said. 'Moss isn't human. He's like a giant squid—always able to hide and protect himself under an inky cloud. Who else but he would have thought to provide himself with an escape-hatch apart from all his other precautions? He spent four hours manœvering to that book table. But all that time he knew an employees' exit behind it led to an outside loading platform and a quick, safe getaway. He left us all looking like fumbling amateurs.'

'Max, there is a bright side,' Thorn suggested, trying spiritedly to find the proverbial ray of cheer. 'Helen is being looked after. Kept out of pain. And the ring is crippled, practically smashed. Those two are vital things you've accomplished.'

'No,' I said, and shook my head. 'That's the whole point. The ring is not really smashed at all. Not for long anyway. As things stand now, if Moss is caught he can be charged only with conspiracy. With a clever trial lawyer, he can wriggle out of that or, at worst, go down for a couple of years. Particularly so, if Garino doesn't talk.'

'I see,' Thorn said, biting her lip.

'Garino won't talk,' I fumed. 'So far, not a lonely word has been squeezed out of him. He claims he found the drugs. That he's never even heard of Moss. Well, it's what we expected.'

289

I sighed, shut my eyes. 'Damn it, Thorn,' I muttered, 'somewhere, somewhere we're standing too close to to see, there's a solution to this mad tangle. It's there, but it keeps eluding me.'

From behind the closed bedroom door, a terrific crash sounded. A thin, piping voice said, 'Ohhhh!'

'Shadow!' Thorn said flatly. 'He's doing that to attract attention. He feels hurt because of not being allowed in here to listen.' She got up. 'I'd better see what he's broken.'

Within a minute, she returned. She reached for my hand and I could feel her trembling. She whispered, almost giddily, 'He has something to tell you, Max. He's almost bursting with it. Talk to him, Max. Listen to what he wants to tell you.'

Shadow's tousled head bobbed out the bedroom door. He took a quick, wary look, then faced me, a secret, excited look in his eyes. 'I wish to help you!' he cried. 'I wish to tell you how to catch Monsieur Moss!'

'*You what?*'

Shadow reached back to rub his bottom. 'Until the chair she slip and I fall down, I am listening from behind the door while you and Ma'amselle talk. I find out you and Ma'amselle are veree sad. I do not like this. So,' he grinned, bubbling all over, 'it is up to me. I must tell you how to catch Moss.'

I stared in astonishment at the beaming boy. '*Are you telling me you know where Moss is hiding?*' I demanded.

In his weirdly childlike, devilish manner, Shadow winked. 'Better than that. Me, I know how to breeng Moss *out* from where he hides. The Mounties they look for five year, but nevair will they find Moss. Nevair. Me, I know Moss. I find him real quick.'

I had the boy by the lapels of his pyjamas. I wanted to shake it out of him. '*How?*' I demanded. '*How* will you bring Moss out?'

Shadow made his usual deprecating gesture. 'It is

veree simple. Nothing at all, Monsieur Max. I will make Moss find me. And all the time you will be waiting behind. You will catch Moss. You will kill this fat pig for me, hey?'

I did shake him, then. 'Quick!' I pressed. 'Tell me exactly what you're driving at.'

'But it is simple!' Shadow repeated delightedly. 'Moss is not a one to run away without his money and jewels. He has many jewels. Me, I know where he keeps everything. I watch one night while he goes to his secret plant. It is in the room of the rats. Moss, he catch me while I am watching. He beat me like crazee. But I know the place of his plant.'

Shadow bobbed his head eagerly up and down. He said proudly, 'It is veree dangerous, my idea. But I do not care. I do this thing for Monsieur Max. I think now maybe he work with the Horsemen, but I do it anyway. Like this: Me, I will go alone to the rendezvous of the addict. I will make the beeg talk there. How I will talk! I will tell how I am going tonight to make the sneak past the Mountie who guards at the house of Monsieur Moss.

'I will say that I go there to make the raid on the plant of Monsieur Moss. Everyone will hear me. For sure, someone will know where Monsieur Moss hides and will send the message to warn heem. Monsieur Moss will be crazee mad. He will for sure try to go after me to keep safe his money and jewels. Perhaps he will try to get inside first. Maybe Moss will figure some way to beat the Mountie that watches at the house.' The boy shrugged philosophically. 'Per'aps he will kill the Mountie.'

Thorn looked troubled. 'I don't like this now,' she said. 'Not that last part of it, at least. Shadow will be unprotected. For some of the time, anyway. Suppose Moss decides to take his revenge on him?'

'Perhaps he try,' Shadow said calmly. 'But Monsieur Max will be near. He will fix Moss. Pow!'

A sudden, crazy desire urged me to shake hands with

Shadow. That is exactly what I did do. When I pushed him towards the bedroom, he was glowing. 'Scoot,' I told him. 'Get dressed right away.' I turned to face Thorn. 'This is the answer,' I said. 'Except that I'm going to let Shadow get rid of the Mountie guard for Moss. Of course, I'll have to take Shadow to Inspector Welch first.'

'Good Lord!' Thorn gasped. 'Shadow will probably spit at him!'

'Well, you'd better come along,' I decided. 'You can watch Shadow, keep him reasonably well-behaved.'

I called Welch and he agreed to wait at his office. For the first time since I'd know him, he sounded tremendously excited. When we arrived at his office he was ready for us. He shook hands with Thorn, nodded curtly to Shadow, then gestured to the three chairs waiting in semi-circle before his desk.

Quickly, I explained Shadow's plan, qualified my appreciation of it by adding in an urgent voice, 'If Moss isn't lured out of hiding he'll hole up for months before you people even get a chance at him. He'll know a dozen hideouts, probably he has spots set up all over the city for a situation such as this. But if he's afraid of losing the wealth he has piled up during the years, he's a mortal cinch to come out and make a try for it. Don't forget. Moss is nothing, if not mercenary.'

But Welch's excitement was altering to worry and doubt.

'Here's another point,' I insisted. 'Moss has a score to settle with Shadow. By now, he knows Shadow talked. Moss isn't a man to forget such a thing. He's so vulnerable now, he can rationalize a bit of risky killing. Even child killing. He'll jump at his chance for revenge.' In a voice grim with conviction, I concluded: 'It's the only way, Inspector. Our best chance, our last chance perhaps, to get Moss. By using Shadow as a decoy.'

Welch remained silent for a full minute during which the only noises in the little office were echoes. He glanced thoughtfully from Shadow back to me. 'This boy would have to be covered,' he decided. 'Covered from all areas. It would be too awkward all around if this turned out to be another fiasco. After all, Dent, you can hardly expect me to trust Moss's boy!'

Shadow pursed his lips, salivated. I glared at him. He swallowed, reluctantly.

'Look here, Inspector,' I pointed out desperately. 'There is nothing else to do. How long can Garino be held without trial? A short three days! Then your own law forces you to send him to court. Can he be stopped from pleading guilty? No. And once he does, and is sentenced, he is a cinch to turn Queen's evidence, demand protection of the Court, then perjure everyone dizzy keeping Moss in the clear. Never involve accomplices! That's the underworld code. And even if most thieves ignore it, we know it is well respected in the drug trade. See what I mean? The longer Moss stays on the loose, the safer he gets.' I slapped my palm on the desk. 'We've got to trust Shadow,' I insisted. 'We've got to let him go to the house alone. If men are posted all over the area, Moss won't budge. He'll know. Don't ask me how, *but he will know.*'

'Sure, 'e know!' Shadow sniffed disdainfully. 'Phew! 'e smell the cop. Easy!'

'Stop that!' Thorn scolded. 'Stop that talk at once.'

Welch snorted. 'So you expect me to dismiss the guard on Moss's house. You expect me to leave the entire area clear. You want me to let you and this, this *enfant terrible* take over. Ridiculous, Dent. I've never heard anything quite like it.'

I came to the edge of my chair. My impatience was complete, but impatience was a luxury I couldn't afford right now. Not with Inspector Welch of the R.C.M.P. 'No,' I retorted. 'That's just it, Inspector, that's the part you don't seem to see. I *don't* want you to dismiss the guard. Clear the area until Shadow gets there, yes. But leave your man posted on door duty. Better than that, tell that constable that now you not only want Moss—you also want his boy, Shadow.'

'Then what?' Welch looked puzzled. 'I don't get your point.'

'You will!' I retorted. 'You will when I get Moss. Just issue those orders. Issue them and wait. Shadow and I will do the rest.'

Welch stared deliberately at the ceiling. I stared at him as if I might will him to reason. 'Issue those orders!' he said with a last burst of exasperation. 'It's a little foolish going on like this, Dent. Good Lord! if I issued those orders I'd probably be struck off strength in the morning.'

'Really, Inspector,' Thorn said. 'I'm very disappointed in you.'

'And why, Miss Ashton?'

'Because,' Thorn said flatly, 'it seems you are so rule-bound you are ineffective. After all, Max and Shadow are willing to take all the risks. Well, really!'

The inspector came on the defensive. 'I'm a police-man,' he protested. 'I'm forced to go by the book. To respect procedure. Please, be reasonable. I don't have the right to issue such orders.'

'You haven't even a clue,' I said, trying to make my voice sound casual, 'not even a suspicion as to where Moss might be holed up. You don't even know if he's preparing to leave the country. Do you?'

'No,' the inspector retorted in a choking voice. 'We haven't, and we don't, and you know it. But that still doesn't give me any right to ignore the book.'

I studied his expression, a small, hopeless movement of his shoulders. 'But you will!' I said triumphantly. 'You've decided at last that you will!'

Welch came to his feet stiffly. 'Yes,' he said wearily, his head shaking in resignation. 'I'll issue orders to clear the area temporarily, and I'll put out a pick-up on this boy.

What choice is left me?' Then he added, irony in his voice. '*A little child shall lead them.* Well—perhaps sometimes the ends of justice are better served by informal methods. But try to remember this, Dent: the force has an interest, too. Whatever finally concludes this nightmare must be official.'

Shadow bounced like a rubber ball from his chair. Smiling a shy, polite smile I had never expected to see, he stepped up to the startled inspector. 'Do not be afraid,' he cried proudly. 'I do not fail my protector, Monsieur Max. And I do not trick you, Monsieur Police. I am on your side. Yes, me, I will make for you the Number One gangbuster!'

Less than a half-hour later, Shadow swaggered down St. Catherine Street to the addicts' rendezvous.

The rendezvous lay in the torpor that had become typical since the beginning of the panic.

Shadow walked deliberately to where two table-chairs stood apart, one chair empty, the other overflowing with the shapeless body of Big Red, Moss's east-end pusher. Two other addicts sat near by. They were arguing violently, gesturing at each other. After Shadow uttered a few loud words, all three men stiffened.

They turned to stare incredulously at the posturing boy.

Big Red rose, and with elaborate casualness walked to a telephone on the wall near the door.

Shadow stayed another twenty minutes in the rendezvous. Flushed and excited, he lingered at every table, boasting over and over that in a matter of minutes he would be on his way to loot Moss's cache. At last, he strutted cockily out to the street, slammed the rendezvous door magnificently behind him, and started along the route planned for him.

I hesitated, eyed the street anxiously, then slipped quietly from the doorway where I had been watching. I ran, shouting for a taxi.

Ten minutes later, I stood at the look-out in the old, vacant building. The same tree slapped against the side of the house with the sound like the distant slamming of an old screen door. But this time no light shone from Moss's house across the street.

A not unknown sense of isolation began to close in on me. Then, below, in the white silent street, Shadow suddenly appeared. His rapid jiggly steps betraying nervousness, the boy marched like a little soldier towards Moss's house. At the foot of the staircase he stopped, looked about, then began climbing quickly. Just as we had planned, half-way to the top landing he slipped. Set up a loud clattering. Then, as if alarmed by his noise, he spun about and ran wildly back down the stairs.

Moss's door exploded open.

The Mountie on guard duty abandoned his post. Obeying orders to the letter, he crashed down the stairs after the boy he had been instructed to bring in. Shadow, the Mountie behind him, ran like a frightened deer.

Then, suddenly, Moss materialized out of nowhere. Where there had been thin air, there was Moss. Bent forward and pounding furiously, he was hurrying towards his unguarded house.

I twisted from the window. In a moment, I was in the darkness of the alley. Circling the block at an all-out run, I came on to Moss's house from the rear.

I flattened myself against the door, so I could not be seen from above, and listened until my ears went numb from the strain.

Satisfied, I took out a lock pick and, holding my breath for fear there might be a tell-tale fall of wafers, worked it.

The door swung as though on ball bearings.

I stepped inside the kitchen, and went as though walking on rotting wood up the inner stairs, keeping my feet close to the wall. Before me now, through a carelessly wide door, I could see the pale glow of the little white bar that shelved Moss's favourite Cyprian. The throne chair gleamed. Beyond it, fingers of light stabbed out from under the door of the animal room.

The balls of my feet carried me noiselessly across the living-room. My ear, pressed hard against the stout door of the animal room, caught the faint sound of squealing and furtive scrambling.

Clearly, I heard the rasping harshness of Moss's breath. I pushed gently at the door. The lock held. I stepped back and booted it and heard the instant click of a light switch as I fell forward on my knees and rolled inside the room, then off at a sharp angle.

I crouched in a silence so tense it vibrated.

Darkness held all sound for an endless second. My hearing reached out and out. Only tiny, scratching feet stirred.

A huge shadow melted ghost-like from behind a row of steel-backed cages, stretched gigantically on the floor, brushed a wall, disappeared.

I cocked my pistol. The sharp, metallic click sounded like a thunderclap.

Wall plaster cascaded over my shoulders. Simultaneous with the shower of chalky flakes came the bright bark of Moss's Italian pistol, like a snapping of a wet towel. Before he could shoot again, I dived for protection to the end of a long line of cages that were now silent but vibrating slightly.

Moss and I crouched across the room from each other. Between us, like a metal parapet, stretched the cage wall. And, between us, lay the long rapt hush, alive and foreboding. Moss fired again, at random. The slug ricochetted madly, rending the dark silence with weird metallic screams. Moss squealed with impotent rage. Another shot hammered metal not a foot away from me and set off a mad scurry. I smelled metal and animal-smell and my own sweat.

Drawing a deep breath, I threw taunts across that wall of blackness. 'You're done, Moss! Done! In five minutes this house will be crawling with Mounties. You're covered so you can't move. End of the road, Moss. Twilight of the mad gods. There's no court of appeal for this. Throw out your gun. Give up. It's your only chance.'

His voice came to me, shrill and amazed. 'You!' he roared. 'I knew it was you! You were in the department store; now here. You've been under my feet for weeks. Who are you? A stinking Mountie? An undercover Horseman?'

'Not a Mountie,' I taunted. 'Not a Horseman, Moss. Only a citizen, an enemy of swine like you. I'm taking you in, Moss. In for the big payoff. Shadow was my decoy. Like you say, I've been on your tail for weeks. Now it's over.'

A shot whistled over the cage wall.

I crouched lower. My lungs were raw from the harsh, acrid reek of burnt cordite. 'That's four,' I shouted at the top of my voice and shouted again, 'Four shots—four misses. I haven't even fired yet. I still have a full chamber. And every bullet in it points at you.'

The end cage slammed against my shoulder as he suddenly shifted position. For part of a second his pistol showed snake-like in shadow form across the wall. 'Never shoot while moving,' I called out mockingly. 'That's an old undercover axiom, Moss. You're wasting ammunition. Soon you'll be holding an empty pistol.'

He screamed at me. 'Listen, you mad fool. Hear me out. I have money here. A tremendous fortune. We'll divide it even. Half for me, half for you.'

Over my deliberately derisive laughter, his words spilled faster, running over each other into the darkness. 'Wait, you fool. I'm talking about a real fortune. Money and jewels, beautiful gems. My profit from years of drug trafficking. Take your half, and let me go. You can live like a king on what you'll walk away from here with!'

I laughed again, and his wasted words fell off into a pleading whine. 'Think, think by God of what can be yours! Women, power, luxury. Yours, all yours. And what do you have to do for it? Nothing, by God nothing at all! Only step aside and let me go.'

I rested the barrel of my pistol on the roof of a cage. I slapped a bullet into the wall a foot from Moss's head.

'You witless fool!' he howled. 'What kind of an idiot are you? Are you an escaped lunatic? Don't you realize I'm offering you the drug connection? I'll fix it so you'll be the Man. The Big Man. The trafficker for all the city.' His voice jumped up a key. 'Do you know what that means? You'll be a despot. Like a medieval king. Can a fool like you possibly understand that? It means power. Crushing power. The addicts—all of them—will be your slaves. You can make them squirm at your pleasure merely by sending a pusher out ten minutes late.'

'Your throne chair is empty, it stays empty,' I retorted, and I sent out a second shot.

He began a desperate, frustrated sobbing. And the animal room began slowly closing in on me. Too much tension was leaving me limp. Too much silence. Darkness. And death waiting as close as the rasp of his harsh sobs, which seemed now to be slicing like a knife into my head.

I undid the lace of first one shoe, then the other.

I kept talking insistently: 'Moss—come out. The Narcotic Squad is all over the street. They're putting out a cordon. Closing in. Do you want *them* to have the satisfaction?'

I threw out a first decoy shoe in a long loop across the room and at the same moment squeezed out a chance shot. Moss wailed with confusion. I called out to him. 'Scream, you snivelling heap of blubber. But remember, you don't ever hear the one that hits you.'

Before he could answer, I slid the second shoe in a wild careening along the cage roofs and leaped for the opposite wall with my hand out for the light switch.

White brilliance flooded the room.

Below the cage stands, Moss's legs stood planted like two tree trunks. I snapped out two shots. Aimed at his knee-caps. He jerked to a full, huge height. Then he crashed forward, sweeping a line of cages under him to the cement floor.

Too anxious, I stepped forward.

Cursing me in a low, savage voice, he shot out a mighty arm and grabbed for my ankle. He got it and my feet went out from under me. He was too close now to aim accurately. He simply shoved the pistol at me and pulled the trigger twice. Pain burned two searing holes in my shoulder.

I saw his face grow white and rigid as he realized his shots hadn't finished me. Slowly, I brought my Police Positive into point-blank range. Moss started talking, then stopped with his mouth hung open on a word. My pistol was one inch from the flat bridge of his nose.

'There is no Court of Appeal for this,' I said, and I squeezed the trigger.

Moss began to die.

And his dying was a wild and terrible thing, full of fury, and ugly as only the death of a body full of hate can be; and even after it was over, he lay there with his great frame shuddering and choked noises coming from his throat.

Though death is not noted for its compassion, it was horrible and a chill had rooted deep inside me. I rolled away from him, and knifed by the pain in my shoulder, pulled myself to my feet by grasping the smashed cage roof over which hung his torn, dripping face. Step by step, I fought nausea across the room to a small safe that yawned wide in the wall behind the toppled cages.

I thrust my hand into the safe. My fingers stubbed against tight stacks of currency. I pulled desperately at the money; threw it helter-skelter over my shoulder until it was a green tide washing about my feet.

Someone once said, *Money isn't clean or dirty, it's only money.* The devil it is! Moss's loot had the feel of filth.

I reached out into the safe again and found a flat steel box, pulled it out. Using full strength of my good arm, I hurled the box against the wall. The box exploded wide open. Jewels cascaded brightly across the room. I jumped over Moss's crumpled hulk. My ears were filled with my own crazy laughter.

A huge diamond in an old-fashioned setting was rolling in bright loops about the floor.

The ring rolled to a stop within one inch of Moss's outstretched paw. It was the Ashton ring; the symbol of Helen's moral disintegration.

I picked up the ring. I thrust it into my pocket. And, dizzily, I weaved out of the animal room.

Voices reached into the living-room from men shouting frantically below. I reeled across the room, reached out for support to the heavy, gleaming arm of Moss's throne chair. The chair seemed to give me no support. To be as unsteady as me.

The voices sounded again. From far away. My heart knotted like a loop that flicks at the end of a long string. A sickness more real than violence, more terrible than disgust filled me.

I raised my left hand to push hair out of my eyes, but the arm wouldn't go above my waist. This was ridiculous. A sob began tickling in my throat. The two distant shots sounded sharply.

I stood weaving, wondering what to do as a loud rush of feet sounded on the stairs. Then voices, more voices, and one louder than them all, crying—'Moss's car was waiting beyond the corner. His two thugs were sitting in it. The fools tried to shoot it out. We went after them and we got them. Both of them!'

The room filled abruptly with noise, with mounties whose lean bodies were weaving, blurred. Voices rose high, and fell, flash bulbs went off in my eyes.

I tried, but I couldn't quite figure out where to go.

301

Epilogue

A scattering of neons shimmered in the darkness, giving wavering invitations to laugh, to love, to play.

Thorn and I stood on the night-wrapped terrace of the Look-out at the western height of the mountain. Below us, the city's midnight pace was beginning to quicken; the tempo of its night symphony to increase. The gaiety that is French, that is spontaneous, was spilling out in carnival mood into the streets of the city of cathedrals and cafés.

For a while, neither Thorn nor I spoke. We stood staring down into the gulf of light and shadows that stretched below us. Then Thorn turned to face me. 'Beautiful. Oh, so beautiful,' she whispered. 'The city at night from here. Like a sky turned upside down and filled with stars.'

'Like a picture postcard,' I agreed. 'In fact, more beautiful than any conceivable picture postcard. But I wasn't thinking about the city.'

'Oh?'

'No. I was thinking about Helen. Helen and Phil. Together. The way they looked sitting in the solarium in the Royal Vic tonight. So busy making plans.'

'Ummm-m. Like Chopin and his lady. No, not really like that. More like an old, very placid couple. Cute in wheel-chairs. But nice, too, together. Max, what do you think about them now? Their chances for a decent life, I mean—once they are discharged.'

'That's what they have. What they've never had before since they became addicts—a chance. They're both too intelligent to keep reaching for a crutch they know no longer exists.' Hesitating, I broke cigarettes from a fresh package. 'As well,' I said, 'there's the wonderful fact that they've found each other. That they're together. And with your father's blessing.'

'And that Phil is filled to bursting with ambition to write music now that he can't play it any more,' Thorn said. 'It's a dream come true, Max. They both feel wanted and loved and needed, useful. I can believe you when you say they have a chance—a big chance.'

A blare of dance music blew high and wide and wailing into the still night air, then died as though a wet blanket had been suddenly flung over it.

'Shadow!' Thorn said, stirring nervously. 'Playing with radio buttons in the car. The monkey, he's filled himself with so much sleep in the last two days he needs to be tied down.'

I said something about what an excellent idea it would have been to have left Shadow at home. At that, a taxi squealed to a stop on the cement apron fronting the Look-out terrace. A moment later, a second taxi pulled up beside it. People tumbled out, laughing. Two couples skipped arm in arm across the terrace to the Look-out railing. Their taxi-drivers sauntered off to a corner.

Two voices, one French, the other thick with Scottish burr, carried on the thin, crisp air . . .

'Cigarette, *mon ami?*'

'Sure, thanks.'

They stood apart and quiet as statues, two glowing cigarette ends burning and mending tiny holes in the dusky night shroud. Then they began to talk; to argue about the new mayor, just as two plebeians of Rome must have argued about a controversial gladiator.

It was a pure, classic scene. And I listened shamelessly.

'You read the paper today, *mon ami?* That we will have curfew? That all clubs and cafés must respect the closing hour tonight—or accept the padlock?'

The Scotsman: 'Aye, I read. Haven't we all been reading the City Hall reform news for weeks? But I filled my tank with gas tonight. Enough for driving until six a.m. I'm one that believes this thing can't work.'

303

'Pouff! You are wrong. You will not burn that gas tonight. This crusading mayor of ours, he has a torch in his hand. Frivolity is his enemy. *Voila!* A large sign in the darkness. 'So far our new mayor has pushed down all his enemies.'

'Aye, he has that. All his enemies. All but one.'

'One? Which one, *mon ami?*'

'The enemy that destroys every crusader. The one inside him. The one that pushes him on when wisdom should tell him to be satisfied.'

'*Oui*, perhaps. It is true that too much is too much. No matter on which side.'

'Shame!' Thorn said, handing me her lighter, and laughing. 'I say, Shame. Listening to private conversations!'

'Wisdom out of the darkness,' I chuckled, jiggling the lighter in my good hand. 'I go along with the Frenchman's campaign for the middle road. Live and let live—within reason.'

I turned back towards the city, bent to light a cigarette against the hungry wind.

When I straightened up, I saw a figure emerge from the shadows on the dark side of the terrace and come sauntering over in my direction. When it was near enough for me to see it was a man, it said, and the voice was amused, 'The Lord and the new mayor watch over the fall of every little sparrow!'

I stared, unbelieving. It was impossible. I was looking for a sodden derelict with an outstretched grimy paw. But no derelict was there. Only a tall, thin young man, clean-shaven and keen-looking, with the indefinable stamp of the Mountie about him. He came nearer and I saw his teeth gleam as he pressed his hand on my shoulder. 'You son of a gun!' he said, laughing. 'You did all right, Max Dent. Not bad at all. I even thought you had *me* for a moment when I ducked my head into the inspector's office. Yes, you did all right. *For a private op!'*

Then he turned away, no longer detailed to be my second shadow and my second right arm, and I heard again his soft, low chuckle . . .

And Thorn clutched my arm.

Shadow, his voice sudden and shrill with terror, was howling from the front seat of the M.G., 'Monsieur Max! Ma'amselle. 'elp. Something happens. Help. I push the wrong button. The car, she goes. I am lost! Save me!'

Slowly, the little sports car was rolling away from us. Rolling back across the slanting cement terrace apron towards the first of an endless run of hills.

I reached for Thorn. Hand in hand, we began running . . . Running to save Moss's boy.